The Fauna and Flora of Distanced Lands

PWN

A Satirical Tale of exploration and adventure
undertaken by a lusty and delusional English scoundrel
during Social Isolation, Lockdown and Shielding.

THE FAUNA AND FLORA
OF
DISTANCED LANDS

PWN

BEING THE FULL, UNABRIDGED AND UNEXPURGATED

ACCOUNT

OF HIS EXPLORATIONS

IN THE FIRST YEAR OF THE GREAT PESTILENCE.

ALL IN HIS OWN WORDS.

WITH NEWLY DISCOVERED EPILOGUE AND AFTERWORD!

Edited by Pavel Nevulski

(Professor of Comparative Expeditionary Studies.)
and with his Foreword, Introduction, and Footnotes

Between the Lines
PUBLISHING

Willow River Press is an imprint of Between the Lines Publishing. The Willow River Press name and logo are trademarks of Between the Lines Publishing.

Between the Lines Publishing
9 North River Road, Ste 248
Auburn ME 04210
btwnthelines.com

First Published: October 2021

ISBN: (Paperback) 978-1-950502-57-8
ISBN: (Ebook) 978-1-950502-58-5

— Unsuitable for minors, or adults, for that matter —

The Editor would like to thank the following:

Peyton Blake, the late Ted Burren, Warren Culleton, Chameli, the late Richard Clayson, Peroline Fauvel, Andrew Garrett, Ylloh Hinton, Chioma Hudson, Sophie Hume, Katie Kiwele, Veronica Kiwele, Loopy, Jo Moore, Tom Neville, Kat Norman, Sarah Norman, Christine Overy, Lisa Piazza, Liz Reed, Joel Sams, and last alphabetically but by no means least: Henrietta Shirazu, without whom this book would not have been written.

Also, my thanks go to Alf Pinch and Horace Pluck of the Norwich and Norfolk Council Waste Disposal Department for an excellent bit of 'dumpster-diving'.

Pavel Nevulski
Editor

My very special thanks go to the Editor's Editors: Liz Hurst, Cherie Macenka, and Penny Dowden.

T. S. Eliot:

We shall not cease from exploration
And the end of all our exploring
Will be to arrive where we started
And know the place for the first time.

FOUR QUARTETS.

INTRODUCTION

It is thought that PWN was born in Shorthouse-on-Stour in the West of England.[1] The family seems to have moved to the Northeast of the country (to one of their several Country Estates), perhaps as little as six months afterwards. Presumably, he had some schooling there but the next record of him is at Galoshes, a 'progressive' Borstal in Lancashire[2]. After that, all records suggest his family removed to the East and took up residence near Norwich, latterly at Leopard Court, a very grand establishment indeed. The House has sadly been converted into apartments and the grounds turned into several soccer-pitch-sized soccer-pitches.

It would appear he was not a distinguished scholar, as once again he disappears from view. There are any number of places he could have been after Borstal, but a good contender is a Technical College to the Northeast of London.[3] We know nothing of him for certain after that but a likely individual with a slightly different name, 'NWP', soon appears, who lives in Ghent in Belgium for a five-year period.[4] Some scholars maintain that 'Ghent' is simply 'Kent' misheard by someone. (I myself incline to that theory.)

It is possible that PWN is the person some scholars have identified as subsequently living with at least one wife and an unknown number of children on a Bird's Eye pea farm in Suffolk for a period of

---

[1] See 'Tall Tales of Shorthouse'. Templeton, D. 1999
[2] This establishment no longer exists, the Home Office having—owing to a collective fit of insanity—appointed a drug lord and pimp as its final Governor. NB. Borstals and Approved Schools have been superseded by Young Offenders Institutions.
[3] See 'Record of Student Transgressions', Notrem Technical College.
[4] See 'Characters of Old Ghent (and other unwanted information).' Ruck, R. 1977

about ten years. The rumours that he attended a university during this period will be discussed in the Foreword.

After this, if his history was not already uncertain, the records fail to disclose anything at all which can be trusted. Some have said he owned or lived at a windmill[5]; others that he was for many years rather odd and removed from polite society. The texts here reprinted would suggest that the former is possible and the latter indeed the case, but until further evidence is found we cannot confirm either.[6]

PWN himself and others tell us that at some point he ordered PWN Towers to be renovated from an ancient property, somewhere in or near Norwich in East Anglia.[7] PWN Towers is now a major sewerage works.[8] No wives or descendants of PWN occupy the House, which in any case has become a pumping station. Though there were undoubtedly many of each, they have completely disappeared from the vicinity. The mystery of why this should be has yet to be solved.

Where and when he began his astonishing career in exploration is uncertain but by his own account, he is a practiced hand at it by the time of what he calls 'The Pestilence' and the journeys about which he writes here. We have reason to believe he cut his teeth as an explorer firstly in Belgium and France, and then Tunisia but this sparse record needs supplementing.[9]

For this edition, the previously known thirteen trusted sources have been used, particularly those emails addressed to Ms. Sarah Norman, as they seem the most considered version sent by PWN to his correspondents, and so to be trusted. Why this should be, we may never know. The explanation may be, in any case, exceedingly dull.

---

[5] See McFever, M. 'DIY Windmill Furniture and its Poorer Makers.' 1998.
[6] See 'The Man Who Thought He Was When He Wasn't.' Yare, C.L. 1997 and see 'The Hellesdon Hospital Records, Norwich.' Various. 1998. And see also 'Northgate Acute Ward Memoirs', Thorell, G. 1998.
[7] See 'PWN? I Deny Ever Knowing Him.' Overy, C. 2020¼
[8] A sad end for a once great property, to be sure...
[9] See 'PWN in Wild Brittany' by Fauvel, P. To be published.

One other name stands out from the correspondents, which is that of Ms. Tina Leslie, who may or may not be the 'Tina' mentioned throughout the text, who appears to have been, if not the first, then amongst the first loves of the author. Ms. Leslie has been completely silent on the matter, except to make a wry face whenever his name is mentioned.

In an exciting development—a fourteenth source has just become known and makes its first appearance in this new edition. In July of the year in which I write this, a computer hard drive was fortuitously discovered at an undisclosed location in Norfolk; this proved to have all the material sent to the thirteen sources plus some fairly small but– in this editor's opinion– important extra entries to the text (given in the Footnotes), plus the extraordinary passages which I have here termed 'The Epilogue' and 'The Afterword.' I have spent much time in verifying this new source and believe it to be the genuine article.

In closing, it may interest readers to know that when a brick hut between the former Pestilential Provinces and the former Badlands was discovered by another Expedition about a year ago, in the far reaches of The Empire, and evidence was found which would seem to indicate that this astonishing 'time-capsule' was used by PWN as the Base Camp for his explorations, there were certain peculiarities which– if the discovery is genuine (and it seems to be so)–would suggest that PWN was not in perfect control of his mind at times during his Adventures, perhaps due to his isolation: a yeast extract of British origin[10] was found in the fridge and single-use plastic in the recycling bin.

---

[10] Our Colonial friends in Australia who claim that it was a yeast extract of theirs which was discovered in the fridge are sadly mistaken.

FOREWORD

I felt greatly honoured when I was approached by the publishers to firstly edit and then write the Foreword for this most recent edition of 'The Fauna and Flora of Distanced Lands' — PWN's seminal work.[11] (Please refer to my Introduction, for those who have only recently begun to read, or study PWN.)

Although most of the documents are extremely well-known, during the course of my research I was able to approach the receivers of the original emails (PWN quaintly or irritatingly calls them 'He-Males'), some of whom kindly provided me with original versions which vary interestingly from those previously in the public domain.

Fascinatingly, as mentioned in The Introduction, one previously completely unknown source was also available for my use in this edition.

There are some simple facts, disputed by none; these include the certainty that the documents date over ninety-nine or one hundred consecutive days, during 2020; and that a terrible plague had broken out in most lands; something almost unimaginable today.

The author tells us within the messages that his home domicile was in Norfolk, in The United Kingdom, and there are indications that his stately home, PWN Towers, was in or near the Fine City of Norwich in East Anglia. He indicates that earlier in life he attended university either there or elsewhere but may or may not have completed his degree. He is vague on the outcome and a thorough search of the records of all universities has disclosed nothing, unfortunately. He may

---

[11] 'Distanced' is here preferred to the previous Shlovskian edition, where the adjective 'defamiliarised' is used. In this Editor's opinion 'distanced'' is by far the more apposite term.

perhaps have used another name when studying, or alternatively a university may have removed him from their records for bringing it into disrepute, as seems most likely.

He tells us he was employed as a young man in the workshops of Hangem and Shaypem but of these employers or their workshop, or even their trade, no trace has yet been found. As his father was obviously possessed of enormous wealth, we can only speculate as to why PWN was reduced to earning a living. Perhaps, as seems only too likely, he had brought great dishonour on the noble family and was at least temporarily cast out?

As to his personality: we may and will deplore his strong libido, but he is demonstrably not a misogynist or racist—or at least it would be a very perverse form of feminist or racial critique that would dare to suggest it.[12] He is such a lover of women, in fact, that he carries his enthusiasm a great deal too far, one feels. However, we should not make the mistake of judging someone from the Past in the same way we would a man of the Present Day, which–in some extraordinary and frankly unbelievable way–is always more enlightened than the day that preceded it, isn't it?

It is clear that he does not believe in the separate development of races. In several places in the text, this is made crystal clear, both by statement and implication.

If he has a fault– though he obviously has some sort of idiosyncratic moral inclination, which might be thought to be a saving grace—it that he is more than a little callous to those he considers to be on the lower limbs of the Tree of Life, as shown by his regrettable collection of hunting trophies, not excluding early human types, although he indicates we are supposed to take his more outrageous sallies into this hobby of shooting and attendant blood-lust, with 'a

---

[12] See 'A Very Perverse Feminist and Racial Critique of the Writings of PWN' by Shirazu, H. and others. (Pamphlet in preparation.)

pinch of salt.' Should we, though? Scholars bicker amongst themselves about this, as scholars will. They are a breed prone to bickering.

The very peculiar zoological and botanical discoveries we may question but we cannot simply refute, as the lands he describes now exist only in corrupt and degenerate forms, after the passing of the Great Pestilence.

His Great Work was never finished, possibly as a result of the tragic circumstances which he relates in his previously last known message. We now know– thanks to the new material, if it is to be believed –that he survived, only for no one at the time, or since, to give a damn.

It is impossible to discover in what form he intended one day to publish. Perhaps he intended to produce a reference book for libraries, or part of a significant collection upon which to found a new Seat of Learning, or a sumptuous book full of colourful illustrations and reproduced photographs to be displayed on the coffee tables of the rich and powerful (for such an edition would be extremely expensive to produce). He may perhaps have intended to weed out all references to his relatives and friends. Thankfully, he did not, as scholars use these as the greatest clues to his identity.

In connection with this, I would like to take this opportunity to refute the scurrilous and absurd claims of some, that I have falsified PWN and that I am in fact the author of his tales of derring-do and quasi-scientific research in the field. They base this accusation–which is entirely without foundation–on the simple coincidence of the initials of our names. His personality and mine are completely different, I should very much hope. *Very* much.

Although I am often, flatteringly, called the world authority on PWN and his Life and Times, from that I demur, for those who knew him must know more of him than do I, and it is to them, now very aged (the youngest now as elderly as ten or eleven; she is–famously– amongst the survivors of the Pestilence) that further enquiry should be made, before any little extra evidence which remains is lost forever.

I have taken it upon myself to correct some spellings and eradicate most of the obvious mistakes from the text, without indication of having done this.

Whatever the public's reception of this edition it is certain that PWN's 'Fauna and Flora...' is already assured of its place as a curious addition to the extremely slim genre of exploration in a time of plague.

In closing, I would like to thank the artist for the cover illustration, which I think brings to life a little the lost worlds of the Guard-Lands, the Badlands, and the Solemn Land. Whilst not of the coffee-table standard hoped for by PWN, it is quite well done, I suppose—if *you* like it, then it is all to the good...

Pavel Wanya Nevulski. Editor

A correspondent to the author:

'I often think of you living alone, having to socially isolate, then be locked-down; then finally having to shield yourself. It must be frightfully dull. I do not suppose you know what to do with yourself or how to occupy your time? Let me know how you get on, will not you?'

The same correspondent to the author three months later:

'I'm a bit sorry I asked...'

WARNING:

As this text dates from the third decade of the 21st century, it inevitably contains completely outdated expressions and attitudes.

A PRELIMINARY NOTE

It is generally believed by modern scholars that by "Guard-Lands" PWN means PWN's back garden and by 'Solemn Land' PWN refers to his local Park. When PWN made his expeditions amongst far-distanced Peoples in the days of 2020 both places were wild and forbidding, full of hostile, warring tribes, and vicious animals. Solemn Land –the Park–was especially a place about which little was known, except by the primitive people who ran, played, made love, smoked joints, or walked their dogs there. Those are the places. The action, it would appear, took place largely in PWN's head.

PWN thought himself to be in the vanguard of the rightful colonizers of both places. Why this should be, one can only guess. A likely supposition is that any Englishman worth his salt and given half the chance, will conquer, destroy, and exploit any area with which he is presented, and subjugate and/or seduce any people he comes across in the process. Therefore, PWN was just the most recent of many, many English adventurers who could make that boast.

[EDITOR: SADLY, NO COPY OF DAY ONE HAS YET BEEN FOUND. [13]]

Day 2

An Expedition to the Guard-Lands.[14] The discovery of a Moai sculpture in a most unlikely place

Disregarding hail and lashing rain and wind, alternating with fierce, thirst-inducing sunshine, and requiring alternate robing and disrobing, I reached Camp Number One from Base Camp (my brick hut) and I pressed on into the Interior of the Guard-Lands, noticing the different textures of the plants the Natives call 'grass.' All the time came the fierce calls of the wild things in the skies, plunging and gliding. Here a tiny proto-bird flew low across my path; there, a goose-like pterosaur was observed, pursued, and mobbed by feathered monsters for all the world like seagulls in our country.

Stopping by the largest water feature [15], I decided to give it the name 'Lake Tina' after a childhood sweetheart. I wondered if–like its namesake–it would be present for only a brief time in my life and then, by disappearing from it, in a similar manner break my heart...

---

[13] The Editor of this edition has not yet given up hope that this will someday be discovered. It is thought to have contained details of why PWN was commissioned to explore the Distanced Lands, together with details of how he came to the brick hut he calls 'Base Camp'. Patient readers will discover that PWN does divulge some details of these matters as the text proceeds. (And see Footnote 29.)

[14] This appears to be the title PWN thought would apply to his adventures, not knowing–as we do with the benefit of hindsight–that he would later discover how to enter Solemn Land and be allowed to do so.

[15] The hard drive mentions that it was almost as wide as one-and-a-half feet in diameter and contained in a pink bowl.

1

At the furthest extent so far reached of my penetration into this World, my attention was suddenly arrested by the astonishing spectacle of a sculpture: a Moai, no less! This artefact was so like that of the statues to be found on that most remote island in the Pacific Sea, Easter Island, that it was easy to speculate that it must have been made by the descendants of those far distant people. You may be sure I will look at this splendid apparition with awe and wonder on each of my subsequent visits. This account I have given into the paws of my Native bearer, Loopy (of the Cat tribe), in the hope that it may reach those of my homeland in due course via the He-Male method.

Day 3

The Expedition to the very ends of the Guard-Lands. The Pool of the Coy Carp, plus my meeting with a Savage

I paused only to look at the moving pictures which the Native peoples here can project onto rectangular screens, and also to break my fast with a foodstuff, so-called, made of bran, called 'Minus' (minus various of the substances which many here describe as poisonous but chiefly 'Minus' discernible taste).

Then, after some rudimentary ablutions (one must present a decent appearance, to raise morale both for oneself and amongst the troops), I dressed suitably for the bush, with tick-proof boots completing my jungle outfit. Gathering my forces and instructing the feline bearers to carry my kit of book, Kindle the gift of my daughters[16], a bottle of juice made from the curious Vimto fruits of this land, and some buttercream candy confections, together with my trusty vaporiser with its remedy for many ills[17], I strode out confidently once more into the little-known world of the Guard-Lands.

Though some of the territory is now familiar to me, imagine if you will, my surprise at-discovering, nestled beneath the Moai sculpture (mentioned in a previous dispatch), a mysterious, large pool. In this pool swim plentiful, large rose-red coloured creatures, which I take to be fish of some sort, whilst the water around them fizzes and bubbles.

---

[16] It is unclear whether the donors were PWN's 'natural' or 'unnatural' daughters (see later in this text). Scholars tend to agree that its source was more likely PWN's natural daughters. In what way the unnatural daughters were 'unnatural' is a matter of great contention amongst academics, with no one theory a clear winner.

[17] **Health Warning**— Use of nicotine products, even in the form of vaporized steam, constitutes a severe hazard to health, destroying heart tissue and being extremely addictive.

'What–' I asked Loopy, my old cat sidekick, 'may be these fish? Are they not perhaps Koi Carp?'

Now, I suppose at this point you may be expressing surprise, if not incredulity, at the fact that here in the distanced Guard-Lands I was soliciting one of my cats to talk? The matter is simple enough. For, as it is true that after a long period of social isolation one finds oneself talking to one's pets, it is only logical and follows that after a further long period one finds oneself quite easily understanding their replies. Not only that but the darn things begin initiating conversations and thus not respecting the position they should occupy as one's inferiors. There is no need to study the language or other communication of animals. Just live with them, and them alone, and pretty soon it will be clear to you what the insufferable things are saying. There was nothing magical going on here, far from it…

So, when I tell you he replied, you need feel no astonishment whatsoever.

'No, Master, they are Coy Carp—called that because they blush from embarrassment when discovered in their state of undress.'

'That almost makes sense, my feline servant,' said I. ' Yet if this be so, why have you and that pretty female fool Meli not eaten them hitherto, for they look plentiful and easy to catch?'

'Not so, master, for look closer and you will observe their pool is covered by a strong grille of wire.'

I did as he had bid and my heart was struck by Terror, for here surely none other than the Hand of Man was observable! So, I could draw no other conclusion than that men, or possibly women, with intelligence, skill and craft inhabit that territory which it is forbidden to enter.

We beat a hasty retreat and after a lengthy march in the Guard-Lands I took my rest on the poorly constructed and crumbling structure which I had previously christened Camp Number One, identified as 'a razed flower bed' (I think he said) by the Native-next-door [18], of whom more in the next paragraph.

---

[18] The hard drive has at this point: 'Presumably at some point someone had set light to it…'

But the Coy Carp were not to be the only surprise this day, for no sooner had I opened a book to while away the time than the Native from the next-door compound came into a partially closed-off area adjacent to where I sat. He greeted me and proceeded to put a cigarette to his mouth and once he had lit it, I became aware of a sickly sweet, perfumed, and soporific smell pervading all the air around me. It was like tobacco but as though some mysterious Native herb had been added.

The Native spoke, and as far as I could make out his words were these— "Nothing like a bit of fresh air, is there?"

I was not overly concerned by his presence as he kept at least six feet away from me and seemed friendly. However, as it is never wise to trust such savages, I finished my own repast of sweetmeats, breathed through the vaporiser one last time (it is a sovereign remedy for many ills), then 'folded my tent' and with my retinue stole away back to Base Camp and Safety.

For many an hour I have been mulling over all the Wondrous Things I have seen today.

I hope this reaches you intact and safely and that you–my Loved Ones–are intact and safe also.

Day 4

Some supplies arrive, though of a strange sort; attacks by pterosaurs and birds also; the tiny metallic dragon; a correction to my account in the interests of complete honesty, a quality for which I am renowned; the first appearance of a Yapper

The days out here begin to blur together, and I can only hope I am keeping correct count of them. As each day passes, I carve a notch into the leg of the camp table, but I fear that all too soon the leg will give way as a result, and then I will no longer know what day it may be, nor even the month. [19]

The day began grimly, with myself in an equally negative mood–but the promise of many supplies improved my spirits. Vast quantities of soup powder of the Native vegetables are soon to be at my disposal, together with powdered milk. One supply of the soup is of a particularly strange vegetable known in these heathen parts as 'Broccoli.' I am assured, however, that despite the sound of it, it is not related to 'e-coli' and is almost harmless, although possibly too salty in its dried form for pleasure or health. In addition to such pieces of good news–all related by messages carried across great distances by the talking-picture crystal screens they have in this place–I received doubly good news that extra funding for my work has come from the unexpected source of a Gas refund. You may be sure that inwardly I

---

[19] On the hard drive, at this point—'In any case, Loopy and Meli obliterate this record with their deep scratchings.'

Day 5

*Of the Expedition to discover the limits of the territory known as
The Guard-Lands. Songs and a Disgusting Disaster*

Here must be recounted 'emotion recollected in tranquillity', as
the Romantic poet put it so eloquently and romantically. Yet again, what
wonders revealed themselves in these fabled but previously little-
known lands! But here I must perforce deal with the many discomforts
and dangers of such an expedition, so brace yourselves. [22]

Reluctantly I prised myself from the warmth of my rough, silk
bed at Base Camp. One of my feline bearers, Meli, took her breakfast but
then refused to accompany me out into the Wild. I remonstrated with
her for her disloyalty but no avail, for she returned not to her bed but to
mine (such indolence and insolence!) and so it was that with the senior
bearer only–Loopy–after a perfunctory breakfast I set foot once more
upon the trails, some of them so familiar now to me that one sometimes
gets the uncanny feeling one is walking in circles.

This time, always taking the paths to the right I went, keeping
up my spirits with a medley of songs popular in my own country and
in my youth. But too quickly I had run through the hits of both the
Beatles and the Rolling Stones. I made an attempt at songs by another
intrepid explorer in his time, Captain Beefheart but after just the first
few notes of 'Sure Nuff 'n Yes I Do' my companion Loopy began to howl,
and to silence him I had to desist. The wild people have no appreciation
of good music, preferring instead their simple, incessant, terror–
provoking 'beats' and jungle drums (Loopy is, I gather, a great fan of

---

[22] From the hard drive— 'Possibly unsuitable for those of a Nervous Disposition.'

the Banana Splits, and his admiration is not post-modern and ironic. Musical Education is wasted on some cats.)

After a time, he too lapsed into silence and the only sound was that of the sweet song of prehistoric creatures in the sky with the occasional drumming of a vehicle in the distance. These crude conveyances we almost never see; it is a mystery upon which tracks or pathways they may run. I have heard talk of a 'main road', but it must still be far off, even though I have now penetrated far into The Guard-Lands.

Much to my alarm–towards the end of hacking our way through the tall grass of one garden, which formed an almost impenetrable barrier to our return to my resting place before the return to base camp– my scout, Loopy, suddenly froze in posture.

'What is it, idiot?' I asked fondly of him, 'Have you detected a wild animal by tracking it here, or observing its spoor, mayhap?'

Said he, ' I certainly observe its spoor, my good master, for you have stepped right in it.'[23]

In fear and loathing I scraped as much of the vile substance off my shoes as I could, only to discover that my trousers were fouled also.

I swore most terrible and eternal curses on the head of the little Yapper, Freebie (for I suspected it of this treacherous deed), and as quickly as I could I gathered up my things at the resting place (hereafter to be called Camp Two) and together Loopy and I made our way swiftly back to Base Camp to wash boots, trousers, and myself.

I am now determined to take back to Civilisation the stuffed head and crossed paws of Freebie to mount in the Great Hall of my Mansion in Norfolk to evoke wonder and terror in the hearts of visitors. The incident has proved a useful warning to me that this sort of thing is

---

[23] The term 'spoor' includes all traces of an animal, including its droppings. See the definition as given by Wikipedia, Merriam Merriam Merriam-Webster Dictionary, and many other sources.

too easily encountered in these Lands, especially if one becomes complacent and fails to look where one is treading.

My Love to you All in my own Dear World. I dare say you yourselves brave dangers and difficulties of which I know nothing. [24]

---

[24] The hard drive has, at this point — 'Nor wish to know, if I am honest.'

Day 6

The Sixth Expeditionary day

I almost feel I need a bit more tranquillity to recollect the events of the day without becoming overcome by emotion — but let me tell you that it involved almost falling into a deadly trap and one left on the trail not by a Beast but by Man...

I have vowed to 'screw my courage to the sticking-place',[25] nail my colours to the mast, conceal nothing, and in short tell you today of the near-calamity.

However, I must assure all those concerned for my welfare (and I hope I do not flatter myself that there must be many in that category) that I emerged completely unscathed, though not a little shaken from a diabolical attempt on my person.

In the course of my perambulations through the Guard-Lands I unwittingly found myself straying just a little from the track, my interest piqued by the three aged and as it proved locked doors set into the artificial stonework in the form of rectangular objects coloured red. Why, I asked myself, were there such doors and why were both ingress and egress denied through them?

This, sadly, was a mystery I would not solve that day,[26] for even as I mused, I began to put my left foot down, only to register a sharp prick in the sole of that foot. Just in time, as it proved, I lifted my foot away. Had I not done so I would have thrust my foot down on a mantrap, consisting of a small iron spear which had been knocked

---

[25] This unusually good piece of writing is not by PWN but by William Shakespeare; it is from 'Henry V' and is so well-known that I do not know why I am telling you.

[26] But see later in the text, for an unlikely explanation.

through a piece of wood and upturned, the whole cunningly concealed beneath tufts of vegetation.

Shaking, I returned to Camp Number One, sat on its razed flower-bed seat, and examined my foot for damage. I had been extremely lucky. The brutish device had left not a mark, though the sole of my stout boot had been pierced through. I had avoided impalement, tetanus, and gangrene by barely a whisker! I had only my leathery sole to thank for the avoidance of a lingering and hideous death far from my Loved Ones in this Dark Continent.

The friendly tribesman who keeps the excremental Yapper, Freebie (some say 'Phoebe'), informed me that the trap must have been laid by that powerful but enigmatic entity known as Count Sil, well known for not clearing away dangerous debris from the usually poor work of his minions. I swore to myself that never again would I trust Count Sil and that all my dealings with him and his tribe would henceforth be circumspect.

My journeys recommenced, I found myself once again at Lake Tina. It had not evaporated, far from it. I now perceived that the pool is enclosed of some dense material, light pink in nature, and that the Lake is exactly circular. It is also full of life of a strange and bewildering variety. I believe I have now found the source of many flying dragons, if not the one who seems to sit for all Eternity atop the post about seven yards away. For from the surface of Lake Tina hang what may be the monstrous larvae of the dragons. The pool is, of course, refreshed by the gentle and not so gentle, rains that form in the fluffy grey clouds that drift across the skies of this world with such bewildering frequency, giving everything and everyone a jolly good soaking as they do so. Is their moisture always welcome? Answer without expletives, please, in no more than two hundred words. As soon as you have sent me all your money, you may begin.

I hope to see more of the Natives of this and the surrounding lands. As it is, this Strange World is made even stranger by their almost complete absence. It is almost as if they are locked in their huts and seldom venture out. All very mysterious…

I bid you *au revoir* for the present! May you all be in good health until we meet again in the dear old Queendom or some other land. Loopy, grumbling because he has had no biscuits for a day (but plenty else), is the unlikely Mercury I send on Winged Paws with this missive.

Day 7

The Expeditionary Tales. Semaj puts on war-paint; the Great Big Boss Handyman

I sit here in glorious sunshine, and I dare hope that you experience the same unusual conditions this early April.

All seems peaceful but it is with a fiercely beating heart that I commence once more my account of the pioneering paths I cut into the dense bush of the Guard-Lands, for there were more sights and sounds to cause alarm to the senses. And yet some peace and repose I somehow garnered in the midst of this primitive new world.

Firstly, yet another correction, in the wall of small man-made red stones the furthest distance from my Base Camp I have discovered that there are four, not three, baffling doorways, of which two seem forever boarded up and the other two, with their original doors, seem to suggest further exploration to be possible beyond—but all, frustratingly, are forever barred to the passage of Man (or Woman for that matter). It suggests that an ancient Civilisation once had more expansive borders and these structures (perhaps stables for horse-motor carriages?) were once the property of such as I who inhabit the lands and dwellings where my brick Base Camp is constructed. Before I came to my Base Camp the people in the dwelling where I make Base Camp must have suffered some terrible humiliation in war to lose the territory beyond the red stone wall.[27]

Now I must tell you of a disturbing new occurrence, and this is not among the potentially hostile tribes which surround the areas so far explored but close to Camp Number One, where I rest, read, and suck

---

[27] There. I told you any explanation PWN gave for it would be unbelievable, didn't I?

peppermints or butter candies each day. I have mentioned hitherto the apparently friendly savage, an aboriginal (in the sense of an original occupier of a territory) from a neighbouring tribe. This person has suddenly changed his appearance and appeared in terrifying guise, for he has entirely shorn his previously lengthy head of hair. Only the follicles show, blue–black at the scalp, like woad or similar war-paint. Though he still speaks in a friendly enough manner, his appearance cannot but strike one with Fearful Anticipation of Maleficent Intent. He appears now to have some affiliation with that aggressive ancient tribe of ill-repute, the Skinheads; one can but pray that his appearance is rather part of some personal ritual and merely a Rite of Grooming, and that he will not suddenly turn and kick seven bells out of me. One thing consoles me: he appears to carry no weapon (unless it be concealed) and I have before now made good account of myself in bouts of fisticuffs, principally by having still a good turn of speed as I run away.

Of my continuing explorations—Upon my trip I was delighted by the sight of a banded, cooing winged creature accompanied by two juveniles. They sat and paced along the border wall of wood slats that denotes the start of the lands of Handy Man. As I approached, they flew up into the sky with much noise of alarm, though I meant no harm, however, were I a meat eater, they looked plump and probably very digestible, perhaps with a red wine sauce.

I saw that the Handy Man has now a pile of the man-made red stones. As these are rectangular, they stack well together. I have heard that they are called 'bricks.' What with Coy carp and cooing pterosaurs, one could not help but feel that Handy Man is singularly blessed and must be a Man of Peace. Imagine then my fright when an enamelled plate he has on a well–constructed wooden hut at the far end of his territory attracted my attention. On it was the one word in our language: 'Boss.' Were this not enough to make the heart fearful, in one corner were the two letters 'GB' and a flag. 'GB' surely can only mean 'Great Big' and the whole: 'Great Big Boss'?

As silently as possible I retreated and carried on along my way, my handsome knobbly knees shaking as my courage somewhat deserted me. But soon enough I mastered my emotion—am I not an Englishman, after all, despite appearances to the contrary, and do we fear such tinpot dictators long? Nevertheless, I will proceed with greater caution when spying out the country of The Handy Man in future, for fear he should actually catch me at it.

I close now and send my love to all My People. May you conquer your difficulties in the same way that I am learning to adapt to the ways of this Strange New World.

Day 8

My identity is questioned

I emerged rather later than has been usual from Base Camp, delayed by certain duties on behalf of the Great Imperial Power that has sent me on this lonely mission. My attempts to secure more supplies were somewhat frustrated by the bureaucracy to which my Nation is prone.

In the event, having done my best, I made the decision to leave the Camp as soon as possible, and clear my head by further exploration through the country that still awaits me beyond Camp One.

Even then my movements were to be initially constrained by the unexpected arrival of a case of beer from Good Old Blighty; this was indeed very welcome, however non-alcoholic it may be, though not so much as the arrival of the long–promised cat biscuits would have been (or 'kibbles,' in American parlance). I also had to remember to unpack vast quantities of that promised powdered soup of strange and acrid flavours and store them in the diminishing space of Base Camp.

I began to wonder if a local foraging trip might not be a good idea. However, I had seen nothing good to eat so far, unless it be the Coy Carp, and I dared not make an outright enemy of Handy Man and his tribe in the Guard-Lands. Anyway, at last, summoning my bearers Loopy and Meli who had been lying on my bed all morning (is it too late to impose some discipline on them? Yes, probably...), out we went into the scrub surrounding the Camp. Who could have guessed at the Encounter we would make in the course of this stage of the Campaign?

Camp One was reached quite quickly, now that our track made by former excursions is quite clear of obstacles and easy to negotiate.

After refreshment had been taken of deep pulls on both my bottled beverage and several drags on the vaporiser, now flavoured with American Gold tobacco and the wondrous berry called 'Wonderberry', out I strode, equipment all tucked into my worn old kitbag, only slightly trepidatious in consideration of what exactly I might encounter.

Past Lake Tina I strode on several circuits, its petite beauty undiminished as the oily waters rippled in the breeze against its pink sides. The midday sun burned fiercely down on the still hairy crown of my scalp (a proud boast of mine) and this mad Englishman was soon joined by that mad, befouling Yapper, Freebie.

No sooner had that fierce beast been called back to her hut by her master, the neo-skinhead, than I was joined by another Yapper, this time a silent one of different colour and fur texture.

I know now that these little beasts come always with a Master or Mistress, so I looked around and saw a portal open in the wooden wall which indicates the start of the Lands of the Handy Man.

And there–striking fear in my heart–came the Boss Handy Man himself. Although we were both in an area of scrubland formally owned by no tribe–I feared Handy Man would pretend some ownership of the territory and be fierce with me, or even launch a weapon of some Infernal type at me.

However, I steeled myself and tried an old English trick for deflating tension in awkward situations: yes, I spoke of the weather.

At this he greeted me fulsomely, in English of a peculiar sort which I have since been told is the 'Norfolk' dialect. Together we went through the accepted ritual of insincere speech upon the subject of the climate.

At last, we both seemed at the same moment to feel the subject exhausted and we each went our separate ways. Before we did so, he turned back and enquired, rather late in the day, if I was 'PWN'? I agreed I was that proud and official representative of the British people.[28]

You may be sure, now that I had seen two Yappers in No–Man's Land, I took extra care to avoid their spoor, especially as my kit had taken very much scrubbing the other day, before it could be at all happily taken back into Base Camp.

There I end for today, much relieved by my pleasant reception by Handy Man. I will give it a day or two before I ask him if I may consume one of his bashful carp.

---

[28] The hard drive has at this point— 'You see how my fame has spread amongst the natives?'

Day 9

From further than I have ever ventured

It dawned glorious, hot, and sunny, here. Nevertheless, I had sworn a terrible Oath to myself the night before to spend the day to come on The Four 'Rs', these being Rest, Recuperation, Repairs and Renewals in Base Camp. I was to break that Oath in short order, as you will see.

How I longed for a petite Oriental masseuse to walk the length of my spine (and that only, erhm...), to relieve the twinges I felt from my old war wound: a slipped, herniated and sometimes strangulated disc in my back, which sometimes prevents me from being quite as upright in stature as a true Englishman should be.

However, in the absence of such a skilled Eastern personage I instead undertook the exercises prescribed for me by a skilled cruncher of bone in my own dear land, so far away. I cannot say that thinking of a delightful imaginary Japanese lady had not disturbed my equilibrium more than a little.

But soon I was once more as nimble as a mountain goat and again as pure in thought, word and deed as my dear Queen bade me be, when knighting me with a six-foot sword and telling me to 'Arise Sir PWN, for now we must discuss the Great Deed you are to undertake for Us, Our united family, and your country, the United Kingdom.'[29]

With the bulk of the maintenance work in Base Camp achieved, I could resist no more the lure of the great grassy plains beyond Camp One, and so, fully prepared against all eventualities, I was soon striding

---

[29] The hard drive has this rather touching, if vain-glorious, phrase at this point—'Mine is no less than A Royal Appointment!'

out once more onto the Plain. Here, surely, when my attention is otherwise engaged, roam great herds of wildebeest, zebra, elephants, and perhaps even peaceful diplodocuses, together with predators, the wolves and hyenas, and the vulture-like pterosaur raptors of this Neglected World? And might there not even be Tyrannosaurs? Have I not heard their terrible roars from Base Camp? Some say that these are merely the noises of Great Boss Handy Man's saw that is circular—but I ask you—how likely is it that such a device could exist in this Primitive Place?!

Eventually I took some rest back at Camp One and consumed my meagre rations for the day, only to glimpse the astonishing sight of a maiden from the unknown tribe to the West preparing to lie out in the harsh sunshine, clad only in a pair of small pink shorts and a sheen of some lotion. You might be forgiven for thinking that after such a long time without the comfort of a female companion I might be tempted to make amorous overtures and more to the maiden but—remaining pure in deed and word, if not in thought—I rejected the idea.

One must be most careful in how one deals with the Maids and Maidens of these lands, for their Menfolk are prone to jealousy, sometimes leading to violence. This is not good for diplomatic relations.

I have not yet encountered the situation which befalls many a Discoverer, I am told, that is— when a Chief offers his daughter to him in marriage, and a refusal often offends. Were this to happen to me I might, in American parlance, have to 'take one for the team.' Or possibly two or three.

There is more to tell but a new day has dawned, and I must once more enter the Guard-Lands and go exploring, so that I may report in due course to you, the erstwhile Companions of my Life.

Until then, I wish you every success in your Endeavours, and great Wealth, Health and Happiness.

Day 10

Once more into the Wilderness

How changeable is the weather in these parts and how unlike my own Dear Country, where there is sunshine every day and only soft Spring showers fall very occasionally to refresh the great woodlands and forests, as any denizen or visitor will tell you. Indeed, I have never heard one word of adverse criticism about the climate there.

But here I am not so fortunate, for it was apparent on Day Ten that much precipitation had fallen, and the skies were as overcast and gloomy as they had been cloudless and suffused with sunlight the day before. I had perforce to clothe myself in my stoutest raiment as I made myself once more venture out into the Border Lands.

I picked my way most carefully along the trails I had already constructed, often employing my Swiss Army machete,[30] for I feared the heaps of ordure left by one or both of the little Yappers, the bane of my present experience. But it seems they choose not to hide these vile traps upon my worn trails but beneath the lush undergrowth. It is only when forging further pathways in the bush of the Guard-Lands that I place myself and companions in Harm's Way.

I encountered two more specimens of the wildlife on that day. Firstly, a feathered archaeopteryx-like creature (a pterosaur with unmistakeable rudimentary plumage) alighted on one of the palisades

---

[30] No official model of Swiss Army knife included a machete. Albany has suggested that a special tool was commissioned for PWN, by Royal Command. It is hard if not impossible to understand how it could fold away into the handle, however. 'Swiss Army Knives and The Famous Explorers.' Albany, W. (Publication TBA.)

demarcating the potentially hostile tribal lands to the East.[31] I watched it in wonder until it flew off. It was a little smaller than the ones encountered the other day and with finer lines and more subtle, pale pigmentation except for a dark band at the base of a neck. Its song was the gentle cooing so beloved of those who wish to relax. [32]

Encountering that ostensibly friendly but now skin-headed son of the neighbouring tribe, he told me 'It is an evod, innit?' I am afraid I doubted his words. For instance, he names himself 'Semaj', which to me sounds like all the right letters but not necessarily in the right order.[33] To be fair, however, I grow a little deaf, and had not got my hearing trumpets with me, for I had forgotten to pack them into my kitbag.

After another circuit of the Distanced Lands beyond the Back Door this same person made friendly beckoning gestures at a distance of six feet. (They are a shy race and do not allow closer contact than that, except presumably for the purposes of mating.) In his hands he held a grotesque yellow creature, which made attempts to leap from his cupped fingers. I took it to be some species of amphibian but unlike any newt or salamander I have ever encountered. I think that Semaj must think I am on some sort of collecting mission for a zoo, for he took care to release it as close as possible to Camp One. However, I took pity on the poor moist, gulping, and croaking creature and simply watched as he (or she, I know not) in small leaps jumped swiftly off the Plain and into the privet–clad Border that separates Camp One from the possibly savage Half-Naked Lady's country. I wished it well, although I fear that unless that fierce woman has a waterfall or other water feature it might not long escape being dehydrated and swooped upon and eaten by one

---

[31] The creature PWN observed is obviously capable of true flight and therefore quite an advanced bird; it probably tasted like something that nowadays one would find, full of lead-shot, in a savoury pie.

[32] From the hard drive—'It is either that or whale-song: 'You pays your money and you takes your choice.'''

[33] Not an original joke but one shamelessly adapted from an old Morecambe and Wise sketch about musical notes, by Eddie Braben. (Credit where credit is due.)

of the ravening pterosaurs. I should not fancy eating it myself, although licking its back as a means of expanding my experience and breaking down the Doors of Perception had—I admit—briefly occurred to me. I do not know where I get these ideas.

You must envy me such sights, but they come with not a little Danger.

And now I must close. It is time to shoulder my kitbag once again and go out into the Guard-Lands in the best colonial spirit and for the expansion of the Empire.

Day 11

Of Trials, Tribes and Tribulations

Despite summoning my feline bearers, Loopy and Meli, they were both conspicuous only by their absence. In a bad temper I hunted through Base Camp for the recalcitrant kitties.

At last, I found my two servants in hiding places in the compartment I use for sleeping. Loopy was ensconced in a cavity beneath the bed and answered my eager summons with a hostile glare and silence, lying flat on his side. Meli, I discovered trying to disguise herself as the fabric covering to my laundry container. For camouflage she has not the ability of the chameleon but more that of the flamingo. However, though both were discovered, they did not quit their stations but remained insolently defying me and the ripe words I used against them. I even pointed out that this very day two enormous sacks of their favourite delicacies had arrived early from across the Pestilential Provinces, from the Middle Lands of my own dear country, and that they should show their gratitude by turning out smartish, take up this English Man's Burden, and assist my progress into the World of the Guard-Lands.

Eventually taking them by the scruffs of their necks, I forced them to look me in the eye, and only then did I discover the reason for their revolutionary behaviour.

It turns out that they were refusing to accompany me because they are too afraid of the little Yappers. They mentioned also the rumours of dog-foxes, but I think there they were grasping at straws to bolster their argument; I am told that no fox has been seen in these parts

26

for two years or more, and certainly not in the daytime. (I am not a complete fool and know better than to explore at night.)

I promised these fearful felines extra rations of Tormentingly Tasty–a very precious savoury commodity–but could not sway them in their resolve to sleep all day at Base Camp, emerging only to urinate and defecate. At least I have managed to civilise them to that extent. Not much to show for years of training...

So, limited by having recruited no servants, I could make but little progress into the bush. I did, however, 'blow the cobwebs away' and was glad of the exercise.

Both the Great Big Boss Handy Man and Semaj came out to greet me. The latter's Yapper, Freebie, had apparently become used to me for she yapped not at all, merely whimpered, and snuffled. Emboldened by this friendly reception I put my fingers through the palisade for Freebie to sniff. Firstly, she did so and then without warning, bit them. Fortunately for the sake of Your Hero she has but little strength in her sharp little jaws and I leapt away, startled but unhurt.

Semaj laughed heartily which I took rather amiss. Seeing this, his heart was touched, and he made friendly noises in his almost unintelligible pidgin-English. Two of these words I took to be 'Wait here!' so I did as I was bid, trembling a little.

When he returned Semaj proffered one of the striking tribal masks the people in The Pestilential Provinces are wearing in their peculiar rituals this season. The mask offered me for free, gratis, and nothing, was not one of the gay ones I had seen on the crystal screen that shows pictures (and no doubt foretells the future at times) but was of an opaque black kind. It covers only half the face so that when I regarded myself in the now still waters of Lake Tina, I looked either like a robber in a children's book or 'Desperate Dan', a character from 'The Dandy' comic of my youth many moons ago. I was, in fact, more of a sight to inspire fear than pity in the heart of any person thus seeing me. I resolved only to wear this piece of apparel when absolutely forced to, perhaps to cross the Pestilential Provinces in search of provisions in the coming weeks. Still, it was a kind gesture on the part of Semaj and his tribe.

I must think how best I may reciprocate for this unexpected gift. Perhaps I could feed the Yapper something laced with cyanide and thus help us both to a state of equanimity.

And so back to Base Camp I made my way to force the feline fools out of their places of rest and get them to prepare my evening meal. I feared it might consist of Miaow Super Morsels and Purr and Fur cat biscuits and so it proved to be. You just cannot get the staff out here in the Misplaced World.

I think of you all, my dear ones, and leave you with this thought: It is always darkest before dawn—except when you get an early morning delivery and a horse-motor van's strong frontal lights, even seen through curtains, threaten to blind one.

Day 12

Of spiders and snakes

Oh, my Dear Readers, what a day I had! Even at Base Camp one is not safe.

As I took my morning contemplation on the ceramic throne, from the ceiling in front of me dropped a hideous black, be-fanged spider, which I judged to be as big as a dinner plate. Admittedly that would be a dinner plate in a doll's house. I feared it would leap at me and bury its fearsome fangs into my flat feet, but I remained still and the vile beast, regarding the one good eye of a True Brit staring back at it without the betrayal of emotion, shrugged its multiple black shoulders in defeat and scuttled away into the shadows behind the pedestal where no Civilised Person had ever ventured.

Suited and booted and coated in a thin layer of 'Handysan' to repel the midges and mosquitoes, I then made my way into the Guard-Lands for which no maps yet exist— though I haven't checked very thoroughly, admittedly.

The Servants ' Revolt is over. Loopy, defeated, has bowed to the superiority of this English Man; without demur he followed me out onto the great plain, formerly called 'The Plain of Jane' but now called 'The Savannah of Savanna' after a young American friend of mine. Above me blazed the sun once more in 'The Sky of Skye' (Savanna's younger sister), whilst in the far distance, as far as a single and myopic eye could see, leaned that unsteady structure of red stones in Handy Man's territory, which I have christened 'The Tower of Lisa' —yes, another American friend and this one the mother of Savanna and Skye, a grown woman with whom I once–many a year ago–considered running away to Spain. Alas, it was not to be. For one thing, I can sprint well, but I am poor over distance, particularly water.

In the land to North, across the track of tar combined with little stones, for at least two hours at midday sported several of the indigenous people, in groups of what I presumed to be families.

Suddenly my attention was drawn to a little girl. Oh, the horror! For was she not wrestling with a bright yellow snake?! Not only that but a man I took to be her father was himself fighting off an attack from a brown serpent—this one was hissing and spitting vast quantities of transparent venom at great force all over the crude outside benches on which this family frequently takes its rest. The father seemed to be getting the upper hand, for the serpent writhed to no avail. At last, it ceased its projectile venom spraying and lay still, strangled by the father. And the tiny daughter too had begun to get the upper hand and the subdued yellow monster drooped from her little hands and lay, quite subdued, over their frontal palisade. But then to my ultimate distress the daughter took the brown snake from the father, revived it, and began to spray its venom over the father and the mother of the family, who had rushed out at the cries of both father and daughter. However, I suddenly realised the family were actually enjoying what would be to civilised people a traumatic event. Truly, these are strange tribes I am encountering, and I despair of bringing to them the humourless culture and stiff upper lip of we, a far Superior People who seldom play with snakes.

After a long day spent in the Bush, upon my return to Base Camp I was shortly to be delighted when a Relief Column came through the Pestilential Provinces, for I now have fresh supplies for the foreseeable future and possibly even enough goods to trade with the Savages here, although I am sorry to tell you that I will keep the unsolicited vast quantity of forbidden prawn crisps all to myself. Well? My doctor is not here to remind me how bad such treats are for me. Does this mean I have Gone Native?

Then the sky of Skye began to darken over the savannah of Savanna, and I retired to my camp bed.

I think of you All, and hope you will spare a thought for me, a lone explorer cut off from his people for as long as it takes me to complete my investigations and as long as funds and health permit.

Day 13

Wounded! Misfortune and Undies

Generally, life on the trail is more comfortable now that supplies have arrived in great quantity and the feline fulminations have ceased, except for the usual sulks one gets from such simple creatures. (I have my doubts that they can ever be fully civilised.)

Once more fortunate in the climate, I set off, now with belly full and thirst quenched, to put the stamp of British beliefs and culture upon this heathen place.

Resting at Camp One I was delighted by a display of winged creatures which fluttered by, for all the world the colour of the shells of the decorative tortoise found in the Mediterranean or the polished shell of certain turtles oft incorporated into fine furniture and musical instruments, in Days of Old.

However, soon my ears were assailed by the melodious voice of the Half-Naked Savage who inhabits the territory to the West. (I should perhaps mention it is the top half which she displays naked— and so far only from the rear.) I could not espy the other person to whom she spoke, so it is possible that she spoke merely through the peculiar devices we have in these parts, which listen and talk and oft display magical pictures of other hideous savages, which the Young Native Peoples so like to rank in order of aesthetic appeal. They live in such luxury in these lands that they have little better to do, or so they believe. However, the Pestilential Provinces do grow in area and threaten their paradisiacal way of life. Ranking each other's beauty may soon become an extinct practice, except for on small Reservations.

To my great astonishment, from a stand with cables strung around it in the Half-Naked Savage 's territory (which is so neat and free of detritus that I almost suspect her of hoovering it) hung many a pair of the savage's lower under-apparel, ranging from very brief items to undies in the French style. I mused for many a minute on this phenomenon until I had come up with a collective noun for this starting assemblage of intimate articles. Eventually I decided upon 'A Pantheon of Panties."

And here I come to the Dreadful Accident which befell me and from which I am still endeavouring to recover —

Pausing for refreshments, I enjoyed the sunshine and the calls of distant pterosaurs, not threatening at that distance. However, little did I know what Danger lurked close to hand!

I took from my kitbag a strange, segmented orange coloured fruit which does not grow in these Parts but which the Natives import in great quantity. It has a skin which usually yields to pressure from the thumb nail. But on this occasion—oh, Cruel Fate!—I tore through that nail, giving me not a little pain and requiring that I take my Swiss Army scissors and trim it back, that nail so beloved of we players of the stringed musical instruments. The pain from a torn thumbnail is second only to that from a compound fracture, a toothache, a bitten tongue, a papercut, a stubbed toe and many another thing.

What was worse, in my solitary travels there was no one there to staunch the wound (Ok, there was not any actual blood since you ask) or kiss it better. My feline assistant—on this occasion, Meli—looked horrified at the mere suggestion, which only added to my chagrin.

Licking my wound, I stumbled back to Camp Number One, making it just in time before Faintness overcame me, and from thence to Base Camp, where I collapsed in front of my Crystal Screen with a can of cold beer from my Homeland to steady my nerve and calm me. Please, no medal—such demonstrations of courage are my occupation, after all...

Yours, shorter by 1/16" of thumbnail but otherwise in reasonably good health and wishing you the same.

Day 14

Of Princesses, Cougars, Friendly Natives, and the Terrible Flying Giants

It is now a fortnight I have spent exploring this Wonderful and yet Terrible Place. Together with the fortnight spent in setting up Base Camp and ceasing the last of spoken communication with the Outside, it is now almost a month since I saw the face of any whom I love from the Civilised World. But am I downhearted? You can bet your sweet bippy I am.

It started in the now familiar way with my smaller and female feline bearer entering my bedroom compartment, jumping up onto my dirty–laundry basket, eager for her exposed belly to be stroked—the wanton hussy. When one considers that she goes amongst her people as a Princess (or so I am informed by unnatural daughters of my acquaintance) and often has the airs and graces of one of that title, it is doubly discomfiting to see such a display and almost turns the stomach in the early morning.

However, I have discovered it is all a Stratagem to persuade me to get up and unlock the secret stash of Miaow Super Morsels sachets, so that she and the more reticent Loopy may gorge themselves on this dwindling resource of hideously expensive nourishment.

Once the bearers and I had both breakfasted–myself on far less tasty delicacies (hard tack with weevils for the protein element of the meal) –and I had downed mugs of both tea and coffee, sweetened not with the harmful sugar of this land but with tiny chemical tablets, it was yet again time to gird our respective loins and depart into the largely undiscovered Back Garden wilderness once more.

The Half-Naked Savage to the West was, to my immense surprise, completely dressed and with protective clothing, and was applying a neat layer of some jungle juice to the exterior of her subsidiary hut, in which she keeps the simple couch upon which she lies Half-Naked for many a day, soaking up the rays of the sun in this unusual spell of bright weather. Everything is neat about her and her actions, but she has a forbidding visage. I doubt that the rumours–that she can magically transform into a Cougar given the right man and the right circumstances–are in fact true.

A member of a different tribe in the West, with whom I have established a reasonably good relationship, Salt Peter by name, came out and kept me company for a short while. He has the unfortunate habit of feeding scraps to the terrible pterosaurs. I say 'unfortunate' because firstly it is the wrong food for the creatures and secondly it brings the smaller of the flying dinosaurs within reach of my usually lazy feline bearers, taking their minds off the jobs I have given them, and tempting them to catch the creatures and distribute their chewed corpses inside my enclosure at Base Camp.

Salt Peter showed interest in my dear Homeland before the Pestilent Times. He was curiously well informed, and I became drawn into a long conversation, despite the World of Wonders still awaiting discovery.

As a consequence, my discoveries were limited. However, settling once more in the middle of the time which I permit for my perambulations to take refreshment and read about the days of our youth from a tome presented to me by my brother, Boston[34] (when, oh when, will I see his dear face again?), I could not help but be horrified by the sudden emergence of giant flying ants, each as big as a little fingernail, all around Camp One. No, really! There must be a Great Nest of the hideous creatures close by. I must say that if the horrifying beasts were emerging for the purposes of finding a mate for procreation, they were making a very poor job of it, for each seemed oblivious of the other and would surely die shortly, without Issue.

I have now seen with my own eyes Flying Dragons, Flying Butters of several varieties, and these flying Giants. All creatures formerly only of Fable. One may only hazard a guess at the Wonders yet to come! But I wouldn't waste too much time on it if I were you.

---

[34] This is the only place in which PWN's brother is named. Unfortunately, it has not assisted scholars. It is obvious, therefore, that PWN has most cleverly disguised his brother's true name.

Leave exploration of the Wild Conjoined Guard-Lands to we professionals with too much time on our hands...

Be of good cheer and be lucky. Until the glad day that we meet again —or at least until tomorrow's Dispatch.

Day 15

In Base Camp for the Greater Part but Industrious

You may be relieved to hear that I did not for long expose myself to the Dangers of the Guard-Lands from which few men (or women) have ever returned and bothered to tell the tale, but rather spent much of my waking hours fully occupied in this crude shelter in one of Count Sil's huts.

One of the Readers whom my messages from this barbaric place has reached–Petroline–sent in return a message of her own, which I was glad to receive as it hailed from Europe (to which Great Britain is so closely allied, of course)[35], although it told of her sheer horror at my fearful encounters, particularly my observation of the serpents a few days ago, and expressing her wish that I take great care.[36] But it is not the life of the committed Explorer–especially one who has been committed on several previous occasions–to shun the risk that an Expedition such as mine entails. After all, do I not forge a way in the name of Progress?

However, it would be a fool who pursued Progress without laying first the foundations of success in the matter of planning. To this end, and because I must placate my Life Insurance company, everything I do must be prudential.[37]

I therefore hereby attempt to reassure my French friend that I try always to remain an observer and not a participant in the animal horrors that surround me and my once-again-trusty bearers.

---

[35] This would appear to be by way of a sarcastic comment, as the UK had left the European Common Market by 2020.

[36] It has been speculated that the correspondent mentioned here is none other than Petroline Wilder, the French aristocrat. See 'French Aristocrats called Petroline' by myself, 2001. Out of print and I never sold a single copy.

[37] It is unclear if this is meant to be a joke. If so, it is a poor one.

However, on occasion–though with due preparation and attention to every detail–I come into Harm's Way, as I cannot think of everything—that surely is the nature of the Unknown?

As regards my speaking of my friend: anyone else seeking a mention in these missives must send fifty crisp pre-decimal pounds, made out to my 'Money for Old Rope Fund.'

I had heard that Music soothes the Savage Beast, so–to that hoped-for happy end–I was careful to pack amongst my belongings long ago in my Dear Homeland a Mysterious Package, the contents of which now adorns my hut at Base Camp, to the consternation and disapprobation of the bearers.

Surely there can be no better (or worse place) to try the truth of the soothing of Savages with music? The Half-Naked Woman is a beast I am particularly keen to soothe, for when she encounters me in the adjacent pathway her face expresses an utter disdain for me and all my doings. I feel her unreasonable hatred as does the innocent fawn speared by the merciless hunter.

And so, at last, out onto the great savannah which is called Savanna (she owes me a quid now, but I will let her off), before the setting of the sun in the sky of Skye (ditto). I had time only for a speedy march around the paths already trod near Lake Tina (she owes me quids and quids! But I owe her more...) but even along this apparently safe trail, I was to encounter–near the Great Big Boss Handy Man's territory– a recent and huge pile of stinking ordure. Who would have thought his own small Yapper to have had so much crud in him? Not I, for one, and so I suspect there has been an Incursion from one of the huge hound-like Werewolves that are at least six times the size of the two local Yappers, from over the border to the Badlands in the North. I have seen these huge creatures in the distance. (Unless they were small and near, of course.[38]) One of these dreaded creatures must have crossed into the Guard-Lands. Its laying of its scent in our territory is no less than a Declaration of War.

In fear and trembling, I returned to Base Camp for rice-based snacks and beer. (I have smuggled in a few luxuries for when I tire of

---

[38] This worn-out witticism is thought to date from Antiquity. Time enough now for it to be laid to rest, surely?

the usual hard tack and brackish water.) But they were to be like ashes in my mouth, for I could not but think of the Monstrous Yapper from The North that might be once again stealing across the border with a full colon, in the Dark Hours!... But be not afeared for me, Gentle Reader. It is true that last night, for me, sleep was elusive and the few winks I got were nightmarish in quality. Yet remember, as I tried to: Werewolves are so rare as to be completely non-existent. You should not worry your Pretty Little Heads about them.

Day 16

Terrifying turbulence in the lands to the North

Once more delayed by musical matters at Base Camp,[39] it was again somewhat late that, on another hot and hazy late afternoon, I set off with my cat companions into the Guard-Lands.

However, I had not long been upon the toilsome trail, heading North–East, when the usual intimidating low throb of the jungle drums was to be interrupted by a never before perceived sound. It was no less than the discordant noise of a fracas in the Badlands to the North, where stands a terrace of Count Sil's huts on the Meadow Rise. (His dominion reaches far and wide in this Pagan Place. Some of the Natives of these huts have, I believe, declared unilateral independence from Count Sil and are now in private hands, which unfortunately seems to mean that their huts become ever tattier, however brave that rebellious move into private ownership may have been.)

To resume: All of a sudden there was an at first muffled shouting in a tongue I do not understand but sounded like Terrible Oaths, which became clearer as the doors of a hut swung open. The litany of Oaths was completed by the worst Curse that can ever be uttered by such Primitive Peoples. Even I could not mistake its meaning for it came at top volume and in old Anglo Saxon (what a peculiar dialect word to find surviving in the language of these Natives of the Distanced Lands!) This was followed by the ear-splitting crack of the door of a hut being slammed shut so hard that one feared for the future integrity of that portal, if not the structure of the entire hut. Many dwellers in the Badlands looked out of their huts, alarmed, or annoyed by this terrible sound.

I had hidden myself as effectively as I could behind the shielding body of Loopy, my old feline bearer, for I feared a subsequent hail of

---

[39] For further information on PWN's musical achievements I refer you to Paddy Tempera's revealing book on this matter: 'A Small Talent to Displease.' Tempera, P., 2023.

stone missiles or even a shower of spears, and that I might be caught at the fringes of the warpath of aggrieved warriors from the Badlands and be collateral damage in a Terrible Battle.

However, strange to relate, suddenly all was stunned silence broken only by the same door being opened, a man looking out at the back of a youth disappearing into the distance, and a female voice from behind, yelling the following strange incantation: 'Leave 'im, Kev, e's not worth it!'

The youthful warrior, mouthing indistinguishable words but clearly expletives, in his own tongue, rapidly disappeared around the bend that descends to the Northeast and towards a place of which I know not but almost certainly had illegal gatherings and alcohol. Then all was still; the civil war, for at least a time, seemed quelled. I peered out from behind Loopy then stood up to my full height (five feet ten and three quarters of an inch, in old money, of superb male flesh), and tentatively began once more upon my penetration of the Dark Exterior which still holds, no doubt, many a wonder and discovery to be wondered at and discovered.

Completing my circuit, I espied both the friendly neighbourhood aborigine, Semaj, and the Half-Naked Woman. Strange to say, on this occasion the Half-Naked Woman was fully clothed and administering water to certain preferred plants she tends in her territory, whilst Semaj was stripped to his waist (unappetising pale grey-blue-pink in complexion as is commonly the appearance of these people), playing with the little Yapper, Freebie, an animal who can never quite be tamed, as I believe is true of all his or her ilk.

After my fright at the Border of the Badlands I was not inclined to engage in conversation, even of the pidgin variety by which we attempt to communicate, and so I retreated via Camp One and a restorative suck at my vaporiser, to Base Camp. I finished my footsteps to the mocking sound of coastal pterosaurs come inland to feast on the crusts of bread provided by Salt Peter.[40]

It was with great relief that I threw myself on my Base Camp bed and closed my eyes for forty winks of fitful sleep before preparing my

---

[40] The hard drive is more dramatic, and states 'Their evil eyes glowed red with the setting sun.'

simple repast of fried potatoes and a fish of the local seas which does its very best in pretence of being cod, which is not to be sourced in these parts except at an expense to which I am not prepared to go.

Day 17

Great Big Boss Handy Man endeavours to make me his handy man

On a chill day with a stiff shiver-inducing wind, far more typical of the Spring weather in these Climes, I packed up my troubles in my old kitbag[41], plus some sugar free mints, butter candies and a bottle of juiced fruit, and once more set out from Base Camp.

Resting once again at Camp One, on the bed raised for flowers by a construction made of ancient railway 'sleeper' timbers but to this date containing only composting coffee grounds, potato skins and fruit peel, I detected with my sensitive and large nasal nerve receptors the vile odour of Yapper dung. I may be wrong, but I begin to suspect that, when my back is turned and I am at Base Camp, Semaj belies his friendly overtures by casting the faecal material of Freebie the Yapper into this trough, intended solely for fruit and vegetable compost and–eventually–delightful, scented, flowering plants of select varieties to cheer my future soul.

The unpleasant niff was wafted by the wind so frequently up my noble nostrils that before it was time, I repacked my necessities and set out upon my Wanderings in the Wilderness. I jest, of course; I do as bid by Her Majesty and do rather plot out carefully the geography of the Dark Heart of this continent where many a Yapper is incontinent.

Each night, in my crude Native brick shack, I pore over fine vellum devoted to the purpose of producing the first detailed map, in the finest cartographic detail, so that those who may come after me may avoid the pitfalls I have encountered and more surely pick their way through this intriguing if dangerous World. (Well, a chap has got to have a hobby.) The borders of the said map I have already illuminated with beautiful decorations in gold leaf, vermilion, azure blue, and lapis lazuli, and within those sumptuous margins, have also represented the

---

[41] This is a strange reference to the famous song from World War One (which is actually only when they started counting them).

many curious and sometimes horrifying Beasts I have encountered. There is surely to be great economic advantage to my successors in harvesting *Garde de Nos* snake skins and Doll's House Spider pelts and suchlike? An established Trade Route could be the making of this Primaeval Place![42]

And so, I come to the meat of this epistle. After much weary toil, I and my bolshy bearers came to the feared border where the grass forest meets the Eastern Territory where dwells the feared Great Big Boss Handy Man, with his Moai statue, Bonsai Forest, Coy Carp, and all. To my terrified apprehension the Handy Man was out in his lands and pursuing the Calling for which he is named. With his almost superhuman strength he was sawing huge timbers, his muscles and sinews rippling beneath his boiler suit. Try as I might to avoid his eye, it was hopeless, for he saw me in the periphery of his vision, straightened up and brandished his saw at me most threateningly. I thought that I was lost, for sure, and would never again see even the ripples on the puddle of water that I have christened Lake Tina, or see the coastal pterosaurs glide upon the wind, or view the handsome blue, brown, fawn and white plumaged proto–birds which squabble over crusts of bread thrown out by Salt Peter, let alone return to the Bosom of my Family. (Mind you, I would prefer to return to the bosoms of someone else's family member...).

However, to my surprise, the Big Boss was in a friendly mood, indicating with certain noises I took to be Words that he was an Admirer of my track-beating work and that he would now like me to thoroughly zig-zag and to chop my way and beat back the Bush all the way to the Centre of the Guard-Lands.

Later, when I thought about it, I thought that he might not have been being as friendly as I thought, for might he not know more what Terrors await the Unknowledgeable Explorer in that Forbidding Forest? Might he not in fact, though all smiles and laughter, be sending me to my Doom? Ah, these Natives are cunning!

---

[42] Unfortunately, this lavish Map has never been found and may never have returned with PWN, if he himself returned, of which there is still some doubt.

Is it not possible that he sends me by such overtures to meet that most fearsome and dismaying monster of all, of whom the aboriginal people here speak of only in whispers—'The Hidden Agenda'?

Watch this space, Gentle Reader, and pray for me, for my danger is compounded by my apparently having, somewhere at Base Camp, or *en route* through the Pestilent Lands, lost some of my precious marbles, carried with me for trading purposes ...

Day 18

I venture towards the Hidden Agenda

As I made my way from Base Camp to Camp One, not a single cloud was in the sky of Skye (ker-ching!), for there were a good many clouds in the sky. The usual Pantheon of Panties was absent on the drying device of The Half Naked Savage, replaced by sensible all–weather clothing taking time to dry in the unpredictable weather. The grass on the savannah of Savannah (and another ker-ching!) waved like the tides as the wind playfully wound its way through it, seeking exposed flesh to chill. Even the Lake of Tina (the pennies are coming thick and fast now...), often so placid and inviting—were it not for Flying Dragon larvae, lakeweed and unnameable rusting wire objects—looked formidable, unfathomably deep, and downright chilly.

Therefore, I determined to carefully traverse the edges of my discovered territory first, before making a tentative assault upon the interior of the grass forest where it is my belief—and that of my feline servants and the Native Peoples – may lurk the fearsome Hidden Agenda. In ignorance, some of these surrounding people revere this monster as though it were a God. Let it not be said of an Englishman, especially one of my calibre, that he is susceptible to such Pagan Beliefs. I am resolved to penetrate, in time, the heart of this mystery and find for it a logical explanation.

Firstly, as I approached the Badlands which border the Northern extremities of the Guard-Lands, I was to perceive two figures miraculously suspended on contraptions of two wheels only.[43] I was shortly to learn that they were one of the two mothers of a family who inhabit one of the huts which face my Camp One at the border, plus her daughter. One of the wheeled contraptions was large, the other small.

---

[43] Unfortunately, no scholar has ever been able to interpret PWN's cryptic description and thus been able work out what these conveyances were. Admittedly, they were a pretty dim bunch of scholars.

How they may perch upon the narrow saddles and balance upon these devilish devices I cannot comprehend. They are surely bewitched to be able to stay upon these machines, which also travel at a frightening speed. Each of the pair wore a hard mask which enclosed their skulls and upon the knees and elbows of the daughter were inexplicable bracelets which looked like black pads of leather or a similar material. These seem of no practical use and are presumably simply talismans to ward off evil spirits.

Dismounting their steeds upon the tar track which has stones in it, they proceeded to lock away their fiendish, magical devices in one of the stables for the equally astounding carriages for which tiny, boxed horses are required for motive power.

Then they removed their masks and war-helmets to reveal their features. The mother in question was the slighter, prettier, and more feminine one of the pair of mothers. The child is a little blonde girl, and so unlike the peoples of those parts that one felt she must surely have been captured by the 'mothers' in some sort of raid on another tribe and pressed into a privileged form of Slavery. I shuddered at the thought, and yet the little girl seemed deliriously happy. 'Stockholm Syndrome', no doubt.[44]

Now there could be no more procrastination, for it was the place and the time for me to take the Swiss Army machete[45] from my clenched teeth (plays merry hell with the amalgam of my fillings...) and begin the careful process of hacking my way through the tall grasses of the forest of the Interior of the Guard-Lands, towards the Lair of the Hidden Agenda. Around me the air was thick with the awful sound of the jungle drums, now joined by a powerful bass line, all treble frequencies failing to carry over the distance from the unknown tribal camps from which they emanated. It was at this point that to a man, woman and cat, the bearers, Loopy and Meli, dropped their packs and mine and retreated in fear and trembling.

---

[44] 'Stockholm syndrome' being a state of mind in which hostages develop an emotional bond with their captors.
[45] See earlier Note.

'What, desert me now, would you in my moment of Greatest Peril, would you, you Perfidious Pussies?' I shouted at their retreating backs, as their tails lashed in Terror.

It was no good; without someone to carry my sugar-free confectionery and my book I obviously could not proceed far. And so, having established a portal into the mast-like grass stems and forged an approach of one zigzag into the Forbidding Grass Forest, I had to abandon the mission for the day.

In any case it seemed as if there were going to be a downpour, so I made my way back to Camp One. Annoyingly, by the time I got there the sun was once more shining and so fiercely that I had to find shade on the other razed flower bed which is Camp Two. There, I discovered my recalcitrant bearers had beaten me to it. They were 'beaters' rather than 'bearers' this time—only a one letter difference but oh -the difference in meaning! ...

And so, hoping to do better in future, I close this Dispatch. May your endeavours be crowned by greater success than mine, and may your pets be more easily persuaded to do their Duty.

Day 19

I make my first foray into the Land of the Hidden Agenda

Imagine my despair, Gentle Readers, when at Camp One I discovered I had set out without a supply of sugar-free mints, and at Camp Two I found my flask of fruity drink was empty but for a few drops.

My nerves were already unsteady as, in the early dawn, when none but the messenger of the Post was yet stirring, I had made my way through a portion of the Pestilential Provinces to send short messages to loved ones—unreachable by other means—on the backs of decorative cards. ('Absolutely Ghastly place. Wish you were here, and I was there.' That sort of thing.) You may believe that I crept out into that unnervingly silent world where angels fear to tread and all others appear locked down in their individual huts against the Lurking Pest after which the Pestilential Provinces are named.

My mission in that peculiar place achieved, with the cards I had written placed in that magic box from which they are spirited all over the Queendom by none knows what means, I silently tip-toed back to the comparative safety of Base Camp.

As I say, still twitchy from that disquieting experience, I now set out upon my quests in the Guard-Lands beyond Camp.

But what was that which I espied upon the roofs of the stable huts for the monstrous machines on wheels? Why, none other than a pterosaur, black and white in plumage. Once again, my heart was assailed by foreboding, for is it not said of Magspies that one alone is a Harbinger of Sorrow? I gasped in my relief when I saw almost immediately that it was not alone, for I had missed its mate who was a little further along the roof. With two of them thus predicting Joy my heart lifted and my mood improved almost at once. I laughed at my own foolish superstition, learned from the simple people who persist in such Pagan Beliefs. All the same, it was good to know that these

49

Favourable Signals suggested much success in my Endeavours that day.

When the two were joined by a third I set off quickly; I feared that there might have been unwanted issue from an amorous dalliance with a Native woman, although I couldn't for the life of me think when this had last occurred.

Instead, I thought I would pretend to myself I had just seen two together and the third had been another black and white blackbird-like creature known in former times—I believe—as a 'Pastorius.' (This is a little-known fact even amongst the people of my Homeland—I bet you didn't know it, you patient Reader of these Epistles of PWN. See? It is bloomin' educational, this stuff.)[46]

So, out onto the trail once more, with a brief rest at Camp Two before embarking on forging a whole new trail into the forbidding forest wherein may lie the beastly Agenda well known for secreting itself, though nothing else of it is understood. I still cannot persuade my feline bearers to venture with me into this Terrifying Territory, but I extracted a promise for them to stay on the border where our track is now well established to await a signal from me. (However, from such animals as they, for whom even affection is an affectation dependent on how hungry they are, I knew it likely they would quickly desert their post.)

I had but hacked a short way into the bush, my courage in one hand, my fortitude in the other and my plucky English mettle in a third, when to my consternation and a thrill of Absolute Terror I came across a Great Highway already constructed. It could mean but three things: People, or a large Animal or a Nameless Something had already gone that way! I stood trembling as I contemplated the Dreadful Danger into which I had precipitated myself without anything like enough precaution, but I have lived to tell the tale, so fear not overmuch for me, my Loved Ones.

Tentatively, I continued along this ancient pathway, through plant species as yet uncatalogued by botanists; here there was a patch of fierce, stinging vegetation and there a patch of vegetation which

---

[46] After an extensive search through the reference books, my associate Arthur Mann PhD, has discovered that Pastorius is an archaic term for an occasionally occurring piebald blackbird. Remarking on sceptical criticism of his discovery, he said 'Well, Arthur Mann is better than none.'

might soothe the stings of the previous plants (though I wouldn't bet on it) until I came to two mountains which I estimate are all of two feet tall. How these could possibly be passed over or through was a perplexing mystery at first until I spotted a stone by my feet which upon inspection proved to have upon its surface, chalked in a wobbly hand, an unmistakeable spear or arrow, although it seemed only to point in the direction of a vast barricade of thistles. Following the direction that it indicated, I came to a Splendid Discovery. For it showed me a narrow passage, too small to be called a valley, more of a cleft in the terrain, by which I might pass, did I but dare.

I knew that as the sun was setting, I could not continue that day but just as I was turning my feet in the direction of Camp One, by my feet I saw lying an object, wrapped in what had once obviously been a very fine skin of the finest leatherette, and tooled into it the following words in imitation gold leaf: 'Lord Little Newton, His Journal.' Trembling with excitement, I stooped and picked up the packet. Why, surely this could be none other than The Journal of Lord Little Newtown[47], an explorer of the early 18th century, who had disappeared into these very same Guard-Lands and was Never Seen Again? I wiped the packet clean of earth and God knows what else, thrust it into my 'Lute of the Froom' tee–shirt[48], and I turned and retreated with my prize to Base Camp, anxious to read Lord Newtown's final words. Was I not with my Expedition emulating this very same Great Man? Pride filled me at the thought.

However, all the way along the trail back to Base Camp I fancied I heard the following footsteps of the fearsome Hidden Agenda.

---

[47] It was, in fact, what it said it was.
[48] If PWN was not paid for product-placement he should have been.

Day 20

The contents of Lord Little Newton's note; fears for my future; the Little Yapper won over

On rising, after a breakfast of the circular dough patties they call 'crumpets' in this place, washed down with plenty of good old British tea shipped all the way from far India, I took the Journal upon my noble knees and read what was inscribed there.

"I, Lord Little Newtown of Happisburgh[49] in Norfolkshire, do here take up my quill, and do prime it, to tell of my misfortune in my Quest for King Solemn's Vines, as a terrible warning to any who might venture into this Gardener-Forsaken land, for though I have – after terrible travails–found that for which I sought, I am surely to perish, for my return to my Dear Old Country is beset not only by the beastly Hidden Agendas of a Great Big Boss Handy Man, of which there is a Vile Colony before I can get to safety, but also a veritable Nest of Ulterior Motives, not to mention the Swarm of Nameless Dreads and the Lair of the deception-loving False Witnesses. All these do now close upon me, and more like them, cutting off the escape of any Unreliable Narrator such as myself. Traveller, BEWARE in particular being drawn into the Temptations of the Seductive Hyperbole! Yours faithfully, hoping this finds ye full of Hope and in Good Health, Lord Little Newtown–signed in his own blood. (I hath had a rotten nosebleed.) My regards to thy mother." And following this alarming missive were the faint red letters 'Little Newt...' trailing off into nothingness...

After this stunning revelation of the awful fate of my predecessor. I decided that day to regroup, rest, and prepare properly for any further investigation of the hinterland.

I sat at Camp One with the melodious voice of the Half-Naked Savage Woman ringing in my right ear, talking on her magic crystal

---

[49] Pronounced 'Hazebru'. This is a coastal village, so prone to erosion that its historic location will no longer exist by the time you read this.

device whilst gently sizzling in the hot Spring sunshine, as Semaj, the friendly representative of the neighbouring tribe (he has an impressive belly on him these days, much like my own) was out be-sporting with Freebie. I seem to have won over not only her owner but the little Yapper, for she came to me, eager to be petted. Luckily, I am not expected to provide the same service to her master.

Despite these distractions I could not but feel compelled by my exploring nature within a few days to once again face the dangers of the Centre of the Guard-Lands, picking up where Lord Little Newton found danger and met his doom. Oh, that I—by contrast—may live to tell you the tale!

Day 21

Of the weather in the streets and light pollution

My Dear Correspondents (although I must say communications from you and from known Civilisation have rather diminished since I have been in this outlandish place—just saying).

The weather changed, forcing me to put off any further assault upon the Interior of the Guard-Lands and confining me either to Base Camp or Camps One and Two on the razed 'flower beds', so called by the Natives (although not a single flower lifts its head in those weed-covered places, the names more redolent of an ambition than an actuality). It is true that sunshine broke briefly through the extensive cloud cover but not for so long as to tempt my Party and I out onto the saturated savannah of Savanna (got to keep the money trickling in) under the leaden sky of Skye (even a few nickels are something...).

Suddenly, much to my surprise, I heard a rhythmic banging in the territory of the Half-Naked Savage Woman's territory. Peering through the barrier of privet, I perceived that woman of Scornful Countenance whenever she encounters me, knocking into the wooden palisade at the Northern limit to her territory, small, sharpened metal rods, with an implement of primitive drop–forged steel on a lathe-turned, primitive wooden shaft. From these rods (like unto the one that nearly wounded Yours Truly on a previous Expedition, which had been negligently left sticking up by one of Count Sil's servants) she then hung marvellous crystal globes of many colours. I was left most puzzled by this activity. Was this by way of decoration of a temple, owing to some religious ceremony of hers, and did these passive, coloured globes represent her Pagan Faith in some way—a form of worship, perhaps?

Still musing on this, my attention was then drawn to a commotion in the Badlands to the North, and so I quickly made my way to a point where the wall of regular red stones dips, in order to stick my noble snoot over, so that I might see what the disturbance was.

At first, as I saw two children of the aboriginal people who live there, on those fiendish two-wheeled devices, which against all common sense stay upright at speed, I thought this to be the same hunting party I had seen the other day. But then I remembered that the couple of women who live almost opposite the wall at this point have but the one child and here before me were two, and neither wore the ferocious head covers or talismanic elbow and knee covers I saw before. They were accompanied furthermore by one adult male and one adult female.

I pitied them, for their hunting technique was hopeless. Up and down the tar and stone track they went, shouting in such a manner that they warned off all prey species for many a yard beyond. Can you believe it? All they would get for their efforts would be fruitless exercise. And yet they kept it up for nigh on two hours!

And then, at the usual distance these people keep between them of six feet or more, they were joined by the smaller child and pretty woman I had seen before, also on the two wheeled contrivances but with the partner of the pretty woman also this time, almost as heavily set as a man and sporting a man's haircut. I do not indulge here in stereotypes, I assure you, I merely report what I saw.

Returning to Camp One, the now friendly Yapper of mixed parentage, Freebie, joined me for a thorough stroking. Unlike my bearers, who had in a cowardly fashion abandoned me at first sight of the little Yapper and fled back to Base Camp via the flap so considerately supplied for them through the back door of that hut, Freebie has apparently no fear of man, nor of beast. Once convinced one is harmless, however, she is the staunchest ally, and did even abandon the backward Semaj, her ostensible Master, for one she suspects of being a Superior Being and one on a civilising mission for the sake of the Great Empress and her Empire. In another word: Me.

At last, it was time to temporarily lay down my Burden for the day and return to the humble comforts of Base Camp and a hearty dinner of fungus and French-cheese pie, with sliced tubers, together with a glass of non-alcoholic beer from the Old Country.

As the light fell, I looked out towards the West, and there, on the Half-Naked Savage 's fortress wall, I saw the coloured crystal globes shining with magical light in the gathering darkness, rivalling the very stars of the firmament. Why this should be, none knows.

Day 22

Astounding news of a Yapper and an encounter with a Siren

When I rose from my simple bed of crude Egyptian cotton[50] and Foam of Miraculous Memory and pulled up my Pioneering Pants, how could I have guessed all the sounds and sights I would hear and see that day? It is as if every day a curtain opens on this world which is trapped between the Pestilential Provinces and the Northern Badlands and reveals yet another dimension to your stunned reporter. You could hardly conceive of all the horrors and splendours of the Guard-Lands hitherto explored to my knowledge by just one other English Man, Lord Little Newtown, to whom I doff my pith helmet in respect. After all, that intrepid explorer came here with none of the modern aids I possess, such as Werther's sugar free butter candies, kitbag of synthetic materials and—most important of all—my trusty if tatty Kindle by which, if by any chance I can get a signal I can order several free or inexpensive books a week, to occupy my mind and to some extent chase away the Nastiness of the Night, temporarily transport me from my Frequent Fears of the Forest, and save me from much dreaded Allegations of Alliteration.

However, I must now tell you of double–barrelled astonishing news of a different nature:

Semaj, he who speaks with backward tongue, that day met me at the edge of his territory and informed me that I was incorrect to call his little Yapper Freebie, to which I replied that I gathered that many erroneously call her 'Phoebe'. But no!

'Her name,' he said with some asperity 'is Suzie.'

'You are sadly mistaken there,' I said, in a kindly fashion.

Sometimes the English Man must be cruel to be kind; after all, these people are just like children and must sometimes be corrected for their own good. He seemed to think that being the little Yapper's master

---

[50] PWN's bedclothes were of silk previously, surely? He may just have changed them—and about time too.

somehow gives him greater knowledge of her than I, his obvious superior, by virtue of my birth in fair England.

'What's more,' said he, now warmed to his argument, 'she is not a Yapper, she is a dog.' This is patent nonsense, of course. Everyone knows that dogs bark. Still, for the purpose of better diplomatic relations, I let this go.

'She got free from your territory into that of the lady beyond–' he then said, 'so she is in disgrace.' I felt this was said as though it were my fault somehow and that I was in disgrace as well. Well, I may have many powers unknown to these primitive peoples, but the command of someone else's Yapper is beyond me. Semaj must control his own Yapper. If Freebie is a dog, which I beg leave to doubt, training her should not be out of the question and is certainly not my responsibility. Personally, even were I a Yapper I would not venture into the territory of the Half-Naked Woman for I fear her savagery far too much...

Musing on this matter, I began my several circuits of the perimeter of the Guard-Lands, when suddenly I was stopped in my tracks, for there over the low wall, coming close by on the paved area that runs beside the tar and stone track of The Badlands, was a vision of loveliness, a bird of paradise, a rose amongst thorns, a veritable Black Venus, Aphrodite risen from the sea, a graceful princess, the answer to a prayer, my heart's desire. In short, this could be none other than a direct descendant of the Seductive Hyperbole.

As I stood, rooted to the spot by scopophilia[51], this majestic maiden, of burgeoning bosom and bottom, youthful and fresh as a drink from a mountain spring, swayed towards and past me. I was vaguely aware of my mouth dropping open and my tongue unrolling down my chin.

And then she spoke, in words as tuneful as the aeolian harp that sings in the wind, or as the tinkling of faerie bells, or the music angels make upon their harps. And her words were these:

'Enjoying the view?!'[52]

---

[51] Not to be confused with 'Scoptophilia', which is crude, nude and rude.

[52] It is unclear whether this young woman is the same as 'The Lissome Black Lovely' who appears later and becomes so important to PWN and his story. The Editor is inclined to think that she is.

I could not answer. I watched her as she went away into the unknown places in the interior of The Badlands, all the time crushing my fingernails into the palms of my hands until they bled, to resist the lure of that mouth-watering creature—a veritable goddess.

When I regained my senses, I hurried back to Base Camp, called for my cats-o'-two-tails and thrashed my back with them to within an inch of my life to purge me of lust. Then I put down poor Loopy and Meli, donned my hairshirt and drank non-alcoholic beer until I was blessedly insensible. [53]

The things I have to do for you, my Correspondents! I leave you now, shaken and stirred as I am—but thankfully all passion spent.

---

[53] From the hard drive— 'It is hard to do but can be achieved if you are dedicated enough.'

Day 23

Of birds, balls, and billowing flags

There was excitement in Base Camp in the morning, for early after I had breakfasted there was a commotion across the floor of my crude shelter, carpeted as it is with poor, stained, fawn rubber-backed stuff through which the floorboards show clearly. [54] When I peered around to see what the commotion was, I discovered that the smaller feline bearer, Meli, was wrestling with a gigantic feather.

And, Dear Reader, this was a genuine feather of some gigantic bird, not the crude little scale-like, fluffy things of the twittering tiny pterosaurs (try saying that with the wrong teeth in) that did so regularly thump into the transparent crystal sheets set in the walls of my Base Camp, in the Days of Yore when I could afford to have them regularly cleaned.

No, as I say, this was a feather of the kind the great sea pterosaurs have for their specialised flight. I wondered that Meli should have one in her possession. Had she perhaps brought such a creature to the ground herself in the Guard-Lands? This seemed too fanciful. It was much more likely that there had been some terrible battle between one of the sea pterosaurs and a predatory dragon or dinosaur which had resulted in the shedding of this large feather, only for it later to come into the possession of my cowardly cat.

Still musing on this matter, I made my way out to Camp One and from thence to Camp Two (to escape the fierce, lukewarm sunshine). After catching up on those wondrous messages that come through the air itself and go by the super-heroic name of He-Males', I once more used my patent loin-girding device to stiffen my resolve; once it was stiff enough I raised myself to my full height and–accompanied by my less than trusty companions–I once more limped

---

[54] From the hard drive—'Camping demands some sacrifices.'

out at a good pace until I reached the lowest point of the wall which separates this province from that of the Badlands.

There I was most surprised to discover the little blonde girl Bad-Lander engaged in an activity with the more butch of its two female parents. Each had in one hand a stick that bore a pierced oval wider shape on the distal end. With these implements they knocked between them a spherical object of bouncy material. What this ceremony denoted I could not tell. However, at one point the adult cried 'Love All!', which sounded to me very like what we are taught in our own country to do, as good Christians. It was thus obvious to me that a missionary from Great Britain must have at one point, probably long ago, reached the Badlands and its barbaric people.[55] [56]

I stood for long milliseconds deep in thought until my reverie was broken by the little blonde child saying, in the strange twang of that much inbred People: 'Mummy—Here is a strange man looking at us!'

I took the child to mean that I was unfamiliar and not that I am peculiar in some way—though I will never be quite sure. In any case, I felt their religious ceremony must be a private one and I should not intrude any longer, and so I gave the signal for my little party to move on.

But the terrors and wonders of the day were not yet over, for as I approached the valley between the hillocks, by which long ago Lord Little Newtown passed into the Way leading to King Solemn's Vines, my way was blocked at head level by challenging flags strung across a stout cord. I could not but suppose that the tribe of the Interior, aware of my former presence at its portal, had posted these flags as a warning against further incursions.

When my face brushed one of the flags, I realised with horror that these hanging cloths—no doubt the military colours of my enemy The Hidden Agenda—were dripping wet and smelled strongly of some Spring-fresh pheromone designed to turn the stomachs of all but those with the strongest guts.

---

[55] The astute Reader will have quickly spotted PWN's laughable mistake here: it is that there is absolutely no evidence that Lord Little Newton was at all religious.

[56] Here, from the hard drive—'Perhaps Lord Little Newtown himself had caused this alteration in beliefs.'

Silently, my bearers and I turned and crept away, knowing that discretion is the better part of valour.

I will return another day but with a force suitably reinforced, ready to tear down those niff-emitting, soggy emblems and to show the upstart Hidden Agenda and his brood of just what a Representative of the Great Empress of the UK is made, and so to gain safe passage to the Vines that once were King Solemn's.

Day 24

Of Savagery and the Territory of Euphemisms

I woke with the lark, Gentle Reader, and once I had shot the little bastard I fled back under my eiderdown for a few precious hours of sleep, for I had tossed and turned all night, as I reproached myself for neglecting my duty of further exploration over the last few days.

Once refreshed by slumber, I rose and broke my fast with a veritable mountain of so-called 'crumpets' with a butter alternative they have in these parts which, though tasting unpleasant, is supposed to be good for one, and is in any case undetectable under a generously spread layer of yeast protein which many do hate but which I love, no matter how bad it may be for my kidneys. There is an Australian equivalent which is never mentioned in Polite Society.[57]

Then it was time to screw my monocle to my good eye, take up my pith helmet and stout stick, call my lazy feline bearers to my side, and step out purposefully once more, with my resolve strengthened to do some actual exploring that day and not merely to indulge in the great sin of observation of the locals.

The sun was high in an almost cloudless sky and so I was not surprised to spot at a glance that the Half Naked Woman was lying once more on her crude couch, face down, the skin of her back now like chestnut tanned leather, which presumably is the look she is going for. Personally, I cherish my pale codfish look and would not care to look instead like my best Sunday shoes—but each to his or her own.

As she looked not in my direction but apparently at the neat, weed-free paving beneath her couch I felt free to examine more carefully her compound or 'kraal'. Beneath the globes that do so magically light up the night, so that the very stars do envy their luminescence, and

---

[57] We have seen stated in the Foreword, that in his brick hut PWN actually had in his possession a jar of the British yeast extract. The corroboration in this passage shows just how absurd is the claim of the Australians to have produced PWN's yeast extract.

astronomers curse the same, in a bed of earth grow neat plants, with ne'er a brown leaf to be seen. Each plant bears upon it blooms of extraordinary beauty; these plants are so unlike the vegetation which surrounds my own territory or even that of The Big Boss Handy Man or Semaj's plot, that one feels they must have been imported lock, stock, and barrel from an unknown Nursery of plants, specifically for the season, which is The Spring here.

And yet—say, what could these tallest of blooms be, whose stalks hid behind the other plants? Why, I realised, they were none other than a regiment of opium poppies! Here, then, is the Dark Secret of The Half Naked Woman and when she must go without that drug which she no doubt harvests from the seed heads, her Savagery towards me increases. There can be no other reason! For I am acknowledged throughout Christendom and even in Pagan lands as an OK fellow, with not a single vice. (I have several vices it is true but not a single one.)

With this mystery solved, I rested briefly at Camps One and Two, but then I levered myself to my feet, left my cowardly bearers to guard the stores of butter-candies and sugar free mints, and–taking only my flask of fruity cordial to refresh me at intervals–strode with determination towards the Dark Interior and the fabled Vines of King Solemn.

I crossed once more the Great Plain, which is named Savanna (tinkle), and upon which move the great herds of grass-eating species under the Skye (likewise the sound of my bank balance increasing by a tiny amount) such as the wildebeest and eland (although on this occasion I discerned only a few ants but of such a giant size that only twenty or so would fit on a little fingernail). Through the untameable bush I then thrusted until I reached the very foothills of the hillocks beyond which it is rumoured the Hidden Agenda reigns in his ancient temples and cities.

But—woe is me—and sad to relate, oh Gentle Overseer of these dramatic Discoveries, over the last few days the way between the hillocks had become impassable with the enormous stinging plants.

I was in despair until I looked at Lord Little Newtown's parchment again. There I saw 'PS. Please see over...'

He had drawn in blood on the reverse a rudimentary map of the hillocks which come before King Solemn's ancient kingdom, and I saw that there was another way of approaching the secret land, beyond the dangers of The Hidden Agenda and the Ulterior Motive and all their kind. But this route is itself not without its own danger, for it passes through the Land of the Double Entendre, or Secondary Meanings.

There was nothing for it but to make a scouting trip at the edge of this dread land. There could be no time for a thorough investigation for already the sun was beginning to sink over distant Lake Tina (bill waived).

Tentatively I took my first steps into the territory that might lead to King Solemn's Vines.

The first thing I saw was a pair of tits twittering on a branch. That is reassuring, I thought, but my surge of confidence came too soon. For at speed towards me came a surely hostile Native with great big balls. 'Do you play soccer – old boy?' he asked in pidgin-English. At this my nerve snapped and I turned and ran the way I had come. However, I tripped on something and fell headlong. Winded, I lay on the rough scrub searching for that which had felled me. Then I saw it: it was the neck of a bottle.

I scrambled to my feet and had a jolly good feel. Ignoring this annoying euphemism, I located and dug out the bottle. It read 'From 100% King Solemn's Vines. 5.6 percent proof. Best served with fish, chicken, or fruit. Enjoy responsibly.'

There could be no doubt that I had chanced upon an indication that Lord Little Newtown had returned this way from the Vines I myself sought! Pocketing the bottle in my voluminous jungle shorts I turned to head back to camp.

Join me again tomorrow for the next possibly exciting instalment especially if you haven't got much of a life.

I send to you both Felicity and Valediction. Look after them for they are not used to strangers.

Day 25

Red breasts and the Agenda Disclosed

Let no man or woman dispute the essential Truthfulness of my Tales of the Guard-Lands. Should they do so, when I return to my dear England, I will call them out for a duel at dawn, weapons of their choosing.

Please note: unfortunately, when in England, I do not rise until the noon bell has been rung. A pity that, isn't it? At dawn you will be on your own.

And so—on with my account of this Strange and Enigmatic land:

When I reached Camp One, I had not long been there before my eyes beheld the startling and rather lovely sight of a chirping pterosaur with rose-red breast, spreading its mighty little wings as it stood like a sentinel on one of the wooden posts by which Count Sil has delineated my external compound.

But then–would you believe it? –upon the next post alighted yet another of these red-breasted fliers, so that two identical fluffy pterosaurs competed for my attention!

Sadly, their tuneful competitive trilling was ended by a startling noise erupting from the territory to the West, beyond that of the Half Naked Savage, and they flew away, soaring to a staggering altitude of at least six feet.

What could be the unholy cacophony that had disrupted this sublime interlude? Why, of course, it was the starting up of the monotonous throbbing of the jungle drums, but louder than hitherto, surely denoting that the surrounding tribes had spotted the presence of a stranger and were beginning to approach— as likely as not, with hostile intent!

However, if only for my amusement and distraction, it must be important for me, today, to carry my own instrument out to No–Man's Land to send back my own message that I come in Peace. Oh, how I hope that they do not find this a further provocation and launch an attack to silence me forever...

Followed by the threatening sound of the slit-drums and their accompanying sneering bass lines, and with the occasional terrible scream emerging out of chanting it was quite impossible to decipher, I hitched up my exploratory jockstrap, once more slung my kitbag upon my shoulder, checked I had oiled and primed my Swiss Army weaponry, and at last once more crossed the unguarded border to the Dark Guard-Land's Interior.

And here I must tell you of how I solved the Mystery of The Hidden Agenda, for too long the greatest terror of this land for me.

It was like this: after much time had elapsed, I saw The Great Big Boss Handy Man open the portal from his land into the Conjoined Guard-Lands and his Yapper entered close to me. Much to my surprise, this animal, perceived close-to, revealed itself as no Little Yapper but a genuine wolf–like animal—a Greater Yapper, in short.

I followed this beast at a distance decided upon by discretion, and saw it go to a corner of this primaeval world and <u>do its business.</u> After the vile animal had returned through the portal to Handy Man's Land, for the sake of Science I followed a huge cloud of buzzing bluebottles and other eager insects to where the Great Yapper had been and there discovered a huge heap, a veritable mound, of the animal's leavings, almost concealed beneath a bush and the huge trunk of a well–fertilised tree (a baobab, perhaps).

It was then I realised my silly mistake—for obviously this Great Yapper is named none other than 'Agenda' and it is his vast heap of dung which has been Hidden by him! The solution had almost been staring me in the face, and very certainly under my nose, the whole time...

And on that bombshell, I leave you, for now, Dear patient and hopefully un-revolted Readers.

Remember me in your prayers, if you would, for there yet remain many dangers in these outlandish lands.

Day 26

In which I deploy my mighty instrument, mark a danger discovered previously and find another clue regarding my Predecessor

I climbed into my new stout boots, of a design unknown in these parts, where only the stiletto, the high-heel, the sandal, the flip–flop, the sling–back and the elasticated side are known, together with the kitten-heel with the primitive strap of Velcro™. Feet once again fully protected from whatever the terrain could throw at them, by thick simulated leather bound to my feet with strong laces, I suddenly realised it would have been a good idea to put on clothes first. One must set an example, and these pagan people (including my feline bearers) sometimes wear too little not to shock the delicate sensibility of a civilised man.

At last, appropriately clad, and shod, I called my feline slaves to my side. They raised sneering countenances only, so I left them nestled into my eiderdown (you just cannot get good help these days) and seizing my usual kit and Something Extra I set off once more to Camp Number One. This is secure and may be counted on, unlike Camp Two, which–though usefully shaded–is sometimes damp and uncomfortable—for seldom does it completely dry out and also its timbers do shed splinters into one's baronial backside. (Try getting someone to come and extract a splinter from one's derriere these days—it is quite impossible.)

After a snack of butter candies, washed down with a good draught of the juice of the exotic Vimto Fruit, I uncased my weapon of peace. You should now know that I had brought with me a neck-fretted, hollow body chordophone, known familiarly as a guitar. After tuning the strings of this melodious implement to the pitches required, I proceeded, against the low threat of the jungle drum and bass, to take up my trusty plectrum and to play not one but three songs of my own composition, and with the music I sang lustfully, as the dear old songs of Blighty rang out for the first time in this wild and neglected region.

By the time I had finished, the drumming had been stilled and all that could be heard was the faint sound of Natives of the surrounding territories stealing away, or closing the doors of their brick huts—in fact, according me the respect I deserved. (Indeed, so powerful had been the effect of my advanced melodies and ululations that the Half-Naked Savage Woman did not re-emerge until I had made my way back to my Base Camp, hours later–though the sun was high and hot and good for tanning— from where I was to observe her take her station once more upon the assembly of metal and plastic one rather dignifies by the name of 'couch'.

It is by such awe-inspiring stratagems and wonders as my music that I reinforce the message of my superiority on the primitive tribespeople who surround me.

After thoughtfully chewing some sugar-free mints, it was time to hitch up my socks and take to the trail once more, leaving my instrument in the cool shade.

I made it my first purpose to carve and drive in a stake, so as to mark both to myself, and for those intrepid souls who may follow one day, the point next to the track where I had previously discovered Agenda's Hidings, so that never again would my boots be sullied by his heaped ordure. I nodded in satisfaction at my work, as I looked upon it and found it good.

Many a weary yard I trudged before I suddenly discerned the corner of something apparently of parchment sticking out from a clump of dandelion-like dandelions. Kneeling down, I took my trusty Swiss Army implement and unearthed and extracted what proved to be a packet, medium in size. It bore upon it marks which I tried to decipher, using my monocle as a magnifying glass.

It appeared to read 'Ken... ucky... ried chick...' and then, stomach-churningly, the words: '... a secret...'!!!

Surely this was no less than a clue left by my predecessor, Lord Little Newtown?! Try as I might, I could not understand the cryptic marks. But there beside the letters was a representation of none other than a face which seemed avuncular and set on placing his Secret in every home across the globe.

Trembling, I literally packed up this latest worry in my old kit bag and–hurrying my steps–made my way back to Camp Number One to recover my musical instrument, and from thence back to Base Camp and at least temporary safety from the fond embraces of Ken Ucky and whatever his dread Secret may be.

May I survive this latest threat–perhaps the worst yet–and live to see again my Dear Ones and my Homeland.

Day 27

I perform open–finger surgery; I perform songs; I perform another death–defying act of lateral thinking

I had not told you of this previously, my Gentle Readers, but for some days I have been in pain from a wound inflicted not by Hostile Man or Poisonous Plant but by my feline companion, Meli, who, making so familiar with me as to leap upon my lap one evening, missed her footing and flailed out with a front paw to get some hold upon me. By the night before last, this wound on my right index finger had developed into a painful, inflamed, and suppurating sore. I waited for lockjaw to set in, resigned to my fate, for there are none other than witch doctors in these lands—a General Practitioner or Accident and Emergency doctor being beyond the hopes of procuring for love nor money (though I have tried neither of these approaches, to be honest).

In the event, when I could see that I was to be spared the excruciating rigor of tetanus, but the inflammation was unbearable, I set to dealing with the matter myself aided only by my knowledge of jungle medicine, my dexterity in wielding my Swiss Army knife, some surgical spirit and the local salve known as 'Saveloy'[58] (other antiseptic creams are available but not here). I endured the operation on the huge ¼" long wound with British pluck but without any anaesthesia, and–clenching my teeth–I first excised, then drained and cleansed the wound before applying the soothing cream.

Despite my agonies of the night before, I am pleased to report to you that come the morning the finger was well on the way to recovery, quite perky in fact, sitting up in bed and demanding breakfast. Yes, I would play the guitar again!!!

---

[58] PWN is surely mistaken here. He must mean a specific or unguent, perhaps Savlon. A saveloy is a kind of sausage. No one would rub one into a wound and I must counsel Readers against so doing.

Therefore, at midday, like an eccentric Englishman, short only of a similarly eccentric dog, I strode out of Base Camp with my kitbag and guitar, in the blazing sun, for the purpose of educating the primitive peoples surrounding me. No sooner had I begun to play and sing than I heard what sounded like a universal sigh or groan, obviously signalling the extreme approval of those neighbouring Aboriginals. Once again, many were so overcome by the sheer pleasure of hearing the ditties of my Homeland–or my interpretation of them–than they had to retire from their small fields, either to spread the word with their families, or people I know not of yet. From those many who must have remained to listen, there was not a single noise to disturb my concentration as I played. Why–if I had not known better–I might have thought the land itself deserted of men, women, and children, so silent and attentive were they!

At last, I put down my subduing weapon of Peace and Love, relishing the reverent silence and sucked at my "Guilty Pleasure" vaporiser (a true friend in one's hour of need). Then I left Camps One and Two to set off on my daily Trudge into Terror. Let it not be said of me that I ever shirked my Duty to my Sovereign.

I found myself, at last, after several pratfalls, at a heap where on many occasion now I have previously espied what look like nothing so much as rotting coffee grounds, tea bags and the peel of fruits and vegetables. Why, I myself have added to this heap, when I have had need to clear the camp kitchen of unusable organic substances. However, I was suddenly struck by a Terrible Thought. It was this: What if the fragments of shell I saw in the heap are not from many, many a breakfast boiled egg, or the shell fragments from eggs used for baking and omelettes but are in fact the fragments of one gigantic shell? Could not this be the egg of the 'Chick' which the grinning 'Ken Ucky' is said to 'ried' (obviously this a spelling mistake and 'ride' is meant)? Might not this so-called Chick be the giant Moa bird elsewhere extinct? If Ken Ucky can saddle and ride a giant Moa, how great and terrible must his other powers be?

My bowels once more turning to water, I turned and fled. Truly, I am not being paid enough by a Grateful Nation to justify all the risks I take in these secretive Guard-Lands. Upon return to my World, I trust

I will be rewarded with a second Country Estate and an enormous stipend to go with it.

I shall return to regale you with further He-Male accounts, my Dear Ones, if I am spared.

Day 28

A concertgoer, considerations of cannibalism and preparation for
Yapper-nets

Semaj–that Native who speaks even his own name with forked tongue–came to the edge of his territory in order to listen to the melodies which I broadcast to all these savages inhabiting the Guard-Lands and the borders they share with the Pestilential Provinces, and the Badlands where those permanently banished from Civilisation live.

When I had finished three of my lovely ditties (but often even in my Homeland this has been like casting pearls before swine), telling of Lost Love (or at least negligently mislaid), he commented in his quaint dialect that he would like them to be louder. I explained that without a power source for amplifying both my instrument and my voice there was no way to act upon his request. I also feel, of course, that I might actually harm my relations with the surrounding tribes, for they are already obviously overcome by the powerful effect of my entrancing playing and increasing their power might lead to injury or death. If not theirs, then mine.

Later, at Camp Number One, as I read further that brother-given book now so dear to me—and rather dear to him when he bought it, I became aware that the Half-Naked Savage Woman was lying prostrate on her couch, close to the privet copse which separates her tribal lands from myself and the Dark Garden lands. Had she then not retreated during my little concert like many another? Her voice sounded startlingly close.

She may have had company, but I think it more likely she spoke at her magical crystal device that does both listen and speak, and sometimes projects moving pictures. To my amazement, she has a most pleasant, friendly voice[59] and a very attractive laugh. Is it possible that

---

[59] In fact, PWN has already mentioned this but seems to have forgotten.

she reserves her haughty scorn for me alone? Why should this be? This is one mystery I must surely solve before I return to Great Britain and if possible, I should establish good diplomatic relations with her and her People, for the sake of the Empire and the possibility of Trade and Cultural Exchange. I would like her to put some clothes on, however, before I open Talks. I only slightly super-human, after all.

In the burning sunshine of a bright blue Skye (I will accept Girl Scout cookies) I crossed the Great Savanna Plain (Postal Orders welcome) until I reached the cooling, deep waters of Lake Tina (that Cruel Girl of My Youth–the 'Young Girl' I couldn't 'Get Out of My Mind'[60]—but a substantial payment to my current account might help me forget...). After resting there, I checked that all was in order, that I had my trusty knife in my kitbag for a weapon, that my pith helmet was clamped down on my Exquisite Nut, and that my monocle was well screwed into my eye-socket.

Then I stood up and began to make my way along my now well–worn track into the Interior of the Dark Guard-Lands where the Malevolent Spirits and Wild Things dwell. My chief fear at the moment is the Great Moa Bird and its terrifying rider, that personage known as Ken Ucky. To investigate this mystery further, I pressed on to where the bush is at its thickest, and to the point where I had discovered that message on a paper packet which had first informed me of this new danger. I picked up the packet and thought to turn it over. There, on the reverse, there was a message which froze my blood. It read 'It is finger–licking good!' If this did not refer to scrambled moa-egg, then it surely could only mean that Ken Ucky finds *human flesh* to be finger-licking good!!!

Discretion being the better part of Valour, and as I needed to think about this Terrifying Development further, I made a strategic retreat to Camp One.

There, I found Semaj puzzling over something at the border between the Guard-Lands and my Camp.

---

[60] A reference to a popular song by Gary Puckett and The Union Gap, out of favour these days, following Geoffrey Epstein.

'You know that Freebie got in from here the other day when off the leash, crossed your compound and got into "her-next-door's" area, and then disappeared up to the West?'

'Yes–' I replied guardedly, 'for an account of this has reached my Beautiful Ears.' (For none may gain-say this about my external auditory auricles). [61]

'What if I stretched a Net across the posts that mark the Eastern reach of your Camp?'

'That I will allow,' said I, with mighty condescension.

I presume he means this will entail the draping between the posts of that same Net by which He-Males' are mysteriously sent. How this will serve to prevent the egress of Freebie I cannot imagine–but I find it best to humour these Savages. They can turn nasty at any moment...

In these Lands fresh difficulties and Horrors emerge each day. Think of me, my Loved and Dear Ones, as so often I think of you. Which is once a week, some weeks.

---

[61] The visible part of the ears.

Day 29

The Moai turns and the Half-Naked Savage nails up more rival sun

---

Gentle Reader: I must here admit that it was not until mid-afternoon that I was able, with a Great Leap, to free myself of the bonds of domesticity and to leave Base Camp, my mighty music tool in one hand, my kitbag on my shoulder and hope in my heart.

For the sense of Freedom dominated over my Fear of the Unknown Outdoors and with a hop, skip and jump–or so it seemed–I achieved Camp One on the slopes of Woodcock Mountain. Here, however, the sunshine was still too fierce; witness the recumbent form of the Half-Naked Savage Woman, lying on her back (but with her modesty just about maintained by a bandeau top). For her still to be tanning herself happily at such an advanced hour spoke not just of Springtime but of the warming of the entire Globe, surely?

After sucking reflectively at my aid to sanity, my vaporiser, I regarded the scene around Camp Two. This I have not described to you yet, I think? I sit there on mighty wooden logs called 'sleepers', for they are the homes of mighty, sleeping spirits. These timbers, I have heard, were culled from some forest of long-ago, where once roamed the great iron dragons that did chuff-chuff as they breathed their fire, smoke, and steam. Of these iron dragons only one remains in these Parts: the tiny one who sits atop the post in the territory but one to the East of my Base Camp, and of whom I have spoken before. (Please Note: There will be a test at the end of these Adventures and woe betide anyone who forgets vital information like this—their pocket money will be withheld, and they may also be grounded.)

As Camp Two is nearly always in the shade, and has much shelter at ground level, it is an excellent place to observe the small mammals that coexist with such as dragons, dinosaurs, and pterosaurs. Examples would be the Shrewd (like a shrew only more so), the

Whistling Wolf; and last but by no means the least: the much-despised Hyperbole (these are not to be feared whilst still little).

However, I had no more time for nature observation, nor taxonomy, for after playing and singing three songs with varying degrees of success, to the exaggerated sighs of the Half Naked Woman Savage (expressing thus how she enjoys my oeuvre beyond words), I sharpened my Swiss Army knife, checked my old service revolver, cleaned my double barrelled shotgun, hoisted the Thompson submachine gun to my shoulder, and strode out to once more proclaim my message of Peace on Earth and Good Will to all men. Or else.

I made my customary way, through the many dangers to which I have almost become accustomed, as far as the palisade to the Far East which borders the Great Big Boss Handy Man's lands. There I idly looked over towards the bonsai forest and beyond that to the Lake where the Coy Carp do swim fishily, when suddenly I became aware that something was different. It was only when I looked up that I realised–with Fear and Trembling–that the great fibreglass or concrete Moai sculpture had turned its aspect relative to the pallet it stands on. Now that dread, simplistic but stern face looked–unmistakeably–directly in my direction...

Doffing my pith helmet and bowing respectfully to the Deity, I retreated, walking backwards as I do when visiting my own Monarch at Buck House. I only stopped this when I got close to the Hidings of that cur, Agenda, for I knew that at that point to look forwards was mightily of advantage.

What can the turning of the Moai mean? Am I in future to fear not only the finger–licking Ken Ucky and his Mighty Chick but also this massive headed Moai giant?!!!

As I returned to Base Camp, I almost fell over a pair of blue balls that had somehow been launched across from the Land of the Secondary Meanings. Whatever their euphemistic message might be, I disregarded them and stayed not to give them a moment's thought but– ditching my unnecessary weaponry–made haste to return swiftly to comparative safety, as the shadows lengthened behind me.

Twilight was descending as I got to Camp Number One. Through the gloom I heard yet more rhythmic banging from the

Northern palisade of the Half Naked One. From Base Camp I looked across from the grassland of my own compound and beyond the wall of privet, only to see the hostile female setting up more of her magic lanterns that by their own agency do light up in the dark. At this rate, there will be no night-time; for all of her compound and beyond will shine like a fierce beacon both day and night.

With that uncomfortable thought and hoping you are not so touched by the poetry of my words that they put you right off your supper, I beg leave to call a halt for now.

Day 30

I encounter new smells, new flames, Old Flames, and flowers

Gentle Readers—I set out onto the Way into the Wilderness at mid-afternoon, for paperwork had detained me at Base Camp all morning. Then I had a snooze to refresh my faculties.

Upon arising, from Base Camp, looking West, I perceived that once more her device had been erected by the Half-Naked Savage Woman and upon it depended not only the Pantheon of Panties but also strange garments of which all I can remember from the Dim and Distant Past is that I never mastered the trick of their removal, despite being shown by Amorous Attachments–frustrated by my lack of expertise–several times, which tended to kill passion in any case.

The Savage Woman herself was laid out like a sacrifice to God Apollo, her skin sizzling almost audibly in the severe Spring sunlight.

Nor was she alone, for as I made my customary pilgrimage to Camps One and Two, I detected the meats of others being burned. I am inclined to the theory that this was not the flesh of other human beings but that of pigs and cattle. These odours assailed me on all sides. From North, South, East and West, my mighty olfactory organ–my nose to wit–detected burning meats. By the way, whilst my nose is gigantic for a Man, it is small compared to that of the Elephant, of which innumerable examples must roam the Savannah of Savanna under the sky of Skye (if you do not pay up, I am sending the big boys round), innumerable because I have never actually seen one to count. How different is this sunny day behaviour from the behaviour of the people of my own country, who are wont to wait until the weekend and until there is sure to be rain and wind before attempting to fire up the barbecue. I defiantly opened my packet of fish paste and cucumber sandwiches, content to be the least of the carnivores who surrounded me that day, not least the feared Ken Ucky, who I greatly feared would be–even as I munched–looking for the next human being to throw on his barbie!

As I approached that vast puddle which is Lake Tina (it never dries up, and is therefore obviously refreshed by some unknown source) I had an unwelcome thought, and it was this: might this splendid and placid body of water not be haunted by the Wraith or Succubus of Unattainable Love? I shuddered with the sad horror of this. I must resist her Siren song and not throw myself in, and thereby perish as the baby-dragon-infested waves close over my foolish and lovesick head!

I have told you much of the fauna of this Forgotten World but not yet much of the flora. As Spring continues, from out of the tall grasses poke the brave stems and buds of flowers, the like of which I have never seen. Their scents do their best to ameliorate the atmosphere of singed substances and their colours are various with blues, blues, and yet more blues. How they came there I know not but I am inclined to believe they have escaped from the Public-Hanging Gardens, which rumour has it once surrounded King Solemn's Vines. Your intrepid investigator will investigate this further.

Back at Base Camp I spotted that on Cocka'wood Lane at the front of my brick hut–at the very edge of the Pestilential Provinces to the South–a Desirable Object of Unknown Usage has appeared, apparently discarded on the paving. I have to venture out in that direction, suitably gloved and juju masked, to perform a task, and I will make it my purpose to inform you as to what this object may be.

Day 31

The attack of the Flower-Pot Men and sundry other matters

Come with me once more–oh Fabulous and Forgiving Esteemer of these Entries in my He-Male Journal–into the distant lands to the North and East of my Base Camp.

But first let me not forget to inform you about the Desirable Item which appeared on the pavement of the Pestilential Provinces. Suitably suited and booted, masked, muffled, and gloved (though in truth I did not expect to see another living being there, nor did I), I ventured South from the front of Base Camp to investigate the slim black monolith that had somehow appeared before the entrance to my brick tent. At first, I could make little of it, as it stood there on great pedestal feet. I observed that it swivelled on its centre on ginormous steel screws through plasticky, apparently self–lubricating bushes.[62] Then I observed that it had once had a long, large door, and that it was divided into several compartments, the uppermost of which was pierced still with hooks of some metal. Then I was struck by a thought: what if its missing door had once carried a full–length mirror, a technology far beyond the people I had encountered this far, and inside the slim case these hooks were for keys? Of the compartments I could make little, but it is possible they were intended to contain 'Useful Things' needed by the original owner, such as driving licences, passports, hairbrushes, combs and so on. Perhaps this furniture piece once stood in the hallway of some strange being long vanished from Earth and whose lineage is unknown. However, it is greatly puzzling....[63]

Despite not knowing its use, I coveted it and thought of taking into my encampment. But remembering at the last the story of the Trojan Horse I decided that this might be indeed very foolish.

---

[62] Linings for a round hole, especially one in which an object acting as an axle revolves.

[63] We may hazard a guess that this was a hall cabinet with mirror and hooks for door and car keys. Far too grand for PWN's brick hut. What can he have been thinking?...

As I reluctantly turned my back on the monolith, I thought I heard it speak in a whisper, 'Stop throwing away the sharp bits off the flints, guys!' but I admit this may have been pure Fancy on my part.

Suggestions as to what the mysterious, slim black object in fact is, should be sent–together with an uncrossed Postal Order for 50 pence or 55 cents–to my bank account in the Cayman Islands. All profits will not go to charity. Your reward will be knowing you have contributed to the Sum of human happiness when I am in a position to spend your money in my own dear country, having laundered it sufficiently.

Now to the Great Event in the Guard-Lands: No sooner had I sat myself for a short rest at Camp One and sucked sufficiently on my "Guilty Pleasure" vaporiser to calm my nerves, than I noticed with a thrill of Terror, that since my last visit, a number of giant to small genuine terracotta pots (accept no substitutes) had moved and were now sitting one atop of each other, ranked in order of size, the largest at the base, the smallest at the top. Now they made a formidable tower of fired orange-red clay vessels. By whose hand had this happened? Who or what had made the necessary incursion into my territory to erect this mocking idol?!

The overcast skies seemed to crowd in upon my poor, aching head as I considered the matter. Surely, at the least, I would have to redouble my defences, set traps for these intruders, and generally prepare for further hostile actions. For it could not be that the pots had done this themselves. But then I had the most fearful thought of all: What if the terracotta pots were now the residences for small malevolent men and that even now–their nocturnal work done–these nocturnal warriors slept inside my pots, waiting for nightfall to advance their terrible tower, like a pottery siege-engine, stealthily, towards my Base Camp?!!!

As if there were not enough Dangers in these heathen parts without a further one complicating matters.

Be calm, my fast–beating heart! How, at times like this, I miss my mother and her wise words: 'How I wish I had never taken you out from under the gooseberry bush...'

A mother's love would be a wonderful thing, do not you think? Yes, my mother was a little severe in her speeches, but they made me the man I am today: A Quivering, Nervous Wreck but with the indisputably finest pair of bowlegs on the planet.

I continued my circuits of exploration until the sun set but for once my heart was not in it, for I knew that even in Camp I was no longer safe...

I hope to live through the night to tell you more tomorrow, my dear friends.

But make your own preparations against the Armies of the Flower-Pot Men; surely the worst threat to face Humanity in a hundred years—the Great Pestilence excepting.

Day 32

The flower-pot-man confesses and nostalgic weather

With low grey clouds and a constant drizzle, I strapped on my waterproof truss and codpiece and adjusted my trusty tackle in general. Clothing my upper body in sou'wester and covering my head with my usual bad weather pith helmet, specially made for when it is pithing down, I strode manfully out of Base Camp, leaving upon bed and love-couch (if that couch could only talk!) my cowardly feline bearers, who do so hate the wet weather, that they resist all but the metal toecap on my boot to show themselves out in the Wild.

For this reason, I filled my canvas and leather kitbag with almost everything I could possibly need and carried my heavy burden myself. I am unsure as to why I employ such lazy cats—and their food bills are enormous, with choice foods being delivered for them through the Pestilential Provinces when supplies manage to get through. This week, if they are not eating better than am I, it is certainly more delicious to smell. If things go on like this, I may be sitting down to 'Miaow Morsel's Tasty Shreds' with an appetite, whilst the bearers may have as much pasta, and as many lentils and chickpeas as they can stand.

To return to the weather: it is so pleasant to a dyed-in-the-wool Englishman to be drenched by soft mizzle and lashing wind once more, so typical of my Homeland. I am practically allergic to the weather so preferred by the Half-Naked Savage Woman, who throws off her clothing with gay abandon and so readily when the sun burns down. For the last two days, when out in her compound, she has been clothed from head to foot, which on her looks all wrong. At night, when, typically, the rain has stopped, her compound's magical lights shine out in their various colours, reflected in puddles, unseen by all who shelter from the elements but possibly shining in the eyes of unfortunate aeronauts as they pilot their awe-inspiring machines that come from who-knows-where and go to who-knows-where. I am under the strong impression that these are solely military aircraft, for their colours are those of jungle camouflage. I am afeared that one day one of these machines of war will land on the great savannah of Savanna from out of the sky of Skye (their debts to me increase) and disgorge hostile forces, as this part of the Guard-Lands must seem attractive as a landing strip.

Is it any surprise to you that I have become just a little paranoid of late?

Which naturally brings me to the question of the invasion of my territory by the Flowerpot Men. There at least there is some reassurance, for I have extracted a Confession from Semaj which explains this phenomenon and quite dispels the threatening impression I had received of the Siege by little warriors, contained–I had thought–within the terracotta pot tower.

Semaj, my friendly Native neighbour to the immediate East, admitted, under pressure, that he had stolen from my Base Camp compound an unused waste–food container and in order to do so he had taken the pots off it and piled them up in order of size, the largest at the base and smallest at the top. What a relief this was to my previously perturbed mind, you may imagine. I had made a mountain out of a molehill, as it were!

Whilst on my usual perambulations of my well-established trail through the bush, I came to the shores of Lake Tina once more and with the rain those mighty waters have expanded and deepened. The Wraith or Succubus was there, of course, but I had taken the precaution of stopping my ears with plugs of cotton wool against her alluring song. For that reason, the sexy beast had taken instead to swimming the backstroke and the American Crawl across the surface of The Lake. In the cold and piercing rain, I felt she was welcome to those swelling waters; I would not be joining her that day...[64]

---

[64] At this point, on the hard drive— 'Farewell and be nice to each other and keep your nether regions dry — or moist, if you prefer them that way.'

Day 33

The Terracotta Warrior Menace renewed, the pterosaurs attack and the Moai turns away

It was a testing day for your Hero in the undergrowth and overgrowth of the Guard-Lands, as I ventured closer to their Heart and the mystery of the whereabouts of King Solemn's Vines and his fabled Hanging Vines, together with the Great Lighthouse, Library, and several other Wonders which I have for the moment forgotten. I think a Pyramid and a Statue come into it somewhere...

At Camp One, as I sat suckling on my vaporiser for the stimulation required to set my foot once more upon the trail into the Unknown, without warning suddenly a pterosaur-like repulsive black creature, flew at my head, flapping and screeching as it came, and it was only by my taking rapid evasive action that the beast did not impale me on its slavering yellow beak. As it was, I so disturbed it by my moving my hands to cover my face for the protection of my noble nose and lily white, marble forehead and rosy cheeks, that it changed course at the last minute and flew away, just clearing the privet copse separating my territory from that of the Half-Naked Savage Woman, still screeching loudly enough to wake the Devil! I cannot yet decide if it was deliberately hunting me or had simply alarmed itself by poor navigation, low altitude, and an unexpected encounter with your handsome Correspondent...

My nerve, temporarily shaken by such an unpleasant interlude, I sat myself back down on the sleeping wooden logs of the Camp, in order to regain some calm and resolve.

However, it was then that I spotted with renewed Terror that the terracotta pot tower which I had disassembled the day before, laughing at my own credulity after Semaj's revelation of his hand in it, had reassembled themselves once more into a tower, and one now made taller by the addition of a further pot in the series which graduated by size, with the smallest at the top.

Surely Semaj would not have had the temerity, in a clear affront to neighbourliness, to have done the same thing a second time? You may imagine, therefore, how disturbed I was by the spectacle, for if no man or woman had created this second tower there could be only one explanation: the Terror of the Cotta Pots is genuine, and I must be wary and watchful from now on. God forbid that the Tower should grow further, by a process like cell division. (Mind you, genuine terracotta pots are so terribly expensive that I might not entirely object to their self–replicating a few more times...)

Machete clamped between my teeth, and my teeth glued in place between my jaws, I then set out upon the track as far as the land of the Great Big Boss Handy Man. The grim weather, so welcomed by the vast parched grasses of the plain and the many herds of creatures which depend on fresh grass, even unto the lowly giant dung beetle, seemed to close down upon my poor intrepid explorer's bonce, giving me a slight headache and I looked upon the Big Boss's territory with something of a jaundiced and jaded eye.

However, when I lifted that same head (well, I only have the one) in the direction of the imposing sculpture of the stern Moai, I was pleased to see that the Evil Deity was once again turned away from me. He obviously knew better now than to try to intimidate an English Man!

With a sense of triumph, I turned away and stepped gingerly across the border into the country of Euphemisms, keeping my eyes peeled, lest I encounter thorn plants with the gigantic pricks that do grow there, erect, and able to penetrate the unwary.

But–Patient Reader–I had quite forgotten to be on guard for the cannibal creature, Ken Ucky, or that I might prove finger-licking good to one of his kind.

I am unable, at the Present, to go on, as not only am I too emotional but the light dims and my finger gets stiff–and not only my finger–so do not miss the next exciting instalment. Unless you are fortunate enough to have better things to do with your time?

Day 34

*Escape from the clutches of Ken Ucky riding on his Chick, and the
Great Pyramid of The Geezer! And sundry other matters*

I left you, no doubt, on metaphorical tenterhooks as to my
encounter with the cannibal chieftain Ken Ucky. What I will tell you
now, which will be to your immense relief, is that whilst I fancied I
heard behind me the stupendous footfalls of the murderous moa chick
on which that dread personage rides down his victims, as the mist rose
and the rainclouds descended to meet it, I managed–by casting aside
the less useful items from my kitbag, and thereby lessening my load–
and dashing back through the Land of Euphemisms (where a man is
likely to slip into a slit at any moment, or make some boob or other), to
escape my pursuers. I stopped only once there and my breath,
somewhat embarrassingly, came in short pants, like those of a child.

Then with one last mighty effort I was back onto my familiar
trail and safety. I briefly hid behind the terrible Hidings of the
degenerate Great Yapper, Agenda, to see if I had thrown off the blood–
thirsty Ken Ucky (whom some know, for his prowess in rubbing down
paint, as the very Kernel of Sanders). But no more did the thunderous
feet of the moa chick sound upon the path. I was free and what's more
would live to tell the tale, however tediously.

But these Guard-Lands contain Wonders as well as Terrors,
Gentle and Patient Reader. Still somewhat pale and trembling from my
ordeal of the day before, I was to encounter one such. It is a thing of
beauty and magnificence such as I doubt any but its maker and I have
ever glimpsed: a creation begun in antiquity and still being added to
today.

In these Modern Times this ancient evidence of the Hand of Man
is maintained and added to by none other than my backwards
neighbour to the immediate East, Semaj. Not content with disturbing
the Terracotta Terrors into reprisals visited upon me, not him, he has

turned his hand to the unending task of Pyramid maintenance and supplementing. I had long wished with all my l heart to see with my own eyes a pyramid but never, in all my dreams, have I dared hope to lay those said eyes upon the Great Pyramid. And yet, by looking over his border's palisade, I got a distant view of this imposing structure.

It appears that Semaj, rather than place Yapper doings in my compost heap, has taken to using the said doings as Yapper mud bricks, in their biodegradable bags, to reinforce a structure wide at its base and elegantly tapering to the top. So many of these alternative–to–mud bricks have he and his forebears assembled that the Pyramid of the Geezer now towers over the plain and can probably be seen from outer space. What can be the meaning of this? Is there some secret passageway and at its end a central space where he is destined to be entombed, from which his soul will leave that Pyramid of Poop to join the Gods? If not, what does he intend to do with the Filthy Thing? So many questions...

I wandered back to Base Camp, musing upon this mystery. In the compound of the Half-Naked Savage Woman her fair-weather clothing hung from her drying device, together with the usual display of Delicates. I never knew there were two parts to her Native costume, though I have seen some sort of improvised strap she uses when grilling herself lying on her back. 'So, she has a complete bikini,' thought I. 'Wonders will never cease.'

Tune in tomorrow for more, Gentle Readers. I cannot promise a Pyramid every day, nor a two-part bikini, but I do think that there is more to tell you of the country of the Euphemisms, where I dare say something is sure to raise its engorged head.

Day 35

A solemn oath and a solemn oaf. Plus: how music eats up the miles and disperses solitude

There have been some complaints in messages I have received recently through the noble efforts of He–Males and other agents in crossing the Pestilential Provinces, and in circumnavigation of the waves of the air. These principally concern the sex and violence which have predominated in my accounts of my exploration of the Tricky Terrain in which I make my Explorations.

Strangely, there have been no complaints concerning the many lavatorial passages, but I object to those myself and have taken myself to task over this low stuff frequently smearing, as it were, my stories.

So, in my tale of the day's doings I will try to elevate my discussion, and concentrate on an Art; in short, the plastic art which is music.

How, you may ask, do I keep what remains of my sanity as I penetrate ever further into these mislaid lands? How do I keep my spirits up and the Vile Vultures of Despair at bay? In answer to these impertinent questions, I will say but the one word: music—in all its many manifestations. Well, OK, that's six words but surely, we have no need for this sort of pedantry?

In short, I have taken to summing up my musical back–catalogue from the moist recesses of my mind. Tunes I do recall well, though sometimes the lyrics evade me.

I have treated my feline bearers to renditions of Elizabethan Aires and to Victorian Music Hall novelties. Moving on literally and metaphorically I have moved musically through blues songs, jazz songs, swing songs, Truly Dreadful Ballads from the 1940s, 50s and early 60s. Recently I have been heard to hum or sing the ditties of the Beatles and the Rolling Stones. Daringly, I have made forays into the repertoire of the (early) Pink Floyd, where few men have gone before.

The lead guitar parts are particularly difficult to imitate so that I must on occasion sound like a stuck pig.

Mayhap I will then dodge to one side of the musical spectrum to sing songs from West End and Broadway shows before pulling myself back to the safety of Abba, via the unlikely avenue of the Beach Boys, West Coast Power Ballads, Steve Winwood, and Captain Beefheart. [65]

On the occasions I carry with me my sturdy tool–I refer only to my trusty acoustic guitar–I will regale the wildlife and the Restive Natives with the songs of Bryan Ferry and Roxy Music, before astounding them with Syd Barrett, and the Sex Pistols (damnation, there is that 'sex' word again!). When I feel particularly courageous, I will play and sing songs of my own composition to the audience of peculiar animal-life which gathers to listen but swiftly disperses, I know not why.

So it was, that Semaj came to listen to me and my music by the shores of Lake Tina, as the sun dipped towards the horizon over the forest treetops. Then up spoke he, in actual English words, no less— 'Would you teach me to play the guitar?' As I hesitated, loath to commit myself to this onerous task, he added, pathetically, 'It will keep me away from weed, women and wine, the which have been my undoing hitherto.'

I ask you; how could I refuse this poor, jabbering, jungle creature his heartfelt request?

So it was that I swore a Terrible Oath to teach him the rudiments of music, or die in the attempt, and with the fearful Assault on Harmony that we will no doubt have to make in the initial stages.

I think we may start with Ian Dury and the Blockheads' 'Hit Me with Your Rhythm Stick.' I think I may there, at the last moment, have unfortunately strayed into Sex and Violence. But luckily nothing Lavatorial...

And so Gentle Reader, I leave you—hopefully 'With a Song in your Heart' and wish you regular bowel movements also.

---

[65] The hard drive has 'It is an eclectic if–admittedly– rather old-fashioned mix.'

Day 36

The name of the Moai's ruler plus the Flags of Surrender

On a Red-Letter day, here in the Guard-Lands, there were at least two occurrences of note.

After I had toiled along the usual paths and trackways and hacked my way through the rapidly re-growing bush, I came to the fiefdom of the Great Big Boss Handy Man. Whilst lingering there for a while, eating my rations and picking the fluff out of my brave belly button, I heard the G.B.B.H.M being called into his brick hut for some sort of crude Native repast (possibly human-being off the bone...); at least a name was called and he responded; the name was 'Rovert'! I cannot help feeling that Rovert is a distorted form of the English 'Revert', which suggests that the clan of Rovert are decadent descendants from an earlier and lost white expedition, indeed from no less a person than Lord Little Newtown! This might well explain the no doubt inbred sense of superiority possessed by this person. Of course! I understand now that it is beneath him to add the Hidings of Agenda to the Great Pyramid, in a neat and avoidable manner. His carelessness in this matter is surely merely a result of being one who is unused to stooping to such menial and unpleasant work.

Somehow knowing a name gives one a feeling of some power over the Named, do not you think? Therefore, without so much trepidation as usual, I boldly looked over his palisade and into his compound. Beyond the bonsai forest and the Moai statue those modest carp swam languidly beneath the grille set to protect them from diving pterosaurs and my felines. I even took the opportunity to see in the distance that Rovert possesses one of those strange two wheeled devices upon which it is my conviction no ordinary mortal can balance. It leans nonchalantly against the neat heap of regular red stones, taking its rest. It seems to need a good deal of rest, for this device I have never seen move beneath the noble derriere of Rovert. Perhaps he keeps it merely as just one of many trophies captured from those he kills and puts in his big boiling–pot? Eventually, I gathered my wits and my gear together and began the long and wearisome toil of the trail back to my various camps. It was then that I spotted, strung up along lines between great poles of steel, flags like those I had seen before, which then indicated the war-like intentions of the tribe whose settlement is in the Far East. However, whereas on that occasion the flags had been damp and of frightening colours now they were all bone dry and white, suggestive of surrender and welcome. I felt extremely gratified on behalf of my Queen and Empress, and of British civilised values. I could only presume that this territory welcomed, no less, myself as the Representative and kindly Patron of their country, now brought under the umbrella of the British Commonwealth, even to the point of embracing Colonisation, as so many nations have unless they want to feel the cold steel of the British Army as it comes in Peace. 'It is for our own good!' I can almost hear this humbled nation say, as I proudly add it like a feather to the hat of the Imperial Power that is Britain (called 'Great' because of the pleasure simple foreigners have in becoming our Subjects).

And so, to my humble present abode and bed, well satisfied.

May you too always be well satisfied in bed.

I love you and leave you, like a casual hook-up.[66]

---

[66] It is interesting to note how in most editions this valediction is omitted.

Day 37

A trap baited for the infant Moa, presumably, and Semaj throws a wobbly

Come with me, Gentle Readers, if you will, into the territory of the vile and vicious Ken Ucky, whose appetite–I am convinced–is for those human beings of the most tender flesh for his Frying Pan and Boiling Pot, and relishes therefore most of all the pedigree fillets of the English Man, milk-fed from infancy to have the palest and most lean meat for the connoisseur—finger licking good in fact. It is said that this Kernel of Sanders (he who grinds slow but exceeding fine) has a secret recipe by which he enhances the disjointed limbs of his tragic captives before plunging them into boiling oil. 'Oh, the humanity!'[67]

Yes, well, as I was saying, if you will take an imaginary trip with me into his cruel kingdom, whilst it is only I who really risks his skin and everything within, you might find as did I, that Salt Peter, a neighbour of mine who lives in an Eastern compartment in my brick hut, had been there before you, laying bait of slices of cooked dough. When on a previous occasion he said he put out bread for the pterosaurs and winked at me I had obviously not understood his true meaning. Now I was struck by his cunning, for surely, he could be doing none other than attracting the voracious Giant Moa chick upon which Ken Ucky travels to perform his acts of murder and cannibalism! And–as if to prove the point (quite literally –when I myself followed the rough path through the bush, along which the products of grain and yeast (with pinches of sugar and salt) had been so carefully strewn, I came to a huge pit cut into that Wild Way and at its base saw-sharpened trunks of the great bamboos that do grow close by!

---

[67] This is a quite unnecessary and rather gratuitous quotation from Herbert Morrison, commentating upon the Hindenburg airship disaster in 1937.

I had never thought Salt Peter to be such a Brave and Noble Native. I suppose for him too Ken Ucky and his Maddening Moa constitute major nuisances.

Unless, of course, Salt Peter really does just put out bread for the small pterosaurs such as infant pterodactyls, and that all else is a product of my fevered imagination. I cannot be sure, for presently I suffer from a bout of jippy jungle tummy. As this is a hundred times easier to bear than what is going on for sufferers in the Pestilential Provinces, I heroically count my blessings.

I retreated from Salt Peter's Moa trap and made my way back to Base Camp with all speed to try to use the primitive facilities there and afterwards to have a cup of coffee substitute, as my real coffee has run out and fresh provision of it not yet secured, although I have issued one of my orders that no man or woman dare disobey. Especially not when money is involved.

On my way back I encountered Semaj, deep in thought and grim of countenance as he walked Freebie on a lead to keep that essentially wild Yapper by his side and out of The Half-Naked Woman Savage's compound. He was not in the mood to talk but mumbled over and over again, 'That bloody Rovert!' All I could get from him further was that Rovert's large Agenda hound had attacked little Freebie and Rovert had had the gall to blame innocent and tiny Freebie for the ensuing battle. Unless I can broker peace between them, I fear that there may shortly be a Tribal War in the Guard-Lands, which might well hamper my further Explorations.

Yours, dosed with crude Native gut-settler and whisky, hoping you are free of such a malady as required me to take it (perhaps brought on by gluttony in my case). Keep your spirits up whilst I endeavour to keep some down.

Day 38

Salt Peter's bait is taken! and thoughts on Rovert's Dinosaur Enclosure. Will the Wonders and Terrors never cease?

I now must tell you the startling news that the fearsome Moa chick was too clever for Salt Peter, for when I finally reached the place in the dense bush where he had laid two pieces of baked goods to tempt the Pusillanimous Poultry onto the sharpened stakes in his pit trap, the bright bird had outwitted the hunter by taking but one of the tasty wheaten morsels, leaving well alone that slice which trembled upon the very lip of the concealed trap! It is obvious, therefore, that I must now apply my Mighty Grey Cells to the matter, if both Moa and Master are to be eliminated once and for all, and the Dangers of the Guard-Lands reduced by two.

And, by the way, the pit was not just the fevered imaginings of my digestion disturbed brain the previous day, for it may not have trapped and dispatched a Moa but it almost did for Me, when–in a moment of foolish forgetfulness–I put my heel into it myself and only with luck and skill avoided falling and being pierced to the quick by the bamboo spears that lay below!

However, with one mighty bound I was free and able to continue on my way, terrified but not terminated...

And so, I returned, via the area marked by the pole on which perches for All Eternity the last of the Little Iron Dragons, to the perimeter of the palisade to the country of the Great Big Boss Handy Man Rovert. Here, I rested my faltering flat feet for a while to gaze at the golden modest carp that did lazily swim beneath the waters of the netted[68] Lake. However, when I looked up and to the left what should I see for the first time but a Puzzling Pergola whose limbs stretched up into the sky and encompassed an area of many square feet. No doubt

---

[68] We have already been told that a grille lay over it, not a net. Our explorer has become confused and not for the first or last time.

you would have come to the same conclusion about this structure as I did: the impressive construction could only enclose a Baby Dinosaur Nursery and Egg Hatchery!

As, if there were Baby Dinosaurs, their mothers could not be far away, I hoisted my shorts, pulled up my socks' suspenders and crept silently away, as the pterosaurs glided overhead, toward the mysterious plateau in the Northeast, surrounded by its cliffs of regular red stones pierced by reflecting squares of a material like obsidian.

I looked back over my shoulder as their magical majesty receded, on my way back to Camp One, until I almost fell into Salt Peter's bloody pit again.

May you avoid being dogged by misfortune but remain with wet noses and shiny coats. Those of you who possess tails—keep them wagging.

Day 39

The baby dinosaurs hatch out, plus a Feral Fearsome Feline of the early Sabre-toothed Panthera species makes an unprovoked attack!

There were disturbing sights on the rolling plain of Savanna under the sun glaring through the sky of Skye (those young American lasses are now immortalised in Literature and Letters both for their names and the amounts of pocket money they will send to support this famous explorer in his ground–breaking studies into the geography, flora and fauna of these Guard-Lands on the edge of the known world — immortality do not come cheap, you know...).

For as I and my bearers made our circumspect way through the vegetation we saw, to our horror, that it was strewn with the dismembered corpses of pterosaurs, pterodactyls, pteranodons and prehistoric small mammals of both shrew and mouse type.

This suggested clearly to my mind two possibilities: either baby hatchling dinosaurs, not of the peace-loving vegetarian kind but of the violence-loving carnivorous type, had quit their shells, and escaped from Rovert, the Big Boss Handy Man's dinosaur hatchery, or that here was another as yet unknown threat to the body and soul of an Off-English Man, namely *me*!

You may imagine with what trepidation my little Party continued to wend its way past the deceptively peaceful waters of Lake Tina, by which the Wraith or Succubus sat quietly combing her lustrous black hair and singing the catchy ballad 'You Can't Help Who You Love'[69] so as to keep her hand in, even in repose, in practice for when next she would fancy luring a young and easily-seduced lover to her side and his Certain Doom...

---

[69] Extensive searches of popular ballad titles (Popular Ballad Titles Database, Clayson and Garrett, 2019) failed to trace the mentioned song. It must have risen without trace.

And so, after hours of my singing to keep up our spirits, with the bearers and Natives covering their ears with their hands in that quaint old Native way they have of showing respect, we came tip–toeing to the palisade of Rovert the BBHM's territory and peered over. Sure enough, there, gambolling amidst broken shells I seemed to see newly hatched dinosaurs looking as cute as only a monster born in Spring can. They were wobbly on their feet and mewed in attempts at roaring like their parents. Occasionally one would, because of yet poor motor skills, stand on the neck of another, or lash another little fellow with a tail not yet properly controlled by its ganglion, or secondary nerve centre.

But some had climbed out from the nest pits where their mothers had placed them for safety and now were trespassing in the bonsai forest, occasionally knocking down a miniature trunk of one tree, inadvertently, as they clumsily toddled, or snapping off the luscious-looking head of another to see if it were good to eat—which it never was for they spat out the leaves and branches with a wry face.

Oh, how I laughed at the charming and comedic creatures but then I set myself to the more serious task of recording the infants of these several species using no more than charcoal on crude Native paper, and a primitive camera with few pixels, for an iPhone or iPad remain just pipedreams. No sponsor of my expedition had cared to run to the expense, so can I be blamed if the grainy images I record in this Land of Wonders will later to be viewed with grave suspicion, almost as much as my words, if not quite as much?

I did toy with the idea of bringing one of the babies, perhaps the runt of the litter, home with me to Great Britain but in the end rejected the idea, as, small they may be, even a little one of these beasts could quite easily take a finger off and perhaps some other impressively protuberant part of my anatomy...

Retreating as dusk fell, and as we felt the thumps and vibration of the mothers' feet, as they returned to their broods, I still felt wary, for I had not, in all these marvels, seen that any mini dinosaur had crossed over into the bush and the plain beyond. So, it was not they who had been savagely destroying rodents and careless archaeopteryxes.

But then, just as we crossed the taller grasses, a huge black cat dashed menacingly from out of the distance and–just missing our Party–it turned its face and growled in hostile warning. I may only have had a glimpse, but it was enough to terrify me. For from its upper jaw protruded two dagger–like teeth, dripping blood! Yes, Credulous and Sceptical Reader alike, it could have been none other than a Sabre-toothed Panther! We were truly lucky it had obviously just eaten, or we would surely have been its victims.

But let not your dreams be haunted by such Terrors. Attacks by extinct Sabre-toothed panthers are many million times rarer than you might think.

By Great Fortune, I lived to write another day and until the white–coated men come with their padded van to take me away.

Day 40

In which I wonder what ever happened to one Wonder of the World, and evidence that the tiny Iron Dragon feeds at night

When I left Base Camp, I could have had no warning what startling things would greet my organs of sight that day. I will not detain you with a further account of my ordeal in reaching my First and Second Camps along the trail, or as sometimes call them First and Second Base, but rather in matters relating to my getting to Third Base and establishing a firm grip there, so that in future I might set up my equipment there as speedily as possible and thus penetrate the Guard-Lands as far and as fast as possible. This surely must be a matter of great satisfaction to all?

In any case, I crossed the great Plain of Savanna (I am now sending the bailiffs for recovery of dollars I am owed) as the pterosaurs did swoop and hover high in the warm up–currents in the Skye (probably a parent's responsibility still, as regards debts, let it be noted) with my knapsack on my back and a song in my heart, the Natives and bearers having pleaded with me not to sing out loud, for the beauty of my voice is such as to break both their hearts and other parts, they say.

Only gradually did it begin to dawn on me that something was missing from the broad horizon, so wide that the curvature of the planet itself can be discerned, on a clear day.

With a shock that caused me to suddenly stand still, so that feline bearers and Native attendants ploughed into my back, I realised just what had gone. It was the majestic and dominating sight where it had always stood, since its first construction long, long ago: the Great Pyramid of the Geezer. That enormous putrescent pile had simply disappeared overnight!

Gentle Readers, you may imagine with what amazement I was filled by the emptiness of the horizon. Yet another Wonder of the World vanished, to add to the list of others no more to be seen, like the Hanging

Gardens of Billabong, the Library at Alexandra's Rear and the Lighthouse of Fairy.[70]

What, I wondered could account for the loss to the world of this latest inestimable treasure?

I continued to travel and–after much of the day had elapsed– arrived at where the base of the Pyramid had been. There, I stood scratching my head and other parts, in puzzlement and sadness.

Only one lonely biodegradable thin plastic packet containing poo there remained. All else was gone—gone for all Eternity! I openly wept for a so–called civilisation that could so high-handedly sweep away both Great Art and all evidence of the industry of its ancestors...

As my own small memorial to the lost Pyramid, I determined to make my camp, or Third Base at the place. I could now say with pleasure that I had gone so far as to get to Third Base and was now within reach of my ultimate goal. Surely soon I would achieve ecstasy as I gazed upon the lost Vines of King Solemn? And yet how could I know how many dangers might yet lie between the intention and the achievement of this feat, perhaps one not even achieved by Lord Little Newton, whose lonely English bones may lie for Eternity near where I found his note. In my heart I fear that King Solemn's Vines lay beyond even his pioneering reach. Perhaps we shall never know...

For the Present, I began my strategic retreat home to my Base Camp (refusing myself the temptation of taking back to England, as a souvenir, the last remaining bag of excrement from the Great Pyramid), for I began to hunger for an Escalope of a Quorn, washed down with 'Hamelin—Genuine German non-alcoholic Beer (brewed in the UK)'.

One last surprise awaited me that day. For as I passed the tiny iron dragon, apparently posed for evermore rigidly upon the pole in a neighbouring tribes' palisade, I noticed that his mouth was full of fluffy feathers or the webs of spiders! It is therefore obvious, is it not, that in the dead of night that miniature beast of legend reanimates and goes a-hunting?

Truly, these Guard-Lands are a constant source of bewilderment, delight, and extreme terror. (Keeps one on one's toes, at any rate!)

---

[70] For an explorer, PWN seemed to have a poor grasp of the Seven Wonders of Ancient Times.

I wish you well in all your endeavours, though your lives are obviously more humdrum and unimportant than that of
The Great Explorer, who remains your humble servant.

Day 41

Of the Half-Naked Woman restored to her rightful condition, and from Third Base I discover, or stumble upon, King Solemn's Great Stone Processional Pavement—probably

As I walked out of Base Camp once more–in full exploring fig and with high hopes of more discoveries in the inner depths of the Guard-Lands–with the sun, for a change, high in the sky and beating down upon a grateful world (for one should not take it for granted – not at my age) I glanced to the West and there discovered that the body of the Half-Naked Woman Savage was already laid out in sun-lotion homage to the ultra-violent rays [*sic*]. It is a wonder she is not partially blackened, like overdone toast and similarly not tasting very nice.

As I took my usual brief look of no more than twenty minutes, she raised herself on her primitive jungle couch in preparation to tying her bandeau bikini-top on and turning over to give the topside an equal incineration. Naturally, at this point I averted my eyes, after ten minutes or so, as any English gentleman would. At that point her eyes opened, and such was the speed with which I snapped my head back and away, that I gave my neck quite a nasty strain, an injury which I carried for the rest of the day.

Did this wound deter me from the mission for which I had been commissioned and upon which so many depend? It did not. I cracked my bullwhip at my recalcitrant bearers and servants and strode manfully on, at breakneck speed (my neck had overall a bad time of it).

I had no time to dally, for it was my intention to reach Base Three before a break to partake of a frugal luncheon of toasted dough, leek and potato soup, an orange fruit which I had to peel myself (one cannot have every luxury in the bush, you know), followed by merely several slices of Emmenthal cheese-and-pumpkin seed crisp-bread, spread lavishly with the equivalent to butter which is used in these primitive parts. After so little, you will not be surprised to hear that I also consumed my daily ration of two digestive biscuits, brought at great expense and difficulty all the way from my Home in dear old England, the land where my Polish forebears were raised if not born.[71]

After a brief siesta of an hour and a half, I summoned my miserable manservants with a single crack of my bullwhip and out we journeyed, from where once the Great Pyramid of the Geezer had stood — out into the unexplored area beyond.

We had gone on but less than one quarter of an hour when, stumbling nastily in my explorer's boots, I fell, and my beautiful white knee encountered–with a hard landing–what was unmistakeably a huge flat stone beneath the sward.

Dumbfounded, I brought the Expedition to a temporary halt in order to more closely investigate this phenomenon. I was silent as I cleared away some of the grasses and groundcover, together with a shallow layer of soil. I had certainly found my dumb for I knew not what to think, let alone say; as I revealed the stone–a conglomerate of gravels and I know not what–it was becoming clear to me that this stone and the one fitted adjacent to it were wrought by the Hand of Ancient Man. I leapt to my feet in celebration and got the recalcitrant carrier-cats to pop open the bottle of celebratory tropical fruit fizz I had brought with me against such a wonderful discovery being made one day. For we, I could have no doubt, Gentle Readers, stood upon the very threshold of the Processional Stone Road of King Solemn, about which no man had ever lived to tell.[72]

More on the morrow, Patient Readers. Kindly wait in breathless anticipation, for as it was, I had need at this point to return with haste before dusk could descend on us. As we returned to Base Camp a flock of those pterosaurs that 'Coo!' rose up out of the Plain and flew away on fluttering wings.[73] They but spoke my thoughts about the day I had experienced.

---

[71] This must be a very important clue to the ancestry of PWN and is still being investigated as this book goes to print, with no results as yet.

[72] Odd that, when you think about it. How did PWN know about it, then?

[73] Pterosaurs —flying reptiles of the clade or order Pterosauria, formerly thought to be extinct.

May your day be one of great discoveries too. Perhaps one of the great things you will discover is exactly why you ever read the messages I send.

Day 42

Semaj wields his great rotary scythe and cunning clippers. Plus, thoughts of revenge on Agenda and Rovert, The Great Big Boss Handy Man, his master

On a day largely overcast, sultry and close, and when the Half Naked Woman Savage could perforce only sizzle herself for a couple of hours at midday, I gathered my band of reluctant attendants and insisting on a forced march of many miles into the interior of the Guard-Lands, along now familiar routes, I made my way towards the definite goal of the likely start of the Famed Road that leads to his kingdom and ultimately King Solemn's Vines. Still, it was not without a little sadness at its loss, at the point where The Great Pyramid of The Geezer once stood, and Base Three is now, I allowed us all a break of a few minutes, to rest our weary legs, and to consume the light rations in my kitbag: diluted tropical juice, and both sugar-free mints and sugar-free butter candies and as much "Guilty Pleasure" as a mere mortal can stand.

I stood for a while in contemplation and meanwhile doffed my sweaty pith helmet in respectful memory of the passing of that Pile of Poo, which once reached almost to the heavens, gone for evermore...

Thus, do the works of even the greatest of mortals perish under the Flat Foot of Careless Time.

And yet surely, somewhere, some God does notice what we puny humans achieve, either individually or collectively, and makes an entry in his immortal ledger, so as to better inform his choices for the Judgement Day? I mean, I expect he or she has angels of some kind to do the actual donkeywork. I do not expect he or she, even with Eternity to play with, really wants to bother himself or herself with the bureaucratic drudgery of filing reports in a ledger?[74]

---

[74] At which point on the hard drive PWN muses—'Perhaps it is all done on a first come, first served, basis...'

Let me now proceed to the point where I had found traces of King Solemn's Processional Pavement the day before. Would you care to imagine my surprise when I discovered that that person of infinitely variable mood, Semaj, had gone before us and had, with considerable dexterity, reduced the grasses and encroaching bush cover with his scythe to reveal that indeed my suspicions were correct?! For here–though Time and the upheavals of the earth's crust had distorted the way–undoubtedly lay that which I sought. In places were still visible slabs both of concrete and stone, some of them precisely jointed together. This could be no accident. I set-to, to record this historical artefact in both photograph and ink drawing, so that the people of my own country should know of my find, for the sake of Posterity, not for any personal benefit (except of course that I might in future make a limited run of an Exclusive Edition of my Discoveries, lavishly illustrated, in full colour and on the finest vellum, for which I would have to ask for a modest donation to my current account at the Screwem and Sodem Savings Bank).[75]

Only a little frustrated that too little daylight remained for us to explore the Road of Solemn further that day, we began the long but satisfied trek back to Base Camp.

Now that the tall grasses and giant herbs had been reduced by Semaj's mighty scythe, it should have been easy to avoid the Hidings of Agenda, but I am sorry to have to report that at one point nearby the Horrible Hound had gone about its nefarious business and I once more fouled my sturdy jungle boots, so that Dettol and a trusty coarse Native scrubber would have to be employed. (I of course paid the coarse Native scrubber to do it for me.)

I know I should–in truth–seek revenge not upon the big Yapper but its irresponsible owner, Rovert, but I feel as though I should like to steal out one moonless night and sew up the offender's offending orifice, so that shortly there might be a single terrible explosion with the result that the problem would be dealt with once and for all.

But fear ye not, no animals will be needlessly harmed in the course of my Expeditionary Adventures—unless ill will should so

---

[75]This bank, if it ever existed, had ceased business before PWN's account of his Travels was first published.

overcome me that I do actually arm myself with chloroform and my curved needle and cobblers' thread. My Boy Scout's Surgical Badge may yet come in useful.

Sleep with one eye open, Agenda – that's all I am saying...

You, I hope, will sleep peacefully in your beds tonight, Gentle Readers. I wish I were with you—and I mean that sincerely. (Offer applies only to unrelated ladies. I must draw the line somewhere...)

Day 43

The eighth wonder of the world is down but not out. Plus, I receive something like a "sext" from the Succubus and other matters

On a glorious day here in the land between the Pestilential Provinces of the South and the Badlands of the North, I noticed that the Half-Naked Savage Woman was ensconced on her portable folding couch, offering her poor burnt body once more to the pitiless rays of the sun. Perhaps this is what she is, in fact: a human sacrifice offered to Apollo by her tribespeople, as they pray for rain? This prayer is quite frequently being answered hereabouts, for when the weather is not such as to produce Third Degree Burns requiring skin grafts, it is deluging us in one day with enough water to supply an oasis and a Saharan desert encampment for 20 years.

As I am not yet ready to establish a Camp Four along my lengthy route into the Kingdom of Solemn (in truth, I dread the exhaustion and predicted *'petite mort'* which will no doubt result from getting to Fourth Base...), I confined my activities to the overdue cartography for which generations will be grateful, as neither Giggle Maps nor any satellite in space has yet discovered or recorded the Guard-Lands and its many fascinating geographic features, some pleasurable, most exceedingly dangerous.

However, with my foolish and lethargic feline fellow–travellers I did get as far along my previously established trail as the sad place of Base Three, where once stood the Great Pyramid of the Geezer.

But–and prepare yourselves for an astonishing shock! –from the wreck of the demolished Pyramid from Posterity now was growing a Second perhaps even Greater Pyramid made by the Geezer people!

Could it be that this is the first recyclable Wonder of the World?! But if so, where does each previous Pyramid of Poo go to be recycled? One mystery is only succeeded by another...

111

Still, it is heartening to know that given long enough there may once more stand upon the horizon, dwarfing each creature–even the elephant and the diplodocus–another Pyramid pointing the way to the stars and the Afterlife...

As our party turned its footsteps homeward, from out of the ether I was summoned by polyphonic bells from my magic crystal device and there I read a message from the Succubus of Lake Tina, stating that she would be sunbathing, at any moment.

I felt my poor old heart and other parts surge at this siren's seductive song and so, urging my troupe on with strategic lashes of my Bullwhip, I made my way back along the trail as fast as ever I could, with the purpose only of recording the watery wraith on either grainy photographic plate, or with my trusty HB pencil on paper. My companions tried their best to restrain me, fearing I was too willing to fall as yet another victim to that mellifluous man-magnet! However, as it turned out, they need not have been afeared *pour moi*, for–reaching the otherwise calm waters of Lake Tina–we were only in time to see the mermaid–tailed maiden vanish back into the fabled fathoms of the Lake, with a flick of the end of her fantastic tail. Soon there was nothing to see there but a few circular ripples emanating from the point of her disappearance. Down at heart at this disappointment, I miserably gathered my ensemble of servants together and we trudged back along the usual route to the initial Camps and eventually Base Camp.

But as I looked over the regular red stone wall, I was to see playing together, in the metalled trackways of the Badlands, the little double wheel balancing blonde and the petite snake–throttling lass. How sweet and untroubled they seemed in that time of the setting sun! My spirits began to lift once more at the innocent sight. It occurred to me that by the time these little girls were full grown, the Pestilential Provinces would have receded (perhaps to nothing), the Badlands retreated, and the Greater Pyramid of the Geezer would once more loom over the Plain in the Guard-Lands, even if I should not live to see it. This thought gave me great hope for the Future. And sometimes we need that, do not we? You may not always have wished to perceive a Great Pyramid of Yapper Poo as did I, but you will no doubt have something equivalent you wish to see. Or might you have your aim set even higher than that, perhaps? Until tomorrow, then, I leave each to his or her own dreams.

Day 44

Rough winds did shake the darling buds of May—if May was
foolish enough to venture out without her raincoat and galoshes.
Plus, Ferocious Feral Felines prowl the perimeter of Base Camp

Gentle and Harsh Reader alike—the climate here changed rapidly for the worse, there was an intense wind which howled over the savannah of Savanna, and the sky of Skye was filled with low black clouds which proceeded to drop rain immoderately on the heads of the unwary. (Something is holding up payment from the aforenamed American lasses, maybe it is just the money-laundering process.)

Only for the briefest moment in the early day did the Half-Naked Savage Woman's Pantheon of Panties appear on its drying device before that Legendary Lingerie had to be ripped down unceremoniously and taken quickly back into her brick hut.

Surveying the scene with the eye of the seasoned explorer, I realised that further ground–breaking discoveries were out of the question that day.

Nevertheless, to clear away the cobwebs (and the cobwebs are gigantic, ancient, and covered in dust at my Base Camp, without a word of a lie) I did make a sortie out between Camps One and Two and on towards Camp Three a little way, after my toilet. (I do not mean I was following my lavatory—do not be so silly.)

But this restricted expedition was wet and dangerous work, for I was, as it were, 'flying solo', for the reason that Loopy and Meli had taken one look at the weather and refused point-blank to accompany me on what they stated in an insubordinate manner was 'the folly of a madman.'

It was true that my rest at Camp One was an uncomfortable, chilly, and wet one and my usual pleasures of sugar-free butter candies and mints washed down with tropical jungle juice were like ashes in mouth. My only pleasure was my Twisted Melon, Tutti-frutti and

American Gold flavoured vaporiser steam, giving me at least some reason to go on.

There was just one discovery in the tall bush which I had not made previously, to wit a flash of blue alerted me to dig out a Native bag from where it was trapped; it was of the sort in which they carry their consumables. How came it there, I wondered? For no sane person other than I walks in these damned regions—and sometimes I wonder if I can truly be called sane after these many days spent in wild territory, where I have had no human company of a civilised kind, or with whom I may hold an adult conversation.

Then the solution hit me! Of course, the Native bag must have been blown here by the wayward wind and the bush had entangled it before it could reach its natural home, the Sea... A tear came to my eye when I thought that no brisk gale could guide me to my spiritual home, for my family home had been sold and now was in the possession of strangers and might even as I write be being gentrified out of all recognition. [76]

However, Base Camp with its limited comforts was calling me and the hour was late, and so I wended my way back.

Of course, my preoccupied mind was responsible for my not spotting earlier that, in the twilight lit Taiga, not one but two of those terrifying sabre–toothed panthers were detaching themselves from the shadows and stealthily approaching me, saliva dripping from their wicked fangs! Well, what would you do in my place, Gentle Readers? I do not mind admitting that I for one–when I finally spotted the beasts–lifted the skirts of my waterproof and ran for Base Camp as fast as ever I could. I had only just got through the back door of the Camp and slammed it shut when both of those monsters came crashing into the magnetic cat flap, trying to headbutt it open and have me for their supper. Luckily, they did not have the trick of it but retreated with very sore heads and a sense of aggrievement...

Really, sometimes I wish that I could just stroll outside my brick hut without a feeling of incipient danger.

I bet you feel the same way, do not you?

---

[76] PWN is not, of course, referring to PWN Towers but to his father's house and estate, Leopard Court, as mentioned elsewhere.

Day 45

A cups and balls trick; Rovert looks rough and causes a pratfall; plus, the approach to King Solemn's fabled land

At Camp One, I noted that there had been no interference with my precious terracotta pots since they had last been placed twice open – side-downwards as tapering towers in some jest of Semaj's. But the blue ball I had retrieved from the Territory of Euphemisms and which I had placed under one had disappeared. How surprised was I therefore when, upon lifting another of the terracotta pots, I discovered that beneath it the blue ball had apparently magically been transported? An idea occurred to me and that was to move the ball from that pot to the one standing next to it.

If there was truly anything odd in its appearance under the other pot it would be interesting to see if it remained when I returned from my travels, although I can see that it depends on your definition of 'interesting'.

At the palisade which separates the bushland terrain from The Great Big Boss Rovert's empire, I lifted my head only to see Rovert in a state of night–time dress and his usually impeccable hair all tousled. His face was stony with bad temper and all his body language suggested that I could expect to receive no welcome from him and that making a silent retreat was by far my best course of action. Unfortunately, as I did so, I tumbled over Loopy who being rather aged now is not as fleet of foot or alert as he was when he was younger. Which of us is? As I fell back my full length, I also knocked over Meli who had stopped to investigate and torment a decorative By-flutter. I had thus achieved a full strike of felines. They picked themselves up, shook themselves ostentatiously and cast upon me surly looks which did not diminish much as we continued on our tiring trail along the tracks which lead to Base Three. Along our way there was nothing but an eerie silence, broken only by a member of a tribe to the Far East venturing out of his brick hut to smoke a pipe of tobacco and stare insolently at our little group as we picked our way carefully towards the Pyramid of the Geezer, now in the process of renovation.

We had brought with us all we required for further exploration of the ancient Superhighway of Solemn, now so dilapidated through the passing of callous Time. So, after a comfort break and refreshments, out we set upon the course that Semaj's great rotary scythes had revealed two days previously. For some time, in awe and reverent silence, we proceeded along that ill-maintained roadway, still redolent of power and majesty. Then we noticed that the course of the Processional Pavement was dipping quite strongly. Down, down it went and into small valley. Ahead of us loomed the Great Escarpment.

At the last we could see a great archway in the cliff. But to my dismay it was obvious that our way through was impossible. An ancient fall of rocks meant that the Subway of King Solemn was forever closed to us!

As there was no other course, at least none other I could see for now, and as the hour grew late, I directed my weary troop to turn and we made our way, most disappointed and low in spirits back to Camp Two, where I remembered to have a look under the pot where I had left the blue ball. Here was almost the biggest surprise of the day: for beneath the pot the blue ball still lay; however, there was now not one but a pair of blue balls from the land of Euphemisms. This was truly magic! Semaj could have had no hand in it as he was not to be seen, although feint laughter could perhaps be heard from within his compound...

I will say nothing more until the morrow although I cannot resist reporting to you that Our Eyes have seen Wonderful Things!

Day 46

A pterosaur hunt interrupted, violently, plus a removal from Base on a gamble. At last, an Approach to The Kingdom of Solemn! A passage about a Passage

A terrible incident occurred as I emerged from the back door of my Base Camp brick hut. For, up from my very feet flew a black and white pterosaur. It soon became apparent that the creature had been corralled there by Meli, for she turned and ran as the beast squawked up and away from the distal ends of my legs. To say Meli was furious with me for my unwitting interference would be an understatement. It took much time and stroking under the chin to earn her forgiveness; words were not enough to soothe her feelings and injured pride. No doubt if I had not stepped out at that moment, the largest carcase ever to have been dragged in through the cat flap would have soon graced my bed compartment's carpet with Meli stood beside it in bloody triumph. Many a mouse and small bird have been left there previously, for me to step on with bare feet at the start of day – but never a Magspy!

But I was anxious to be off and out, mounting that day my greatest attempt on achieving the fabled Kingdom of Solemn, and somewhere within it his Vines, the source they say of the World's Greatest Ever vintages. To this end I required that enough utensils and provisions be packed and carried to the red stone escarpment, together with knives, spears, guns, missiles, and atomic warheads to show we came in peace. For it was my intention to reach the land beyond the escarpment by any means, even should it mean camping out at the base of the escarpment until we might find some way to progress.

It was a cool day but not unpleasant as we bestrode the plain and passed Lake Tina, from which could still be heard that siren voice. But I would not be diverted from my important task, after all the pride of Great Britain depended on my essential work in that wild place. Without a thought for the dangers of Agenda or Ken Ucky, or his mighty infant Moa, ever onwards we pressed as the Native drums throbbed through the bush, seeming to say 'Beware, beware, English Man and cretinous cats!" No Bullying, bad tempered Rovert could have held me back (nor did he) and as we arrived at his territory's border with its dreadful pointed palisade, I called a temporary halt so that we might satisfy our thirsts and hungers.' Twice as Tasty' sachets downed, the feline bearers set themselves to some serious catnapping, for it was midday and the sun beat down on us as mercilessly as one entirely obscured by grey clouds may.

As they snored, I crouched on my haunches puffing from my precious, dwindling stock of vaporiser juice. Who knew whether in the Land of Solemn they have such things or if I would have to go 'cold turkey'?

On, on we went. I drove my bearers relentlessly, so that some useful light would remain by the time we reached the foot of the escarpment.

Once there I did not pause. I had decided to follow the base of those tall cliffs by the convenient public footpath, not yet overgrown in these many years of disuse. It was not I but wise old Loopy who spotted, behind a tangle of thorn, an unmistakable door shape. Above it there were strange hieroglyphs, which I was at pains to translate. At last, I deciphered their meaning! The words written there, embossed on a rusty metal panel, were 'King Solemn's Subway— Service Tunnel. Authorised Service Personnel Only.' The iron door was locked with a giant padlock, but I would not be frustrated now, not at the eleventh hour! I took my secret weapon out of my kitbag: a pair of miniature gentleman's bolt-cutters (no, not for miniature gentlemen—you are silly!). It was the work of only a moment for me to sever the padlock and then we stood upon the very threshold of entry into the Kingdom of the Great Emperor, Solemn.

I peered into the ancient passageway and upwards at its far end there was a dot of light. Then that light was momentarily almost obscured. What could it mean? I had the happy notion of taking my telescopic rifle-sight and peering through it. As the light began to be revealed again, I suddenly realised that something had briefly partially stopped it. Yet–wait–it was not a something but a someone. It was a fabulously dressed hominid female![77]

---

[77] A primate of the family Hominidae that includes humans and their fossil ancestors.

Day 47

Amongst the Solemn People! I theorise with the use of my compass; we cross a Confusion of dwellings and merchants on the outer edge of Solemn's land; and a Luscious Lake to the North

Overnight, I had given some thought as to the relative geography of the escarpment and the tunnel leading up from the plain. Taking my trusty compass, I plotted the points and to my surprise I came to the inescapable conclusion that the passage could not but take us back, under and beyond the Badlands, so that the Kingdom of Solemn in fact lies due North of Base Camp and the Badlands.

Excited but nervous, I ate my simple breakfast of roughage and sultanas, followed by two digestive biscuits, all washed down by plenty of strong 'Twinnings' Assam Tea for Explorers.' Then, after a final –for now–lungful of 'Guilty Pleasure'-suffused steam, we hoisted our various burdens, leaving much at the Cliff Camp, under the watch of the two felines, who point-blank refused to come further, having heard probably baseless rumours of King Solemn and his People.

After as long as a long ten minutes, we emerged blinking from the distal end of the tunnel, panting at the altitude we had gained. As I looked back, I could see the brick huts and pathways of the Badlands rising still further above us, menacingly. How strange it was to think that our passage penetrated below those uncouth people, all the way from the Guard-Lands!

We knew we must press on and so we did. After not long of a forced march through an area of straggling brick huts, bearing a little East, our way dipped down considerably and past a row of merchant's houses. Advertised on large crystal frontages, were such choice goods as exotic flowers, savage cosmetic goods, and the work of barber–surgeons for both males and females. Strangest of all, perhaps, was a merchant who specialises in selling miniatures, and in particular tiny versions of the many kinds of flying war machines which are obviously used by aggressive tribes in the Solemn Land.

These merchants formed but an outpost of traders and soon–after we had crossed a great silent track–ahead of us lay the vast wild hinterland, with giant trees like sentinels. After much difficulty, we succeeded in entering the great greenery through a gate of oak, at which point we observed signs with Terrible Warnings about the times this wilderness would open and shut and instructions that to properly observe the Customs of Solemn Land one must preserve a respectful distance of twin-fold yards from any other person. Here indeed was something strange and unnatural.

Still, we pursued our way to the North, past a fenced-off area which the hieroglyphs informed us was forbidden to Yappers and certainly to other predators, where only infants might eat their lunches, undisturbed.

The road of compressed sand wound along the Eastern edge of a forbidding forest, where wild things called, and pterosaurs nested. Occasionally bushy tailed rodent-like creatures ran out and–for no good reason I could see–buried their nuts in small holes. Imagine if I had to keep stopping to bury my nuts! Why—we would never make any progress...[78]

At last, in the North, we came to a large lake, which I have dared to name Lake Tina Superior, for it entirely dwarfs Lake Tina, although I fear that where Lake Tina the First can boast a Succubus or Siren, Lake Tina Superior may have in its depths nothing but shopping trollies, bottles and the occasional skeleton. But these are superficial impressions and no doubt more will be revealed over the days to come.

Obviously, you will not be making such impressive discoveries, but I hope you are now experiencing some minor freedoms of your own.[79]

Watch this space for more stories of Exploration.

---

[78] Really, this passage is in very poor taste and it is omitted from several editions.
[79] It is believed that here PWN refers to a small degree of the lifting of Lockdown regulations. Historians have suggested a date six weeks after the start of Lockdown.

Day 48

Under the Greenwood Tree. A call back to Base Camp. Then a return to King Solemn's Land and more of its sights and sounds

In the morning a swift-footed messenger came with a note in a cleft stick. In turn, one of the servants I had left there hurried up the Service Tunnel and followed our trail to Lake Tina Superior. (I had thoughtfully laid a trail behind me of toilet roll and pasta, things which no one could possibly want very much.)[80]

It appeared I was requested to return to Base Camp forthwith, to receive a large shipment of musical and other supplies, for which my presence was necessary, though no signature required, for the supply train had come from the Pestilential Provinces.

Cursing in a manly way, I did as I was bid but after many hours of this retreat, I was rather glad to be in Camp when the entry bell tolled, for I had been for many days eagerly anticipating the arrival of these Goods. After taking in the packages, and leaving instructions for their safe keeping, I hastened back to my fearful attendants by the Lake in Solemn Land.

However, when I got there, it was with shock, horror, and awe that, at a distance, I at once saw something was amiss. For seated there beside the Lake were two not just solemn but surly Natives of this Land, challenging all who came there by the daggers in their eyes, and drawing upon great cigarettes. There were the unmistakeable spicy, herby smells of the mixture Semaj likes to smoke when he can get hold of it. *Of my servants and supplies there was nothing to be seen!*

I was in a quandary, Dear Gentle and Patient Readers, for I was a foreigner, alone and conspicuous, and without status of any kind,[81] and with my companions having vanished. A bead of sweat formed on my brow and dripped its way down my noble Roman nose, falling off

---

[80] There, sadly, PWN was to prove very much mistaken.
[81] The hard drive has—' ...except my innate nobility.'

the tip of it onto my prominent, manly chin and then doing a backflip onto my aristocratic Adam's apple. It was a good trick, but I was at my lowest ebb.

At last, I gathered my thoughts and began to wonder; if they had survived at all, where was the most likely and prominent place for my party to have regrouped? At once the answer came to me.

Away on the Eastern horizon stands–and has stood for many centuries at my estimation–a solitary great tree, very like the redwood or sequoia tree of North America. Surely there could be no better candidate, if my servants had any sense, for a reunion with their Master?

And it was so, for as I approached, I could see, beneath that splendid specimen of wood-hood, my dear displaced Serfs all rejoicing and dancing at my return, bringing back to them the authority and leadership each so requires.

How different is our cooperative adventure to the solo, distanced solemnity of the sad people of Solemn Land! For each one seems as though he or she carries the weight of the world on their shoulders, though any hostility on their part is belied by their broad, sad smiles. A strange and contradictory place this is, to be sure.

I rested beneath the widespread, shading branches as a chill wind whistled around my private regions. Looking up the hill to the North, I suddenly spotted, in a break in the clouds, a Great Residence, like a Stately Home of the country of my birth, for which one pays a steep price in order to torment and bore one's children for an afternoon in the Holidays. Yet examination of this Wonder would have to wait for another day. It lies at a great distance and atop a steep incline with forests clinging to it, hiding who knows what angry creatures? It is certain that blood-curdling noises emanated from the woods, like a Tyrannosaurus 'in heat'.

It was time to slowly retrace our steps, giving Lake Tina Superior a wide berth for now, as we returned to the Service Tunnel of Solemn and down it to the relative safety of our Camp, and a glad reunion with Loopy and Meli, as ever demanding Miaow Super Morsels with the threat of severe reprisals if they didn't get it.

May you also get what you most desire this night, Gentlemen and Ladies.[82]

---

[82] From the hard drive—'As for me—chance would be a fine thing...'

Day 49

My ablutions; Lakes and Blondes; the nymphs at Lake Tina Superior and their doppelgangers on the track through the Gigantic Grass Meadow. Plus, our first encounter with the wild and domestic animal life of Solemn Land

It was our third day of forays into the Kingdom of Solemn, from the Cliff Camp below the escarpment beyond which it lies.

To mark the occasion, I had Loopy and Meli draw me a bath—but the picture they produced was useless for bathing purposes, so I had more sensible servants put water into a tub. I washed my long locks, then watched too many of them float on the water towards the plughole. I trimmed my beard and shaved beneath my chin and over my neck until the skin was as smooth and soft as a baby's bottom. I kept a Native baby beside me as I did it, for comparison.

Arising from my bath as lovely as a bearded Venus, I quickly donned my explorer's uniform and heavy boots and then, anxious not to waste more of the glorious day, I produced my bullwhip and mustered my troops together with their packs of provisions and whipped them up to speed as we made our way through the passageway and the small brick settlement of Emporia, and into the vast wilds of Solemn Land.

After a trek through a copse where pterosaurs perched and rodents rambled, we came back onto the Superhighway of Sand leading deep into that Long-Lost World. It was not too long before we approached the shores of Lake Tina Superior, where the waters of that inland ocean lapped against its banks through a blanket of lakeweed. However, being able to take our rest there was again prevented but not by the barbarous blaggards of the day before but by the presence of glorious blonde nymphs or minor deities, doubtless those creatures heard of in legends but never hitherto seen: the Vestigial Virgins of Solemn. I confess that I had never really believed in their existence and had assumed that they were simply the heroines of stories told to the children of the Pestilential Provinces, The Guard-Lands, and The Badlands in the hopeless hope that our own children would emulate the Virgins' basic qualifications, at least vestigially.

Backing away from these magical youthful creatures, lest my coarse Native bearers in some way sully them, I made the democratic decision to once more make a temporary lunchtime camp for rest and refreshment beneath the ginormous redwood tree. But on our march, we saw not only some more Solemn people, keeping their distance as usual—possibly because it is their custom, or possibly out of respect to such a distinguished visitor to their land.

Suddenly, from behind a pair of these people dashed an enormous loose hound—no Little, or even Greater Yapper was this. It may have been my imagination, but I thought I discerned slung around its thick woolly neck a small barrel of brandy! I drew back in a protective gesture, but this dog only rubbed itself in a very friendly way against my waist. Most relieved, I stroked its amicable if slobbery head. Here, at any rate, was one Native of Solemn Land who was prepared to break the rule of social distancing.

The redwood camp made, I downed my backpack and permitted my bearers to do the same. After taking my healthy lunch of butter candies, sugar–free mints and tropical juice, I relaxed with my vaporiser in the tree's shade, reading an interesting tome until suddenly my attention was drawn by the sound of voices to a pair of ravishing young blonde creatures walking towards me on the pathway. To allow them their privacy, and for the preservation of their modesty, I looked once more down at my book but could not resist gawping at them from another aspect as they continued down the path. However, I was most surprised, not to say embarrassed, to discover that they had turned to look at me!

To hide my confusion, I made the–I thought reasonable–observation, ' Did I not see you at the Lake just a while ago?' They, however, denied it, whilst giving an attractive if somewhat mocking peal of laughter. I made some sort of gesture, between a wave of farewell and of regret, and I manfully turned back to my book, thus allowing them to proceed peacefully on their way.

How beautiful are the maidens of Solemn Land! I suppose they cannot all be Vestigial Virgins...

Calm yourselves, my friends, as I had to—until I address you again tomorrow.

Day 50

In which mention of the Stupendous Causeway of King Solemn is made; reflections on the Alternating Sylphs of The Lake, and the Magic Trainer Trick, amongst other things; plus, from Ivory to Ebony

Firstly, I must observe that a couple of Correspondents have mentioned–though praising other content– that they found my missive, about the day before, somewhat fruity. In my defence, I would like to say that for a lusty explorer in the Prime of his Manhood like myself (myself, in fact) who has been deprived of female company for many a week, except for Meli and the Half-Naked Savage Woman (and I do not count the former as she is a feline, or the latter because her hostility is altogether too savage), to suddenly come into reasonably close proximity with many examples of the fairer sex must be something of a delightful novelty. I can for that reason not promise that today's Expedition adventure will not be peppered with the same sort of manly, 'locker room' talk.

Firstly, we shouldered our kit and bestrode the passage up into Solemn Land and here we encountered, separating us from The Kingdom, something I have neglected to mention so far, although we have had to traverse it on each occasion. Cutting across our freedom to gain entry into Solemn's Land is a great thoroughfare which the locals tell me is known as The Outer Circle. This was once no doubt, in ancient times, where stood an outer circle of Sarsen stones and formed the perimeter of a temple dedicated to the King, transforming him into a veritable God. Whatever it once was, it has fallen into sad disrepair, with the Sarsen stones replaced by wonky poles with coloured lights on them in a tawdry display. These coloured lights can mean nothing now, for neither horse-motor carriages, nor people using the feet the good God gave them, pay any attention to those frequently changing colours.

On the sticks there are useless buttons which I have christened 'Pedestrian Pacifiers'.

Once more within the Amazing Kingdom we set our course for Lake Tina Superior, for surely this time we would meet with success and be able to camp on its shores where her mild green, sludgy waters slop against her shores? But no! We were once again to be denied our objective, for lying in attractive poses on simple benches beside the body of the water were the bodies of a pair of new Goddesses, these ones as black of hair as the ones the day before were blonde. Am I to understand that that these minor deities alternate in some sort of goddess guard duty, day by day? Howsoever that may be, I dare not approach further or make suitable, or indeed unsuitable, overtures—for one thing, the unspoken rules which govern proximity of each to each in that place would not allow it.

And so, for I do not as yet dare to penetrate the Interior of the Kingdom further, we hied our steps once more unto the Giant Redwood, to seek the safety and shade beneath its vast canopy. As I sat on a great fallen bough, purple in hue, with my carriers setting out the luncheon upon special Adventurer's gingham tablecloths, I started up in fear, for heading towards me at considerable speed was a White Hell Hound, swiftly joined by another of the same ilk. They looked for all the world as though part of a snowdrift had suddenly animated and detached itself. As they ran toward me, they barked huskily. Swiftly into view, in the nick of time, came their two owners, who commanded the monsters to cease and desist. They fortunately did as they were bid, and I could breathe easily once more. And now comes the astounding part–if what I have related was not enough to have you gripping the edge of your seat—the male and female humans had called the names of these vile creatures to bring them under control, and those names were 'Ulterior' and 'Motive'! At last, those fear-filling names mentioned in the Guard-Lands near Base Camp made sense...

Trembling from the encounter with those less pleasant creatures from Solemn Land I turned upon the log upon which I sat to eat the tender butter candies and mints my servants proffered on silver platters (standard jungle ware supplied for my Expedition like so much else by

Throns of Norwich[83]). As I did so, my eye was caught by a pretty, raven haired maiden who sat on an oaken bench close by. She dangled one shapely leg over the other and I noticed that on her dainty foot she wore a little blue and white boot which told me in letters written on them that her name was 'Nike'. Nike sat there almost all the while my own Party rested there but just before she left, she was joined by a boy, who by certain signs revealed he was her mate.

I looked away to allow them their privacy. When I looked back it was to see them walking away from the bench together. But here was the very strange thing. He seemed to be shod in boots also bearing Nike's name! How this could be I cannot understand. Do both youngsters call themselves 'Nike'? Some mysteries are almost too difficult to explain.

If you have an answer, Gentle Reader, this should be written on a ten-pound note, placed in a brown manilla envelope, then sent to my offshore account in Switzerland. (That's a joke—I mean my offshore account in the Cayman Islands, of course.)

The Winner will be automatically disqualified.

---

[83]A superior hardware, tools and machinery store of a similar name still plies its trade in that Fine City.

Day 51

Of brunettes and a late arrival at the Lake, at last. Also, Ulterior and Motive attack once more. Plus, observations en route

The sun shone with unmediated power, and as I passed through to the North of my compound outside Base Camp, I noticed that the Half-Naked Savage Woman– even that early in the day–lay prostrate upon her couch in her territory, roasting in its rays, clad only in tiny pink shorts. Her skin is now darker than her shorts and though of Caucasian extraction–her short blonde hair is proof of that ancestry unless it be from a bottle, as possible–she seems to do her best to simulate the colour of a school satchel. And yet, whenever I see her face, it is white skinned and with a deadly expression in her eyes. I mean, if looks could kill...

Passing the Badlands to the further North, as I went East towards the Service Tunnel of Solemn, I was aware of the voices of excited children. And there was the little blonde girl of the two-wheeled conveyances and also her friend, the junior snake strangler, playing together, running to and fro on the metalled trackway of the Badlands, at the frontage of their brick huts. It was a very sweet sight but how sad their plaintive cries when they were summoned back into their respective brick huts by their parents. It was as if they would never see each other again and tore at the heart as one looked and listened on.

On, on, we went until we achieved Base Three, where we paused to catch our breath and take some refreshments. But then we hit the trail again to eventually pass up through the secret Service Tunnel and into Solemn Land. There are so few people using the stalls of the merchants that one wonders how their Emporia stay in business. In fact, I could see only three of these functioning: a place that sells frizzled marine life with sliced tubers; a purveyor of general foodstuffs; and a seller of exotic flat dough discs with various toppings. The last mentioned also promises on its crystal frontage that it sells slices of re-formed baby sheep. This may be a foodstuff from a foreign land but it sounds and looks absolutely revolting, Gentle Reader. I hope the mere mention of this has not turned your delicate stomachs.

But we had no further time to dwell upon such attacks on a weak constitution for we had to press on, hopeful that today would be the day we would again achieve the shores of that great water-world which is Lake Tina Superior. For surely that day it would not be occupied and guarded by yet another Goddess?

But how wrong could I be? For there in languorous pose lay the trim figure of not a blonde, nor a raven–haired Naiad but this time a brunette! Truly, they were running the gamut of hair shades and styles by the rippling stream's end that is Lake Tina Superior. We have lacked there but a skinhead and an Afro to have the full set of hairstyles and colours, I think.

Once more prevented from reaching our goal, we crept silently away, for fear of startling that exquisite creature of the Gods.

But, as we courageously walked in the wild grass towards the Sequoia that climbs towards Heaven, and where we have been wont to take our rest, and–those of us who can read–to read jolly accounts of man's inhumanity to man (with a fair few women thrown in for good measure), we were once more subjected to an unprovoked attack by those huge white terrors, Ulterior and Motive. What were the odds that we should once more arrive at our tree of shade at the same time as those horrific spikey-haired, white coated parcels of vicious belligerence?

But I have become cunning now in the ways of the man and woman who control these slavering savages. For I had noticed on the previously occasion that Ulterior and Motive have long but not infinite leads which attach them to their owners and all one has to do is to stand beyond an arc described at this length from their controllers, so that the hounds of hell are thus at the end of their tethers. At this point one is entirely safe, and one is free to mock the desperados, however high may go their crescendos of howling!

And so, to our second rest at the base of the trunk of the redwood, enjoyed for the protection which it affords against the sun and rain, both.

Along the trail from time to time would come thin and pretty and not so thin and pretty girls in couples (some have never heard, it seems, the droll expression: 'Lycra doesn't lie'). They seem to go everywhere in pairs, one fair and one plain, and this defies all explanation.

At last, as daylight began to dwindle, we started on our long trek back to Cliff Camp, and from there on to Base Camp. But when we reached the greenery that encircles Lake Tina Superior, I had suddenly the idea of seeing if the brunette goddess still lay there, guarding that mythologised mass of two parts of hydrogen to one-part oxygen and one part of sludge. She had gone! This then was our moment, if late in the day, to stand upon the shores of Lake Tina Superior for the first time.

And so, approaching with Stealth and Caution, my two best men, I proceeded, and in a short time we had at last penetrated through to that Lake of Perfection. In the dusk we stood, lost in admiration of its fine coat of pale, green lakeweed.

A smell of the finest bilge water assailed our nostrils. A triumph was ours; one that would go down in the annals of history, if I have any say in the matter.

But even as we stood in glory on the bonny rubbish-strewn banks of Lake Tina Superior, a deafening row burst upon our ears and a huge Black Beast rushed from nowhere and plunged into the Lake from the far side, spoiling the silence. At once our glory turned all to terror and we turned and ran for the safety of the sandy path of Solemn!

I end this by wishing you triumphs of your own—Dear, Patient Readers. But beware the Black Beast, for we have looked into its bloody maw and were truly fortunate to have lived to tell the tale.

Day 52

A human barometer; a meeting in Solemn Land; first news of an astonishing Old Cat and his possession of a grand property

I have astonishingly late in my travels realised that I may divine the weather for the day from whether the Half-Naked Savage Woman is prepared to strip to her foundation garments and beyond, in preparation for crisping further large areas of her sun–scorched skin. Nay, not even that, for if she approaches her subsidiary hut to get out her sun-coddling couch this is enough of an indication that I may forego my sou'wester, galoshes, and umbrella for the day.

It was one of the days that by the instinct which no other possesses, she had begun to broil her flesh (threw herself on God's barbecue, as it were) and so, after coating my few exposed parts in Factor Fifty coconut and olive oil embalming fluid, I set out early with my companions from Base Camp towards King Solemn's Land.

This day it was my intention to explore further and so, after climbing the Service Tunnel and descending through the row of Emporia, then crossing the treacherous Circular Way, I directed my bearers and myself along the course to the East, through the field reserved for infants' lunches. Here we observed a strange construction of logs which I took to be King Solemn's Outpost; a fortress for enforcing the regulation of travellers seeking to penetrate further into Solemn Land. I fully expected guards to intercept us and that we must at least expect to have our Passports and Permissions inspected but this was not the case.

I believe the casual way our appearance in Solemn Land was treated and the neglect of this Outpost both indicate that the whole country has fallen on hard times. Who knows whether the fabled Lost Vines of Solemn are still in existence or have fallen into noble rot?[84]

---

[84] If there is still anyone there to make wine from the grapes, with the advent of *Botrytis cinerea*, the 'Noble Rot', a delicious, sweet dessert wine vintage should result.

Our travel to the East proved to be a dogleg, in that after a short distance the pathway began to turn to the North again and then came the great revelation of the day. For the coarse path of compressed sand came up to, and was succeeded by, an astonishing true metalled road composed of stones set in bitumen and as broad as two men lying down one next to the other, head to toe.

It was not too long before we came across a Traveller going in the opposite direction. I stayed the respectful distance from him demanded by the unfathomable rules of that country whilst I asked him to tell me, if he would, where this impressive Highway might lead. He mumbled something like 'Boy —it leads, dun it, to the Old Cat's Hall...' but I could make out no more, for he hardly spoke English and his accent was too thick.

Who is this Old Cat? Is he to be feared or not? Is he old and frail, or is he immortal and in fine fettle? Perhaps all will be revealed in due course.

However, we had no time left for further exploration that day and instead we headed West across the enormous meadow, whose grasses must surely be kept short by grazing herds of Mammoths. My intention was to quickly attain the banks of Lake Tina Superior before striking for Base Camp once more.

All faery creaatures were absent, be they dryads, sylphs or naiads—I think their shift must end at 5.30 PM each day.

Present and seated at Lake Tina Superior was a very strange human, who proceeded to ask me if I had purchased a rainbow and a fake finger for pressing things so as to avoid the Pestilence? It was a great relief when this madman–with his talk of rainbows that might be purchased and the employment of false fingers, and crazy talk of standing out in the street, applauding the coming night each Thursday–took my stunned silence as assent and he got up and went away.

There was just enough time for me to take a little silent rest, during which time, to my delight, I saw a juvenile gold finchosaur, before we had to leave the magnificent Lake, a micro-droplet of whose beneficial waters is said to either heal or kill—but I have forgotten which, which is a shame.

And so, I close my journal but only for one night. There will be more. Threat or promise—you decide.

Day 53

I suggest a simple system of signals for distancing; the nymph of the Sequoia in residence once more; the terror of Ulterior and Motive continues unabated, and sundry other matters

On my way to Solemn Land, on a sultry and not particularly sunny day, I noticed that Semaj is now digging pits in the ground in front of his palisade; it is a mystery as to what purpose these may serve. They will certainly be troublesome for travellers such as I in the conjoined Guard-Lands, for we will be forced to circumnavigate them. One wonders if they have some connection to the pitiless, unending sawing he has been doing in the last couple of days. At least whilst he is so occupied, he will not be interfering with my terracotta pots by turning them into towers or, within them, giving me blue balls.

There seems to be no clear rules as to one's motion in the outskirts or the heartland of King Solemn's Land and this is causing me some perturbation. In order to remain at the prescribed distancing of approximately six feet (roughly two metres in new money) one is forced sometimes to swerve in a most undignified manner, sometimes with accompanying alarm.

I therefore propose that the population adopt the signalling system of the earlier horse-motor carriages and still oft used by those who can master the ludicrous two wheeled machines. That is, if one is thinking of turning left one should make a clear signal with the left hand and arm, with the right arm for a right turn. If one intends to continue on a straightforward path, then one would extend the whole of the right arm with fingers pointed in that direction. One should never, however, raise that arm in a straight attitude above shoulder height for fear one might seem to be indicating an intention to invade Poland or launch an unwelcome Blitzkrieg.

Reversing should be indicated not with an arm signal but by turning on one's heels in a smart manner and proceeding in the reverse direction, thus going ahead of the pedestrian to whom you are in that manner making the signal. It is important in this manoeuvre to make sufficient progress so as not to narrow beyond permissible one's distance from the other or rely on them applying brakes to their feet.

I offer these suggestions entirely free on a trial basis of one week to the citizens of Solemn Land, in the certainty that they will want to take advantage of this once-in-a-lifetime opportunity, which is afterwards available on the purchase of an annual licence from my office. Somebody has to pay for my phenomenal expenses in exploration of these lands, after all. The gratitude of these puerile people is simply not enough.

Once more too nervous to take on the Old Cat and his ilk, I set our party to proceed across country to the shelter of the redwood tree. We could not help noting that the offences perpetrated by the little Yapper, Freebie, and my nemesis, Agenda, are as nothing compared to the piles of spoor left everywhere in the Solemn Country. In the oddest tradition, the humans on many occasions bag up their Yapper's doings but then strew the little festering bags across the countryside. I can think of no explanation for this quaint rural custom, can you?

At the Great Redwood we found Nike, the spirit of that place, again installed on her ceremonial bench. She always has in her hair a pair of strange devices from which one can occasionally detect the sounds of a weird music, something between talking and singing and with a most unnecessarily heavy beat. This is no doubt a miniature version of the jungle drums and ululations I often hear emanating from the Badlands and to which, by their near-universality, I have become accustomed.

Despite my varying our time of arrival in the Solemn Land, I was once more, almost unbelievably, subject to a charge by the suddenly emergent pair of clouds with mouthfuls of sharp teeth, in other words: Ulterior and Motive. Although I did now know that their joint charge would be arrested by the lengths of their leashes, I could not help an involuntary reaction which had me screaming and leaping up the branches of the Great Redwood to avoid their carnivorous embrace. How foolish I felt to discover that the eyes of the fair Nike were upon me as I made my fast, cowardly ascent and slow, embarrassed descent.

Yeah, like that's really the way to impress a girl-dryad, PWN... Grasping at straws, I felt she might have been just a little impressed that an explorer of my maturity still had the speed and strength for a feat of such prodigious levitation.

Nor was that to be my only humiliation, for we encountered on our way back through Solemn Land a new Enemy, an unpleasant and ignorant Native with the name of 'Pester John', of whom I will tell more tomorrow, for I cannot bring myself to speak of the Vile Creature just now.

Still, I survived our meeting in order to leave you for now with All My Love to the Women—and a grudging nod to the Men.

Day 54

Of a Piddler; Pester John; the clocking–off time for Lake Tina's Vestigial Virgins; sun-dried pterosaurs and a narrow escape from Ulterior and Motive!

Held back by administrative duties and practical matters at Base Camp, it was not until the late afternoon that I reached King Solemn's Land with my reluctant bearers. Before we set out, I had to attend to my large, horny, in–growing toenails, for I have not my usual Foot Specialist, Mrs Sirhc Fallopian, to see to these comforts, nor have had for many a month. I was forced to employ a circular saw and industrial angle-grinder, with shards and sparks flying everywhere.

As usual, I left Loopy and Meli at the foot of the escarpment, for as yet they will not go further, despite reassurances that it is safe to proceed up the Service Tunnel and into Solemn Land. Indeed, they refuse even to cross the Great Circular Causeway where once stood sarsen stones to rival Rovert's single Moai, it is thought (only by me, admittedly—but I am rarely wrong).

I mentioned Pester John to you. This is a horrible, bald, and stocky character whom I have come to loathe and try to avoid in these outskirts to Solemn's Kingdom. Unfortunately, our paths keep crossing and worst of all he considers me to be a friend. His great fault would be that he thinks the cruellest of insults he emits to be merely banter, if this fault was not exceeded by his formidable ignorance of almost any subject you might care to name and his inability to remember anything you tell him which was intended to ameliorate, or improve, his stupid state of mind. He is accompanied by a poor old dog who looks as though he longs to die—and so should I, if forced to bear for long the company of Pester John.

An example of Pester John's ignorance would be that he believes that men and dinosaurs once bestrode the Earth together. The fact that this is so in Solemn Land and the Guard-Lands but nowhere else on this planet, the which I have informed him many a time, never sinks into his thick skull. What is more, Gentle Reader, he is convinced his ludicrous opinions are a matter of fact when everyone knows that this holds true only as regards myself, your sage correspondent. In all modesty, there is no doubt I rank amongst the wisest of men.

I was late into King Solemn's kingdom; I had hoped that the lateness of the hour would mean Pester John might be safely in his brick hut, walled up with his ignorance and curled up with his poor old, long-suffering dog.

I may have avoided Pester John in this fashion, but I was not so lucky with regard to missing a group of young men with one young woman. This was unfortunate, for I was treated to the sight of one young man calmly detaching himself from their number, to urinate into a lone bush upon the Central Veldt. This is an inexcusable and French sort of behaviour. Do I not ensure that I and my companions all 'go' before we leave (if you see what I mean), so that nature does not call us, whilst away from camp? Surely, this vulgarity is a sign of the general *laissez-faire* and moral depravity which has come to the people of Solemn Land since the glory days of the first King Solemn.

I arrived, sick and weary of travel at Lake Tina Superior at 5:35 PM and twelve seconds, approximately, and was just in time to see some very attractive young ladies–Vestigial Virgins, every one–move away from its wicket gate. Obviously, it was time to shut up their watery Temple and go home, as chaste as they were when they had arrived, one hopes. Or chaster, with any luck.

I had no sooner taken my seat upon the bench that was still warm from those goddesses' Holy bottoms than there was a terrible commotion and bounding toward me were the vile creatures of candyfloss with vampire teeth, Ulterior and Motive. However, I was protected from falling victim to their savage jaws by the fence around the Lake and I could afford to laugh at their frustration. If they should ever learn to manipulate the latch to the gate, however, I might be in dire straits.

As calm and dusk both descended, within the quiet environs of the Lake I was treated to the sight of several miniature pterosaurs, in particular a robinosaur and a bearded-titosaur, as well as several other species whom I shall feel free to name in any way I choose, flying down to relieve their thirsts–but for now, finishing this communication as we returned with weary steps the whole long twenty minutes it took us to get back to Base Camp–I must leave you. May your hearts be lighter, and your fears reduced, for your Hero is safe and well—and I am getting a bit fed up of people telling me to keep so.

Day 55

A roasting hot day brings out both the Pantheon of Panties and their wearer; the adventure of the feuding pterosaurs; and a Meditation upon the three principal tribes of children in King Solemn's Land

Taking our signal from the early taking to her sunning-couch of the Half-Naked Savage Woman, I instructed my servants to have all in preparation, for another reconnoitre of the Kingdom of Solemn, so that we might leave at the earliest opportunity for that fabled place (which turned out to be 5 PM, as it happens). Still the sun beat down on us as we made our way there, wary of the Sabre–toothed Panthers which had been observed once more in the vicinity, and recently joined by a more piebald, raggedy animal with a very mean visage. Their close proximity was indicated more by the arched back and spiked-up fur of Loopy and Meli than by any sighting. They growled incessantly for a large part of our march along the previously cleared trail. However, as soon as we reached the Camp at the foot of the escarpment from where we take the Service Tunnel to the Solemn World, both lay down contentedly to snooze, making up for lost catnap time, presumably.

On, on, I pressed with my bearers and scouts. As we emerged from the tunnel up into the plateau immediately beyond it there was suddenly a great commotion in the sky and on the ground. Unwarily, I had jettisoned from my hand, onto a shelf of rock, a slice of unwanted bread from my ration for the day. Immediately, down upon this provender, or morsel, swooped a whole flock of disputatious white and grey pterosaurs and they argued noisily about who should have the greatest portion. But this was as to nothing compared to the cacophony that arose when an enormous black pterosaur flew down and into the mass of creatures, scattering them as a bowling ball does a set of pins. He was such a bully that he dispersed the others quickly. But a moment of great humour arose, for as he continued to drive off the others, one of them crept up behind his back, picked up the whole slice and flew away; to the victor did not go the spoils!

Thankfully, as we proceeded, there was neither the sight, nor the sound, of Pester John. No one I encountered on the Highway to the Heartland looked furious and shaken—a clear indication that someone has met with the man. Perhaps his dog has died— an extreme measure for escaping his Master, to be sure, but were I him I might well think it was worth it.

As we circumnavigated the legendary Great Meadow we passed or were passed by several groups of children of that place, some in small groups attended by adults.

I have given the matter considerable thought, and these are the suggestions I would make, based upon my observation of these infants: Firstly, the children seem divided into three tribes. The first tribe, however tiny, wear the ritual masks so common in the Pestilential Province sand the Badlands. They pluck at them constantly as though they are not yet used to those facial obstructions. My conclusion is that these children are Novices in the predominant religion of Solemn Land. Their accompanying Instructors do not wear the fearsome masks, presumably reserving their costuming for formal services to appease their Gods.

The second group of children are unmasked and dart hither and thither, uncaring of the rule of keeping a six-foot distance from one another and adults. They run wild, I conclude, and either disobey their instructors, or they have not yet entered the period of formal religious instruction.

The third group of children, all female, are the most formidable to my way of thinking. They may be aged as young as nine or ten years, but they bear already upon their faces paint like unto the form of extreme warpaint their elders wear. These children are obviously novitiates in a Warrior Class, beginning early their training in the endless Sex War which has brought many a man to destruction, even the first King Solemn himself, it is rumoured. For the story goes that once he had met the Queen of Sheba, he let his kingdom fall to wrack and ruin...

Musing on this and many another deep thought, I found myself at Lake Tina Superior and entirely alone again, except for a large number of pterosaurs and prehistoric true birds. There were juvenile Bluetitosaurs and Chaffinchodons. Most impressive of all was a mighty fawn, black and blue Jaypteryx—a beautiful true bird. Who could deny this? After all, the creature has plumage of colourful feathers. It is very handsome but has an unpleasant cry, like a human baby being strangled—and kindly do not ask me how I know. (I was released without charge after payment of an enormous backhander.[85])

I shall shortly commence the Work which will, I trust, make me the name for myself in History for which I long: 'The Astonishing Fauna and Fauna of the Guard-Lands and the Solemn Land'—a book of the anthropology, zoology, and botany of this barely explored World.[86]

Order your advance copy now. Over thirty-six years it will build into the standard, fascinating, illustrated textbook on the subject. It is sure to impress your friends and cause your library shelf to fall down.

---

[85] Once again, we can only hope that this is a complete fabrication...
[86] No previous editor has used this title for the unfinished diary that forms this collection, and nor do I—because it is a lousy title.

146

Day 56

Dishes-duty, delays in departure, and stores order cause disorder (and similar tongue–twisting morning responsibilities) before Progress proceeds at a proper pace; also, an alarm is caused by the possibility of inadvertent infant baptism at Lake Tina Superior

The morning was a frustrating one; the first of which frustrations was that no servant has been keeping down the mountain of washing–up at Base Camp. In fact, upon inspection I discovered that it was not a single mountain of dirty dishes and pans but a whole mountain range, or massif.

From the aperture I could discern that the Half-Naked Savage Woman predicted a day of fair, indeed glorious weather, for almost at break of day she did her barometer trick of getting dressed in the morning only to get undressed again almost immediately to lie upon her couch face-down, thus no doubt squashing her exclamation points. But I could not take her cue to get under way; there was so much washing-up that it would have tripped us up as we left.

I complained mightily to my servants. 'Why–' said I, with asperity 'keep a monkey and crack one's own nuts?' Meli and Loopy looked at me scornfully and held out their little paws.

'Look, oh revered white master,' they chorused, 'Do you really want us to try?'

Clearly, they could be of no help. They rarely are.

There was nothing for it but for me to get started on the nursery slope of the first mountain–the dinner and side plates–and proceed doggedly to pour water on them from the piped, underground stream, together with a quantity of grease–dispersing and emulsifying magical liquid made–so it said–by a fairy.

I found my scrubber but decided I had better leave her until a more opportune moment.[87]

The work took a good many hours, which may give you some idea of how things had literally gone to pot recently at Base Camp.

That done, do you think I was I able to don my kit, reign in my bearers, issue rations from supplies and head off to the Guard-Lands and Solemn Land? Would that it had been so, but such was not to be. For the time had come round again for me to stock-take and then order essential supplies to be brought to me across the Pestilential Provinces by the slaves of the Adsa food-chain. It is hard work but someone Adsa[88] do it.

I thought better of the champagne, caviar, and truffles I have so relished recently; I feared my sponsors at The Royal Society for The Unnatural Sciences would baulk at sending me such luxuries more than twice. Truly, I had pushed my luck the second time and my order had arrived with a stiff note from the President of that august institution, which read, simply, 'Third strike and you're out!'

I took the hint and confined my list to those things essential for the sustaining of life: coffee from dark Ethiop and far Amerikay, crispy morsels of humble rice extract by Primgirls, many another such basic food and most basic of all, economy baguettes. At last, satisfied that, with the short list of just ninety-seven items, my expedition could pull through until the next time stores might arrive (and who can know when that will be?), I laid down my digit-operated crystal device and– at last–turned to the main business of the day:

I will not delay you with an account of our travails overland to reach Solemn Land once more, for little of note occurred except an attack by the Sabre–toothed Panthers, a mass melee of mastodons, dive–bombing by faeces–hurling pterosaurs, and so on; these are the everyday hazards faced by intrepid explorers like myself, although I dare say, in all modesty, there has never been an explorer as intrepid as myself. Anyone who says differently I will meet outside for fisticuffs. Just give me twenty minutes to run away in the opposite direction.

---

[87] This poor excuse for a joke has been used elsewhere in the He-Males. It didn't raise a titter then and it has failed once more.
[88] Spare us...

At Lake Tina Superior, as we took our rest and I puffed on my vaporiser filled with the delicious liquid mixture of Twisted Melon, *Tutti-frutti*, and American Gold, we were at length surprised by the arrival, one at a time, of bands of adults with tiny tots. No doubt spurred on by their knowledge that the Vestigial Virgins had once more blessed those waters during the main part of the day, the Parent Priests took those little tots to the very brink of the lakeweed covering the Lake. I sat with a heart full of fear, for I suspected that their holy parents intended the Total Immersion of those innocent little creatures in the dark, polluted and icy waters of the Lake. I could hardly concentrate on my book; I was so scared. The truth is, I felt l might be called upon to elegantly dive into the depths of Lake Tina Superior, to retrieve the little mites, and, having submerged myself there, inadvertently, once before (I have kept this secret from you before out of shame) I did not overmuch fancy doing it again. But all was well in the end and though I could see they were much tempted, the Parent Priests all left with the same number of toddlers they came with. For I must remind those of you who have the little blighters—children are a blessing. Hard to remember sometimes but true.[89]

---

[89] The hard drive closes this sentence with a question mark.

Day 57

Upon the inaccurate magic of weather forecasting; the cruelty to children of a man in a van in the Terrace of Emporia before the Old Circular Route; more cruelty in the clothing of young people in Solemn Land, etc.

Gentle and Esteemed Readers: I was tempted into my man-kini and a thick layer of sun cream for the first time this year because I had listened on the squawky box to the ceremony of the casting of runes this morning and it had promised, and I quote, 'sunshine and a light breeze' were to be expected of the day ahead.

In the event, by the time my party and I were under the Sequoia, with its protection, freezing rain was lashing down which had been preceded by a true gale. Now, if only I had let myself be guided by the non–appearance of the Half-Naked Savage Woman...

However, the day had indeed promised to be a fair one, with an early mist, as moisture was forced out of the grasses in the Guard-Lands by a high temperature even at an early hour.

As we made our way past the row of brick emporia to the East of the trail that took us to the crossing of the Old Circular Causeway, there was suddenly a terribly loud sound, as of a music box amplified many times, playing the tune of 'Boys and Girls Come Out to Play.' I stopped a passing pedestrian at a distance of six feet, by raising the palm of my right hand with my arm held out before me.

'Pathetic Peasant –' I said, 'What, pray, is that tympanum-crashing cacophony?'

'It is only the Eyes Scream Van coming for the children,' replied the beer–stoutened, bucolic peasant.

How cruel must be the people of the Badlands and Old Cat's Village to countenance this savagery: vans sent around to make children's eyes scream? I reached for my crystal device and at once summoned 'Save the Children' to inform them but–strangely–they seemed unconcerned and quickly terminated our dialogue. I ask you, is this the sort of discourtesy one is to expect these days from charitable causes? Things have come to a pretty pass.

'If *I* were you–' the peasant said, for he still awaited my order that he might proceed on his way, 'I wouldn't be caught standing about near an Eyes Scream Van dressed like that.' I took his advice and let him go whilst we turned our steps to Solemn Land proper.

Within Solemn Land, it was noticeable that casual cruelty to young persons may be widespread. Many teenagers are clothed in costumes that are slashed and ripped, with occasionally a pathetic attempt to repair such slashes with an inappropriate zipper at a diagonal. Sometimes it seems that their bodies are only decorated by strands of textile and not enclosed therein. It brought a tear to my eye to see that many pretty young women were sent out by their mothers with blouses of too little material to cover their midriffs or blossoming bosoms. My impulse, of course, is to bring clothing with me on the morrow to cover their sad nakedness but on reflection I felt this would be tactless and the parents and the young people themselves might think this a patronising gesture and I find myself in a dangerous position. Could it be that the young people do not want to be helped? Hard to believe but there you are...

To proceed: we had retreated to the Great Redwood, not purely for its protection from the elements but because Lake Tina Superior had been occupied by rough looking young warriors passing around a long and fat cigarette, shaped not unlike a carrot, stuffed with all manner of fragrant weeds, the smoke of which formed a low cloud which drifted across the sacred green surface of the Lake.

As the wind and rain abated, we observed two Scandinavian-looking maids, sadly dampened by the rain and with hair blown about, run with shrieks and giggles to an elongated version of one of those two wheeled conveyances and, mounting it together, pedal off into the distance. We took this as our cue to head North up the Highway to the Heartlands of the Solemn Country. For it was my intention to continue North towards the Holdfast of the Old Cat.

And before we had to once more turn South to return to Base Camp, Dear Reader, I did see upon the far horizon the Lair of the Old

Cat! This is a formidable fortress, when seen through binoculars. It struck me that here was a fine medium sized House in the Georgian style, mutilated by Victorian-style extensions and balconies. The Old Cat obviously has little aesthetic appreciation and taste. The whole mélange has been further mucked up by all the bricks and stones being painted a pale pink and cream, so that it looks more like a forbidding birthday cake than a building.

Here, without a doubt, resides that fearsome beast, the Old Cat of the North. He is obviously permitted some autonomy of rule within the deteriorating government of King Solemn's Land.

I hope in future days to discover more of this old tyrant and his Reign of Terror, and to be able to educate you on the matter in turn, should I live to tell the tale.

Shall I live to tell the tale, do you think? Send your answer at once, together with a signed blank cheque to me.

Day 58

I join the mass debate on Nature versus Nurture, in particular regarding gender, using the illustration of the act of skipping; plus, the conquest of two wheeled conveyances by the young of Solemn Land, despite evidence that to ride them is impossible; matters pertaining to the South Side of The Old Cat's Hall

Sunshine was in abundance, although a gusty wind blew around at various uncomfortable angles. As we made our way to Solemn Land, within hearing were discernible multiple Eyes Scream Vans plying their disreputable trade. Unbelievably almost, there is something about experiencing screaming eyes that attracts the children of the Badlands and the terraces of brick huts all around the row of Emporia. As strong as the pull of these fiendish transports is for the infants, despite the horrific clangy tunes of the vans (enough to make the ears bleed as well as the eyes to scream), the force is equal and opposite for their parents, who pull upon the hands of the kids, or sometimes literally tear them away from the vile vehicles, with the youngsters wailing in their deep frustration. Little do they know, it is only thus that their safety can be assured!

Luckily, as we hurriedly turned our footsteps to the Great Circular Causeway (seemingly a relic of prehistory), the screams of both successful and unsuccessful children diminished almost to nothing. However, they were replaced almost at once by a terrible ululation as several horse-motor carriages coloured white but with stripes of blue and yellow flashed along the metalled trackway before us. Startled, I almost missed a legend written on them. But I did catch sight of it on the final identical vehicle— and it read 'Ecilop'. Who or what are, or is, the Ecilop and why must they, or it, flagrantly disregard all the rules of the road, as ancient as the rule of King Solemn? For instance, they pay no attention to those lights hung high on poles (although nor does anyone else it seems, but at least others do not disobey them at high speed).

Stilling somewhat the raised beating of my frightened heart, I summoned all my party together, for the servants and bearers had dispersed in all directions, as if the Ecilop had been after them and not just passing, no doubt on pressing business.

'It is as if you all have guilty consciences,' I said in remonstration of my cowardly colleagues. And perhaps we all have. After all, I had hidden in a bush myself.

Comparatively calm Solemn Land achieved once more–by passing through the substantial oaken gates of its guard–post–we set out upon the Highway into the Interior, eschewing the shores of Western Lake Tina Superior, and heading due North along King Solemn's Highway towards the Old Cat's Hall, for much remains to be investigated there.

Whilst upon our way, I was not the only one to notice several little girls skipping along beside their parents, and also beside their non–skipping brothers. I realised that I have never seen a little boy skip and yet all little girls do it, invariably and compulsively. This must be a matter of their Nature not of Nurture, for I believe no one has to show a little girl how to skip, nor does anyone forbid a little boy to do so. I think it most unlikely that mothers show their little girls how to skip (that would be an ungainly spectacle, methinks), nor are there skipping-schools or lessons for skipping, and yet each little girl does it and does it well. Do their older sisters show little girls how to skip? No, they do not, for at about the age of nine all girls suddenly stop skipping. [90]

Therefore, in my reasoned opinion, skipping is hard-wired into the brain of all little girls but they either forget how to, as puberty approaches, or they are taught not to, at around that time.

I concede there may be skipping boys, but I think you will find these are the least manly of creatures, so that even to call them 'boys' is probably a misnomer. And—whilst I am on about Nature versus Nurture: all little girls and little boys can apparently ride those temperamental two-wheeled contrivances of which I have written before, but none can stop their progress elegantly. That seems to be an

---

[90] From the hard drive—'It is, as it were, a negative secondary sexual characteristic.'

154

art that must be learned. Therefore, their balancing is natural but their stopping a matter of nurture. Discuss this in no more than two hundred words and then burn the paper and with it your fingers, immediately.

On the South side of the Old Cat's Hall, as one approaches, is a substantial iron-framed construction with panes of clear crystal in it. One feels that this must be the wicked Old Cat's Sunning Salon. Beside it is an extensive lawn of short green grass. There we observed a solitary human being in ragged clothes tending to the edges with a gigantic pair of scissors. How horrible! The Old Cat has *human* slaves!

Mind you, I sometimes think Meli and Loopy also think they have a human slave...

Day 59

A Flag Line and A Tent in the Guard-Lands; about the Wild Western Wood in Solemn Land and a Mysterious Plant; about a Grand Gate to The King's Empire, previously unseen; and a number of other matters

The sun scorched down, and in the compound of the Half-Naked Savage Woman could be seen not just the Pantheon of Panties but a veritable Flotilla of French Knickers. What was more, for the first time ever I saw the Woman assume her position on her crude couch and then whip off her bandeau bikini–top! As I am a gentleman, I almost immediately averted my gaze, for it can hardly have been a short half hour before my interest was otherwise captured by my observation that an explanation now existed for the pits that Semaj had been digging disrespectfully the other day, into the grasslands of Savanna (open your piggybank, dear American miss, and send what is in there, as my need is greater than yours). The backwards Native had been producing the holes into which to lower metal poles. From these, he stretched covered and twisted, thin metal cables. No doubt he intends to hang flags in the same manner as the neighbouring people further to the East of his family's brick hut. I must consider this as an act of aggression but luckily not directed my way, as he was all gap–toothed smiles when displaying his handicraft to me.

With a fellow Native friend of his, Semaj then proceeded to another area to build a grey and black tent and very amusing it was to see them struggle with its erection. However, I was perturbed by this proceeding. Why is Semaj thinking of camping out on the Plain? A vast number of alternative explanations flickered across my Bulging Brain–Box. But I had not come up with the definitive solution when– Semaj and his friend having gone back to his compound–the bally thing blew down again when caught by a tiny breath of the wind, more of a whisper than a zephyr. From this I concluded that Semaj and his friend are new to the art of tent construction.[91]

I was laughing still at this, just a little, even as I entered Solemn Land some twenty minutes or so later. But the laughter stopped when I considered my mighty purpose for the day, which was to head neither East, nor North, but to go West and thus to plunge into the dense dark woodland there and follow one of several trails until an opportunity might arise to trek Eastwards to that bank of Lake Tina Superior.

And so, we set off, our hearts in our mouths, as we moved as silently as possible beneath the great limbs of ancient trees. For a long distance we travelled, as eerie noises emanated from the undergrowth, and always–still further to the West–could be heard a low rumble with the occasional hoot of either a gibbon, or a horn being blown by a primitive anthropoid. I shivered with Terror at each warning blast.

We found at last a clearing formed by the convergence of four trails; a jungle crossroads if you will permit the preposterous notion.

Obviously, we were not the only people who had ever been there. As we sat, partially concealed by the greenery, our blood seemed to freeze, for coming along one of the trails, in our direction, was a group of animals very like the orangutan of far Malay. However, the hideous truth was that these were some sort of human creature, for though their massive chests were bare, their head hair long and they walked only partially upright, they spoke words of some coarse language to each other and wore blue trousers with rivets in them!

Luckily, we remained hidden, and these loathsome creatures continued bounding away along one of the trails, making their horrible noises and trailing a scent of something that seemed to come from the anal glands of a lynx transported to Africa.[92]

As our heartbeat rate declined and we began to breathe more easily my attention was suddenly drawn to a strange fence–like thing to our left, beneath a mighty old evergreen. It had the appearance both of a plant and of a human construction. For its verticals grew from the

---

[91] Frustratingly, PWN never gives an explanation for this behaviour by Semaj and his friend. It remains a mystery to this day. Perhaps the failure of the experiment meant that Semaj and his friend went completely off the idea?

[92] This seems very specific, as though PWN himself had once used the self-same preparation himself.

ground like pollarded limbs do grow but across were woven laths of thin wood. Here indeed is a mystery: is this the nest of a dwarf race, or what is it? If it is a plant which naturally grows fencing panels, what a boon this could be for all humankind![93]

At last, it was time to use my compass and take us via the Western shore of Lake Tina Superior back across country to the Highway and thence home to Base Camp. But as we headed South, what should we see in the Southeast but huge ornamental iron gates with finials of precious gold? This was more in keeping with the lost Greatness of King Solemn and the Road to the Vines. I had always thought it odd that we entered Solemn Land via a wooden gate. I now realised we had been using the Tradesmen's Entrance round the back!

However, any idea we might have had about staying longer to investigate these wondrous gates was curtailed by a terrible attack of vicious midges, each as big as a small fly, as the evening closed in.

May you be spared little bites, Gentle Readers, unless, of course, you would welcome them.

---

[93] It has been suggested that PWN has confused botany with infants' den-building. See 'Plants and What They Cannot Do.' Persimmon, Q. 2019.

Day 60

I am awoken by the Dawn Chorus from Hell; the servant problem; two messages from Beyond appal but in different ways; I make a resolution

You can hardly be said to have experienced the Dawn Chorus until you have been awoken by it in a Camp by The Guard-Lands and King Solemn's Land. Two nights ago, I was so hot in my crude jungle four–poster[94] (which, kindly note, I had to construct myself upon the evening we had arrived at this God–forsaken place, as at that time neither Loopy nor Meli had yet been hired—not that they would have been of much use; their talents do not lie in that direction) that I had to leave open the crystal pane which looks out upon the Pestilential Provinces to the South.

By doing this I had indeed made cool my bed compartment, but I was to pay a price, for at about 4.30 AM my sleep was not so much disturbed as destroyed by a hellish cacophony of proto-birds and pterosaurs, both pteranodons and pterodactyls, all of whom began to sing or squawk at the top of their leathery little lungs.

I ran on tippy toes across the rush–covered floor to slam shut the crystal pane but in doing so managed to so mightily stub my right big toe on my Explorer's Chest as to cause a lightning bolt of pain to shoot up my leg and into my groin.

Hopping and howling, as if I performed an improvised war dance, I may have uttered a frightful curse upon those flying creatures whom I held responsible. I hope the Lord Above had his ears closed or better still had not opened his heavenly crystal pane overnight and still slept the sleep of the Just.

(There may be a Lord Above and it is always wise to keep open all diplomatic channels. Especially with my record.)

---

[94] I refer you to a previous Footnote.

I retreated to my crude sleeping contrivance and closed my eyes. As soon as the pain diminished sufficiently, I was once more exploring the Land of Nod—a place even more full of possibility than the land where King Solemn once grew his famous Vines, and which I believe I am presently the first in several hundred years to visit.

Upon my awakening, I was surprised to see by the sundial on my wrist just how much of the new day had gone. My servants Loopy and Meli were sore aggrieved at my neglect of their stomachs, for they are incapable of providing themselves with sustenance. Indeed, at my Camp, things are somewhat topsy-turvy in that the Master serves the servants. Although All Nature rebels at this reversal of correct roles there is nothing for it but for me to slice open their jellified rations and top up their teeth-improving kibbles, or else the servants would summon the RSPCA and I should be ignominiously dragged before the Magistrates. Of course, one might gamble that they would be overcome by starvation and exhaustion before they could ensure such a retribution but that is not a gamble I should like to take. In addition, I quite like them at times and when it is evening and they sit on my lap (one at a time, of course–do not be daft) and they turn on their purring motors it is a comfort to this otherwise companionless Explorer.

And so, at any rate, it was late in the day that I arrived at Lake Tina Superior, having brought with me correspondence which had been hauled through the Pestilential Provinces and the Badlands by the officers of the Royal Delivery Service. As the hot sun began to retreat over the horizon and the world began to cool (and, in her compound next to Camp Number One, the Half-Naked Savage Woman would, no doubt, be slithering off her canvas couch greased by sweat, before taking herself, charred at the edges, back into her brick hut) I began to examine my disinfected deliveries.

Good Lord! – (presumably now awake and observant above)–I am guaranteed a major prize if I will only answer a few simple questions and pledge myself to a formidable contract to buy a property in Spain, which I can withdraw from at any time in the next thirty days! Tempting though this is, as I am a traveller in a more distanced land already, I hardly feel it necessary to avail myself of this 'once in a lifetime' opportunity.

In the same post I was told that a certain destitute young person in Africa requires my sponsorship. Sadly, until I have made my fortune with the forthcoming 'Flora and Fauna of The Guard-Lands and Solemn Land' I am hardly in a satisfactory financial position to commit myself to such a proposition and to be such a benefactor.

At the very moment I was thinking this, a mother and a roly-poly child entered the environs of Lake Tina Superior, and I compared the picture engraved on the missive in my hand of a skeletal, wide-eyed and appealing little girl with the bulky, complaining, spoiled brat in front of me, and this seemed somehow to concentrate my thoughts wonderfully.

As I made my way back to Cliff Camp and onwards to Base Camp and my blessed bed once more, a certain melancholy crept over me and I resolved that as soon as I am in a position to, I will–no, not pay the Poor from my own pocket–but set about, like Robin Hood before me, robbing the Rich to help the Poor. [95]

In fact, I will start doing it now to get some practice. Stand and deliver! This message will cost you a guinea or your life!

---

[95] At this point the hard drive states 'I will be the first beneficiary. After all, PWN Towers is a money-pit.'

Day 61

The escutcheons, or shields, at the top of the wrought–iron gates tell a tale of the deposition of the Head of State of Solemn Land; the captive trees; and, how to create a basic workshop with tools from the Animal Kingdom

I was determined, should I do nothing else, to examine the splendid wrought iron gates to the Kingdom of King Solemn the Present, which form the official gateway to that much fabled Land, by which I and my companions–and many another–might have hitherto gained access had we not instead entered by the coarse oaken structure originally intended for tradespeople only.

And so it was, that with our steps we traced part of the periphery of that Lost World by getting to the wooden gate and then making our way East and around the bend at the bottom of the dense forest until we found ourselves heading Northeast. Now, by dint of a sharp turn to the West, we found ourselves after a short, gravelled driveway approaching the splendid semi-circular structure which was the enamelled and iron barred gateway for VIPs, now fallen into a little disrepair, and with no attendant or guards to check our credentials or passports into that mysterious land, or to send word of our coming by fleet messenger to the Overlord of that land.

I noticed, with my keen red eye and the employment of a monocular telescope, that atop each huge main metal pillar, forged who knew where and who knew when, or in what hellish furnace, there are sited great gilt bronze escutcheons, each with an oval hole. As these make no sense as they are, one must presume that formerly each enclosed a large enamel or porcelain portrait of each of the lineage of the Kings, and possibly Queens, of Solemn Land. Sad is their loss and how much to be regretted.

Perhaps there are yet fragments of these oval masks to be found if one dug into the gravel track at the base of the iron pillars. However,

I cannot but help thinking that this would not be the way to make friends or influence people. And perhaps a Solemn King had been so unpopular, that in their fury his people had thrown down all images of him, including these ones which had once crowned the heads of the iron gates? [96]

After at least several seconds of pondering these matters, we then proceeded for a length of time across the humongous Heartland of Solemn Land, occasionally–for a little sport–putting up courting couples from where they laid in the artfully constructed 'covers' (where the few still employed gamekeepers of Solemn Land do confine them). Then there would be a great burst of gunfire from myself and my companions. Most of these surprised couples are intended for the pot but I intend to use their heads to decorate my Entrance Hallway when finally, I return to my Stately Homeland. And I must say, the sport was good. My game-bag was positively stuffed with the unwary young creatures, many of them caught in the Atrocious Act, or at least so engaged in heavy-petting that they caught not the light step of the homicidal maniac who was in no way the light of his late parents' proud eyes. Yet I felt the spirit of my father within me as I carved another notch in my walking stick for each kill. I knew it had been a special day of hunting when finally, with too many notches in it, my stick gave way, pitching me snoot–first into the heather.[97]

Despite the blood lust, we almost silently glided across that landscape–apart, that is, from thunderous bursts of lethal gunfire–after which any spared or lucky lovers crept away, glad to live to tell the tale of such a Great Hunter.

We could not help noticing that at intervals grew medium sized trees, each wrapped around with a cage of rusty iron. I can only speculate that these trees come horridly to life at night and try, triffid-like, to shuffle away on their rasping roots to join their fellows in the

---

[96] In his 'Wrought-iron Gateways of Foreign Border Posts' Arthur Smelter suggests that PWN is entirely wrong in his interpretation of these pillars as once bearing enameled shields of the Kings and Queens of Solemn Land. He explains this by saying, in his expert opinion, 'I do not know why—I just think He is wrong.' Smelter, A. Publication TBA.

[97] It is thought now by Scholars that this is passage more reliant upon wishful thinking than actuality. We must certainly hope so. They point to the fact that it PWN has declared himself to be a pescatarian and that therefore he could not have been shooting for the pot.

forests. How great must a civilisation once have been to have been able to spare the men and the resources to go around caging individual trees? Truly, I doff my cap and bow my head to some ancient King Solemn and his army of tree–cagers.

At last, it was to Lake Tina Superior that we made our now weary way. There, as we relaxed, dipping our calloused toes and blistered feet in its green waters, I noticed a flurry of wings and across the Lake I spotted a beast like a proto-woodpecker drinking from that fouled water–source. Whatever it actually is, it fills the evolutionary niche of that modern bird of Britain. I shall call it the 'peckersaur'. I had only previously heard these creatures before, tapping like a hammer drill up in the branches of the trees of Solemn Land, and never seen one come down for water.

Is it just me, or would it not be possible to create a useful toolkit to equip a jungle workshop, with beasts with such notable evolved skills? [98] I now have a wood–driller; I think animal cutting tools will be no trouble for many have evolved to cut or gouge their victims. Where my plan may fall down, I freely admit, is in the provision of a lathe, for I have yet to find an animal that revolves at high speed; I have, however, high hopes of coming across a Whirling Dervish in my travels. Then there will be absolutely nothing to stop me.

---

[98] It is just him.

Day 62

Repercussions from the Lovers' Hunt; of the Lovely Black Woman and how her genes may be preserved; the agitation of a noble proboscis by pollen and its aftermath; and a new phenomenon of young adult primates

Firstly, Gentle Readers, I must deal with the alarm I seem to have caused among my readership by my account of the apparent decimation of innocent (well, that's debatable) Young Lovers, the day before, upon the Meadow of the outlying area of Solemn Land. Of course, I was <u>only joking</u>! Did you really think I would—or suffer my company to—fire with murderous intent upon these young creatures, after startlingly them from where they lay, in partial concealment, with only the occasional naked bouncing rump to be seen?! No, indeed. Our idea was simply to morbidly maim as many as possible and leave it at that.

As for 'stuffing my game–bag with their corpses', nothing could be further from the truth! I simply picked up the ones that were accidentally slaughtered by the less accurate shots amongst us. I mean, I am an Englishman, and we are known to 'play up, play up and play the game'. [99]

I hope that will now lay to rest all the horrified accusations which have come my way in the last twenty–four hours.

And you must remember, those people passionate about my

prose, that I take as my dictum the following: 'A foreign country is the Past; I do things differently there.'[100]

We had no need of a signal from the disrobing and prostrating of the Half-Naked Savage Woman to tell us that the day was set fair for

---

[99] As the hard drive states—'To do that, one has first to bring home game.'

[100] Here PWN seriously misquotes L. P. Hartley and the first line of his novel 'The Go-Between.'

further exploration. After a long morning once more ensuring that sufficient supplies might reach Base Camp in the evening, it was something of a relief to pull on my best jockstrap, hitch up my khaki shorts, clamp my pith helmet upon my bonce, and then give the signal to be under way to my feline bearers and other servants (all of whom worship me as a God now, having seen me use my spectacles and arch supports to good effect, in the field).

As we made our way through the Guard-Lands, we came upon a singular sight of which I will write more tomorrow. I will say that it was big, spherical, and orange, and leave it at that.

Having mastered the Passageway up to the Emporia Terrace at the edge of Solemn Land, we were approaching the Great Circular Causeway when we saw approaching us a small war–party of fine young maidens. One I looked upon with particular favour. Indeed, I seemed to recognise this graceful, or lissom, black girl from a previous sighting, for she was a splendid example of her kind, and in no way overdressed. One of my servants rolled up my tongue and put it back in my mouth, whilst a particular scheme came into my ever-active mind, and it was this: would it not be wise to tranquilise this fine creature, to return with her to England and PWN Towers in the County of Norfolk? I could easily transform the attics of the West Wing so as to provide a safe enclosure for her. Now, do not think I would be doing this to keep her in some sort of high–class zoo. No, not at all—how could you think it?

As I have never seen such a fine specimen, my idea is to establish with her a captive breeding program, by which her manifold progeny could later be returned to Solemn Land and released into Nature. It is possible that I might forget to bring back a male of the right sort for my enterprise, in which case–short of cloning her, with all the pitfalls that entails–I might have to supply the deficiency myself. Honestly, the hardships a Benefactor of the Human Race has to put himself through...

At Lake Tina Superior once more, I temporarily dismissed the servants, who set to, playing their heathen games upon their crystal devices, and I breathed in deeply of the rustic zephyrs that did waft across the top of the green waters and out of the surrounding trees. As I did so, several Natives of Solemn Land, adults, and children, approached through the rickety gate in the Lake's perimeter. Unfortunately, at that very moment the abundant pollen in the air brought upon me a Truly Terrifying Sneeze, which had those persons falling over themselves in their retreat. No doubt they assumed that I carried with me the Pestilence of the Provinces to the South. However, I was pleased to have so simply and effectively purchased some privacy.

This was not to last, however, for soon into the enclosure loped some vile, dirty–looking primates, approximate five of them, with their two–wheeler conveyances. They proceeded to follow the fence around to the North, all the time screeching and hooting and issuing the occasional macho challenge to me as I sat innocently, planning the capture of the Lissom Black Lovely, and reading my book, whilst puffing on my vaporiser.

It was obvious that at last I was seeing a band of almost inarticulate Teen-Apers. I had heard rumours that these coarse animals existed and here they were before me! It was also obvious to me that they had too much income and too much free time. Add to this that they did not observe the correct distance between them, and you can understand why my heart began to palpitate somewhat. However, I sat my ground, and in time their threatening behaviour diminished. Why, they were nothing but young male Bullies, whom, if one does not respond, soon lose their bravado! They slunk away, looking and no doubt feeling foolish. Once again, I was the Hero of the hour, and my dander was hardly up during the whole episode. What is a dander, and why does it go up? Answers on the back of your best credit card, which together with your PIN number should be sent to me.

Day 63

The sudden appearance of a futuristic Orange Sphere in the Guard-Lands; a second entrancing encounter with the Lissom Lovely and her Gang; I make a Nebulous Plan for her Capture in short order, and for her long–term upkeep; other matters arising from my exploration of the surrounds of Old Cat Hall and the Black Forest to the Northeast

As the Half-Naked Savage Woman grilled herself in her Compound, and consequently a faint, savoury smell of roast woman permeated the air, my Expeditionary Party prepared itself for a day of concentrated exploring.

But how could we have anticipated what first met our bleary eyes as we made our ways along the red stone wall between the Guard-Lands and the Badlands? For lying there, as mentioned before, was a large orange sphere made of some incredibly smooth and hard material, the like of which has hitherto been unknown in these parts. Is it some sort of Message from Beyond? Could it herald an invasion from Aliens? Might this sphere not be the forerunner of a Frightening Force from the Future? So many questions... (Meli and Loopy's suggestion that it is just a ball kicked over from the Badlands is so preposterous as to be immediately struck out of the record. I am surrounded by numskulls...)

But I had no time to ponder such things, nor much inclination, for our itinerary for the day was a tight one.

It was at about the same time as the day before that we emerged into the Terrace of the Small Emporia and having passed those mercantile premises, we were at much the same point when our path once again crossed with the gorgeous Ebon Maiden and her attractive attendants. Some of you may argue that though my conscious mind had no suspicion that this might be so, my subconscious may have anticipated or even contrived it. Whatever the case may have been, here I was and here they were. But this time I was bathed and shaved, pimped, primped, and preened, and I walked with almost a swagger of confidence. Beneath and below my pith helmet my long and dark curly locks which yet owe little to artifice except the occasional sousing with a gallon of 'Do or Dye for Men', were like enticing fronds, the sort of shining curls that girls like to run through their fingers through. (You may take my word on that.)

This time there was an immediate encouraging response from the Lissom Lass and her white acolytes. For that little War Party turned all to shy giggles.

Perhaps in the near future, luring the Lissom Lovely to a point where I could use just the correct dose in a tranquiliser dart in her fabulous fundament is now not beyond the realms of imagination or possibility. Or might I even so tame her that she comes willingly to me?

I now–on a closer inspection–begin to think that the dark damsel may have a touch of the Asian about her. It would be interesting to perform a DNA test upon her in due course, although there are other more pressing matters, quite literally so. For I wish to earn her trust and affection and I have found in the past that after I have paid them concentrated attention, and bribed them considerably, women do begin to quite like me.

As the young women passed, one of the Black Nymph's maidservants turned ostentatiously to take another look at me as I bestrode the tarmac, like a veritable Colossus of the Road. I raised a Roger Moore-like left eyebrow, and as the girl turned once more there was another round of giggles, like the tinkling of fairy bells, if fairy bells sound like girls giggling, which I very much doubt. No, they did not mock me! How dare you suggest it?

How may I separate the Desired One from her protectors? If I had some sheepdogs and a shedding ring it might be contrived, I suppose. I wonder if two felines and a roundabout might serve the same purpose? I must try the experiment.[101] As it was, I had to go onwards but for many hundreds of yards it was with a pronounced limp...

We approached at last the Hall of the Old Cat, from the East, and got a closer view. I am convinced that what we see from the Highway

---

[101] As far as can be ascertained he was never to do this. Experimental archaeology suggests it is not possible.

to the Heartland is only the rear of the building, for there is no driveway or path and no impressive door, merely a number of small doorways, and there are outbuildings whose terrible purposes one can only guess. Perhaps here the slaves who do the gardening are housed? However, there was not a soul to be seen, although the hedges and a gigantic lawn spoke of much industry. It is possible that all this is tended-to at night when the Old Cat sleeps the sound sleep of the Truly Wicked.

We finally achieved the banks of Lake Tina Superior via a Southerly march through a frightening Black Forest, to the West of which there is a mysterious set of buildings, like a deserted school, with playgrounds, etc. Could this be an institution preparing servants/slaves as employees for the Wicked Old Cat? But why is it presently deserted?[102]

A chill breeze blew across Lake Tina Superior and a jaypteryx flew across the Lake so close to me as almost to be touched! I tried to concentrate on my book but visions of the Lissom Lovely kept drifting across my mind. I may be of a certain age, but the blood still flows red in my arteries! There may be a dusting of snow on the roof but there is still a hearty fire in the grate...

My having had too much excitement meant that Loopy and Meli felt it necessary to send me to my bed compartment at Base Camp, without more for supper than a sandwich to keep me sustained until breakfast, by which time they hoped my behaviour would have improved and my blood pressure have gone down.

You may say I just need to get a grip; in fact, I have avoided that only by chaining my arms to the sides of the bed.

---

[102] The Editor suggests that it had a less sinister purpose and was, in fact, a school for those with learning difficulties. See 'Education in Remote Places Where Difference is Feared.' C/f Hydem. and Gagem, 'Why the Disabled are Concealed in Modern Society.' 1999.

Day 64

A worry about Salt Peter in the neighbouring compartment of Base Camp; the mysterious late appearance of the Half-Naked Savage Woman in her compound; a discussion of what capabilities the Orange Alien Probe has on board; the double lady couple of The Badlands, together with their blonde little girl, encountered in the Terrace of Emporia; a raucous party in Solemn Land

I was in receipt of an item to decorate my Loving Room [*sic*] at Base Camp. However, I was not in a position to take in the wall-hanging myself and so it was put into the hands of my kind neighbour, the usually garrulous Salt Peter. When I retrieved it from him, I could not but help noticing he did not look at all well. It is possible he has tarried too often and too long in the Pestilential Provinces to the South. I will have to keep an eye on him, although how I can do this through No Man's Land and two locked doors is a problem yet to be solved.[103]

I awaited the appearance of the comely but aggressive-faced Vest-less Virgin of the territory to the Northwest but she appeared only quite late in the day, for what reason I do not know. But as soon as I saw her upon her couch, basting herself with the usual unguents, or lotion, which I suspect is composed of furniture-stain and sea-salt, I called my colleagues together and off we set, quite coincidentally timing our departure so as to very likely intercept the Lissom Lovely and her companions, close to Solemn Land, as we had done on the previous two days.

Firstly, my attention was drawn to Freebie (the Yapper whose owner, Semaj, continues erroneously to call Suzie), who was squatting and opening her bowels close to the Orange Space Probe sent by Aliens

---

[103] Salt Peter must presumably have recovered, as there is no more mention of his ailment. Either that or he died; who can say? The truth may never be known.

to see what life is like The Guard-Lands. I hoped that of the many sensitive instruments which must be aboard that futuristic craft there is not a high-quality camera sending back to the Mother Ship circling overhead movies of such an unedifying spectacle. Yappers, dogs, and hounds seem to have been put on Earth for the purposes of eating and defecating, and in between those activities chewing upon unsuitable things like small children. The larger monsters like Ulterior and Motive do not limit themselves to infants but have an appetite for Intrepid Explorers, as I know all too well.

At the Terrace of Emporia, I was surprised to see, outside the shop that was selling battered marine life with fried sliced tubers for the instant gratification of the locals' appetites, the little blonde girl of The Badlands together with her two lady parents. They had a hound with them, who had recently no doubt been evacuating its bowels in Solemn Land.

Another little girl shouted to her and blew a kiss and I seemed to hear the name 'Ylloh!' called. I believe I have, amongst many, a natural daughter of that name, myself. For a moment I thought of her poignantly, so far away across the Pestilential Provinces but then I stopped for it came to my mind that she might disapprove of my current intention to further my plans to capture the Lissom Lovely. A father with an active sex-life is, after all, a quite disgusting thing to his children…

But sad to report, either we had set off too early or else the Beautiful Ebon Missy only traverses that section of the trail beyond The Terrace of the Emporia on weekdays; whichever it was, she and her war party of Attractive Amazons were nowhere to be seen. Several other delightful damsels were to be seen—but the handcuffs which I keep in readiness for her are engraved only with the name 'Lissom Lovely'. I am not fickle in my affections...

Mind you, I am not yet in possession of the correct dart gun or anaesthetic–although they are on order–and there is some talk that I might have to have a veterinary qualification and know something about anaesthetics and their reversal, as well as possess the correct licence for the sport. These problems do not seem to me to be insuperable. I could just disobey those Rules and there would be no witnesses to say otherwise but obviously I must stay my hand for the present and content myself with luring my quarry ever closer.

On the way to Lake Tina Superior my attention was drawn to a large assembly of Teen-Apers, together with females of the species. They were a raucous group of Great Apes and seemed many of them to be under the influence of brewed drink and quite possibly smoked herbs as well. The females seemed in part to civilise the rough and vulgar males but also to stimulate them to foolish gambolling.

Nowhere was a six-foot gap to be observed between any of them. Far from it, for occasionally the tongue of one was seen to be deep within the mouth of another! I think a social distancing score of minus four inches might be disapproved of by the Ecilop–the Guards of Solemn Land– but they were entirely lacking upon the Mammoths' Meadow, as indeed were the largely nocturnal Mammoths of Solemn Land who spend the daytime hanging upside down in the oak trees, I am informed.[104]

The beloved surface of Lake Tina Superior was well studded with floating bottles and cans. I suspect the raucous party of primates observed in the Meadow had previously been enjoying the waters there. I cannot prove it, though.

---

[104] He should, I feel, tell us just who are his informants, do not you?

Day 65

*A Tracking Collar as a better first option for the Lissom Lovely;
is she, in any case, a Mirage? The adventure of the ten-legged
spider; a discussion of too-short shorts; 'Hallo, Young Lovers —
you're under arrest!'; [105] my pineal gland comes under scrutiny;
plus, sundry extras for your pleasure or alarm*

I was frustrated by the non–appearance once more of my Dark
Lady, the Lissom Lovely, at the usual rendezvous. Not even her
Amazonian, pink-pearl complexioned companions were there. One can
only hope this was because the weekend continued, and Normal Service
will be resumed as soon as possible.

I have in the meantime had a concerned telegram from the
Worldwide Fund for Nature, which informs me that not only am I not
licensed to tranquilise wild specimens but that in any case removing the
said Lissom Lovely or any of her ilk to PWN Towers in the County of
Norfolk is something that at this stage they are unconvinced is
necessary, as the numbers of this glorious creature in Solemn Land have
not yet been ascertained. They suggest that if I must interfere with her
in any way, it might be better to persuade her to wear a radio collar, in
the first instance, so as to trace her movements. This sounds alarmingly
like stalking to me, but I bow to their superior wisdom in these matters.
I must now lay my plans differently. I think, however, we shall find she
is a unique specimen and eventually the only correct course of action
will be for me to rescue this endangered enchantress from Solemn Land
and take her back with me for the breeding programme I originally
suggested. [106] Still, I do not want to betray any impatience, although it
is tough when the original discoverer of a New Species has little to say

---

[105] This is believed to be a reference to a very old Tom Lehrer song, itself referring–but
satirically–to a Rodgers and Hammerstein song 'Hallo, Young Lovers.' (I sometimes think they
do not pay me enough for the research that goes into these fabulous footnotes.)
[106] The hard drive has 'I will have to risk breaking a few Laws in the process.'

in what then happens to it. If she were a Bigfoot or a Yeti, or other cryptozoological species, I might not feel so chagrined.

What was worse, was the disbelief in the tone of the spokesperson for Worldwide Fund for Nature. He or she seemed to imply that I might have had a touch of the sun, and that the Lissom Lovely and her dawning interest in me is all a sort of mirage brought about by Base Lust under the cruel heat of the sun over Solemn Land. My feeling is that only by getting her into an attic in PWN Towers, that ancient pile in Britain, and showing her to doubters, will my word be taken as honest in this matter. But in the dark of night at Base Camp even I am assailed by doubt but of a slightly different kind: what if this pitch-black Goddess has only been shown to me by God above as an example of what I could have had in Paradise, if only I had been Good?!

The debate amongst our party, as we traversed the Mammoth Meadow and followed the various pathways into deeper Solemn Land, was this: How short can a lady's shorts go before they become the lower half of a bikini, or even a thong? This matter, I am sure you will agree from your own observations, is one that urgently requires resolving. My estimate is that starting at about the age of sixteen and up to about the age of forty years, the women of Solemn Land resolve that they will enter a competition to cut away the legs of their jeans or other trousers, or even reduce the legs on pre-existing shorts until they can cut away no more without risking an inadvertent gynaecological procedure.

On some of these ladies–a distinct minority–the effect is pleasing, and undeniably so, but on others so much terrain of vast hindquarter is exposed that precious little mystery remains and I rather long for the days of my youth when the exposure of an inch of ankle would scandalise the community and lead to the ruin of the lady in question. (Some of you may doubt I had a Victorian childhood and suggest I was a child when the mini skirt was all the rage but if so, I have complete amnesia about that.[107])

The sunshine has also brought another clutch of young lovers into being. We seem not really to have had an impact on their numbers.

---

[107] This is merely a refashioning of the hoary old chestnut that 'If you can remember the 1960s, you were not there.'

One is likely to trip over a pair doing their mating rituals wherever one goes in the Mammoths' Meadow.

How sweet they look just before I produce my hunting licence and give them both barrels. Better that than a life trapped together in Young Parenthood, do not you agree? I act out of kindness, really. [108]

As I sat in the shade of the Old Redwood in the periphery of my vision, I spotted a Thing of Horror. For creeping towards me on the fallen branch on which I sat was a huge ten-legged spider! It was as big as my two hands put together and as dark as sin.

I quickly moved away in alarm but later had to go back for my gloves. Luckily when I picked them up the hideous spider had gone and only my black gloves were there. Yes, I may need to see an optician—what's your point?

I spotted two people in the grounds of the Old Cat's Hall. Are they more servants, or are they acolytes? Do they supply the greedy Old Cat's great feeding bowl with 'Twice as Toothsome, (Human-Being Flavour!)'?

An Oriental/Latinate Beauty, midriff on display, turned twice to look at me as I sat under the Sequoia, shaded both from the sun and the wind. Perhaps I should get a tracking collar on her also? It is always wise to have one Mate to wear, one spare, and one in the wash...

I kid you not, I also had admiring glances from a bunch of blonde women, with giggles and whispers between them, as I departed Solemn Land; I have not had so much admiration since I was a boy of fourteen and my voice broke and the sap first began to rise, a mere half a century ago.

One concerned correspondent writes to ask am I not perhaps receiving too much sunlight on my vestigial third eye, the pineal body in the brain, and might it not be wise to add a parasol to my equipment or more bromide to my tea?

A second correspondent, my doctor, writes to ask if I am still taking my medicine, as these sound like the ravings of someone requiring medical intervention.

---

[108] Once again, one must doubt the veracity of this statement. I suggest that you keep the salt ready, for pinches of it when PWN says such things.

I suggest I may just be looking and feeling well and that the many admiring looks of women I encounter are for that very reason. Here before them is a virile male specimen, with a confident swagger, in the midst of a time of worry and pestilence.

A third correspondent, this one from the Jehovah's Witnesses, writes to ask what are my intentions towards his daughter, Lorraine, and do I intend to do the honourable thing by her?

I immediately discount this letter as it has arrived twenty years after the event in question. I am sometimes glad the postal service is a little erratic…

Day 66

Of the Half-Naked Savage Woman's pact with technologically advanced Aliens; the familiar family from the Badlands make yet another appearance in these Dispatches; on the scarcity or otherwise of Lissom Black Lovelies; and how on Lake Tina Superior I discover and name a new variety of aquatic Pterosaurs

Though a very fine day again, with a soft, refreshing breeze, there was no Half-Naked Savage Woman to be seen for many of the hours of sunshine. This was a puzzlement to me until as we made our way through The Guard-Lands, I saw that the mysterious orange sphere had gone. No doubt, having gathered much information, it had taken off to rendezvous with its Mother Ship, very likely on the Dark Side of the Moon. And it was then that I perceived that The Half-Naked Savage Woman was in her compound, fully clothed, setting out yet more of the lights which come awake at dusk. Her small territory is now chock-a-block with these brightly coloured devices. I fear that the Half-Naked Savage Woman may have gone over to the Alien Power which sent the probe. Her compound is now no less than an illuminated landing-site for Alien Craft.

Then I was struck by a brilliant notion, and it was this: Might not the Pestilence be the doing of this evil futurist force, softening us up for a full–scale invasion? [109] If there is no Gigantic Fleet of Spacecraft assembling behind the Moon, before using the Half-Naked Savage Woman's light display to guide it to Planet Earth within just a few days, I shall be very surprised!

Still, in the meantime Life must go on, and so I shall relate to you that on our approach to Solemn Land, we again saw the little blonde girl (who may bear the name, Ylloh) and one of her mummies, the more svelte one, together with their hound, returning from Solemn Land to

---

[109] This is one of PWN's less-stupid ideas— it is stupid but less stupid.

the Badlands and their home, via the Terrace of Emporia. Their mastery of the Circular Route is not as good as mine, and so they were left stranded for several minutes on an island in the middle of the route, with horse-motor carriages going past them at speed.

There was–I am sad to relate–no sign of my Lissom Lovely but imagine my surprise when I spotted another one upon the Great Mammoth Meadow! Perhaps they are not as rare as once I thought. What is more, this distant, picnic-grazing specimen was accompanied by a small one, obviously a toddler. Where there is a baby one suspects there is likely to be a father. Quite suddenly it was revealed to me, in a flash of genius, that I now know of four specimens of the species. I begin to wonder if the need to capture my first Lissom Lovely is quite as pressing as once I thought it to be. Although I still do rather yearn to have the first and most Lissom one safely beneath the roof of PWN Towers...

That day the Mammoths' Meadow was full of groups of young girls, not infants but not yet Teen-Apers. I had nothing to do with them for they were not accompanied by lusty males, being not yet nubile, and therefore provided no sport for my always-primed shotgun. Nor would they yet be interested in the Neanderthal-like male of their species. 'That will all change,' I thought to myself, 'I must return in a couple of years. Then there should be sport enough and I will be able to pick off a whole new generation of Young Lovers!'[110]

When we arrived at Lake Tina Superior my attention was instantly riveted by the sight of three large pterosaurs on its banks. Two were of fancy colours and one of a pale brown with a blue and black flash along her side. As I approached them as quietly as possible so as not to give them alarm, they made their way in a waddling manner down into the Waters and began to glide over them in a tight–knit group, emitting a very strange noise. I have for this reason named them 'quackosaurs'.

They slowly drifted, propelled who knows how, between the assorted floating trash of the Teen-Apers, pecking down into the lakeweed surface. I took several photographs of these prehistoric creatures to take back as proof of their discovery by me to my

---

[110] This is presumably another one of PWN's jokes. But it hard to be sure.

Homeland. But I know it will be to no avail. In these narratives it is invariable that all proof is destroyed in some freak accident, so that all that remains is one's word against the sceptics one encounters.[111]

By the banks of Lake Tina Superior, I had the company for just a few minutes from a tiny but determined little blonde girl and her father.

Later I was temporarily joined by a gorgeous youthful woman, long of leg, a bob of lustrous blonde hair and with a winning, toothy smile when I greeted her. She ran around the Lake with an easy accustomed stride. She spotted the quackosaurs but was not so impressed by them as I had been. As she left through the distal gate, she adjusted her disruptive pattern camouflage shorts in a most alluring manner. I did wonder if it had been a totally chance meeting, as she looked over her shoulder one last time, tossed her hair, and winked. I winked back but with my glass eye—I am no fool; I wanted to keep my good eye on her, taking in the alluring vision.

Then two young women turned to stare at me several times as they went by, safely superintended by a matronly woman. I returned the hussies' bold looks. I can bide my time. I may bring my guitar on another occasion to further entice such ravishing specimens by exhibition of my small talents. It is trick which has worked on many a previous occasion, and after all Science calls for no less than that I employ every method at my disposal to closely study the denizens of Solemn Land.[112]

---

[111] How prescient this proved to be. PWN's photographs, now kept in a basement of the Natural History Museum, are a sorry bunch of suspiciously poor images, derided by scientists during their lunchtimes, and upon which they often place their wine glasses.

[112] Was it really Science which demanded it? Most commentators beg leave to doubt it.

Day 67

A Neanderthal in the Badlands; a bad-tempered Narrator; the vanquishing of Pester John—his poor old dog hangs on by a thread; a contrasting couple in the Mammoths' Meadow in Solemn Land, etc.

On a hazy but still bright and warm day as we made our way down from the escarpment behind the Badlands into the valley before the Terrace of Emporia and thence to Solemn Land, a Horrible Gangling Neanderthal youth of prominent low brow–not even a Teen-Aper–came up right behind me, invaded my space, and breathed his warm wet breath in my ear. If this were not enough, he then dropped his still-lit cigarette butt as he passed me so that I had to step aside to avoid it; then he spat copiously on the paving, so that I had to once more step aside to avoid that as well. He then proceeded to invade the space of every person he encountered until he got to the Terrace of The Emporia, where he suddenly responsibly socially distanced himself. Presumably the fool thinks the Rule only applies to the act of shopping and not elsewhere. It goes without saying that his kind will go extinct. It is just a matter of how many Homo sapiens undeserving of extinction they take with them.

Some palaeontologists say the Neanderthals are underestimated and that they may have Culture and Art. I doubt it, personally. [113]

At the turning of the trail to the second avenue of Emporia whom should I see, with sinking of heart, but Pester John. As I time my excursions into Solemn Land largely to avoid this brutish individual and his so-called 'banter' I steeled myself for yet another encounter with the ignorant person I would call an ape, did I not know that most apes exceed him in intelligence, by far. However, to my amazement the vile body would not meet my eye but rather cowered before me. It seems

---

[113] The hard drive adds—'Not these ones, at any rate.'

that after many attempts to show him that I consider him to be as dirt beneath my feet, this proto-ape has at last got the message that I want nothing to do with him.

And so, we continued on our way, with much rejoicing. As I looked back briefly at this creature, who could hardly qualify even for the status of a Neanderthal, I saw his poor old dog. He had a look in his eyes that seemed to beseech us to liberate him and to take him away from Pester John forthwith. However, the Laws of the Land being what they are, we were forced to ignore that poor hound's silent, imploring face. It seemed to say, 'Do not leave me with this brute!' but our hands were tied in the matter. One can only hope that one day the hound will rise up against his master, kill him and bury the tyrant's bones in several locations. Not that I wish any man ill but as Pester John hardly qualifies as one, that doesn't apply.

Yes, despite my victory in the contest of wills, I was disproportionately angry and remained so very bad-tempered that I began to wonder if I might be coming down with something.

However, on achieving Solemn Land through the Tradesmen's Entrance, I did begin to calm down somewhat and by the time we had crossed the Mammoths' Meadow and observed the little children and their parents playing such games as 'Find the Land Mine' and 'Step in the Gin-Trap' my pacific and placid nature had reasserted itself.

Upon the sward of green grass I observed a fifth representative of the Lissom Lovely species. She was accompanied by a Pasty White Partner who exhibited the savage marks of a bad sunburn. He is obviously melanin–challenged in a way she is not. If ever there was an argument in favour of interracial relations it is surely this: one race burns in the sun, the other does not. As much more sun is predicted with Global Warming, the former–the whites–are therefore obviously rapidly becoming the inferior race and it is my unlucky lot to be numbered amongst them. We must quickly breed ourselves coffee-coloured at the very least. And I have already done my bit to start the ball rolling.[114] I am willing to do more of this noble work if I can only persuade the Lissom Lovely to take up domicile in PWN Towers.

---

[114] This is, possibly, an interesting autobiographical revelation, if you think about it.

Day 68

Jungle fever! A Witch Doctor prescribes sleep and in large quantity; once in Solemn Land a change in the mode of dress is perceived; the little blonde girl plus parent doppelgangers; an alien probe is assaulted on the Mammoth's Meadow; observations of a naturalist and swimmer at Lake Tina Superior

In the morning, Jungle Fever was rife throughout Base Camp. This manifested itself as a deep melancholia plus sleepiness, together with an ulcerated gob. It was hard to detect if the feline bearers had the illness as their natural state is one of lethargy.

A Witch Doctor was called for a consultation on my crystal device and the advice given was to close the curtains on the camp's panes, turn off the sound on my crystal device and then to sleep the sleep of the Truly, Deeply Mad for as long as Nature wished, and an aging bladder allowed. This was very successful and with an ancient analgesic swallowed, and a tincture applied to my ulcerated mouth, after a late luncheon was taken, I was able to fit in a speedy sojourn in the Guard-Lands and Solemn Land.

Outside Base Camp, the day was dull with a chill wind. Only the hardiest and most exhibitionist of the young hominid women were prepared to wear the tiny shorts, whilst most were dressed head to foot in many layers of imitation Dalmatian skins or Michelin Man style parkas and trousers.

By the Terrace of Emporia, I thought I saw once again the Little Blonde Girl, whose name may be Ylloh, from the Badlands behind the Guard-Lands, plus a parent. But later I had doubts, for one little determined blonde girl is very like another, as is one rather masculine looking mother.

Upon Mammoth Meadow I was startled to see that a group of male Teen-Apers was foolishly kicking about an identical orange alien probe to the one we already know from the Guard-Lands. What the

Aliens lying in wait of Invasion behind the Moon will make of this insult to their species and their technology, heaven alone knows! Mind you, if the Aliens descend and take out all the male Teen-Apers first, I for one will not be shedding many tears...

At Lake Tina the quackosaurs were back, having missed a day. I wondered where they had gone the day before.

Then not one but a pair of wood-peckersaurs visited Lake Tina Superior. I felt lucky to see the one the other day but how blessed was I to see a pair this day? I can practically feel your envy.

In addition, there were numerous small creeping pterosaurs and proto-birds at the water's edge.

The quackosaurs are now so used to me that my presence does not disturb them whatsoever and they gather before me in humble appreciation of a true naturalist who, however, keeps his Winchester rifle and sawn-off shotgun beside him on all occasions in case a herd of marauding stegosaurs or other unreasonable beasts come suddenly to drink or swim.

You have not lived until you have seen a stegosaur with armbands or a diplodocus with a polystyrene float in Lake Tina Superior. It is something I shall often speak about to my children (all girls) [115], in my dotage, should I survive all the Trials and Tribulations of my dangerous days in this Mislaid World.

'Never–' I will add 'get beneath a brontosaurus when it is diving in at the Deep End. They think they can dive but actually all they do is make a huge splash and for this 'bombing' and other misdemeanours, like heavy petting, they are often sent out of the Lake and banned from swimming there for a month.'

How fortunate my children must be to have such a wise and well-travelled father, do not you think?

---

[115] Is PWN to be congratulated, or pitied?

Day 69

A very British day in foreign lands; the lives of the smaller pterosaurs; the actual abundance of Lissom Black Lovelies becomes clear; a dilemma over admittance of other explorers to these newly discovered Lost Worlds; the many Messengers in Solemn Land, the variation in them, and their Mysterious Journeys as well as their quaint outfits

It was a typical very British June Summer Day in the Guard-Lands, the Badlands, the Terrace of Emporia and elsewhere, with cold grey skies and lashing drizzle. Periods of nostalgic dinginess were interspersed with extraordinary spells of startling blue sky. No weather forecaster or computer model could work out what would happen from minute to minute. One would not have been surprised should hail fall on the land beneath, or the sun scorch us. The sky of Skye and the savannah of Savanna varied enormously as the jet streams above vied for dominance. The meadow of the Mammoths was at times suitable for a picnic, at others suitable only for sliding about in mud.

The lives of the pterosaurs and proto-birds were not affected however, for having begun to build their nests or feed their young, every leathery or feathery thing doggedly went about its business. There were chaffinchosaurs on the trail down from the Badlands and by Lake Tina Superior a handsome juvenile jaypteryx came down to drink and bathe.

On our way to Solemn Land along the trail past the Terrace of Emporia we saw another Lissom Black Lovely, sheltering under an umbrella. She had dismounted from a giant horse-motor carriage with many seats (most of them empty). These beasts make the most terrible growling noise as they increase in speed and I am of the opinion that though they are said to have a horse-motor, deep within them is harnessed a great monster, like a Tyrannosaurus, and it is this that provides the motive power.

To return to the Lissom Black Lovely. I am now of the opinion that Reports that the species is represented by very few individuals in Solemn Land are obviously erroneous. Some Complete Idiot must have been responsible for spreading the rumour...[116]

An Exciting Development: I have had communication from an intrepid explorer, herself a Lissom Black Lovely, which promises a rendezvous by Lake Tina Superior next week, if I will provide the coordinates and a description of how my almost daily position there may be achieved. The question is: do I keep all my discoveries to myself, or do I share them with this colleague (who is Ghanaian-British and an unnatural daughter to me)?[117]

Part of me wishes to keep my marvellous findings to myself and part of me desperately desires to converse in my mother tongue once more and also to have a non–Native witness to all these Miracles, so that none may say in the future that I have made it all up for vaguely comic effect. I have replied in the affirmative and long to see her, even should it mean my having afterwards to share the glory of the discovery of Solemn Land...

I have noticed over the days in Solemn Land that there is a single group of runners, with a sort of uniform. They typically wear a singlet and shorts, with bands on the head and wrists. They have expensive-looking footwear, very like that which the Spirit of the Sequoia, the maiden Nike, wears. Some of them are svelte maidens upon whom it is a delight to look, others are individuals upon whom the Lycra continues to refuse to lie, and shows rolls of supplementary fat, much as would be disclosed should I so dress myself. Do they carry messages from these outmost reaches of Solemn Land to the Mysterious Interior? Are they in fact servants in the employ of a ruler, one superior in rank even to the wicked Old Cat?

As I prepared to leave Lake Tina Superior in order to make my way back along the arduous twenty-minute trail to Base Camp (much of the way uphill, do not forget) a wonderful, adult, banded pterosaur

---

[116] It would seem he has no one to blame but himself.

[117] This is another fascinating autobiographical piece of information. Some commentators suggest that the young woman in question was called 'Ytteh'. See 'Daddy issues: Having an Unnatural Father', Shirazu, H. Publication TBA.

flew into the bank at the far side of the Lake. Then it was joined by another, and then yet another. It is my belief I had seen these creatures before in the Guard-Lands. From them, as they pecked at the ground, came a soothing noise. But it did not fool me one bit. If I were the Old Cat, I should fear that my reign might be close to ending, for I believe these birds speak of nothing but their intent to carry out a *Coup*.

Day 70

The Old Giant Tortoise Men: my interest turns to the Elusive Non–Dumpling of the North Folk; a mere look from your author prevents a minor crime at Lake Tina Superior; more on the Flora of these Mislaid Worlds; a hoard of coinage of the reign of Eliza-of-the-Bath, is uncovered

The weather at Base Camp, The Pestilential Provinces, The Guard-Lands, The Badlands, and in Solemn Land remained grim, and if anything, grimmer. Whilst I am the first to enjoy a grey, even black daytime sky, and cooling rain in the Summertime, I was forcibly reminded of the old joke about the Yorkshire priest who in a drought prays in his Sermon one Sunday for God to let it rain so as to refresh the crops he and others tend in their Guard-Lands, and the farmers of the parish in their fields. When the next day, whilst the priest is hoeing his poor withered plants, the sky grows dark, lightning flashes, the wind howls and a great storm is unleashed, drowning the earth, so that the plants in the dry earth begin to wash away in the ferocity of the downpour, the soaked priest looks up at the heavens and shouts, more in sorrow than in anger: 'Nay, Lord, have a bit of sense!'[118]

Despite the inclement weather, we trudged our way through the dust which was rapidly turning to mud, through the Guard-Lands and up through Solemn's Service Tunnel and came out at the rear of the Badlands.

In the Terrace of Emporia, we met with a most unusual sight: to wit a number of Giant Tortoise Men. These elderly specimens, many perhaps as old as one hundred years of age, have long, wrinkled necks and sharp beaks. They carry not shells upon on their backs but packs. They smoke pipes of a very strong and rich tobacco. Their trade seems

---

[118] The Editor: I myself first heard this joke recounted by the late, lamented, Edward Burren of Lyminge in Kent. He told it better than PWN does.

to be gossip, and their words– those that can be distinguished– start always with 'In my day...' or variations thereof.

I have begun a new hunt, now that it is clear that the Lissom Black Lovelies are in no need of my assistance. No, I am now in hot pursuit of the even rarer Thin Blonde Beauty of The Broadlands of whom I saw one out of the corner of my eye. It is said that the mere glimpse of one such drives men to madness. It would have done so me, were I not already at that destination.

She hides, it is said, amongst the many Norfolk Dumplings. The latter are not savoury simmered islands floating on a stew, as they may sound, but are the many over-generously proportioned women of the North Folk. A willowy blonde, or BBB, is indeed a rarity and would make a marvellous addition to my menagerie of 'Natural Wonders of Womanhood' at PWN Towers. Let the hunt begin!

My eventual presence at Lake Tina Superior–which was only slightly wetter than its surroundings–put off a group of rather uncouth looking youths of both sexes from coming closer but shortly afterwards a strong smell of narcotics drifted from the nearby forest.

Of the flora of Solemn Land: In addition to the Sequoia and the Solemn Oak already mentioned there are Prehistoric Pines with reddish purple cones, as well as historic holly trees, together with willows and giant beeches with copper-coloured leaves. In addition, there are ground plants that one can watch growing in real time—sending out exploratory spirals to seek out larger plants on which to hang. Everywhere grow individual strange specimens, as if transplanted from another place and another country. I have heard tell of King Solemn's Land Designer long ago, called–at least in legend– Toemass Wraptoe; no doubt parts of his design remain in remnants in the landscape, though much has been superimposed by nature and inferior Landscape Gardeners.

Just before we had to head back, I discovered in the muddy earth at my feet a real treasure: a number of shiny coins of Eliza-of-the-Bath (and her consort, whose name seems to be Reg) who reigned in the last century and beyond. On the coins is the head of that monarch, looking as though she is aware that the Kingdom passed to her from King

Solemn through many generations, is not what it once was, and as though she is not pleased about it.

On showing this cuprous cash to Meli and Loopy, they said the old gal looked like she has either indigestion or a seriously bad temper. I cannot help but feel that this smacks of treason—but I cannot help agreeing with them about the artwork.

Day 71

An incompetent duo-wheelist; a Beautiful Blonde Bombshell eludes your Author; strangers at Lake Tina Superior; a band of Teen-Apers leave the shade of the Sequoia in a downpour to play in the forest; explorers from my Homeland expected in the next seven days

As we made our way down from the escarpment and passed behind the Badlands a disreputable-looking bearded young person in tatty clothing was weaving his way up the trail on one of those two–wheeled conveyances. He threatened, as he passed beside a parked carriage, to scatter us like skittles, his course was so erratic, literally weaving in great loops from side to side of the track. Though the way was broad enough for us to pass, his wobbling motion made us fear for our limbs, if not our lives. Eventually, we thought it best to stay stock-still and let him look up and take avoiding action. At last, he looked up and just in time he moved aside to let us pass. He then issued the ridiculous words 'Sorry, mate, I am all over the place at the moment...' He spoke only the obvious, for he was literally so, whatever the state of his mind, which I suspect was somewhat intoxicated by drink or drugs, or both.

Between the slope down from the escarpment and the Terrace of the Merchants' Emporia, upon the plateaux we observed a prime example of that rare thing, a Beautiful Blonde Bombshell, running swiftly for exercise and to keep herself in peak condition. She had particularly lovely eyes and two of them, which is often considered a bonus, though I have only the one, following a tussle with the rare Ghanaian equatorial polar bear (but my glass eye is a triumph of the craftsman concerned).[119]

---

[119] Note well: Here are mentioned both a rare reference to a former expedition by PWN and a detail of his physical appearance.

Unfortunately, I could think of no way of arresting her progress, for she went at terrific speed, and was light upon her dainty feet. Not only must I furnish myself with suitable words to bait my trap and a large butterfly net to scoop up this lovely, rare creature but I must remember to stock up with gold jewellery, champagne, strawberries and such dainties, plus roses, chocolates, and lingerie, for –though little is known of this species– what is known is that they are High Maintenance and can waste away too easily and often in captivity, if denied a constant supply of such luxuries. They are also thought to be ultra-sensitive to their surroundings and I think Base Camp is a bit too base a Camp at present to accommodate one of them. I think I may have to make some adjustments there if I want to ensure that any I capture will thrive. Should I bother, I wonder? Send advice to this address, post–haste, Gentle Reader, if you would, together with three first-class stamps.

A group of swarthy-looking people speaking in a tongue unknown to me, were present at Lake Tina Superior. They were pleasant of manner, however, and only one lingered for any time, speaking with great animation into his crystal device.

Though I tried to settle and read my book, soon the sky became very dark and increasing rain forced us to pick up our things and head to the comparative shelter of the Giant Redwood. Nike, the spirit of the Sequoia, was not present, no doubt having slipped into the trunk in such inclement weather. Even spirits can do without being soggy, I suppose, and need to shelter from the despicable advances of the Rain God Indra and that horny old God, Zeus.

On the other side of the redoubtable giant tree there was a group of Teen-Apers, female and male, who increasingly like to gather there, I have noticed.

Though I was dry where I was, as the downpour increased, the Teen-Apers retreated into the forest to the Northwest, either because of my intimidating presence, or the rain. From there I could hear loud whooping, both the higher excited shrieks of the females and the rival challenges of the Males, beating their chests in contests of dominance.

At the Sequoia, I received the exciting news on my crystal device that there is to be a follow-up expedition by Zow Bunny of the Daily

Asperger, sent out to find me next week in Solemn Land. I hope that if he is successful, he will greet me at Lake Tina Superior, with words to become immortal: 'PWN, I presume?'

Then came further news that one of my unnatural daughters may come to Lake Tina Superior next week, and two others with my unnatural grandson Nitram, will venture as far as The Guard-Lands. How delighted and yet nervous I will be to share some of my many Discoveries with them!

If I have seduced, captured, and caged a Beautiful Blonde Bombshell by then I will have to hide her, as I suspect neither my unnatural daughters or others are yet ready to accept that PWN has been doing such active field and conservation work. There may even be censorious looks and harsh words, believe it or not.

Day 72

A Pastoral Fantasy: upon the actual pasture, the arrival of a camouflaged tepee heralds the annual Mammoth round–up and count; the Teen-Apers and their primitive, syncopated music; the Wicked Old Cat puts up bunting on the veranda of his fortified Hall; his Wicked Purpose?

Imagine if you will, Gentle and Harsh Reader alike, your Hero skipping about the Mammoths' Meadow in pursuit of fairy-like Beautiful Blonde Bombshells, waving his giant butterfly-net from side to side in the hope of snaring one or two of these ravishing creatures to take back to Dear Old Britain purely in the interest of science.[120]

Well, you will have to imagine it, for the day dawned with weather as miserable as the most miserable thing since Eve said to Adam, ' You have got to try this new fruit! It is more refreshing than a mango and with a lower sugar content.'

Not only was the cloud low and grey, with moisture being wrung out of it at regular intervals by an unrelenting wind but I have not yet constructed my human-net, not mastered the art of skipping, for which I require instruction by a little girl (see a previous Dispatch).

It was all academic anyway; not a single BBB could be spotted anywhere as, by the time my party emerged into the Terrace of the Emporia and thence into Solemn Land, the best of them had scurried for shelter in their humble brick huts, and the worst of them into Luxury Dwellings called 'Penthouses' with their Protectors, the fabled and foul 'Sugar–Daddies', who I gather are like the Old Giant Tortoise Men but with huge pots of money which come very largely from the Mysterious Money Laundries and also from the long-lost Loopholes in Tax Laws.

---

[120] PWN has used this justification before; it was not convincing before and isn't so at this point, either.

If I can rescue a pair of the Luscious Ladies from this Fate Worse than Death, and possibly save a Fallen Woman or two for myself in the process, that can be nothing but a Good Deed, surely?

The reality was that when we emerged into the Mammoths' Meadow there was not a soul to be seen as the precipitation precipitated relentlessly down upon our all-weather garb. (Even this was not enough, for occasionally a cold puddle would form upon the back of my neck and trickle down my back, inside my waxed jacket.)

What was actually present on the meadow was a conical green tent. This I suspect is the tepee or yurt of the Mammoth Herders, engaged upon their annual Mammoth count. As the Mammoths here are largely nocturnal, the occupants of the tepee were also not to be seen, no doubt sleeping soundly until darkness falls and the Mammoths flutter down from the giant oak trees where they have been hanging and drowsing all day.[121] One night I must risk the intervention of the Ecilop and go to watch this spectacle at dusk through the infra-red lens on my rifle, my trigger-finger itching.

To return to this day: the Teen-Apers had returned to the Sequoia, well wrapped and a very few wearing savage face masks. In a brief period when the rain stopped there was an outburst of loud syncopated music with much bass. I could not see if they made this frightening music themselves or if they summoned it from some Device. Whatever the truth, I soon was glad to leave, and my Party made its way to the Northeast area of the Old Cat's fortified Hall.

Ulterior and Motive passed by, lunging at me on their long leashes to no effect. See how blasé I have become about these former threats?

But then an identical pair of wolf-like creatures also passed me but with different human master. I have christened this terrifying pair 'Nameless' and 'Dread'. These beasts ran around their master in contrary

---

[121] The eminent anatomist and expert on mammoths, Professor Entwistle Halt, derides this claim, stating that '...not only is there no proof that any mammoth was ever nocturnal but they could not possibly clamber in trees, not being possessed of prehensile limbs.' However, the esteemed and rather super bone-specialist and wild-swimmer, Professor Roberta Malice, however, has pointed out that not only does PWN's account have the ring of truth about it but those mammoths were certainly possessed of a prehensile nose, or trunk, being a relative of the elephant. She added— 'And PWN was twice the man you are. So there!'

directions, so quickly that soon they had him lashed up with their leashes like ribbon wound around a Maypole. I was heartily amused by this.[122]

I noticed that The Wicked Old Cat has put out bunting, which hangs from his veranda's eaves. I have been told that the Tyrant has invited all small rodents to a Midsummer Party. My feeling is they should decline the Invitation.

---

[122] The hard drive shows that here PWN was of a mind to add—'...and my blood pressure reduced at once at the sight.'

Day 73

Another grim weather day; my attitude to the Teen-Apers begins to alter; a female almost falls in Lake Tina Superior; after my strategic retreat to the Giant Redwood, I am pursued by the huge band of adolescent Apes; initial Terror turns firstly into Intrigue and then to Delight

I have been, over the last few days irritable and bad-tempered at Base Camp, hardly able to bear the incompetence of my feline servants, who seem incapable of rational thought and one of whom thinks it is fun to present me with a vomit-covered compartment floor each morning and even proudly draws my attention to it. So far, I have avoided putting a naked foot in the product. I have no doubt that he is shortly to be the proud producer of a large fur–ball.

This has given me paws (mirthless laugh: ha, ha) for thought: do Lions, Tigers, Leopards, and the Sabre–toothed Panthers who prowl around Base Camp also groom themselves so assiduously to arrange their fur and to free themselves from tics and fleas, that they too produce (presumably larger) fur–balls? It seems likely. And why are we never informed about this in the many wildlife programmes on our crystal screens? I suspect a conspiracy of silence. The wilds of Africa, Asia and South America may be littered with huge fur-balls for all you and I know...

On this, another grey, drizzly day, I plodded with my Native bearers through the Mammoth's Meadow to Lake Tina Superior. There had not been a human soul to be seen all the way from King Solemn's Service Tunnel which is an unheard-of phenomenon.

For twenty minutes I sat peacefully on the crude wooden bench to the North of the Lake, reviving myself with sweet lungsful from my vaporiser, when suddenly the air was rent with the deep voices of young male Teen-Apers from behind. To this was then added the loud sound of their Atavistic Music (like jungle drums mixed with the white noise produced by the Big Bang) and swiftly almost upon me was a group of male Teen-Apers. As I looked around, considering my options for escape, from the South Side came an equal or a greater number of female Teen-Apers!

Gentle Readers, I was trapped, with the Lake to my left and a precipitous hill up to the forest to my right. What was I to do?

I knew that my only course was to use my powers of persuasion.

'Please be seated, dear ones–' said I, in calm and measured tones, 'for I was just about to go, anyway.' (This was a lie.) I had wondered if they even spoke any English, but I was in luck, and they do have a smattering of the language, despite the language they use between themselves being formed mostly of grunts and obscenities, as far as I can tell.

I seemed courageous but inside my sturdy Korean walking–boots of synthetic leather I shook like a leaf. For the troupe now numbered at least fifteen and it was possible I had only a few minutes to live and breathe the sweet, stagnant breezes which emanated from the surface of Lake Tina Superior.

But I should have had more belief in the aristocratic bearing both natural to me and refined through the generations of my family. For, in a moment, the atmosphere changed from hostility to politeness, with these untameable creatures suggesting I stay! However, my nerves were too shaken, and I shook my head and said 'No, you enjoy yourselves, kids…' There was a chorus of thanks and suddenly I could see that these Teen-Apers were as shy of me as I was terrified by them. Indeed, as I headed South, and their ranks parted one young female almost fell in the Lake in her haste to allow my safe passage through their ranks. She looked at me with awe and adoration in her eyes after I had quickly put out a strong and masculine hand to stop her falling in the icy water.

We took ourselves off to the lonely Sequoia by a forced march and there I settled once again, marvelling at the recent events. Perhaps, I thought, the Teen-Apers are not so much Bad as Misunderstood. I was just relaxing again, when suddenly the whole troupe, now augmented by more females, were upon me once more. I am not kidding you when I say that there were at least twenty now of these youthful primates. Either there is some coincidence of our movements or else they have begun to follow me! I suppose you cannot blame them; to them I must seem like some sort of God: an adult who is quite nice to them. For it is true: I have begun to warm to them.

And here is a thing you may at first marvel at, or even doubt (it surprised me very much at first): amongst their number, hidden deep in layers of voluminous clothing, were slightly older females very shortly to reveal themselves as my Lissom Black Lovely plus a Beautiful Blonde Bombshell! The life–cycle and age affiliations of Solemn Land women was beginning to reveal itself to me.

There was no hostility as the troupe settled around me. Once again, I excused myself as the raucous music started up and once again, they implored me to stay. But I felt at least one of us should keep to the Solemn Land Rule of a two metres separation, and I also wanted to leave them with the impression of myself as something of A Man of Mystery.

I am forming a plan to wean them off their present rackety music by singing to the lovely, young, impressionable females in due course, and impress them with how I manipulate my instrument. (Oh, and I may bring my guitar, as well...)[123]

---

[123] Give it a rest.

Day 74

The Half-Naked Savage Woman displays a human victim's head! Of the Robbers' Copse and a further encounter with my young friends, the Teen-Apers, and one in particular; a potential grave insult to the Beings from Space and how my Power of Thought solves the problem of a lack of retribution by the Alien Invaders; junior Neanderthals at Lake Tina Superior

On a day with improved weather — though the Half-Naked Savage Woman was not roasting herself in the rays in her compound, to which she has now added the hanging head of one of her enemies (although my eyesight is not good without my glasses, and it could possibly be just a basket of flowers) — we made our way to Solemn Land by the accustomed route.

At the Tradesman's Entrance there is a patch of dense woodland to pass through, where great rats with bushy tails forage on the ground, bury their findings and then dash up into the emerald conifers all around. Some steal from the others and for this reason I have called this area the 'Copse with Robbers' (just my little joke).

As I made my way, followed by my noiseless and obedient Servants, whom should I see coming towards me but a portion of the troupe of Teen-Apers. I stood aside, smiled, and waved them on. Several acknowledged me and the Bountiful Brunette stood back from the group, smiled broadly at me, and said 'Hallo' in perfect English, to my surprise and gratification.

I am conceiving a great fondness for these harmless if noisy young creatures and I am even more glad I did not dispatch them with my trusty Winchester or Swiss Army Death Ray when first I encountered them.

They were heading toward the Terrace of Emporia, and I speculated that they are omnivores and might have been going to purchase a meal of battered marine life and fried, sliced tubers. This would argue that they have disposable income and can use it, at least to a limited extent. Perhaps in the official record of the fauna and flora of this land I should name them something other than Teen-Apers, as they are obviously as high above the male Teen-Apers as a Homo sapiens is above them.

My feeling is that the way to further infiltrate into the roaming troupe for the sake of studying them, is through cultivating the acquaintance of the Bountiful Brunette. Once again, I must sacrifice myself selflessly for the sake of my devotion to the Natural Sciences...

I did rather wish I had looked and felt at my best, not having brushed my hair, or splashed on some deodorant, and I hope to be on better Brunette-charming form on another day. Still, I had not done too badly, unprepared as I had been.

Up on Mammoth Meadow a terrible sight greeted my bloodshot eyes: a group of Solemn Land men were kicking around a white sphere. Whatever can the Alien Would-Be Invaders make of such a gross insult to one of their probes, and an important one judging from its rare colour? I expected at any moment for a lightning blast or space torpedo to hurtle out of the sky to decimate these sacrilegious and disrespectful humans but–strange to tell–there was no retribution by the Forces doubtlessly marshalled out in Space. Then it came to me that I was being foolish. For it is obvious that the spheres turn to white from orange when their useful life is over. I chortled at my stupidity. How fortunate it is that my powerful brain, housed within a small skull like that of a human, is able to work out these problems in a calm and rational manner!

As we settled ourselves on the bonny, bonny, banks of Lake Tina Superior, a party of three anthropoids entered through the picket fence which surrounds this vast body of water (where plesiosaurs and ichthyosaurs dart and gambol—probably—and certainly quackosaurs and peckersaurs are a not uncommon sight). These representatives of Man at The Dawn of Time were thin, dark, and surly looking and wheeled two–wheel conveyances with them. My strong impression is they have them for status only and are incapable of riding them. Such poorly made primates surely have no ability to balance properly, judging by their loping and unsteady gait.

I thought for a moment they might be a portion of the troupe of my friendly Teen-Apers, but it soon became clear that they were not but were older, hostile and meant no good. However, with a look of British steel I quelled their impious insolence, and they did but smoke one reefer on the Easterly bank of the Lake and then were off, throwing a metal receptacle for a barley-based alcoholic beverage (judging by the smell) into the virgin jungle. What despicable behaviour! My conclusion could only be that these were immature Neanderthals, and–let us face it–even mature Neanderthals are not much to write home about. And yet I have done so—and several times now.

Dearly Beloveds—keep well until this, reaches you. And afterwards, of course.

Day 75

The cowardly attack by a National Emblem; at Lake Tina Superior I enjoy the company of two male Teen-Apers who pay me a Great Compliment; my fears as to the likely outcome; the rain it raineth; messages from Beyond require my attention; the hunt for a bewildered Correspondent is crowned with eventual success

As I was preparing to cross the Great Circular Causeway in order to gain access to Solemn Land Proper (as opposed to the Badlands and the Terrace of Emporia, which might perhaps be called Solemn Land Improper), I swung out a hand simply in the act of perambulation, or walking, and what should happen but that a snarling poisonous viper of an Overgrown Thistle, hundreds of miles from its Native land, should dare to pierce my Explorer's anti-pestilence gauntlet?!

My Dear Readers—the sharp pain unfairly tested both my fortitude and my resolve, but your Hero merely winced and gritted his acrylic teeth, before pressing on with his retinue towards the Tradesmen's Entrance to Solemn Land. The only evidence of the hurt done me came in some choice epithets by which you would be surprised and might think could never issue from my cherry lips.

Perhaps you will be surprised that I did not take instant retribution? But I am better bred than that. However, should I find that treacherous specimen of plant life lurking at the trackside today to wound me again, I will have no hesitation in taking my blunderbuss and blasting off the swollen purple head of the monster. Such an unprovoked attack as the one by that impertinent invading Scot, especially upon an ambassador-of-sorts of the English people, should not go unpunished. As well as blaming the entire Scottish nation, I blame the negligent tenders of the verges of the Causeway who are these days conspicuous by their absence.

At the Tradesmen's Entrance a new sign in red warned of the likelihood of fires and that all visitors to Solemn Land should not light bonfires or barbecues and should carefully put out all cigarettes. The likelihood of a devastating forest or heathland fire to me seemed little, as it was raining hard and had been drizzling for days, and the ground was sodden. The sign therefore amused me; I wondered if it had been posted that day by the Solemn Land Ministry of Sarcasm.

In fact, it was to be a Red-Letter Day for me and for Science and Mankind, for I awaited the presence, at last, of a distinguished visitor from my Homeland, of whom more in due course.

At Lake Tina Superior I made temporary Camp with my Inferiors (the bearers of my kit) to await that significant encounter. I had the meanwhile to deal with many administrative matters using the Mobile Data incarnation of my crystal device. But my duties were to be interrupted by the arrival of two skinny Teen-Aper males whose first-whiskered faces I recognised. When I said I was expecting a Distinguished Visitor they hazarded the guess that I awaited a female of my species. I disabused them of that absurd yet flattering notion, but I said would they mind roosting elsewhere when joined by the girl Teen-Apers (who had hovered shyly outside the picket fence)? They smoked a perfumed paper-wrapped stick of an herb probably originally from South America and then good-naturedly wished me 'Good Luck' and left to seek shelter from the rain at the Giant Redwood.

Then the full significance struck me! Had not perhaps their enquiry about my having a mate been but a stratagem for discovering if the field was open for a marriage to the Lissom Black Lovely?

The situation may call for all my skills in diplomacy if I am to emerge from it with my virtue intact and friendly relations between our peoples maintained. If the worst comes to the worst (or the best comes to the best) I will lie back and think of England...

At the appointed hour there was no sign of my Distinguished Visitor, who I will now inform you was to be none other than Zow Bunny of the Daily Asperger, the newspaper to which I am giving the scoop of having discovered me in Darkest Solemn Land, having sent him instructions as to how to find me. At length, I buckled up my belt and went to find him for he was obviously lost. Soon enough I spotted him, wandering in circles at the far side of The Mammoth's Meadow.

His first words were not the hoped-for 'PWN, I presume?' but 'This is where Giggle said the Lake would be.' He looked cross with me about it as if the Lake and I were in the wrong!

We returned to the banks of Lake Tina Superior, and we spent fifty happy minutes together before I had to return to Base Camp to feed Loopy and Meli. I have no doubt that his account, together with his grainy photographs of Solemn Land taken on a primitive crystal device will shortly appear in the Daily Asperger and on various social media sites to hint at the Wonders I have discovered in my now lengthy Expedition. Of course, not a soul will believe the story, and many will declare the photographs to be forgeries.

But you know better, so look out for Zow Bunny's homage to Your Hero, my Dearly Beloved Readers!

Day 76

An insult to the Aliens; the passing Ecilop provoke a crisis of conscience; the fires of Hell predicted for Solemn Land turn out to be a damp squib; an apparent canine causes unnecessary alarm and actual harm to my famous foot; the Teen-Apers gone for now but not forgotten; a crisis in supplies

I noticed that the orange sphere in the conjoined Guard-Lands had not after all blasted off to rendezvous with its Mothership behind the Moon but has in fact been captured and imprisoned in the compounds of Semaj. He will surely rue the day he committed this act of interplanetary larceny. If he is not at the top of the list after the destruction of Planet Earth's centres of power, and if the alien ships do not take him and his compound out with a short, sharp blast of their plutonium pistols, I shall be very surprised.

Later, as we proceeded down from the Escarpment that divides Solemn Land from the fringes of the Badlands, where stands my Base Camp in its humble brick form, the carriage of the feared Ecilop came down the hill with all of the horses they cruelly imprison beneath their bonnets whinnying, and an extra noise, as of banshees who have been on a recent refresher course.

At once all my past sins rushed to my mind, as if I were confessing them to the dread Ecilop, or a priest, or to God itself. One thing I must do, upon my return to PWN Towers in Norfolk, is to release my many wives from the Castle's harem and give them their freedom, or at least a chance to breathe some fresh air. I really have let that little hobby get out of hand. It is one shameful secret too many...

The weather continued as foul as may be. Once again, I read incredulously the notice at the Tradesmen's Entrance that predicts a Fiery Inferno in an apparently parched land, if people do not take great care with their naked flames and preferably not make any. The predicted conflagration could only be, I reflected, if the constant stream

206

descending from the heavens and running down inside the neck of my sou'wester were of lighter fluid or liquid methane— and I do not think things have yet got quite as bad as that on our dear little planet.

There was an almost total absence of hominids upon the vast vistas of these outlying areas of Solemn Land, nor signs of other life.

That was until I spotted, lying across our path, the form of a recumbent, prostrate hound. Even as we got close the animal-like profile and colour convinced me that a great dog had collapsed across the trail. My mind became very active as I considered what best to do. Was the hound dead or only injured? Should I try to resuscitate it?

Only when I had given it a tentative sharp kick to see if I got any response, did I realise that it was part of a stout branch that had fallen there. As I nursed my throbbing big toe, I truly understood the meaning of the phrase: "Let sleeping dogs lie' and would add 'For often they will turn out to be logs not dogs.' Especially if one has not visited one's optician for a long time.

Under the Giant Redwood, Nike, the dryad–in–residence, sheltered me, leaving only occasionally for romantic trysts with her poor, hopeless swain. (For what mortal can hope to unite with a minor Goddess? I tried it myself once and no good came of it—but that is another story.) True to her name the dryad kept me remarkably dry. I remained as dryad as anything.

The inclement weather meant that the soft-living, fair-weather-preferring Teen-Apers were absent from any location I yet know, and probably sheltered in their brick nests, driving their parents to despair with their absurd sleeping pattern, loud music, hardly comprehensible grunts, and too hearty appetites for fast food.

However, in their absence my thoughts turned to the male Teen-Apers and the ritual scarification by Cruel Acne which they exhibit, poor fellows. It adds to the unpleasant scowl which they so often adopt.

I wondered also where the Fattening Sheds for the pubescent females of the species may be, as many tribes have in Africa, or does this species of hominid not require to learn the arcane skills of rapid bloating followed by intense periods of slimming as evident in too many of the adult females of Homo sapiens?

As I sat in the dry but chilly shade of the Sequoia, Ulterior and Motive passed on the adjacent track, together with their black-waterproof clad Master and Mistress. Though Ulterior and Motive are still the fluffy white clouds with a set of sharp teeth they were before, I now fear them not, for they no longer lunge at me. They have probably decided that my meat is too tough and stringy to be worth the effort of ingestion. They, on the other hand, rather appeal to me in their resemblance to candy-floss. I could do with something sweet as my Witch Doctors absolutely forbid sugar.

After time had passed and we had become so damp that actual rivers had condensed from the saturated air to run steadily down our legs and into our boots, I gave the order to pack up and return to Base Camp, there to await delivery of supplies to supplement the meagre rations to which we have been reduced, from our stores and from foraging in the surrounding land. The arrival of the sustenance was none before time, for our cupboard was so bare that Old Mother Hubbard would not have found even a bone there to give to her dog, who might in any case, Gentle Reader–as we have seen–have turned out to be a log.

Day 77

I revise my ideas concerning Ken Ucky; a terrible accident averted; signs and portents; the skipping boy; a fortuitous encounter with the female Teen-Apers; a pterosaur of prey and the Mysterious Eastern Forest

Our passage into Solemn Land was fairly uneventful, except for two notable incidents, and they were as follow:

Firstly, in the track leading to the Terrace of the Emporia a large conveyance passed me with its power of horses hidden inside and like the Eyes Scream Vans but with no terrifying music issuing from it. Though it passed by me at speed, I could not help seeing that on its side was a picture of that avuncular personage spotted before on a greaseproof bag in The Guard-Lands, Ken Ucky no less! But now I saw my error, the name of this friendly threat is actually Kent Ucky, and he does not ride a Moa chick but has a partner called Fred Chicken (if my eyes did not deceive me, for they passed at some speed). I am sure you will forgive my previous error and I am sure we are all glad to have got that honest mistake cleared up. Now, what it is that Kent Ucky and Fred Chicken get up to with their van is one mystery that yet remains. To me it sounds like Kent has a ventriloquist act and Fred is his puppet. This seems the most logical solution, doesn't it, Gentle Reader?

As my retinue passed by the battered marine life and fried tuber shop there was almost a dreadful accident, for in preserving the distance prescribed by Law over the desired distance between people, a gentleman stepped out into the trackway and a passing horse-motor carriage had to take emergency action to avoid the hapless chap. I have noticed this problem myself and call upon the Authorities for a solution (if there are any remaining persons of authority in the sunken form of civilisation in the borders of Solemn Land these days, which I very much doubt).

The sign at the Tradesmen's Entrance to Solemn Land has now been revised to 'Be Carfull of Cigarettes.' To me came the unpleasant notion of a vehicle full of cigarettes and cigarette stubs. Is this really what is meant by such an instruction? I have heard of taking your litter home with you, but this seems a bit extreme.

I must here make another apology. I have told you in a previous missive that only girls skip, and it is a talent not found in boys. However, with my own eyes I saw a boy about twelve years of age exercising to the extreme; hither and thither he ran on the Mammoth's Meadow, and round and round, barely stopping. With him it seemed almost pathological. When finally, he came to a halt it was only for a moment before he began to *skip*, expertly! That is not all, Dear Reader, for I regret to inform you that following the skipping the same untutored youth broke into a high goose-step, chillingly reminding one of fascist youths. The skipping was bad to witness but this was worse. Has a gap occurred, with the degradation of the Kings of Solemn, in which this sort of hell's spawn may prosper? I shudder at the prospect. Even so much exercise as this beardless youth undertook filled me with horror and despair.

Despite this disturbing sight, I rallied, and on I went. There were small bands of male Teen-Apers at the Lake and at the Sequoia but no sign of the young females.

As I was not in the mood to swap banter with the males, in their primitive patois, I proceeded up the steep hill towards the Old Cat's Hall when with whom should I cross paths but the Lissom Black Lovely, plus 'my' brunette and a Beautiful Blonde Bombshell, those firm friends of hers. I now have the possibility of capturing the Complete Set! (Unless they can be persuaded to add a redhead to their number.)

I said with a grand gesture of recognition 'Hallo, youngsters! Nice to see you again' and they all replied in chorus, 'Hallo, nice to see you too!' in pretty well recognisable English and not insincerely, I dare to think. The brunette once more paused not a little, to drink in the sight of her lordly PWN, only a tad too plump from too many minimum rations over nearly three months and wrinkled through wisdom which is only gained by experience and which no doubt she feels only adds to my charms.

How my heart lifted to see them, after a rather depressing day when a rendezvous with my unnatural daughters had not happened, though expected and longed-for.

I supposed I was old enough to be these beauties' father (if not their grandfather, knowing how things go in the Badlands) but seeing them sends youthful blood to the major organs and seems to reinvigorate me, and–as I reminded myself–being old enough to be someone's father has never stopped me before.

I have, by the way, coined a new term for the delightful young female Teen-Apers, which seems more to reflect the affection I hold for these representatives of the Pongo species, which is 'Orang-u-Teens'[124] which translates as—well, nothing that makes any sense, so I will not bother you with it.

As we turned back South towards Base Camp, a kestrelosaur or other wind-hovering pterosaur, flew over the Eastern part of the Mammoths' Meadow, hunting the small rodents who have been invited to the Wicked Old Cat's Midsummer Jamboree. But it was unsuccessful in its hunt, as we can only hope will be the Old Cat in turn, and it flew off further East, possibly to perch in the branches or find its nest in the Mysterious and Vast Forest which lies there and to which I must devote many an hour in exploring in due course. And to think; these are only the mere fringes of Solemn Land which some suggest is just a large part of the Earth itself! These same people also suggest the Earth is flat, which is too obviously true to require mentioning to you: my Exquisite Readers with the softest of touches—if I remember correctly.[125]

---

[124] In fact, this is a singularly inappropriate name. PWN seems not to understand, or have forgotten, that 'Orang' means 'People' or 'Man' in Indonesian. He would be correct about the name 'Pongo' which applies to the various species of the Orang, were it not that nowadays zoologists agree that both Teen-apers and Orang-u-teens were in fact post-pubescent Homo sapiens.

[125] PWN must be being 'arch' here. The first thing which is taught at Explorers' School is that the Earth is a slightly flattened sphere. A dull fact it may be—but a true one.

Day 78

A suitable candidate for the redhead my group of Orang-u-Teens lacks; two–wheeled conveyances and the matter of balance; the Aboriginal Child and the Lying Father; a disturbing sight of flesh seen from the Sequoia; saving the Over-Exercising boy from ruin

Day dawned with a bright blue sky from the off and it was early that the Half-Naked Savage Woman was out on her griddle, like the character on one of those complex clocks they sometimes have in old market squares, whose appearance out from behind an archway denotes fine weather.

You do not know this but–following more thought on the matter–I had set myself the task of finding, were it to be the last thing I did, a redhead for my charming Orang-u-Teens group, to supply almost the only deficiency. I had looked high and low but not a one had I seen for many an hour. However, when I had almost given up hope, the most suitable candidate turned up in the most unlikely place. For, as I drank a simple breakfast cup of primitive Guatemalan cafetiere coffee and gazed out of my Base Camp's crystal pane in the morning, whom should I espy walking up the track on the hill in The Badlands opposite and to The North, with a well–formed woman who was apparently her mother? None but a simply gorgeous Orang-u-Teen redhead!

I ran to fetch my monocle and trusty telescope and a closer view did not disappoint, although the lens annoyingly rather quickly steamed up.

Well, this young specimen of what we scientists call 'a woman' is actually strawberry-blonde but that only adds to her appeal in the mind of your correspondent, so let us not quibble about it...

I should say she is of the same age of my young friends in Solemn Land and so my ever-active mind has now turned to how, firstly, I may separate her from her family group to capture her from the wild (sedation may be required), and secondly how she may be introduced to the group of friends. I would have to be careful to protect her from the already established pecking order. I am not entirely sure who is the Dominant Female at present, but my money is on 'my' brunette, who has a very confident and rather determined manner about her (as I know all too well) and to whom the Lissom Black Lovely and Beautiful Blonde Bombshell seem to defer a little.

I must give the matter some thought in the coming days.[126]

Of course, my whole entirely scientific and intellectual enterprise relies on whether the Strawberry-Blonde was only passing through on an annual migration, or if she is a Native species. I could kick myself for not getting out to the Badlands there-and-then with my illegal tranquiliser dart gun. The Royal Society will certainly be displeased if I return without the news that I have observed a complete set of Orang-u-Teens in the wild when I had the perfect opportunity.

When, finally, my Expedition was prepared, and we had made our way to the bottom of hill from the Badlands on our way to Solemn Land Proper, the Strawberry-Blonde Vision was long gone. Disappointed, I put away the tranquiliser gun, stowed the nets and continued on my way.

At the base of that hill there is a small rank where the Authorities have placed two-wheeled conveyances for use by the populace. For me a question was here answered, for I had long wondered whether it was the passenger (such as the little girl from the Badlands) who balanced rider and conveyance, or conveyance who balanced the rider, if the whole notion was not impossible, which I had at first thought. Two of the five two-wheelers lay on their sides and the others were supported by a strut. So, I conclude, it is the hominids who do the balancing of both themselves and the conveyance, unlikely as it sounds. I marvelled that a member of my genus could do it, for I am sure that it is beyond me, especially now, with my poor back. (I have concealed from you hitherto that I carry an old campaign wound of a prolapsed and sometimes herniated disc in my vertebrae which I got when fighting the

---

[126] How ironic it is—for we know he hates the Neanderthals with a passion— that the strawberry-blonde young woman PWN hopes to introduce to his favourite Orang-u-teens almost certainly bears a large quantity of Neanderthal genetic material. In any case, SPOILER ALERT—PWN never does introduce this specimen into his set of Solemn Land Orang-u-teens.

hostile Dreaded Manual Labour Tribe in Ghent[127] many years ago, and which flares up from time-to-time.)

In Solemn Land, a boy child of the Native human tribe threw a boomerang (so this weapon may be found outside Australasia, it is clear) while his father sat reading and not looking up. 'Daddy, Daddy!' cried the little aboriginal, 'Did you see that! I threw it a long way!' 'Yes, dear,' the father lied, as fathers will, all over the world.

The Lissom Black Lovely and the Beautiful Blonde Bombshell sat on the bank of Lake Tina Superior but not 'my' Bountiful Brunette, as I like to call her now, and they looked up at me, nervous without their leader, so I did not disturb them further for fear I would put them to flight, and my party moved on to the shade of the Giant Redwood.

I soon became aware that on the Northern part of the Mammoths' Meadow there was a sight more often seen on the beach at St. Tropez! For there were two lovelies in tiny black string bikinis, one a Beautiful Blonde Bombshell and the other a Raven–haired Rapture and they displayed themselves in a way one feels was calculated to attract the male Homo sapiens' gaze. In their briefest of black apparel, they looked very like the diagram commonly seen on a butcher's wall, showing how to neatly joint a carcase.

They would not do it at night when the Mammoths descend from the trees and rampage over the countryside.[128] A black string bikini would be but poor armour against a Woolly Mammoth in a bad mood, methinks. Unless these shameless hussies can also bewitch Mammoths, my bet is on the Mammoths.

At the sight of these immodest maidens, you may be sure I firstly scourged my back with whips and then had my bearers bring me my hairshirt, for such temptations should not be placed before an Innocent Explorer and especially one of repressed English stock!

The Over–Exercising Boy, passing by, surprised me by asking for tobacco but I could not assist him. Nor would I want to, as tobacco,

---

[127] To my mind, and that of many scholars it is this reference, which may be a simple spelling mistake, which caused the confusion about PWN's domicile earlier in life, referred to in a previous Footnote.
[128] See a previous Footnote. How they managed their descent is a topic which has spawned many an academic Paper. PWN later refers to them 'fluttering' down. How this could be managed without wings is anyone's guess.

strong drink and too much 'self–attention' ruin the constitution and set a boy on the path to Moral Turpitude, Self–destruction and Eternal Torment. I should know; I only just pulled back from the brink of doom myself and it is still a Daily Struggle. However, I have to say that my time in Moral Turpitude was the most enjoyable period of my life…

Day 79

An unnatural daughterly let-down; the birthday of my youngest correspondent and a claim on her birthday money; a spread of Half-Nakedness; the mysterious appearance and nature of 'a skip'; paper diamonds in the sky; what to do with your spare real diamonds

You may ask, Gentle, Sensitive and Exquisite Reader, how it is that I can take being without family, friends and indeed anyone of my own elevated form of Homo sapiens, considering the already lengthy time I have spent away from them in the Guard-Lands and Solemn Land? The answer is, I manage tolerably well most of the time but there come times when a dark cloud seems to descend upon me, and the only solutions seem to be to bounce a cat off the walls of Base Camp or over-indulge in supplies which I should mete out to myself less liberally.

It was 'one of those days', for once again my unnatural daughters had failed to cross the Pestilential Provinces to spend some of the daytime with me at Base Camp. Had they done so, we might perhaps have ventured to my Camp Number One, my First external Base in the Distanced Lands, and Camp Number Two, my Second Base, and even Camp Number Three–my Third Base–although I feel it would be a great error to ever get to Third Base, with one's own daughters, do not you? Although I believe Norfolk in England has a reputation for such strange and unnatural goings-on.[129]

I wondered if something dreadful had happened, for my dear unnatural daughters not to have fulfilled their promise to relieve me of the Terrible Loneliness but in my heart-of-hearts I know they just had a better offer, for the fine white sand of England's beaches must have beckoned to them, if the sun shone (as it did here) over my Beloved

---

[129] This is a terrible slur, repeated so often that one begins to suspect there may be some truth in it.

Country whose flag I am truly honoured to plant in these foreign places and whose mighty Empress Queen I am honoured to represent.

Although a fine day, as I say, there was a certain haze to the sky of Skye as I strode, magnificent in my manliness, across the savannah of Savanna. (By the way, it is Skye's birthday this very day, so she will not mind sending me the greater portion of the birthday money she will no doubt receive, as her debt for being mentioned is becoming so great. Being a modern girl Savanna may prefer to pay me in crypto-currency.)

I had observed that the Half-Naked Savage Woman was revolving at great speed in and out of her brick hut, uncertain as to whether it was really sunny enough to souse herself with various sticky substances and lie down on her roasting couch to achieve a good crackling by the end of the day.

However, as I looked to the North, I noticed that her influence is spreading even unto the children of the Badlanders, for the little blonde girl and her snake-throttling friend were running about in the carriage–less trackway, in imitation of the Half-Naked woman, without a stitch on, on their upper halves! Why, if this continues, I may be tempted to strip off my own upper apparel in similarly gay abandon. However, I fear that my lily-white skin would suffer both from the fierce sunlight and attacks by gnats and other nuisances in the Guard-Lands; also, should I do so, I fear I might make not such an impressive sight for the ladies of Solemn Land; as it is, when we cross paths, I have to suck in my burgeoning belly most mightily! Yes, when I look down, I see most clearly the pernicious effect of Lockdown, which even my exertions in the Guard-lands have not kept at bay.

As we descended the Escarpment behind the Badlands, we saw a most interesting sight. Various topless men (you see, it is infectious), of almost as dark a brown hue as the Half-Naked Savage Woman, were throwing timber and bricks into a large metal container wider at its top than at its base, which was now placed upon the verge of the trackway. We enquired of a passer-by what was the name of this strange receptacle but received only the mystifying command 'Skip'.[130] Although my Native bearers took this as an order and proceeded to cavort

---

[130] Whilst of many subjects PWN does seem to have an impressive grasp, this is one of several where he has an almost willful blind-spot.

unimpressively, I declined to join in such a disgraceful exhibition of silliness, although of course I now know it is possible for one of the male gender to skip.

My retinue found itself following the Raven-Haired Rapture and the Beautiful Blonde Bombshell of yesterday's micro-bikini display into Solemn Land, but I was doubtful that they would so thoroughly resemble a dissection guide on this day, as the weather–though good–did not seem appropriately Mediterranean. I should mention that these ladies are not Orang-u-Teens, like my young friends, but fully grown–and I mean fully grown–women.

I resumed my usual place at Lake Tina Superior, as the hour was getting late, and all its visitors had gone. From there I noticed yet another beautiful Blonde Bombshell running around the tracks of Solemn Land. What was my surprise when I realised this was the self-same girl with the disruptive camouflage shorts, I had seen once before at Lake Tina Superior! She would be worth the chase, but I doubted whether I could match her stride and would, no doubt, lose ground on her all the time. Even if I piqued her interest–and the wink I had received from her before seemed to indicate that I did–no doubt that admiration would fade when, by the end of less than one circuit, I would be wringing with perspiration, my generous midriff would be wobbling uncontrollably and I would, in all ways be a broken man and no good for a tryst but more suitable for the Knackers' Yard.

On the front of her vest was printed the word 'Verily' and on the back 'Forsooth'. Truly strange, I thought.

Once again, I saw the OEB, or Over-Exercising Boy, as I returned towards Base Camp down the Highway to the Heartlands. This time he was on one of those two-wheeled conveyances. I wonder if he had persuaded anyone in the end to give him tobacco. If he must imbibe nicotine, he would be better off sucking at a vaporiser as do I. But I fear his future is to be 'cigareets and whusky and wild, wild women.'[131] Oh, how I wish I could prevent him taking that sorry path which was my fate before him. Mind you, it was an awful lot of fun while it lasted — before all three wrecked my health.

---

[131] From the song of a similar name by Buck Owens and Buddy Alan.

Over the Southern part of the Mammoths' Meadow a strange sight met our eyes. Several people of both sexes were busy throwing into the sky slim rhomboids, apparently of something like paper. Most simply crashed back to the sullen earth, not escaping the bonds of gravity. But just occasionally one of them was caught by the breeze and ascended into the sky, to some extent–but not much–controlled by the thrower. What, I wondered, was the purpose of these flying lozenges? It is a matter that needs further investigation. Whatever their function the throwers certainly need to improve their method.

By the way, and to finish this account: why is it that when one looks for a redhead teen for one's group of Orang-u-Teens one is lucky to find one, but when one has stopped the search, three or more come along, and all together, like London buses?

Answers with an envelope of genuine diamonds should be sent to me before the closing date, which has been infinitely extended.

Day 80

I walk aboard an alien spaceship! A Killer Werewolf; the habits of workmen in this Brave New World; how even athletes and dancers are pulled by gravity to the Earth; I muse upon the mating habits of pterosaurs and humans; I go all philosophical until my little brain hurts

I had an adventure in the Pestilential Provinces this day, which was a very fine day again but perhaps too hot for comfort. I had no warning of the weather, for recently the weather forecast by the Half-Naked Savage Woman has been a bit unreliable and is only certain at the weekend. This argues that she may be in gainful employment elsewhere during the week now. Perhaps she is once more called into the Pestilential Province to risk life and limb in the pursuit of money and the happiness it arguably brings?

To continue: To my great surprise and alarm I was summoned in the late morning, via an ancient communication device attached to my brick hut, to attend at a certain place in the Pestilential Provinces, and at a certain time, by a voice I did not recognise. I was told to come alone, to wear the tribal mask in fetching black given me by Semaj weeks ago, and that if I did not do so there might be dire consequences. With this vicious threat hanging over me, I had no option but to agree and so, at the appointed hour, properly suited, booted, and masked, I took only my second steps out into the Pestilential Provinces since I had come to The Guard-Lands and Solemn Land. My breath sounded in my ears like Darth Vader in that jolly series of 'Star Wars' movies. My spectacles with each breath clouded with steam and then cleared. I thought that this must be very like taking a spacewalk.

Imagine my extreme shock, my Over-excited Readers, when at the appointed place I found what was very like a Great Spaceship lying on the ground, protected by a series of stringent hygiene measures. It took several minutes for me to receive permission to board, and then to pass through a series of airlocks, before I stood before the first alien I had ever seen, in real life. This creature wore a suit of light blue clothes and was gloved and helmeted, and a visor prevented me from seeing all but its piercing eyes!

It ushered me into a compartment, the door slid shut and I was then subjected to a brutal interrogation about my health, my lifestyle, and my mood, before the alien began to apply a Hideous Machine to my upper arm. This clamped down tightly on my arm, almost until I could stand it no more and just when I felt I might faint, the pressure suddenly was released.

'This is not satisfactory,' snapped the cruel creature, before– horror of horrors! –pushing a needle into the same arm to extract tubes of blood from me for who knows what diabolical purpose?!

Issuing terrible threats about my life (and did I wish to prolong it, or not?) the creature then took me to the airlock and tossed me back into the Pestilential Provinces once more. I breathed a deep sigh of relief, for I had feared that in that shiny laboratory my end had been nigh.

I suddenly had a thought and turning back and using the intercom supplied, summoned the alien once more. 'Is it your people who are sending out the orange and white probes all over the Guard-Lands and Solemn Land?' I asked.

'I think it might be time for you to see one of our mental health specialists, PWN,' was her terrifying reply.

'Forget I mentioned it!' I implored, releasing the communication button, and quickly floating away back to the safety of my brick hut. I supposed I had been lucky not to be subjected to an anal probing, a technique much beloved of Aliens, I gather, and applied too often by my own species to my own poor colon, in the recent past...

Nor was that the end of the Terrors that assailed me, for later, on the way to Solemn Land at last, there was an attack on me by a Killer Werewolf, named Milly. Its owner merely laughed and said, 'Milly wouldn't hurt a flea, do not worry.' I forbore to say that it was not whether she would hurt fleas or not, that bothered me.

Near the trackway beyond the Terrace of Emporia, three builders were putting up a brick post for a gate. One worked whilst the other two watched. I have learned that this is the method by which things are done in the land beyond Solemn's Service Tunnel. Sometimes none work but all stand around gazing in something approaching sorrow, at a partly finished task.

As I proceeded to the banks of Lake Tina Superior, two bonny runners, like insubstantial feathers or dandelion clocks carried by a slight breeze, came towards me. However, as I stepped aside so as not to impede their path and they passed me, the earth shook, and small creatures did wonder and startle at their noisy and heavy footfalls.

I was reminded of my late father (curse him!) and his suggestion that even gossamer-looking ballet dancers as they land or jump make the joists and planks of the most robust stage creak and complain. He added that they sweat profusely and there is a feint smell of body odour and flatulence. How my father came to possess this knowledge is a mystery which may never be explained. [132]

As I sat at Lake Tina Superior, two svelte runners came past doing an anticlockwise circuit. Using the seismic calibrator on my Swiss Army Knife I was able to work out that they would only have shaken the foundations of any nearby brick huts but not have caused major damage to the structures.[133]

In addition to this disturbance to my senses, I then watched a handsome woman pass by, whose shorts were so high-cut that there remained but the waist band and some rudimentary leg parts to save her modesty. It would only take a stiff breeze to blow for modesty to be beyond rescue. Patient as I was, the air remained still until she had passed.

In the trees, the banded, cooing pterosaurs either played court, with a great flapping of wings, or else they squabbled over territory. How like human couples they are—they firstly woo each other, briefly 'love' each other, raise a chick or two, then squabble over territory and possessions before going their separate ways, leaving strangers to invade their territory. It is the Circle of Life, I suppose...[134]

---

[132] At this point the hard drive states—'My mother was never a ballet dancer, although she was possessed of many other skills.'

[133] Truly, this was a very unique Swiss Army Knife but all record of its manufacture has disappeared from the records of the Swiss manufacturer of such knives with many folding tools.

[134] This is a very cynical and skeptical view of human relationships, isn't it, Reader?

As we trekked back to Base Camp, I began to think about Homo sapiens and how little progress we have made since first that prehistoric fishy thing pulled itself out of the Primordial Swamp and shouted back to its mate, 'Come on, Fred—we can just about breathe this stuff!'

Do you know—I do not wonder so much if we will ever find intelligent life elsewhere in the Universe, but if we will ever find it on Earth?

Day 81

The diseased hound with the terrible rash; flowers of many kinds spot the Mammoths' Meadow; how the largest mammals of the meadow may construct routes through it and various questions arising; I unwittingly may have given myself a chill; two odd characters and my thoughts on observing them

On entering Solemn Land Proper, after crossing the Great Circular Causeway and coming up onto the area adjacent to the designated Children's Picnic Area, my retinue and I were approached by a great gangly hound leading its two human slaves. This hound was like a diseased albino Werewolf, as it was covered with black spots, and what looked like a bum-bag on its neck, which may have been some sort of poultice to draw out its infection and return it to its pure white state. Its male slave remarked, in passing, 'Did you know they were specially bred to run alongside fire engines in the olden days?' I said I did not know this, but I supposed it would have made a fire easier to *spot*. (Insert Hollow Laughter followed by the howl of the wind across a wasteland...)

There was an intense display of wildflowers all across the Mammoth's Meadow. This included giant daisies, buttercups, and little purple flowers I wouldn't mind betting are unknown elsewhere in the world. But here a marvellous sight met our eyes. For throughout the Meadows, South and North both, regular paths have been created somehow overnight, to indicate where the citizenry should walk. Speculation was rife as to how these paths had been created. I favoured the theory that the Woolly Mammoths and Woolly Rhinoceroses must have fluttered down[135] from their perches on the Ancient Oak Trees, and munched out these trails all night long, before retreating once more for their diurnal slumbers in the trees. This theory only raised further

---

[135] See previous Footnote on this matter.

questions— If it is, to the Mammoths, an established and precise eating pattern, were they so trained in infancy and if so, who trained them?

And where are their piles of dung? How much worse might it not be to fall into a heap of Mammoth dung than into the Hidings of Agenda, that loathsome Big Yapper belonging to Rovert of the Guard-Lands? I tend to the answer that nothing could be worse than the deposits of Agenda, though it is true that I have not yet had to scrape the ordure of a Mammoth off the bottom of my Brave Explorer's boots. But they are vegetarians, so–though plentiful–their dung should be less repulsive than that of a Hound.

Eschewing the broad paths in the sward provided by the considerate Mammoths, I decided to cross the tall-grown wild country, forging my own path. Unfortunately, my fragrant Explorer's socks and stiff linen shorts got soaked as a consequence, leaving me with fears that I will catch a terrible Summer Cold whose symptoms might easily be confused with the Pestilence.

Many a Profound Thought I had, as I ushered my Party through the lush grasses and flowers of that Central Vastness, crossing Southwards again to skirt the Wicked Old Cat's Hall and to eventually reach Lake Tina Superior. For instance, I wondered if babies born out of wedlock, nor from civil Marriages, three or four months after the Pestilence has passed and the rule enforcing distancing has been lifted, may come to be viewed with grave suspicion, as may their parents, should they not be of the same household, and how there may have to be a Slaughter of the Innocents and the not-so-innocent parents. 'Desperate times call for desperate measures.' [136] Such flagrant breaches of the Rule of Law surely cannot go unpunished, even here in Solemn Land?

Perhaps I had better not even remind the Authorities that such infants will be absolute proof of wrong-doing. Even if they were conceived during a permitted outdoors visit, the act of their conception is surely forbidden by various statutes, not least those Bylaws governing lewd behaviour in public and the possibility of scaring horses? And what if the young lovers disturbed the Mammoths in the

---

[136] A saying believed to have been coined by the ancient Greek physician, Hippocrates in his work 'Amorphisms'.

trees? A Mammoth stampede, particularly an aerial one, must be terrifying, beyond even my imagination.[137]

I approached the great Sequoia–where I saw a stranger whose stern expression had obviously scared away the Dryad–and then the Superior Lake named after my Unattainable Love, I realised that it was three days since last I saw the Teen-Apers and my dear Orang-u-Teens. I began to think that they have moved, *en masse*, to another roost. How sorry I should be if it were confirmed that this is indeed the case.

At Lake Tina, a bluff and hearty bearded fellow I swear I do not know, hailed me as if we are old friends. I do hope he is not going to prove to be a nuisance like Pester John was once. It took me an age to rid myself of that excruciating human example of living excrement, so I do not want to go through all that again.

A woman with purple hair went past and I wondered at her. Is this a colour found in nature amongst the Solemnites or does it owe something to a bottle and artifice? And–anyway–why do it? It seems to do nothing to promote aesthetic pleasure in the observer. Perhaps it is accidental and comes from excessive imbibing of a drink made from the waters of the Cassis— a wide purple river with swirling black currents, which is rumoured to run out of the Central Massif and down past the capital city where it joined by the river which waters King Solemn's vines. How much is myth, and how much fact? Stick with me, kids, and I will lead you unerringly either toward the Truth, or over the edge of a cliff.

---

[137] This is more unlikely even than the 'fluttering' descent of the mammoths previously alluded to. Your guess is as good as mine...

Day 82

The dangers of the connubial aftermath; a clinging dress causes havoc in my facial attentions, plus references to pygmies and a certain American movie actor; letting in the Forest in the Badlands; the Orang-u-Teens reappear, to my happiness; another purple haired woman initiates a brief discussion with myself of how one 'Makes a Pass'; the return of Zow Bunny in these pages

This day, in these God-forsaken lands, it was sizzling hot, with the Half-Naked Savage Woman at her post from early on, getting caramelised and crispy at the edges. I may not wish to enfold her in an amorous embrace (not least for fear of being consumed afterwards, as are many poor male spiders following the act of procreation) but I cannot help thinking she might make a tempting fried meal, and, like bacon, a gateway food back to carnivorous ways for many a vegan, vegetarian or pescatarian like myself.

As I trimmed my grizzled but distinguished beard in the bathing compartment at Base Camp, in an idle moment I looked out of the crystal pane and whom should I see but a young woman in a miniature dress walking along the trackway in the Badlands, which we all now know eventually leads the Terrace of Emporia and all points of the compass in Solemn Land. The dress she wore, decorated with thin black and white stripes, clung like a second skin to her curvaceous figure, and even from my high vantage point it concealed very little and if one had been a pygmy at street-level in the Badlands all the Mysteries of Woman would have been revealed. It is not often that I have wished to be one of the people of the phenotype who have restricted growth, who inhabit parts of Central Africa and Myanmar in Asia, but this was one of those times. Had she dressed with attention or lack of attention? It is certainly a fascinating question and one which I predict anthropologists will debate for a long time, should I return to pose the question at a meeting of The Royal Society.

It was not of course the girl's fault, exactly, that, whilst looking at her intently, I had unintentionally carved a very strange shape into my beard with my cutthroat razor. Now I think about it, it was unwise of me to have continued my toilet whilst distracted by the sight of the young woman walking down the hill from the Badlands, as her bottom described a hypnotic pattern, with the stripes of her dress firstly converging and then diverging. I had to shake myself most mightily to come out of my dangerous hypnotic trance, but if anyone is able to break such a spell—never fear—it is your Hero who can do so.

In the Badlands, as my brave band of one Explorer, bearers and scouts made our way to Solemn Land, the little blonde girl and her snake-throttling friend played together in the middle of the carriageway. This tarred track is so clear of traffic, it is like going back fifty years in my own dear Homeland. How long can it be, one wonders, before the Forest begins to take back all these roads? It will only take one modest weed to get a hold and soon there will be a riot of tropical trees and vines, for without doubt Nature is always looking for ways to overturn and humble even the greatest Civilisation.

At the Great Causeway I had—much to my relief and undeniable pleasure—a close sighting of the trio of my favourite Orang-u-Teens. I experienced a flood of pleasurable emotion at the sight of them. Although the Lissom Black Lovely and the Beautiful Blonde Bombshell did not look at me with more than polite interest my Bountiful Brunette once more gave me a broad smile of perfect white teeth and said 'Hallo!' even as the word formed on my own lips and my abdomen clenched to its best advantage. I wish like a late certain movie actor, that I now wore a male corset. Just as on him, it would not make me look less stout, but it would at least show I knew I was a bit portly and wanted to do something about it.[138]

There will be a reference to the late American movie actor in the Extensive Notes to my 'The Flora and Fauna...' as he was partly responsible for inspiring me to devote my life to Exploration of the Dangerous and Difficult Places on Earth, my having watched him in a

---

[138] The actor referred to seems to be the late Robert Mitchum.

certain mini-series set in Africa. Perhaps he is to blame for the fact that in doggedly pursuing my vocation, I have unfortunately neglected to ever get a Proper Job.

I awaited the arrival of a guest at Lake Tina Superior, and as I did so another purple-haired woman passed by on the track alongside the Mammoths' Meadow. I fear I do not find this hairstyle of the Solemn Land women attractive and would certainly never make a pass at one who sported it. As I had that thought, I could not help but wonder what a 'Pass' is exactly and how one makes it? Is it in the mind of the passer or only in the eye of she who is passed at? I am sure I was never taught about this either at school or University, and if it is a skill, surely one should be able to achieve some sort of qualification in it, or if not that, a disqualification?

At length, and when I had just about given up on him, Zow Bunny of the Daily Asperger arrived, and we sat at the recommended distance while he reported on how news of his discovery of me last week has been received in England and elsewhere. Apparently, my discoveries in the Guard-Lands and my penetration of the Mysteries of Solemn Land are being considered as Supremely Uninteresting. From this I have taken only the positive of the superlative. After all, being Supreme at anything is pretty good going, do not you think, my tender-hearted Readers?

Day 83

A cataclysmic summer storm delays play; avoidance of the Land of Euphemisms; a speculation on the possible delights of a Diversion; evidence of a Dangerous Cult and a vow to explore the Eastern Forest which may reveal more about this wicked Religion; a massive Gathering of Teens; the danger of Mammoths dropping at dusk

A torrential downpour, like Sabre-toothed Cats and Yappers falling, stopped play and indeed work until late on in the day, confining me to Base Camp.

When finally, the sun burst out and the clouds dispersed, rapidly drying up the outside world and myself, and we could take up our Exploration gear and make our way to Solemn Land, we observed the little blonde girl in the Badlands, as naked as the day she was born, if she was born wearing an embroidered white skirt, playing out where a Forest will be shortly, unless Count Sil gets his workers back to work to hack down the weeds fairly soon.

We skirted the Land of Euphemisms, keeping it to the right and paying as little attention as possible to the lewdly shaped trees, many of which were erect and thrusting, in that region.

As we came down the hill from the Escarpment toward the Terrace of Emporia, we came to the place where four tracks cross and where we usually bear left. Here we noticed signposts in the tracks for a Diversion. I imagine the Diversion was in the nature of an entertainment with music, do not you?[139] Sorely tempted as I was, I commanded the bearers to take me on to Solemn Land Proper.

On entering Solemn Land, to the East but before the Great Eastern Forest, I spotted a totem pole with an impressive statue of a pterosaur-of-prey at its top, all hewn from a single huge log, upended,

---

[139] No, I do not.

with one end buried deep in the earth of Solemn Land. My eyes were attracted to it because it appears to have just received a fresh coat of paint or wood stain. This argues that the Cult it represents is still active. The Cult of the Chainosaur Carvers was rumoured to have existed –that men and woman who wielded the ever-growling beast that is the Chainosaur, once carved statues with them—but this was my first clue that this vicious practice, suppressed elsewhere, was still practised in Solemn Land.

The exploration of the Great Eastern Forest was well overdue, I told myself, and I resolved, despite the dangers, to undertake that mission in the next week, for as long as it took to understand its geography, its botany, and its zoology including its hominid inhabitants. There may be Formidable Terrors involved, so wish me the Best of British Luck!

Far from having moved on, as I feared in the last three days, there was the largest gathering yet of the Teen-Apers and Orang-u-Teens at the base of the Giant Sequoia, including–as could be seen even at a distance–the Lissom Black Lovely, for she is distinctively different, even if dressed in the same white short-sleeved blouse and skimpy blue shorts—a uniform they are all adopting this season.

Can these gorgeous creatures really be intended as brides for the lumpen and incoherent Teen-Apers, and not for a wise, noble, and courageous Explorer such as myself? Oh, cruel is the Fate that has our destinies at its disposal! [140]

I wondered if Nike, the dryad spirit of the Sequoia, ever slips out unnoticed to join these young hominids, of much the same age as she must have been when saved from some metamorphic appearance of randy Zeus, by being transformed into a tree spirit by one of the major goddesses?

If only I had left the shores of Lake Tina Superior five minutes earlier (where I had sojourned with my vaporiser and reading matter) I would have definitely been able to fall in step with my favourite three Orang-u-Teens, who preceded me by fifty yards or so and never turned back to see the Explorer and Great White Hunter hot upon their trail.

---

[140] Here, on the hard drive—'But is Fate fixed, or could I perhaps play fast and loose with it?'

When I reached that gentle giant of a tree, whose branches all slope down to prevent Mammoths from getting a good grip, requiring them to fly at dusk to perches in the oaks whose branches all tend to the horizontal, whom should I see but *two* Lissom Black Lovelies, my familiar one and a simply fabulous spare, and even a Lissom Black Male Lovely, in case your interests lie in that direction—an unusual and very fine specimen of young Teen-Apery with finely chiselled features. Sad to say, my Favourites all looked in the other direction so that all I was treated to was a back view of the Orang-u-Teens, not in itself something at which to sneer. But I should have liked at least one of those uplifting smiles from my Bountiful Brunette...

And so, with the short day of exploration over and the sun declining in the sky, we wearily made our way Home, as the Mammoths stirred and those with a poor grasp[141] fell with a thud from the trees where they had been concealed by the dense foliage, shaking the earth, and narrowly missing falling on our heads. However, our luck held.

I hope the same luck may go with you this day, although a falling Mammoth is unlikely to be one of the problems you encounter, my Gently Glowing Readers.

---

[141] See previous Footnotes.This is too frustrating. All we want to know is with what were they grasping branches? Their trunks or their tusks? Sometimes you just want to shake PWN, do not you? I know I do.

Day 84

Before Solemn Land all seems deserted; games turned to one's advantage; an attack-craft from the Mothership in Space; an infant forever blowing bubbles; I describe my intention to rush into print my book on parenting

We observed almost no one on the way to Solemn Land Proper. Even for these days, this was most unusual. All the way down the hill from the Escarpment to the Terrace of Emporia the only two hominids we saw were two Mini Orang-u-Teens. No doubt they spend much of their time longing to be one of the womanlier Orang-u-Teens and be the apples of the eyes of the vulgar, whooping and spitting Teen-Apers. Time and again these age-old tragedies have played out, probably since the Dawn of Time when first sexual selection began in the primitive creatures possessed only of a mouth, a distal vent and the first ill-thought-out reproductive organs.

As we came up onto the plateau that leads to the large Picnic Area (very rarely used for picnics, by the way–I can count on the fingers of one finger the times I have seen it used for that purpose–I saw a child with its hands being held by an adult Solemn-lander, turned so quickly with the adult as the fulcrum that it was lifted clear of the ground and flew through the air. I wondered to myself why is it that the adults do not just let go and rid themselves of these nuisances once and for all?

There were only the hardiest and ugliest examples of the Teen-Apers at the Great Redwood. They seem to live only for two things: to inhale Class C narcotics and bother the poor Orang-u-Teens. I should hope the Orang-u-Teens know they can do better but inside I know that so often it is the handsome but rough young males, constantly vying to be the most dominant, with rippling muscles, who most appeal to the females of nearly all species. Indeed, is there any species in which the female is made weak at her knees by the presence of an ugly wimp, or one who can boast only charisma or brainpower? I think not. Luckily, I myself possess the perfect combination of qualities.[142]

At Lake Tina Superior a hideously noisy flying machine passed overhead, representative of some advanced technology. Is it one of the Aliens' scouting machines, flying at a low altitude in order to spot people who have identified their probes and by pointing an atom gun at them, eliminate them so that we may not tell our tale far and wide? I trembled in Terror but feared they would be only more likely to spot me should I dive for cover on the banks of Lake Tina Superior. Instead, I did my best to imitate a miserable proto-man like a Teen-Aper or a Neanderthal, a Homo not yet sapien, as it were. I whistled nonchalantly, with the occasional ape-like grunt in the hope that the alien pilots could pick this up on some super sensitive auditory device they may have developed out in the far reaches of Space.

Outside the fence demarcating the exterior of Lake Tina Superior, a little girl happened along, dipping a magic wand in a bottle held by her father, and creating multi-coloured bubbles which floated in the air. Her parents stopped for many minutes, to capture her activity, upon their crystal devices. Their progress along the trail was painfully slow, for they had a little black Yapper with them, who sometimes leapt to bite the bubbles and pop them. Thus, was all the good work of the little magician girl undone. The whole process, whilst charming, struck me as pointless and unreliable, as many times her wand failed to produce any bubbles. But then most magic tricks are pointless and unreliable, if you think about it; this is probably why most activity on this world is not achieved by means of magic. And the parents had obviously made a rod for their own backs, as their walk was going to be (possibly infinitely) prolonged.

When I got to the Giant Redwood the Teen-Apers had in fact been joined by a couple of the less dazzlingly attractive Orang-u-Teens, without doubt taking their chance, since my favourite trio of beauties were not present, to use their lesser charms to secure themselves a mate from the unprepossessing but male Teen-Apers, who were engaged in smoking and drinking alcoholic barley-based beverages and fighting amongst each other for dominance.

---

[142] Modesty might be another appealing trait?

The Orang-u-Teens may have been superior to the Teen-Apers, but they seemed happy to attract them and they seemed to be doing it. It is obvious from this that in this world there is someone for everybody. As proof you may take the example of PWN Towers in Norfolk which has attics and dungeons chock-a-block with desirable women, some of them there by choice.

As I returned South by the Highway into the Heartland, I spotted once more the little bubble-blower magician girl and her poor parents. They had made very poor progress because of the little girl's insistence that they stop every few feet so that she could attempt to perform her feat yet again. My suggestion to them is that they leave the magic wand at home next time and instead do the flying game with the little girl, being sure to let go of her hands at the fastest speed they can achieve. By this method they can be sure to end the problem once and for all. I really should be an Authority on Parenting.

And they should not be sad; for the little girl may survive and grow up admirably independent and relying on no one but herself and her own talents, as every modern woman should. Either that or she will be brought up by wolves, which could be a whole lot of fun, although I am sure wolves would not encourage her to keep up her foolish magic tricks, for these do not put raw meat on the table.

This and many more sensible parenting skills can be gleaned from my forthcoming book "Lose Your Child in the Wild." [143]

---

[143] This manuscript is lost, although the Editor has hopes that it may one day be found. With luck, it will then be swiftly lost again.

Day 85

A day of indifferent weather; Semaj imparts news of a somewhat terrifying nature; exit Loopy pursued stage left by a Little Yapper! The creeping nightmare of politeness and kindness; birthdays here and there; Yappers and proto-wolves attack me and themselves; the wonderment of woman at my beauty and its long-lasting effect

For much of the day before we left Base Camp, as the wind came from that direction, we could make out the sound of Rovert, the Great Big Boss Handy Man's saw which is circular.

The day was not so fair that the Half-Naked Savage Woman was laid out in supplication to the Sun God. However, she lay clothed (and how inappropriate clothes seem upon her now) upon her roasting couch, as it was warm and dry out, if not of a broiling temperature.

We met Semaj on the hill down from the Escarpment. He was coming up as we went down. (I had previously little idea that he knew his way to the outskirts of Solemn Land. It appears we are not the only ones who know about the King Solemn's Service Tunnel.) With faltering words, he told me that his brick hut, which is adjacent to my Base Camp, is suspected of harbouring the Spectre of Creeping Damp. This is an alarming development, as I do not want to face this monster in turn. Semaj said Count Sil had been notified.[144]

He also told me that earlier Freebie the Yapper had been chasing Loopy around the Guard-Lands. Loopy is the original Scaredy Cat; were he not, he could turn and swallow the Little Yapper at one gulp, I should estimate. I reassured Semaj that Loopy seems none the worse for the experience and indeed had not even reported it to me, and he had had ample opportunity.

---

[144] Of this Menace nothing more is found in these pages. Perhaps it was a false alarm, or not as serious as at first feared?

A little boy just beyond the Terrace of Emporia said 'Thanks, mate!' very loudly as I made way for him and his parents or prison-warders, whichever they might have been.

Will this outbreak of niceness and kindness to each other never end? How glad I am that in my Homeland far to the North, across the Pestilential Provinces, the general spirit of the British suspicion of polite behaviour holds sway, and that we would rather spit on a stranger than commend him or her for good manners! The innate belief of each English person in his or her own superiority is our God-given birth-right and one that every English man or woman should defend to the death.

In Solemn Land Proper a party was being held upon the sward of the Southern Mammoths' Meadow. Young women were wearing becoming cone-shaped hats in gold and silver. This poignantly reminded me that far away in Britain one of my unnatural daughters was that day celebrating her twenty-first birthday. I have known her since she was seven years old. Not quite two years ago, she presented me with an unnatural grandson, and what a surprise this was, since I had only just guessed she was expecting, and it had hardly been confirmed before the event was upon us. I haven't lost an unnatural daughter, but I have gained another dependant. And just when you would think I could get some well-deserved rest and have the pressure eased on my poor long-suffering wallet...

Just as we left the bonny, bonny banks of Lake Tina Superior there was an insufferable attack by a small white Yapper, yapping loudly enough to almost shatter the eardrums. [145] I decided on balance not to blow it to Kingdom Come with a prolonged blast of my Kalashkinov AK-47/submachine gun, which I had slung upon my back before leaving Camp or seize it and cut its throat with my Swiss Army knife, but I was sorely tempted.

Later I was to witness, from the Highway into the Heartland, an internecine attack by one superannuated wolf on another, when Ulterior and Motive were set upon by the diseased spotty Werewolf, much to my satisfaction.

---

[145] The hard drive says—'They are a very belligerent species.'

To my sadness, but not to my surprise, there was no sign of the decorative Orang-u-Teens, nor yet the plug-ugly Teen-Apers. It is my conclusion that they are a species which can only tolerate the fairest of weather, and at all other times must hide away in various nooks and crannies constantly sending each other pictures of themselves in various stages of undress and scoring each other on their looks alone. What a degenerate species and how God-forsaken! No wonder civilisation in Solemn Land seems doomed. If only I could save one Solemn Land girl from this Fate and bring her back with me to PWN Towers in Norfolk, as Lady PWN—no matter what the neighbours might say...

Heading back to Base Camp, there was a young human female surrounded by a gang of Neanderthals, who were stripped to the waist and kicking a dead alien probe about, in the Picnic Area.

Upon my arrival she seemed riveted by my appearance.

How could any woman not be, I thought, as I crossed before her, with my glass eye rolling wildly in its empty socket, my state-of-the-art acrylic teeth glinting greenly in the sun and my replacement ears spasmodically opening and closing in their coverings of synthetic skin? [146] I could add to those my now legendary ear trumpets, bowlegs and flat feet, but I must stop before the list of my attributes, reading like those of a Greek God, causes the Ladies amongst my Readership to swoon.[147]

Let us just say that I am told that once seen I am never forgotten—even after years of therapy for PTSD.

---

[146] Unsurprisingly but touchingly, at this point the hard drive has—'Exploration takes its toll; it cannot be denied.'
[147] The Greek God PWN has in mind here is surely Hephaestus, the only known ugly God. By way of compensation, he was the craftsman to the Gods.

Day 86

The courageous little girls of the Badlands and Solemn Land; I get high but through no agency of my own except normal breathing; the disaster of all manner of deregulation in these lands; I remain undaunted in the face of an attack that would unnerve a lesser man; evidence of how far the previously Great Kingdom of Solemn has fallen; unsuspected, there turn out to be yet more specimens missing from my Collection

As we descended the slope from the cliffs that surround the mysteries of Solemn Land, we could not help but observe before us a little girl of some ten or eleven years I would estimate, dressed in animal leggings, constructed from something like Leopard Skin crossed with a werewolf affected by the Spotty Plague which we have seen previously in the wild.

I continue to applaud the courage of the little girls of the Guard-Lands and Solemn Land. Some wrangle snakes and others conquer and subdue the conveyance with two wheels. I imagine this one had trapped the beasts required for her leggings with her own hands, lying in patient wait at some waterhole for the animal to present itself and remain still until the kill was made. Or was the animal skin provided by a brave father or mother? Might they even have had to go into slave labour to afford such clothing for their progeny, whilst the clothing itself is produced by a separate class of (possibly unfairly and poorly paid) hunters and artisans? The skills demonstrated not only in the hunting of these beasts but in the production of leggings of such a fine, delicate nature must be truly formidable.

In Solemn Land our progress, which might otherwise have been swift, was delayed by two smoking Neanderthals. As I was in their wake, little time elapsed before I ended up as high as one of those rhomboid things people try to fly in the Southern Mammoths' Meadow. Indeed, all forms of law and order seem to have broken down, for the consumption of that sickly, fragrant herb seems to be going on now in open defiance of the Authorities, with people– principally but not exclusively the Young–openly smoking that powerful stimulant of laughter, hunger, dilated pupils, and sleep. It is second only to the consumption of brewed liquor in the list of non-medicinal drugs which are quaffed by the degenerate populace. Where, oh where, are the once proud and dignified denizens of King Solemn's Land — the same people who once probably confined themselves to a bottle of the product of the King's Vines once a week on a Sunday, together with a traditional roast meal? Truly, these feeble inheritors of this magnificent land would descend into anarchy if not barbarity, if they could only be bothered. Perhaps it is a good thing they are all too tiddly and stoned to actually do anything as practical as question their inept leaders. The present ruler of Solemn Land, unless I am much mistaken, must be merely a constitutional monarch and content to remain in his or her palace engaging in pointless ritual, such as circular waving, making the occasional polite enquiry of its subjects— 'And what is it you do?' and not really being interested in the answer, unlike our own dear Queen.

At Lake Tina Superior, suddenly, with a blood-curdling cry by the only adult male, there was an unprovoked attack on me by two adult humans with a pretty Mini-Orang-u-Teen. They came bounding toward me but on seeing my calm demeanour and unstirring defiance the war cry was silenced in the male's throat. They proceeded in reverent silence away around the shores of Lake Tina Superior until they were lost to sight.

I commend the stiff upper lip I exhibited to all those who may follow me. And, with luck, the stiffness in your upper lip may spread around to other parts. (I have always found that courage in battle leads to courage in bed. Or is that just me?)[148]

It has been a question in my mind as to how came the mossy, cracked, and in places missing herring-bone tiles around the Lake's edge. At first one does not see them, for they now so resemble the natural parts of the banks. One becomes aware of the nature of their slippery glazed surfaces when first one ventures too near the water and then slips inexorably down into the cold green water which then closes

---

[148] It is just him. Do not try this at home.

over one's head. You may take my word for that; listen to one who has had the experience and do not try the experiment yourself, Gentle and usually Dry Reader.

The tiles speak of a Great Civilisation doing Monumental Public Works. Once again, I seem to detect evidence of the time when the greatest of the Kings of Solemn reigned, with such marvellous things fallen into disrepair under the governance of subsequent weak leadership.

Around the Sequoia were no Teen-Apers or Orang-u-Teens but instead families with players of musical instruments. I was amazed that they possessed an advanced instrument very like a guitar, and not just one but two. My only explanation for this is that my predecessor, Lord Little Newton, introduced these fine things to the ancestors of the coarse Natives, and taught them to make and play them, centuries ago. Almost certainly a secret society passes on the secrets of their construction and the method of playing them. It is certain that no Neanderthal or Teen-Aper possesses the Art, though–annoyingly–one cannot stop the Teen-Apers from trying, and still worse adding their discordant ululations.

As, returning to Base Camp, we approached the area adjacent to the Main Gates to the Kingdom of Solemn, my scouts fell on the trail of a different type of Orang-u-Teen to any we had so far met. One of the scouts remarked that he believed he could detect the mouth-watering perfumes of the Orient. As we rounded a bend, we found ourselves extremely close to five extremely pretty and shy Orang-u-Teens from the Mystic East, in extremely short skirts. We had to be very quiet so as not to startle them and put them to flight. For many a yard we slunk in the nearby bush, photographing the herd—the Case is to be heard next Thursday.[149]

Oh, how much I would like to capture one as a valuable addition to my collection and–in the course of time–after she has enjoyed a long and full life in captivity–decorate the Grand Entrance Hall of PWN Towers with her superb head as one of several trophies of the excellent hunting to be had in Solemn Land.

---

[149] As PWN discovered, it is probably not a good idea to do this with human females, even if you think they are a new species, and could get you into a whole heap of trouble.

But this sort of thing is frowned on in Great Britain, these days. And yet we are famously supposed to be a tolerant nation![150]

---

[150] Might this not be a serious argument against the widespread notion of 'toleration' in a humane society such as the British one? Perhaps we should, rather, refer to an attitude to behaviour as 'approval'? On the latter ground, PWN would be found lacking, whereas he has a point in saying that 'toleration' could apply even to the hanging of human heads on public display.

Day 87

Various theories concerning the education and the nature of girls emerge in the course of one day; the savage repast of The Neanderthals; into The Great Eastern Forest and more on the Fierce Chainosaur Carver tribe; plus, my former enemies humbled

Although there was glorious sunshine, no Half-Naked Savage Woman lay upon her couch, turning into overcooked brown meat but to the immediate North, in the Badlands, the little girls played on the verges of the trackway, enjoying the warmth and brightness. They seemed not to have a care in the world, which is just the way people say it should be for infants, although a gradual training in disillusion, puzzlement and depression might be a better training for adult life, do not you think, Gentle Reader?

I am for that reason initiating my University Diploma in Rapidly Growing Misery for Children over the age of five. I intend to teach the course myself, in the first instance, before putting it into the hands of suitable tutors such as Messrs Thwackum and Gradgrind. Soon there will be no child over the age of nine (when the Course will terminate) who can say they were not warned about adult life! Talented students may want to go on to the MA (Mostly Awful) post graduate course, or even on to a PhD degree (Pretty horrible, Darling). I myself am at the level of Without Merit Professor in the subject. I intend there to be a Passing Out Ceremony at which I am so horrible to them that the young people actually do pass out. All forms of kindness will be banned from the Campus, of course. At my establishment one will always be cruel to be kind...

But all this is for the future, so back to the immediate past—

There was a barbecue party of Neanderthals in the proximal space beside the Terrace of Emporia. These primitive hominids talk exclusively of 'Bodacious Babes' (but do not mean new-borns—one trusts) and Footballs, for which, in their profound and woeful ignorance, they mistake the orange and white alien probes.

As I promised you last week I would, at the Picnic Area in Solemn Land Proper, I turned my band of 'brothers' firstly to the East and then the North to penetrate the Great Eastern Forest.

Here, towering trees of all sorts, some positively primaeval, rushed up high into the sky, closing ranks above us to produce darkness and gloom on the forest floor, penetrated occasionally by shafts of sunlight and the rare clearing where one of those giant trees had fallen, having either been destroyed by lightning or having collapsed from its possession of far too insubstantial roots.

As our eyes adjusted to the much lower level of light in the forest, on a tree trunk here and there we could see, fixed there by the unmistakeable hand of Man, small wooden boxes serving as signs which instructed birds to box, and bats also. These imperious commands inciting pugilism caused me much alarm. Are they the work of the cruel tribe of the Chainosaur Carvers, you ask? They may well be. Only further investigation may reveal the answer.[151]

A track to the right led to a spacious field where horses grazed, temporarily relieved of their irksome duty under the bonnets of those Ecilop carriages that come screaming along the Great Circular Route.

If our nerves were not already jangling, I then spotted in a small clearing the terrifying spectacle of two, grandly carved, living-room chairs. They seemed totally out of context and confounded my senses. Who can it be who takes their seat there? Surely, they are none other than the thrones of the King and Queen of the Chainosaur Carvers!

It was therefore with much relief that, coming toward us on this main arterial track in the Great Eastern Forest, I at last discerned members of my own species, including a little girl, unmistakeably almost human, at least for the present.

It was then that a new theory came to me with regard to little girls in the Distanced Land. Do they not all harbour the genes for turning into either real human beings, or precocious Orang-u-Teens, or–

---

[151] An investigation by the Editor reveals that the 'box' in question is a noun not a verb. The author's fear that they are commands by the Chainosaw Carvers is therefore quite unnecessary.

worst of all–Neanderthal women, with all their dirty and loathsome habits?! Who can say how, with the slightest of different spins, that particular three–sided coin may land?[152]

There is so much more to explore of the Great Eastern Forest; we have barely scratched the surface. But for now, we had to accelerate the pace of our march, in order that there still be some daylight for our return across the Upper and Lower Mammoths' Meadows.

I had only just realised that along the main trail in the Great Eastern Forest we followed, no running messengers from and to the Interior of Solemn Land dared to venture, perhaps because of the mud and ground made uneven by tree roots, when we at last emerged in the North to travel West to beyond the Wicked Old Cat's fortified Hall. Here we were to see another splendid Gate, before we had to head once more South and towards Base Camp, firstly coming to the Sequoia, where, despite the glorious weather, there was not a Teen-Aper or Orang-u-Teen to be seen.

On our way back to Base Camp, finally, we encountered a subdued Ulterior and Motive, not the same fierce clouds of pointed teeth since their bruising encounter with the plague dog. They trotted next to their Master and Mistress, eyes on the ground, and each tried to stifle the cowardly whimpers which formed in their throats.

Thus, how are the mighty humbled!

---

[152] A three-sided coin would be a most interesting object, do not you think?

Day 88

I am exposed to terrible danger by the partially exposed Half-Naked Savage Woman; investigation of the Western Wood in Solemn Land Proper reveals evidence of an ancient civilization and its buildings; terrible sex–pestery amongst the young of Solemn Land and my scheme to eliminate it (once I have completed my own Collection)

With the weather only debatably fine, for though the sky was cloudless, and the sun beat down mercilessly, such important decisions as starting out to Solemn Land must not be made on a hunch alone, I glanced across to her Compound and saw that the Half-Naked Savage Woman lay face up on her griddle with almost all parts exposed to the merciless orb in the sky. Obviously, it was safe to proceed on our way to Solemn Land.

However, at that very moment her eyelids snapped open, and I was transfixed by a vicious stare from her steely eyes, like that of the Basilisk of legend, the monster which is said to kill with a single glance. However, your Hero, whilst certainly rattled by this naked display of aggression–in every sense–simply drew himself up to his full height and turned away instantly in confusion and embarrassment, and thus the assassin's eyes missed their mark, and I survived the encounter, if only just.

En route to Solemn Land proper, coming along the trackway beside the Terrace of Emporia, I saw upon an omnibus carriage, with its internal growling monster, a poster for an 'Invisible Man' Moving Picture. I could not help but reflect that this is the only sort of picture where one pays not to see the star. Does the principal actor even have to turn up for the filming process, or may he just sit quietly at home and wait for the cheque to arrive?

In Solemn Land Proper we made our way this time, for only the second occasion, through the Western Wood, for the sake of its shade.

All the time I remained alert, for it is a known haunt of wild mammals. Certainly, everything ranging from a weasel to a grizzly bear may on occasion appear there, from out of the deep shadows. Even Sabre-toothed Cats are suspected of patrolling the paths, on their way to taking a chunk out of a Mammoth or other large vegetarian browser, from the hippo to the stegosaurus, which may be frequenting the watering hole of Lake Tina Superior on moonlit nights.

I felt the chances of our being set upon were very low, as this activity must be principally nocturnal, for reports of these carnivorous beasts hunting in the daylight hours are few—but it pays to be eternally vigilant, just in case of the first exception to the rule.

I have recalled that the day before I saw something in the Eastern Forest which I have not mentioned to you: this was a large stone base obviously for a statue, but the statue had long gone. Was this missing Colossus a graven image of King Solemn the First himself, or was it a homage to a predecessor to the present Old Cat? But here in the Western Wood were no statues or even the mounts for such. Yet there were lengths of age-old iron fence enclosing nothing and even at one point–most mystifying of all–a lightning rod can be seen, buried deep in the earth, the building or tower it had once protected being long gone. This surely requires more investigation in due course, either in a later Expedition by myself or perhaps by Explorers yet to be born.

As we emerged from the Wood, unmolested by ape, hominid or any bear that may have been visiting in the wood for its own arcane purposes, our eyes met on the Mammoths' Meadow the charming sight of a little blonde girl and a dark-haired boy of her own age, chasing each other, and generally sporting, until, of a sudden—oh, horrible sight—the girl leapt upon the boy and kissed him!

It is surely none too soon that this sort of thing is eradicated in the young, and why stop there? My plan is to roll out my plan for Sex-Pest control to all adult hominids, even myself, as I already have numerous wives and concubines whom I took under my wing, and now require support. I graciously provide for them by sending them out to work.

The vast majority are at present all housed in a vast old warehouse in Petersfield, Hampshire,[153] while I am away, so that all the dreadful, dark secrets at PWN Towers are given a much-needed airing and the entire place is fumigated from top to bottom. This is in order to rid myself of all the less precious Fallen Women I have charitably picked up over the years, but who now hide in the top corners of rooms, drop on me from the ceiling, clog the floor-sucker, and have generally become a nuisance.

My pondering of the need to escape such responsibilities, then brought me to reflect on the other and main reason for my current heroic exploits in opening up the secrets of Solemn Land, and I finally recognised the fact that I do it for the simple reason that, like Everest, it is there, and it is the impulse of a manly Hero to accept the challenge until there is not a place on Earth that I cannot say 'Been there, done that, got the t–shirt!' [154]

Once more at Lake Tina Superior to rest ourselves, with my bare feet and ankles dangling in the cool, pond–weedy water, I looked up to see four gorgeous Orang-u-Teens pass by, dressed in the ubiquitous uniform of tiny denim shorts and skimpy blouses, in which they shamelessly display like Birds of Paradise.

Perhaps I will suspend my Plan for Sex-Pest Eradication everywhere, until I have just a few more for my Collection. Can I help it if I attract these fabulous creatures as a magnet does iron filings?

That was a rhetorical question, Gentle Readers. Kindly do not fill my He–Male Inbox yet again with outraged comments.

---

[153] Once again, no record of this can be found. Several large warehouses in the area were destroyed by fire, however, and all paperwork lost.
[154] The hard drive declares—'Also, it gets me out of the Great House once in a while.'

Day 89

The Half-Naked Savage Woman prepares an ambush; keeping mythological creatures as pets; a daughter frustrates my plans; administrative systems in a poor state at Base Camp; I encounter a Dark Lady for the first time; the Terrible Torment of the Lissom Black Lovely and her apricot dress; Zow Bunny reappears to jot down my Adventures on his crystal device; a first and second encounter with a Dark Lady— I muse upon the vagaries and whims of Fate

The sun so beat down upon my brick hut, that even the opening of the crystal panes and being constantly fanned by the more attractive of my servants was of little relief. When I glimpsed across to her compound, fearful of her painful death stare, I could not at first see the Half-Naked Savage Woman. At first, I was relieved simply to escape from a similar Basilisk glance to the one she had given me the day before.

Then, tucked right into the corner of her territory, I discerned a small patch of skin, like a taut brown drumskin stretched over the shell of a drum. Was it possible she hid in order to ambush me and once more cast on me that baleful, murderous look from her blue steel eyes? Whatever the case may have been, it was not long before she was tempted out by the sunshine into its full glare and she sat, back towards me, on her roasting dish of a couch once more. Her long spine presented itself to me, with her back now as brown as that of the pigmented wax from a tin of Cherry Blossom boot-polish. I must admit I was to a certain extent relieved; I have grown accustomed to the sight of this figure, formerly known only from myth, and found inaccurately portrayed in heraldry.

So, must it be for the fortunate few who keep a Cyclops, Medusa or Gorgon as a pet. After all, it is only a few steps up from owning a Komodo dragon (and I house one of those already, in the stable block of PWN Towers). Dangerous pets are almost *de rigueur* these days and certainly provide a delightful frisson of horror when visitors call. My Komodo dragon serves also as rather a fine guard dog, when I send it out to patrol the boundary of my extensive Norfolk estate.

I had waited in Camp for the arrival at last of one of my unnatural daughters, Acinorev, who had contacted me to say she was coming that day with her swain, through the Pestilential Provinces by way of the tracks I had myself pioneered, to spend some time with me at Camps One and Two close to the Badlands, but she once again failed to turn up. I stilled my rising panic and told myself firmly and realistically that this was almost certainly because the day was too hot. For such, Gentle Reader, has been the Pattern of the Past. She is a zealot of that bizarre religion which holds that making a promise is the same as keeping it, if not better. All the young people are followers of this religion, I think.

The day got worse when I discovered I had missed acknowledging the birthday of my friend, Oj, with the breakdown of systems at Base Camp. I determined to do better and at once sent off for a Birthday Book. I have ordered the delivery of one with a cover depicting a swimming pig surmounted by a seabird. This is a common enough sight in Solemn Land, and I was glad to see the phenomenon had been spotted elsewhere in the world. Soon there may be no pig or wild boar to be found that is not surmounted by a seabird. It is their tern to shine. (Joke, in case it was so small you didn't spot it.)[155]

As we made our way, late in the day, to Solemn Land once more, I gallantly stepped aside for two maidens of the Badlands, coming up the hill toward the towering cliff of the escarpment, which rises higher than any other point in this notably hilly landscape.

At the entrance to Solemn Land Proper, I once more stepped aside, this time for a maiden dressed in a low-cut black vest, who acknowledged my gesture with the age-old gambit of 'It ain't half hot, innit?' Whilst I acknowledged her ploy, I refused to use the standard reply of the interested, which is 'Yes, it is! Do you come here often?' Even as I felt the words form on my lips, I bit them back and replied only with a gentlemanly nod. That's all I need, I thought: more complications...

---

[155] No, we spotted it alright but didn't dignify it with a laugh.

My little troupe walked through the dappled shade of the Western Wood towards the South Side of Lake Tina Superior. Here I found ensconced, two smoking Teen-Apers, polluting the place with their presence and their vile droppings of plastic bottles and fag-papers, and so I eschewed the bonny banks and instead sat with my back against the wooden boundary fence.

Because of this I was treated to the sight of the familiar group of Orang-u-Teens under the Sequoia across the Meadow, with just one or two weedy specimens of Teen-Aper, one with a practically skeletal and white body. If he is not an albino, I will eat my pith helmet.

Imagine my pleasure in spotting the Lissom Black maiden in a wispy dress of pale apricot which clung becomingly to her every curve and which, because it had no straps but hung on her solely through the weak agencies of Elasticity and Hope, she had to keep pulling up before what little of her remaining not on show was suddenly revealed, like a seventh veil descending. I may have emitted an involuntary groan at the thought...

Then came a sight to disturb me in another fashion, Gentle and Empathetic Reader, for I saw quite plainly my Bountiful Brunette take the paw of one of the most brutish Teen-Apers and lead him into the woods in the Northwest, to grant him one hardly dares think what dreadful pleasure! About twenty minutes later they returned, with their arms intertwined and wreathed in satisfied smiles. Oh, Cruel Fate—that I had not netted and secured her for my Collection previously, for I fear that in those dark woods she may have met A Fate Worse than Death! He, on the other hand, probably had experienced a Fate Better than Life, the vile fellow.

I had a purpose in not exploring further, for I was expecting once more a rendezvous with Zow Bunny, the adventurous reporter of our Expedition for the Daily Asperger, which has exclusive rights to my story.[156]

He arrived, late as usual and we discussed matters and he showed gratifying incredulity at all my latest discoveries. Several times

---

[156] No 'Zow Bunny' ever reported for 'The Daily Asperger'—a newspaper that never existed, as far as can be ascertained. One can only speculate as to who this imposter was and what he might have been up to. Perhaps he was just a somewhat maladjusted person needing a friend, and even PWN would suffice?

he shook his head and said, 'They will never believe this back in the UK or anywhere else for that matter!'—which made me glow with pride.

After parting with that strange bald man from Good Old Blighty, I and my party made our way slowly back to Base Camp, indeed following the Orang-u-Teens, though not deliberately so. (Honest.)

Would you believe it? Fate then conspired to have me meet my Dark Lady once more at the entrance to Solemn Land Proper. All that was different was that we had reversed our directions for I was now leaving, and she was entering.

I said to her 'We meet again! What a coincidence!'

But–Ladies, Gentlemen, and the Undecided–I sighed inwardly at the event, for it seems that however hard I try to resist Temptation, Fate always has other plans for me.

Day 90

The Half-Naked Savage Woman puts out more flags; a theory regarding the baleful glance of the Basilisk; a serious mistake in a much–quoted piece of poetry; the subordinate Teen-Apers and their menacing presence; an Imposter forces me to reveal my True Identity

As I looked out on the Guard-Lands, with Glorious Sunlight giving the lie to their name, I was swift to realise that the Half-Naked Savage Woman's device for drying things was once more showing a significant Pantheon of Panties but now with a New and Improved colour variation. This is a fascinating change in style, and I wondered what has tempted her away from the subdued white and pale pinks towards a riot of fuchsia and orange? Then a most dreadful thought crossed my mind: might not the Half-Naked Savage Woman be, as it were, putting out flags in celebration of a forthcoming Alien Invasion?

Before venturing near her territory, as we strode purposefully to Camps One and Two, I had equipped myself with tinted shades so as to scientifically survey the Half-Naked Savage Woman laid out in the centre of her territory, in tiny shorts, in the once more glorious sunshine.

Here is the Science Bit, which is a matter of conjecture and needs further experimentation: Is the poison of the Basilisk's stare, the evil power she possesses, transmitted by wave or particle? Would my clip-on sunglass attachment afford me some protection against that fearful weapon of hers? We crept along the palisade separating the Guard-Lands without her noticing and so, luckily, I didn't have to put to the test this hypothesis.

I was preceded down through the Badlands by an unfamiliar Beautiful Blonde Bombshell. Her hips didn't lie but instead spoke of the Eternal Verities: Truth is Beauty, Beauty Truth. The poet Keats tells us 'That is all ye know on Earth and all ye need to know.' But I think he is wrong; knowing a Third Party who could introduce one to the Beauty might be rather a good thing to know, do not you think?[157]

Rather to my relief, the Dark Young Lady who seemed to be in pursuit of your Hero the day before, was not present in the little wood of conifers adjacent to the Tradesmen's Entrance. The only living things in evidence were the bushy-tailed rodents, cheekily running about almost under my feet in their desperation to find their nuts and bury them. Not for the first time, I told myself that never would I be reduced to spending all day finding my nuts, as they do, or burying them. My nuts are always kept out for easy access by visitors, at PWN Towers.[158]

Once more the vile young Teen-Apers who form a separate smaller bunch from my favourite troupe (the ones who flirt or besport themselves with the lovely Orang-u-Teens) were in occupation of the banks of Lake Tina Superior. My theory is that they are probably miserable, outcast, inferior males whom the Alpha Male, the Lissom Black Lad, has defeated in several skirmishes when they challenged him and tried to wrest away his harem.

I fixed them with an attempt at a Basilisk's stare, but I must need more practice, or else am not fitted by Nature to exude such poison as does the Half-Naked Savage Woman, for my ocular attack dropped short, disappointingly; the shabby, just post-adolescent, hominids were neither affected, nor offered to leave and let me have to myself that place, so redolent of my Unrequited Love.

And so, I reluctantly regrouped my Expeditionary Force, and we crossed the Mammoths' Meadow, casting our eyes about us for pitfalls and snares, until we came to the base of Nike's American Redwood tree. Here, where only the day before the Lissom Black Lovely and her friends had been decoratively enhancing the little grotto of shade formed by its lower branches, was but one older woman, reading a book. She looked up at me in an unfriendly manner but what was that to me, one who now, by repeated inoculation, has some resistance even to the look from the Half-Naked Savage Woman that would kill a lesser man?

---

[157] All male commentators on the text seem to agree with this sentiment. Female ones have been noted only to roll their eyes toward heaven.
[158] I think PWN has probably got as much mileage as he should be allowed out of that.

Finally, as the sun began to dip towards the horizon, we came away and we had gone about half a mile before I realised that I had left my gloves. And yet I could swear I checked to see that I took all my kit with me when we left the Sequoia. I can only conclude I must have glove-blindness from some of the Half-Naked Savage Woman's Basilisk glance having splashed into my eyes two days before!

As we approached Base Camp I began to long for a cold drink, even an unrefrigerated one would do—a beer made cold only by running under a mountain stream, albeit one that has entered a river, then a reservoir, and then been piped to a faucet in Base Camp. For I had forgotten to put a can in the jungle icebox earlier.

I must finish today by warning you that I have discovered that I have an imitator, who goes by the unlikely name of H. Rider Haggard. Defenders of this blaggard Haggard even have the temerity to suggest that I am *his* imitator. The truth of the matter is that he rushed into print much as Darwin did to beat a competitor to the Theory of Evolution by Natural Selection.

The matter is quite simple: Rider Haggard is only my predecessor in the sense that John the Baptist preceded Christ.

For such comparisons I once found myself enjoying a protracted stay in a Special Facility and treated to a feast of electricity which made my head light up as if suffused by LEDs and all my limbs dance as if joining in with *Mardi Gras* in Rio, until I started keeping such thoughts to myself instead of telling the world.

But even the stoutest and strongest dam must one day burst and Truth, like floodwaters, flow unfettered. It is at last time to blow my own trumpet. For without doing so, my fear is that someday, like the scattered small remains of great things in the Western Wood of Solemn Land, I will only be known by a few fragments, like my glass eye, my acrylic teeth and my arch supports. It is even possible that, in the end, all that could be left of me may be my initials appended to my Great Work. So, for that reason, in closing, I give my name and title here in full: **NAME AND TITLE REDACTED ON BEHALF OF HER MAJESTY'S GOVERNMENT.**[159]

---

[159] What a shame it is that this information was censored by a sensitive monarch or her government before this Work's first publication

Day 91

The yellow shorts and what they mean; portraits in light and taxidermy; Freebie the Yapper trespasses and Semaj almost dies as a result; the sad fates of slaves and elephants; the Albino Teen-Aper isn't one and gets the girl

On yet another day of relentless sunshine the Half-Naked Savage Woman had put on tiny deep yellow shorts. As these are obviously a new purchase from the market far away in the Pestilential Provinces, I can only assume that like the departure from the pale panties on the Pantheon, these constitute another symbol (yellow being the flag of the coward) with which to signal abject capitulation and subjection to her alien masters, whose arrival must therefore be imminent, I fear.

In the Badlands the Half-Naked little blonde girl–for she is firmly a convert now to the Tribe of the Half-Naked people–and one of her mothers, carried from their horse-motor carriage into their brick hut a large, tinted family-portrait photogravure, a likeness etched onto metal, into their brick hut. As the portrait is as big as the little blonde girl herself, I can only assume that the walls of their brick hut are not entirely covered as mine is with representations of some of my many young women—natural daughters and unnatural daughters, sharing the space with the many recent stuffed heads of my kills in the Guard-Lands and Solemn Land. I have a particularly fine specimen of Mammoth, which I have stuffed and mounted in the attitude of clinging at night to a bough of an oak tree, as if just about to fall onto the unsuspecting heads of a couple composed of a Teen-Aper and an Orang-u-Teen. Never fear, Gentle Reader, I did not kill either but merely injected them with a powerful and lasting paralysing drug. I am a humane man, never doubt that.

When I saw the Little Blonde Girl's family photogravure, I did briefly consider the possibility of commissioning a painter with light to capture my likeness with my bearers and other loyal subjects, in positions of abject supplication, ranged behind my throne made of Mammoth ivory, together with the Lissom Black Lovely and other of the more photogenic maidens of Solemn Land sat upon my several knees, looking up at me in deep reverence. I decided against the idea as I do not light-capture well, being too strong in the profile department and there are other tiny faults which also show up. However, if there is no such thing as perfection in the physical world, only in Paradise, in all modesty I must claim that I am pretty darn close to it, if the Lissom Black Lovely is–admittedly–much closer.

On the trackway verge down to the Badlands I met Semaj, who told me that Freebie the Yapper had crossed my territory and found a hole in the privet bush defensive palisade, ensuring separation between my compound and the territory of the Half-Naked Savage Woman. Freebie had not returned, despite his calling her, and so he had gone to the ceremonial entrance to her brick hut to explain the situation. At which point she had uncoiled like a cobra, hissed her displeasure, and attempted to fix him with the hypnotic Basilisk glare that brings a chill to the heart and soul, even unto death. Semaj and I talked temporarily as equal companions, our stations in life temporarily forgotten, about our unpleasant encounters with, and escapes from, that dread creature; one so keen to get naked but so lacking in showing any naked emotion except Grade One Hostility to her fellow human beings, if she is indeed human, and not some monstrous survival from the time of the Ancient Greeks.

Because the day was hot and close, I did not sit out in the open in Solemn Land, but I walked through the Western Wood for the shade, and rested in a cool, secluded bower there. In that enchanted place, I read about Africa before the civilising influence of the White British man, who brought those dual wholly beneficial great enterprises of slavery on an industrial scale and a belief in a God so kind and egalitarian that any amount of man's inhumanity to man can be tolerated in His name. In my opinion, His image should not be of a kindly old man but of a stern one who is easily able to turn a blind eye to those who purport to act in His name. But each to his own, in the matter of Gods...

I read also of the elephants' mutual sorrow at the death of many hundreds and thousands of their fellows at the hands of my predecessor explorers, and how only the lucky ones escaped being turned into parts of a piano, to seek in the end their natural deathbed at the fabled Elephants' Graveyard.

There is a similar place I have heard tell of in Solemn Land, but there, it is said, the pachyderms go only when it is time to seek their ultimate reward: a river of sauce for their nut-roast-and-two veg, and it is called 'The Elephants' Gravy Yard.'[160]

The Lord is on occasion merciful (not often, but it is nice when He pulls out His finger) and I recovered my gloves at the place of The Giant Redwood). They were obviously beamed up for inspection by the Aliens but returned overnight to the same place, once the Interplanetary Idiots had discovered that they were not a life-form in their own right.

Returning to Base Camp at last, near the area designated for picnics, I saw the Albino Teen-Aper. Close-to, I saw that he was actually not an albino, merely extremely fair. I was astonished to find that his companion on the sward was one of the Beautiful Blonde Bombshell Orang-u-Teens. They sat in silence together as something sinister and vaguely related to music issued from an old-fashioned device, which I have named a Squawk-Box. The girl looked at me with more than passing interest; it was like an intermittent distress signal which issued from her eyes; but I was pleased that the non-albino Teen-Aper had found himself a little happiness and I left her to him, as his legitimate prize. Anyway, the rooms and attics of PWN Towers are all taken up by previous similar conquests and the feed I must provide for them requires me too frequently to seek the intercession of a kindly bank manager, prepared to overlook the amount by which I exceed my arranged overdraft. It was indeed partly to avoid the Pestilence but mainly to satisfy my bank manager that I set out upon this very Expedition, fraught as it is with Horrors, Terrors, Accidents, Injuries, and all manner of Alarms, and so dangerous that no Insurance Company would take on the risk.[161]

---

[160] I do not believe this, do you? It is figuratively and literally a little too much to swallow...

[161] This information was verified recently by the Screwem and Sodem Savings Bank, which is still seeking redress in the matter, despite being urged by their legal advisers to 'let it go.'

Gentle Reader, I perform here doing all my own stunts, and without a Financial Safety Net![162]

---

[162] As the Expedition was by way of a Royal Commission, it seems surprising that PWN had no bursary.

Day 92

I adopt camouflage which has the unfortunate effect of ruining a perfectly good sail; how my charisma transcends even my camouflage; is a Neanderthal army arising? The angry probe; a discussion of the diurnal behaviour of Teen-Apers and Orang-u-Teens; I amuse a small audience

The Half-Naked Savage Woman appeared only briefly in her territory and on that occasion with a thunderous look on her cobra face. Had not this been enough to convince me that all was not set fair for the day, the rain overnight and the casting of the runes by the weather diviners, which I had caught upon my crystal set in the corner of my compartment, intimated to me that in the Guard-Lands and Solemn Land, attacks by piercing lightning, and the sound of thunder should be expected in the course of the day.

However, as you now well know, I am a courageous fellow, and am seldom daunted by the terrors of the land, or the sea, or in the sky. Having discovered a 'window of opportunity', as they say in these degenerate times, in a debased language, I determined to proceed to Solemn Land not long after dawn so as not miss a whole day of Exploration.

I dressed myself with circumspection, and then added a layer of clothing.

(…Pauses for laugh. Laugh doesn't come. Carries on—)

Now, it may surprise you to know that just recently I have adopted the Native dress. The reasons for this are several. No, I have not 'gone Native' in the sense of being absorbed into the Native culture but being dressed in a safari suit of starched white linen with pith helmet had meant I had begun to stick out, in the more populous parts of these new worlds, like the proverbial sore thumb. Not only that but bright white is a poor camouflage in most landscapes, and if ever an outfit proclaimed 'I am an English Man and an explorer; eat me now' to

Sabre–toothed Cats, Cannibals and other predators, then a suit of bright white is it.

Camouflage is often essential to a predator or his prey, but it is also essential for one who intends largely to observe. And I am more usually an observer than a participant in the events of the Guard-Lands and Solemn Land. There are exceptions, of course, as when I am noticed, admired, and engaged in delightful conversation by the Orang-u-Teens, or any number of the Exquisite Ladies of these Mysterious Places.

You may wonder about what it is I do now wear. Hold your horses, and I will tell you:

I have, as it were, substituted one uniform for another. On my chest portion I have been provided by my servants with a black garment universally known as a 't-shirt' and over this I wear an unbuttoned lumberjack-style shirt. Many of the more mature male hominids wear this style of attire, so I have cracked that particular problem. From the waist down I have the usual knickerbocker undergarments and hosiery, over which I wear trews made of sailcloth. As my servants took the material for these trews from the sail of our Expedition Dinghy there are now two trouser shaped holes in it (for the front and back of the garment). I fear that 'running with the wind' in the little boat will now be almost impossible but we should be able to perform the complex manoeuvres of 'luffing' or 'coming-about' with far greater ease.[163] I was not greatly pleased when I saw what Loopy and Meli had done with the sail but when I saw the result I was impressed, and even more by their ability to use a sewing machine, as they have no opposable thumbs and I have no sewing machine.

To resume, when we got to the Terrace of Emporia, I saw several Neanderthals patrolling. The awful thought came to me that these hairy and heavy-browed males might be beginning to organise themselves into an army. What might this signify? I will keep my eyes open (always a good idea when not actually asleep) and tell you more when I know more.

---

[163] This nautical terminology suggests that PWN had some slight familiarity with the skill of sailing. Also, why has he not mentioned previously that at Base Camp he keeps a sail-boat? Why has he not used it to explore the waters of Lake Tina Superior? These are questions probably never to be answered.

Then came the Terror of the Day (like the *'soup du jour'* or Chef's Special of Horrors), for on Lake Tina Superior an Alien Probe awaited me. Such probes must be waterproof and contain flotation tanks, for it lay calmly atop the waters of that beloved Lake. I suspected that beneath a single black heptagon, it trained its baleful camera eye upon me. I do not mind telling you it unnerved me.

It was red with anger. I can only assume it was sent there to be a special warning to me. Can there be any doubt now that the Aliens know I have 'sussed' them and worked out what they are up to? I think not.

However, I soon regained my *sangfroid* and *élan*, and any number of other French attributes, and sat, heroic and cool as a cucumber, in its menacing presence. At my dismissive attitude it began to wander across the surface of the Lake before returning at intervals to fix me with its furious monocular stare once again.

It was too early and the weather too dismal for the Teen-Apers and Orang-u-Teens. It is thought that they do not stir in their shabby nests until noon, when still half-asleep, they reluctantly arise and swing across the floor from object to object, avoiding the piles of dirty clothing and bottles full of dubious liquids, whilst an angry parent hoots and yelps at them from the place of food preparation. After the Teen-Apers' eccentric meal–a cross between breakfast and lunch–in these straitened times, the parent may try to teach them things it is essential for a Teen-Aper or Orang-u-Teen to know, whilst horribly conscious that they know little of the subjects themselves.

I sat, alone in the whole of the Old Cat's Domain, and felt almost as though I was King myself of the entire country. I was soon made aware that I was mistaken for a middle-aged couple comprising Early Man and Early Woman, had come to stare at me in the Early Morning, through the boundary fence, as if I was some sort of prize exhibit of previously unknown Ape. It was a strange feeling to be the observed and not the observer.

However, I did not let them down. I did a few of my best tricks before turning my back on them and retreating to the back of the enclosure with a bunch of bananas, to scratch my bottom, leaving them to return to their own Early People with a scarcely believable Tale of having encountered a Future Man.

And–Gentle Readers–What A Man, eh!?

Day 93

An al fresco *dining experience for Semaj's tribe; discovery of a Northwest Passage; an investigation of a village to the West cut short by the activity of the Ecilop and the terrifying result of that activity; yet more terror at the first glimpse of the Old Cat's town; is the flight of the Red Alien Sphere an Augury of Invasion? A very exciting episode, even though I say so myself*

Although the weather was changeable, Semaj and his Neanderthal friend enjoyed roasting meats in their compound upon a machine which looked not unlike a flying saucer on a Martian tripod's legs. Semaj's friend–who possesses a giant hound with a glossy coat, tan in colour–looks exactly like the cartoon of Matthew Muggins, the Cats' Meat Man in Hugh Loftus's books of Dr Dolittle, which I used to read under the bed covers utilising a torch, when I was a nipper at my father's country seat. That is, he has a face that seems to have been run over by a steam roller and the flattened article then stirred with a blunt stick. But we all have our defects. I, for instance, though I am somewhat of an oil painting, have rather too large feet—although you know what they say about large feet. It does mean that I am almost freakishly equipped in another department, although I hate to blow my own trumpet—no, I can usually find someone all too willing to blow the 'trumpet' for me.[164]

As no period of the day could be said to be especially sunny, there was no sign of the Half-Naked Savage Woman (now darker in hue and with a glossier coat than Semaj's friend's dog), although occasionally the sun came out from behind the scudding clouds and mercilessly burned down on the Guard-Lands.

There is nothing to report, in all honesty, of our trip into Solemn Land Proper but–for shelter from the wind this time–we made our way upwards in the Land by starting in the Western Wood. Going further

---

[164] It is unsurprising that this passage has often been removed from editions of the book.

West than ever before, we began to hear the unmistakeable sound of whinnying horses under the bonnets of carriages and then, peeping out carefully from behind the tree trunks, I was surprised to see a Giant Northern Causeway (not to be confused with the Giant's Causeway of Northern Ireland, of course) which came up from the Ancient Circular Causeway and headed Northwest.

We dared to cross this enormous track and we discovered that a settlement named Fiddle DeeDee was revealed to us behind a curtain of trees. (There was a signpost with faded letters.) At this point, though, we thought it best not to push our luck, for a surprising number of stern-looking gentlemen of the Ecilop were patrolling up and down. And so, we retraced our steps and beat a hasty retreat to the verge alongside the Western Wood of Solemn Land.

Pushing our luck, we decided to see what might be revealed by walking always uphill on this verge.

Beyond Fiddle DeeDee to the West it appears that rural Solemn Land resumes, whilst to the North the Northwest Causeway leads to the West of the Old Cat's fortified Hall. Here, a dreadful portent of doom appeared in the form of a plaque set into an obviously ancient flint and brick wall. It proclaimed that the brick huts here belong to the dreadful Old Pussy himself, for there is a grinning representation of the old feline reprobate and the eroded but dread words: 'Old Cat's Town'. This surely means he is always on guard for intruders and is a Terrible Warning to those who would enter his fiefdom that he will deal severely with All.

We had only just retraced our steps, and found a path that my measurements and calculations told me should allow us to cross the West Wood to gain the banks of Lake Tina Superior, when from the Northwest Passage behind us came the most fearful noise, as of a horse-motor carriage being pursued by a number of the vehicles of the Ecilop, their bonnet–capped horses snorting and neighing most terribly. Suddenly there came a terrible squeal from the horse under the bonnet of the carriage in the lead, followed by a double explosion of its rubber hooves being popped!

'The Ecilop have spiked it, Master,' one of my bearers replied.

I enquired in the measured and not at all frightened tones of a Hero — 'What the b***** h*** was that?!'

He added 'They do it to stop drugs running.'

I was a little enlightened by this information after I had worked out that he did not mean that pills had grown little legs and sprinted off into the distance. I feel I must point out that, as I have told you, there seems to be a plentiful supply of narcotics in Solemn Land, so the Ecilop are not doing a terribly good job of it, are they? Mind you, I should be saddened if they were to arrest every Teen-Aper and Orang-u-Teen and throw them in chokey. They can do whatever they like with the Neanderthals, however, as far as I am concerned.

There continued for some time to be much excitement on the North-Western Causeway, with several Ecilop Carriages surrounding the spiked carriage, and, even when its occupants had been marched off in handy cuffs, the stern looking officers of the Ecilop remained, making light-capture pictures, and so on.

When all was quiet once more, we continued cutting across the Western Wood until we reached Lake Tina Superior, with the late afternoon light twinkling on its beautiful sludgy and bottle-strewn surface. How I have come to adore this body of water, as I adored the person for whom I named it! One wonders just how many skeletons of disappointed lovers lie concealed under that water...

I sat in silence, consumed by a feeling of nostalgia and loss, until I suddenly realised that the red sphere was no longer there to spy on me. It must have flown off, no doubt to make its report to the Aliens on the Mothership hidden behind the Moon.

It is with fear, trembling and a loosening of the bowels that I await the possible retribution for my astounding intelligence which has penetrated the Mystery of the Spheres. Have I, by my actions, accelerated an attack on Earth, my beloved home planet, or might I have in some way dissuaded the creatures from launching the anticipated Final Assault?

Gather all those precious to you, Gentle Reader, and batten down the hatches, for we may be in for a bumpy ride.

Day 94

A Bad Night and Deep Thoughts are succeeded by a pleasant breakfast; the route is altered; Semaj attempts to do wizardry with a wand and a miniature carriage; the unpleasant secrets which may be revealed by a monster digging on the corner; a distinct absence of hominids in Solemn Land Proper causes me to give advice to all those prospective owners of Teen-Apers and Orang-u-Teens

For some unknown reason, I had spent a restless night—with blood–chilling sounds from the Guard-Lands coming through the open window: the whisperings of the monster that is called Guilty Conscience that occupies that land in the small hours. I finally dropped off to sleep, only to awake a very few hours later feeling jaded, listless, and liverish, which no amount of patent pain killers and cups of Kenyan Arabica coffee could do much to dispel.

I set myself the task of discovering the deep reasons for this sense of miserable listlessness and decided that more than anything I am hungry to once more walk freely amongst my own people, for all their many flaws, in the Land of my Birth. Of course, the grey, overcast nature of the weather did not help. If I were in England, I could simply book myself in for a tanning session in a salon and lie, as the Half-Naked Savage Woman does, exposing myself to a few ultraviolet rays of the correct wavelength so as not to burn out the retina of my good eye; my eyesight is not what it was, and I would not want to make things worse. And I dare say it would be hard to list 'Explorer' as one's profession if one has to use a white stick or give employment to a Guide Dog. Perhaps it can be done but I beg leave to doubt it.

I decided that throwing myself into the activities of the day must be the best medicine, even for homesickness and the lack of company of the equivalent intellectual capacity to myself. I even laughed at this: thinking that such a person or people could be found here, in these God-forsaken parts, when they are thin on the ground even in Great Britain and the Colonies![165]

The normal ablutions undertaken, and a spartan breakfast consumed of bran, sultanas, wild boar cutlets, quail's eggs, and Beluga caviar, all washed down with the finest champagne—I pulled on my togs and called upon my trusty bearers and servants to prepare my sedan chair, and we set off for more Feats of Exploration, the extent and courage of which the World has never known.[166]

However, our progress was to be baulked at the very first (it was obviously going to be 'one of those days'), for we were diverted from the Guard-Lands into the track in the Pestilential Province before we were able to access King Solemn's Service Tunnel, due to Count Sil's minions attending to a line of fencing in the Guard-Lands. For this reason, I was not to see if that stripping phenomenon of the Basilisk was at her usual station, but it seemed unlikely on such a chill and sad day; when all heaven seemed to be about to weep in a kind of universal sob-fest.

In the trackway in the Pestilential Provinces where we were forced to go, we immediately saw Semaj playing with a toy horse-motor carriage that screeched at an even higher and more annoying pitch than the real ones. For this reason, I suspected that it was powered by a guinea pig in pain, or possibly a weasel or stoat. After all, there could only be room for a horse of Lilliputian size beneath its bonnet, and one would have then to believe in the truth of the preposterous adventures of Gulliver, unlike my entirely factual accounts of worlds previously unknown, except in Legend.[167]

Semaj tried to control the miniature apparition with both hands on a magic wand, to little avail. It whizzed along the trackway only to suddenly turn too tight a circle and flip over onto its back with its rubber hooves turning uselessly in the air. He yelled to me that it needed 'tuning up'. As it is not musical in the slightest, I think he is in error; in my opinion, shooting it would be merciful.

---

[165] PWN has a high and very likely erroneous opinion of himself, does he not?

[166] Ditto.

[167] Have you noticed how PWN seems to be under the impression that a 'horse-motor carriage' is one that has no visible horse, but that these are present, housed under the bonnet of each vehicle? Will you be the first to tell him, or shall I?

I suspect he has spent the money he was supposed to be spending on purchasing a guitar for lessons from me, on this miniature mobile monstrosity. To an extent this is a relief; I fear he would not make a good pupil.

At the corner, where this most unmusical of Diversions ended, I noted that an enormous monster Bull now dozes in the front garden of the corner property with the fence behind it recently removed, so that it appears a high bank there is going to be dug out and removed. As I had heard rumours about the disreputable people who formerly lived there, who were far too interested in intoxicants and gave house room to far too friendly young women, I wondered how many corpses will be disinterred as this mound is levelled.

I had Great Fortune in crossing the Junctions of the Causeways as my Party did not have to stop once but we went on our way unhindered by the silly lights on sticks with the pedestrian-pacifier buttons.

In Solemn Land Proper we turned our footsteps towards the East and proceeded around the misnamed picnic area, for almost no one ever picnics there—but Messengers from Inner Solemn Land still run around it, most likely carrying News far and wide, whilst achieving their Personal Best Times, which they check by consulting devices on their wrists, which seem to be hard taskmasters, for they never grant the messengers any rest. 'That sort of servitude would be illegal where I come from,' I told the servants, who were struggling to carry my sedan chair over particularly difficult ground.

The heavy cloud and cool conditions had put off all but the hardiest of the little sundress wearers and also the Teen-Apers and Orang-u-Teens. These are very sensitive to the cold and cloud and must be kept in temperatures not below 27 degrees centigrade, with low humidity and a breeze no stronger than would disturb a paper tissue.

I suspect it is largely because of the difficulty of achieving these conditions that few keep them as pets successfully, although I have in the past been a notably successful owner and even–on occasion–been able to breed them. However, in order to achieve this astonishing feat, I have had to face ruinous feed and heating bills. It is not a hobby into which to enter lightly. Once you have one or more Teen-Apers or Orang-u-Teens much of your waking hours will be spent in their care.

Preparing a vivarium for an Orang-u-Teen is more difficult than for a Teen-Aper, who will put up with and actually increase the filth of the habitat provided for him but still live there very contentedly.

An Orang-u-Teen's tank on the other hand may appear superficially like the make of the male's one but there are crucial differences: it will generally be cleaner, but a huge wardrobe must be provided with large quantities of brand-new clothing each season; this vast resource will supply the very little that the Orang-u-Teen actually wears. You cannot get away with the sensible amounts of clothing the creature will actually wear. Too many owners of Orang-u-Teens report trying to limit clothing in this manner, but it leads only to the Orang-u-Teen pining away and sometimes making the dramatic statement 'I might as well die! I hate you!'

What else do the Teen-Aper and Orang-u-Teen need to flourish in captivity and prepare for adulthood and reproduction? Well, a constant and generous supply of the magic substance of 'The Internet' is essential; you will kill a Teen-Aper or Orang-u-Teen almost instantly if this is not on tap at all times. Those who are interested in breeding pedigree ones should note that many Teen-Apers are called by the Orang-u-Teens, but few are chosen. You should, however, be prepared to chuck out straightaway any unsuitable Teen-Aper who looks like a dead-loss to you, however much your Orang-u-Teen appears to go weak at the knees in his presence. You should then put netting over the crystal panes and doors.[168]

The best method of disposal of a Teen-Aper you catch, who is up to no good,[169] is to snip off his head and put him down the loo. In no account should a moribund Teen-Aper be disposed of without first removing its head as they frequently only imitate the dead but will revive when given a cigarette and a beer.

The owner of an Orang-u-Teen needs eyes in the back of her or his head and the usual couple at the front. Eternal vigilance is required.

---

[168] As the hard drive suggests— '...to prevent ingress, egress and congress.'
[169] The hard drive is unequivocal— '...which is all of them...'

In particular, beware of Homo sapiens men like me, for it has unfortunately been known for an Orang-u-Teen to cut out the immature specimen which is the Teen-Aper, and go straight on to an unpleasant creature called a 'Sugar-daddy.'

In short, the successful nurturing of a Teen-Aper or Orang-u-teen to adulthood is more difficult than successfully growing bonsai trees—and that's hard enough…

Day 95

The adventure of a stinky cat; the returning Silver Van and a Competition; the Corner Bank and the Cutaway; another Alien machine patrols threateningly; I put on a show for Homo Erectus people; the Orang-u-Teens come into close proximity, and I consider a future for them at a relocated PWN Towers; the adventure of The Tattooed Woman

With visions of portraying the evil mastermind, sitting in his grand chair, stroking the pure white pussy cat on his lap, I took the old feline bearer Loopy onto mine and he suffered being stroked for a moment or two.[170]

But then–Sympathetic Reader–the most dreadful odour penetrated my noble beak and registered in my poetic consciousness, dispelling all calm and pleasure of the senses. There was no doubt that the creature had either been indulging in carrion, as is his despicable wont, or he had trodden in the Hidings of Agenda in the Guard-Lands. I leapt to my handsome feet and deposited the creature upon the crude matting of my brick hut. But–horror of horrors–the filthy moggy had still the filth upon his paws, and he had christened my sailcloth Native costume trews with traces of the muck. It was but a matter of a moment for Your Hero to run to the cooking compartment and procure sheets of absorbent plant fibre and a spraying bottle of sanitising fluid and I then proceeded to chase Loopy, capture him and–despite his protests–cleanse him, and then turn to myself to do the same. I opened the crystal panes throughout my brick hut and yet still the malodorous niff lingered for many an hour.

As a result of this adventure, I was forced to stick my head out of the cooking compartment crystal pane in order to breathe sweet air

---

[170] Students may be interested to hear that this point, the hard drive states—'Loopy is black with white paws, with many scars of battle and illness.'

and it was while I was doing this that I saw that a silver horse-motor van was parked up upon the wide verge of the trackway through the Badlands. It stood, apparently abandoned–for I have never seen a hominid within or beside it–with its back doors open, as always. What can be the answer to the mystery of the visiting silver van? All answers written on a postcard with your name and address on the reverse side and accompanied by a money order for £2.50 sterling or its equivalent, will go into a lottery with the money banked by me and no winner ever announced. Terms and Conditions apply— and not announcing a Winner is number one on the list.

As we set out upon the march to Solemn Land Proper, I turned at the top of the Escarpment to look once more at the bank being carved away. Once again, the Bull monster was dozing but it was clear that it had, when awake, eaten away a neat cross-section. To my surprise, there were not to be seen so many syringes or quite as many human bones as I had expected there to be. Nor was even a single archaeologist or representative of the Ecilop to be seen at the site. Might the mound therefore be entirely natural: a terminal moraine perhaps left behind from a prehistoric glacier?

Overhead, as we walked through the Terrace of Emporia, one of those Alien craft which go slowly across the sky of Skye (her debt for my mentioning of her name has had to be written off) with noisy rotating wings, came close overhead so that its menacing underside could clearly be seen, showing that it has skids for landing. I wondered– and still wonder–if there are Aliens aboard and if they seek more subjects for their mind and body probes. Well, they can jolly well leave me alone! I have been their captive once before, and proved such a thorn in their side, with so dangerous a blood pressure, that they were forced to release me after less than an hour. I think they know better than to meddle with me again...

Once in Solemn Land Proper, there were more people there than on the day of bleak weather that preceded it, with Early Men and Early Women walking around with their Early Children. I wondered if they were types of Homo Erectus, for they seem–though certainly more 'Woke' than the Neanderthals–still too primitive to be Homo sapiens, their pleasures are too simple and, by their inability to keep to the Rules of Social Separation of Solemn Land, they show they are too irresponsible.

They appeared once again to look at me in the enclosure of Lake Tina Superior, like a zoo exhibit, and they watched with wonder as I puffed upon my vaporiser and used my opposable thumbs to open a packet of diabetic sweets and I almost got a round of applause as I took off a wrapper from a single one, which is admittedly a terrific show of dexterity.

I was joined by three Orang-u-Teens who declined to sit near me but shyly huddled together on the opposite back, making their chattering and laughter like the tinkle of klaxons warning of an air raid.

To my delight, the Bountiful Brunette was one of them. Close up, they are younger than I at first thought, and not quite of marriageable age, even for yours truly, unlike the Lissom Black Lovely and her two more frequent companions.

While I tried to apply myself to my book, the Orang-u-Teens continued to chatter and giggle with the occasional scream of delight at one vision or another on their crystal devices. Oh, the sheer wastefulness of Mobile Data! They obviously do not pay the bills.

I managed the hard task of ignoring them so well that, in the end, when they finished their stay, they waved and shouted all unison 'Goodbye!' to me over the water

It took me some time to register the fact (plus I had not my ivory and gold ear trumpets in place). I suddenly realised they were smiling with lots of fine teeth on display, and waving, so I did the same back, wishing them well and urging them to 'Take care and stay safe!'

'We will, they replied, 'See you again soon.'

It is rather nice to be liked by these jolly, pretty girls. I suppose I had better live up to their trust and not make any one of them Lady PWN for now. That would be invidious, in any case. No, I will have to wait the requisite number of years, then marry them all. (What do you mean "If they will have you?!" The matter is beyond question. What girl would not want to be the Mistress of such a Master? Why, my seven-figure overdraft alone is sure to make each gasp with respect.)

As we walked back from the Terrace of Emporia, in the stretch of trackway before the ascent to the Escarpment, I was riveted by the vision of a Tattooed Woman. She was a delightful sight, with arms, bosom and midriff all bare except for the entrancing, dancing tattoos. I was just craning to examine her lower back, when unfortunately, she turned and fixed me with a glare. In vain did I explain 'I was just trying to follow the story of the Norse God Thor and the Mermaid to its natural conclusion but unfortunately that's where your leggings start...'

As I did not feel I was improving my case, I stopped 'digging', smiled with a flash of handsome acrylic teeth in what I hoped was a winning way, waved (to which she put up a middle finger in understanding) and I went on my way and she hers.

Day 96

A dream prompts memories and reflections; a Ferocious Fungus is defeated; a Dozing Bull and a single discovery; a meeting with Zow Bunny proves unsettling; a philosophical flourish

What, I wondered, as I awoke in the early morning, would Freud have made of a dream in which I was back as a humble young gentleman apprentice in the workplace of dear old Shaypem and Hangem, and in which Shaypem's then young wife came into the workplace with a Scandinavian friend, the friend wearing but a short nightie and needing a big strong man to open one of those enamelled tin pots, the lid of which had got gummed up with dried coffee? Not only that but what would the sage therapist think of me, as a weedy young lad, pausing in his work and–as there were no big strong men around–taking the coffee pot and–whilst kneeling at the feet of the lovely Scandi lady to wrestle with the coffee pot–taking the opportunity to peek up her nightie?

I suppose, as no doubt you are thinking, he would wonder if I got the coffee pot lid off. Indeed, I did, Gentle Reader. I was weak-looking and thin in those days but surprisingly strong and determined.[171]

As the young women admired my strength and pretty looks, I then found myself, like the renowned author Proust before me, in that state between dreaming and wakefulness, regretting the gradual disappearance of that world of my youth, however surreal and distorted it had appeared.[172] It had felt so real; I could experience once more the smell of the workplace and see the tiny dents and burns on the sides of the red coffee pot my Swedish, Danish or Norwegian vision held.

---

[171] I do not think that is what Sigmund Freud would be wondering and nor does any other commentator.

[172] See Proust, M. 'Remembrance of Things Past' Vol 1. 'Swann's Way', 1912.

It took a good deal of real not dream coffee, and shaking my head and pinching myself, to fully awake me from that nostalgic dream world. How could it be that I have come from that anonymous, ambitious, pretty, home-loving boy to this: a handsome but grizzled Explorer, famed throughout the Known and Unknown World, and one who is seldom in his own country. How truly unpredictable is life.

That morning I was suddenly made aware that I was under attack by a Ferocious Fungus I must have picked up in the Guard-Lands or Solemn Land but recently. This Giant Enemy, somewhere between a plant and an animal, had secreted itself in-between my toes and suddenly made its presence known with a dreadful ticklish irritation and blistering as it moved around biting out great chunks of my flesh. However, was your brave Hero to be daunted by this Fierce Foot Pest, even though it attacked the very parts of my anatomy so precious to my profession? Indeed, he was not.

Just as I have methods for dealing with plantar pain of my handsome heels and collapsing arches, I has a method for dealing a smart blow to the horrible hopes of this Fiend. I have carried with me into the wilderness beyond the Pestilential Provinces a spray which deals death to all Fungal Foes. You should have heard the screams of the creature as I squirted the targeted poison into its vicious eyes! In no time it was in retreat, especially when I took the advantage to follow up my attack with tea-tree lotion, thus smothering the vile chewing mouths and tickling claws of the monster.

It was almost too much excitement, this battle with the Fiendish Fungus, and so I rewarded myself with a glass of stimulating cordial before setting out once more on my Explorations.

It was an overcast a day and so the Half-Naked Savage Woman did not lie upon her person-burning settee but instead she had filled the Pantheon of Panties with mysterious flags aplenty, and she was busily nailing up symbols all over her domain, of various sun gods and signs in the Aliens' language. Perhaps we should inform the Authorities about this traitor in our midst?

The Bull dozed on the corner above the hill from the Escarpment, and yet it must have been active, for it had chomped away still more of the bank there. If anything of interest had been found, it had long since been taken away for forensic analysis, as the bank now revealed only geological layers, redolent of the times when Homo sapiens moved freely across the face of the Earth in a way which is impossible now. I instructed my little band of brave servants to pick up my sedan chair once more (I rested therein only because of the suffering I had been caused by the Ferocious Fungus, and to give the servants their daily exercise).

There were two quarrelling Neanderthals on the road that leads to the Od Cat's Hall. One said angrily, 'It is a room, innit? It is no big deal!' Was he being criticised by the other for showing interest in renting a room in the wicked Old Cat's fortified Hall? For there have been rumours that the Old Cat is running out of prey and cash. and therefore, may be willing to take in lodgers. A tale of mice and men, as it were.[173]

I had an appointment to meet Zow Bunny at Lake Tina Superior. He duly arrived and I informed him of my latest marvellous discoveries. However, it was evident he had little interest, however, as he just played a 3D game upon his crystal device the whole time. I recalled that before leaving for the Guard-Lands and Solemn Land I had never heard of his newspaper, 'The Daily Asperger', nor of him. Is he perhaps not all he says he is?

He then upset me by telling me that my beloved, romantic Lake Tina Superior is to his knowledge a Witches' Ducking Pond, and as he did so he drew a terrifying pentagram in the dust at my feet. Not only that but he began to tell me Tales of Haunted Solemn Land, mentioning Ghosts of Disappointed Lovers, said to haunt Chaos Lane to the Northeast. It all seemed pure invention, whereas I deal only in the unvarnished Truth. I have become most suspicious of him, even though he seems quite an affable person.

After he had left, I recalled that I had seen that day no sign of the Teen-Apers or my dear Orang-u-Teens. Really, it was unsurprising; the weather was not conducive.

I have had yet more thoughts regarding the Bountiful Brunette. With regret, I think I shall stay my hand about taking her back to PWN Towers just yet. I suspect she has not yet taken her Advanced level

---

[173] A reference, perhaps, to 'Of Mice and Men'—a novella by John Steinbeck, 1937?

exams, and as the Philosopher almost says: 'The unexamined wife is not worth living with.'[174]

---

[174] This is close to a saying reported to have been made by Socrates at his trial for impiety but it is not anywhere near as profound.

Day 97

Appearance of bed-things in the Pestilential Provinces; reflections on Trebla; a few facts in connection with your Hero's romantic life; matters concerning the ominous Ecilop; my mother's sweet but impractical beliefs; a theory concerning the Turin Shroud; two women who should know better behave like the Orang-u-Teens they were half a lifetime ago

A mystery has arisen at the frontage of my brick hut, that aspect which faces into the Pestilential Provinces: to wit, a sleeping pallet and large, springy person-cushion have been propped up next to the entrance. I think I see the hand of Semaj in this, but it could be the work of Trebla, a kindly but extremely private individual with a vast moustache. He is the chief of a large tribe in the territory adjacent to Semaj's. Or the work may have been that of his younger and muscly nephew-by-law.

Both Trebla and his tribe have an almost impenetrable accent and dialect. This reminds me forcibly of the denizens of Norwich, where stood the magnificent Leopard Court, near the Choking Art inn. The old family home of Leopard Court became impossible to retain, so I had to flee to PWN Towers, acquired in order to escape an impetuous and violent girl called Aron, who, my having sworn to marry her three or four times, supposed there was some truth in my declaration, whereas they were vows made only to preserve my lordly life and limb. Once in PWN Towers, I quickly transformed it from a Gothic castle into a comfortable home for myself, and a pleasant *seraglio*, or sequestered living area, for my many wives.

But even escape from Aron was no guarantee of safety, for at PWN Towers I negligently became engaged to marry yet another girl and conducted a secret affair with yet another. This sort of thing is very fatiguing, as you may imagine.

Perhaps there is some operation I could and should have, to get the volume of my animal magnetism turned down...

But back to the Present—In the last two days, despite their inactivity in the matter of the dozing Bull's eating away of the suspicious mound at the corner before the descent from the Escarpment, the Ecilop have been noticeable by a strong presence in the collection of brick huts to the South of the trackway (Cock-o'wood Avenue), about half way down it, and also at the smaller Parade of Emporia behind the towering saplings of the Chestnut Grove, immediately to the South-East of the cross-tracks.

As we proceeded to this junction of trackways that lead to all points of the compass, I saw a black clad, bare headed member of the Ecilop force, running from one of their conveyances into the Southerly collection of brick huts, looking swarthy and intent, with one hand on the hilt of his weapon tucked into his utility belt, like a disreputable Batman.

I cannot help but feel—and not for the first time—that it is unfortunate that the Ecilop dress all in black, like super-villains, creatures of the shadows and the night, and not in all white, like heroes representing goodness and purity. It is true that they are somewhat personalised by shiny silver figures on their jackets, but these are numbers, not a name; they are therefore not as individualised, identifiable and approachable as, say, your average person manning a service-till in your average Super-Emporium.

When I consult Natives of the Badlands on the matter, I receive the information that they trust these upholders of the Solemn Law about as far as they can throw them—that, in fact, they fear them and are not comforted by their presence in the slightest. They particularly dislike the screeching, woo–wooing and clashing noises of their horse-motor carriages, like vastly amplified versions of the terrible primitive sounds of over-excited Orang-u-Teens. And at least the Orang-u-Teens are charming in appearance and give some warning of their arrival, gradually ramping up their noise, whereas the Ecilop are visually unappealing and are upon one in a loud moment, righteous and sinful citizen alike.

They may be compared to the medical vans for their similar howling but at least, as my mother used to say, 'a medical van may be conveying a woman in expectation of a happy event', whereas the Ecilop are rarely engaged in such matters but usually intent on work involving someone's worst day: the innocent who has been murdered, assaulted or robbed, or else the villain who has fallen into a life of crime for reasons we cannot know, and about which the Ecilop care little.

Talking of my mother and her habit of looking for the best reason and outcome for the employment of the medical vans, I recall that she applied this philosophy to every area of human existence. Nor did she confine this optimistic, rosy philosophy to people but also to things. Despite being a realist in most things, sentimentality and superstition still lingered in her; she was no cynic. She literally and metaphorically searched always for four-leaved clovers and if she found none, she would say that one ordinary one showed 'great promise' which would come good in the next generation. That this is not so could plainly be seen in her own offspring, no more than three-leaved all of them in the matter of goodness, and in my case probably only two...

Back to the Present; it started fine enough but by noon a blanket of clouds shrouded the sun lending a grim aspect to the sky, like the cloth that wrapped Our Saviour and ended up somehow in Turin. Perhaps it was sent to the cleaners and that was subcontracted to a firm in Italy who couldn't get out the stains and so never sent it back to the Holy Land?[175] It is the sort of thing which often happens.

There is little to tell of my day in Solemn Land Proper. It passed off without delight or dismay. However, on our way back to Base Camp, going towards Solemn Land Proper as we headed away, near the Terrace of Emporia two handsome mature women stopped and 'gave way' to me, so as to preserve the correct distance between us. They backed up into someone's driveway to do this and I proceeded through the length of verge they thus liberated.

But–Here is the thing–as they did so, they giggled and wiggled just like a pair of Orang-u-Teens, especially when I bowed and told them I had just been about to give way to *them*. Well, I suppose I did

---

[175] See 'The Socks of The Saints and other Holy Laundry.' Milksop, A. 1930.

have my Devastating Mode turned up to the max, dressed as I was in sailcloth trews and jacket, and my black t–shirt over my ravishing if slightly protuberant belly. I mean, really, who could blame them for losing their heads?

Day 98

The end of the second Pyramid; the mound falls to the onslaught of the dozing Bull; the Angry Ageing Hippy; a Delightful Encounter with Orang-u-Teens in triplicate and the methods by which I keep and even improve my envy-inspiring good looks; an Ordeal by no "Guilty Pleasure" sent from the Gods; I begin to work my devilish wiles upon the Orang-u-Teens; how I intend to wear down the resistance of my Lissom Black Lovely

I see I have neglected to tell you, Gentle Readers, how the second Great Pyramid of Poo fares? Alas, though at first the combined Native tribes seemed enthusiastic about recreating the marvel that was the eighth wonder of the world (or somewhere in the Top Ten, at least, Pyramid-pickers!), they soon abandoned their work on the plain of Savanna, and no more than a rude (in every sense) square was placed as a foundation before they abandoned the work and stole away in the night, back to warring amongst themselves and so on; it is apparent that the Great Civilisation which created the original Pyramid is no more—destroyed by divisions amongst the peoples who made it.

It is enough to make a grown man cry. I must have been one of the last people to stand at my Third Base, and see the sun set over the finial of the great mound, whilst pinching my nose in the correct manner, as demanded by tradition and self-preservation.

At the corner of the trackway down from the Escarpment, the cut away bank has now been entirely digested by the Bull which is never seen awake but always dozing. Like the working men of the area, it is impossible to catch it actually doing its work. Where once was a mighty hillock, it seems as if there will be just another parking space for horse-motor carriages; its proud history of being the fabled place where naughty young women met their clients, and syringes were deposited, lost forever. Perhaps not a bad thing, as some ideas lose their appeal with time.

I have been remiss in not telling you about the least peaceful Hippy I ever encountered, who is the sole survivor of his tribe and who has his territory not terribly far from my Base Camp, where he grows Gigantic Snails and Slugs, much to the displeasure of neighbouring tribes, for the massive molluscs are no respecters of garden borders.

He was perched on his two wheeled conveyance as it came up the incline. I was relieved that he was crossing my trail, for this meant he would not harangue me once more upon the subject of the harm I do to the Environment by wearing shoes, or clothes, or having a kit bag, or breathing the air. I was very glad not to have to talk to him; I cannot think that with his abrasive manner he wins many friends or influences many people, although in many cases I happen to agree with him. I have always thought, however, that one wins more minds and hearts by the 'softly, softly catchee monkey' approach than by hitting people over the head with the Big Stick of Blame. I am such a pacifist that it crossed my mind to blast him to bits with my blunderbuss. That would ensure future peace and no mistake.

Oh joy! Rounding the bend into the Terrace of Emporia, I crossed paths with the original and only truly Lissom Black Lovely and the Original beautiful Blonde Bombshell, plus a handsome Brunette Orang-u-Teen whom I did not recognise. They were going toward the Chestnut Grove Parade of Emporia toward the Southeast, no doubt for more supplies of the beauty products which they unnecessarily use— unnecessary because they have that most attractive of all cosmetics— Youth.

I myself shower from time to time in the Fountain of Youth, or bathe in the Eternal Flame, or inject monkey gland juice, or have a transfusion from a small child, to stay looking and feeling like the superb specimen of Manhood I am;[176] one who is in pretty good fettle, whatever my GP and consultants may say. By the way, I always take a shampoo that washes and conditions, into the Fountain of Youth. You may think this unnecessary, but I ask you, why take two bottles into the Fountain of Youth, when you can shampoo and condition with just one, whilst–at the same time–genetically revitalising oneself?

---

[176] I trust PWN is joking about the child.

By lip-reading I could tell that the Beautiful Blonde Bombshell whispered to the others, 'Oh God, it is Him!' I am flattered that they think me a Deity, but I must correct their natural error at some point. I gave them as wide a grin as I could with my shining, lupine, plastic teeth and said, 'Good afternoon, young ladies!' and they replied 'Hallo!' with reasonable enthusiasm, although not enough to match that always exhibited by the Bountiful Brunette, who, sadly, was not with them.

On reaching Lake Tina Superior I was terribly displeased and dismayed to find my minions had not packed my 'Guilty Pleasure' vaporiser, but I supposed I was being tested by the Lord and felt determined not to hurry back to Base Camp for the thing. Does it control me, or do I control it?

I gave up resisting its call after a quarter of an hour and–humiliated at my rapid defeat–began to return to Base Camp.

On moving North briefly to get onto the Highway heading South, I spotted the Beauties I had seen already that day, now back at the Sequoia, soon joined by two other Orang-u-Teens whom I did not recognise. They seem these days to have entirely renounced the Teen-Apers who–disconsolate at their spurned and clumsy advances–have taken themselves off to sulk, either in the forests or their odoriferous nests.

With the spurning of the Teen-apers, my intense appeal now gives me the possibility of winning the heart of the Goddess-like but haughty Lissom Black Lovely, looking even more Lissom and Lovely with her white top, black trousers and with her taut, dark brown midriff on show.

If I win her, at PWN Towers I will build for her the greatest mausoleum of marble which the world has ever known, not excepting the Taj Mahal, when she inevitably succumbs to the gloom and damp, as is the sad fate of all beautiful specimens transplanted from their own land to the miserable atmosphere of England. It is that very miserable atmosphere that has made us the envy of the entire world.

But first to wear down the heart of stone of the Lissom Black Lovely with the constant drip, drip, drip of my longing.[177]

---

[177] It has long been suspected by scholars that PWN was a bit of a drip...

Day 99

A truly British day but in Solemn Land; an exercise in exorcism during which two shameful episodes fall under the red pencil; an outdoor yoga class and a brief reflection on the same; the larcenist in me is overcome but to what good? More information about the Superior Corner House in the Badlands and its Bearded General

It was the sort of dank, gloomy day to gladden a True Britisher's heart and I was busy much of the day in Base Camp, excising material from the account of my Travels and Adventures. For instance, I simply cannot have in the public domain the slaughter I wrought at the fortified Hall of the Old Cat, last night, when I was invited for dinner, only to discover that it was the cruel old feline's intention that I should constitute all the courses, except for pudding. Though I allowed him to keep his life, in order to escape I had to rob very many of his attendants and soldiers of theirs. It is possible I lost my famous 'cool' and ran amuck in a way that might well be frowned upon by my Queen, fellow countrymen and the Cats' Protection League–although I should have been commended and elevated to an Earldom in former days of the Empire–and so I took out my big red pencil and struck this tale out of the record.[178]

Also, I censored all mention of my brisk but efficient affair with the Queen of the Chainosaur Carvers, which so nearly led to my dying in the most horrible circumstances, with a face not even my mother could love. You do not want to betray the confidence of a Chainosaur-wielding King, is all I can reveal of this particular episode, and especially not to be found to be carving a special place in the heart of his Dearly Beloved.[179]

---

[178] But not entirely, as we see...
[179] What a loss to the world are these passages!

Then, also, there was the occasion when I led the infamous raid upon the Solemn Land Gatehouse, using my Swiss Army knife to open the safe there, to extract all the new brochures for holidaymakers in Solemn Land and then alter the dates of the Festivities, plus the Honoured Guests' invitations, so that none might arrive on the right day. Not–as I had supposed–just a harmless prank, this, as it meant the Lady Mayoress of the City to the East arrived in due course for a kiddies' Teddy Bears' Picnic and not a meeting of the Solemn Land Women's Institute, and Father Christmas turned up at the Midsummer Jamboree. On both occasions many innocent lives were lost. The Lady Mayoress is well known for her catastrophic losses of temper. What is less well known is how murderous Father Christmas can be when unnecessarily woken up in Summertime.

As I cannot be proud of these and other episodes, I have decided to suppress them. What would our own dear monarch say of them? And how harmful might the revelations be to my place in Posterity, however amusing they may be to some?[180]

I think I can, however, mention that in the Solemn Land, as we made our way North, in a glade, we saw assembled a group of women taking a yoga class. It seems odd to me that the people I saw doing yoga were the people least likely to need to do it, for they were each one slim and their muscles toned. It seems likely to me that all the hard work is done in private and only when perfection is already achieved, do the yoga students display themselves *al fresco*.

And there can be no harm in mentioning that as we returned South in Solemn Land Proper, I discovered a pair of spectacles on a public seat and with scrupulous honesty, though their magnification would have very much answered my needs, I left them, in the hope that their original owner would retrieve them, although that seems unlikely, for how would he or she find them without his or her spectacles? In addition, the likelihood of their surviving the night seems slim with an oak tree's branches overhead, no doubt sheltering a Mammoth or two.

---

[180] It seems likely that the Monarch did find out about these incidents; she must have had a reason for stripping PWN of his knighthood later that year. See 'Regina v. PWN'—Honours Court Pipe Roll, 2021. Special permission is required from a Monarch or Prime Minister to examine this record. As permission has so far been denied, we only know of its existence, not its particulars.

Mammoths are not well known for daintiness and might well drop onto those delicate instruments of sight.

There was no sign of the Teen-Apers, or the Orang-u-Teens for that matter, tempted as they may have been to venture out to scour Solemn Land for their Hero.

As we returned to King Solemn's Service Tunnel on our way back to Base Camp I had it in mind to see what more the dozing Bull might have done to the bank when briefly awake. What was my surprise, when I discovered that the entire thing has been remodelled and now slopes in the opposite direction? Thus, has been revealed an ornamental archway next to the adjacent Brick hut; this is a grand touch not normally seen in the Badlands. The people who live there must indeed be unusually wealthy for the area. One wonders if they have some sort of supremacy over their neighbours. I have met the bearded gentleman of the hut casually, but we are not in a state of such familiarity that I have discovered his position in the Badlands, but he has all the bearing of an Army General. I rather get the impression he looks down his nose at me. If this is so, he must watch his back for I can be a Terrible Adversary, although I am a real pussy-cat most of the time. I am only homicidal in brief, totally justifiable episodes.

NB. FROM THE POSTMASTER:
The following has been forwarded to you, as one of its intended recipients, from a list found on PWN's crystal device.

Day 100

This could be the end

Well, it is A Red-Letter Day, being the 100th day of my ongoing Exploration of the Guard-Lands and Solemn Land, and so I have decided to write this account of this day whilst here at Lake Tina Superior, and not in the evening, as usual. Yes, I have, as it were gone 'live', though I will send it tomorrow.

It being a gloriously bright and warm day, if a little on the windy side, with the sun at its zenith, I had no doubt when I left Base Camp today that the Half-Naked Savage Woman would be splayed like a spatchcocked chicken might be on a bed of vegetables, on her green crisping bed. So she was; as my party passed her, she may have shot a poisonous glance at us, but I was fully protected by my sunglass spectacle attachments. What I did notice was that she immediately reached for a communication device from the ground beside her. I dismissed this from my mind, however, as on we pressed into the Interior of the Conjoined Guard-Lands and on towards the Badlands and Solemn Land Proper.

Stepping carefully past the Hidings of Agenda, Lake Tina Inferior and the man traps possibly set by Kent Ucky and his ventriloquist puppet Fred Chicken, we finally reached the territory of Great Big Boss Handy Man, Rovert. He was out in his compound, feeding the flakes of his innocent victims to the Coy Carp. No wonder those fish grow so gigantic and how glad I am that I did not in the end feast on one, thus absorbing second-hand human protein. Mother always counselled me against cannibalism, however tempting, saying 'Eating people is wrong, even when they are in a desiccated state.'

I looked back, when we had moved away a little towards the Land of Euphemisms, being sure not to get too close for fear of another attack of the Blue Balls–and caught sight of Rovert picking up a communication device. Merely a coincidence, I am sure, for the Half-Naked Savage Woman and he could have nothing in common.

Leaving Loopy and Meli at the Cliff Camp, through King Solemn's Service Tunnel we ascended to the Escarpment. When I looked back to the corner brick hut with the dozing Bull monster, I could see its Bearded General—how odd! He too was lifting a crystal device to his ear and speaking with urgency into it.

Down the hill through the Badlands to the Terrace of Emporia we progressed. There was quite a queue outside both the battered marine life and fried tuber slices shop, and a shop where stands a life-size, ferocious but somehow amiable character with a handlebar moustache, in a blue-striped apron, holding a fearsome looking cleaver. Further along, a shop for miniature aeroplanes and such still stands locked, with a shattered safety-crystal window. I could only guess that some person desperate for a miniature flying machine in the middle of the night (and we all experience times like that) had attempted to take one without paying for it. It may even have been a pregnant woman with a particularly strange craving who was responsible for the damage or her desperate-to-please partner.

It was not long before we had achieved Solemn Land Proper and had taken the trackway North, which runs more or less parallel, but to the left by many hundreds of yards, to the Highway to the Heartland. Away, across the Southern Mammoths' Meadow, a team of what I took to be the Old Cat's gardeners were mowing short trackways across a profusion of wildflowers[181]; pterosaurs of all types flapped their leathery or feathery wings as they circled above, gaining height, or assembled in flocks in the blue, limpid sky. It was truly a day when one felt most alive!

Still, ceaselessly, the singlet-and-shorts clad messengers of the Solemn Kingdom ran on their perpetual task. I wondered what

---

[181] It is unclear whether the gardeners were tending to the Old Cat's Lawns or to the Northern Meadow tracks but earlier we have been told these were created by nocturnally grazing mammoths, so the likelihood is that PWN refers here to the Old Cat's Lawns.

messages they actually carried in their bottom-bags? Could it be just a message warning anyone who finds their bodies, worn out by dizziness and with joints destroyed, not to take up such employment?

And so here we are, at Lake Tina Superior, resting, and looking at the water as the cooling zephyrs of the breeze fail to disturb its deep lakeweed. I have spotted that the buds of waterlilies are poking through that matted meniscus, like rude pokers. All is good. It would only take the vision that is the Lissom Black Lovely and her Orang-u-Teen friends to complete the picture.

When, as if summoned, here they are coming from the North Mammoth Meadow toward me!

But what is this? They are not alone. In fact, there is a great mob behind them, including the vile Pester John, the bearded General, Rovert, the Half-Naked Savage Woman, Kent Ucky and his puppet chicken Fred, and many another. And horror of horrors! All are brandishing scythes and other weapons. Rovert has even detached his great saw which is circular and twirls the toothed blade menacingly at me.

And now here comes the King of the Chainosaur Carvers with his Chainosaur growling and its teeth revolving in its mouth; he pays no heed to his Queen who clutches at his elbow and begs for mercy for me.

Last but not least arrives that terrible Old Cat of the Hall, bearing scars from our battle. He does not look as though he can be appeased by a saucer of milk or a sachet of 'Tasty Ocean Treats', should I even happen to have one concealed about my person.

My bearers have fled, and it looks as though I will have to swim for it to escape, across the wide waters of Lake Tina Superior. But *no*! Even that route of escape is barred to me, for the enormous Alien Spaceship is descending from the sky to settle on the Lake, surrounded by angry red probes.

And now the mob are almost upon me, and they do not look as though they are about to break into a flash-dance. Well, I couldn't think of a stranger bunch of assassins if I had made them up myself.

But what is this? They come to a halt in front of me and the Lissom Black Lovely steps forward. 'Thank Goodness –', I think, 'the lovely young woman has come to intercede for me.' But then I notice that she is drawing a large, sharp dagger out from behind her back.

'"Et Tu, Beauty?!"' I say, not a little dismayed.

Over her shoulder I notice that of all the crowd only the Bountiful Brunette has tears in her eyes for me.

Well, all this is a tad unfortunate—but never fear, Gentle Readers, I have been in worse scrapes in my time...

MESSAGE ENDS.

Electronic signature: PWN

Editor:

And with that email ended the He-Male messages, which were the only formerly known source-texts by PWN.

It therefore seemed unlikely he could have survived his predicament, with the forces then ranged against him. On the other hand, he was a resourceful and experienced Explorer, if a bit of a miscreant; he was also possessed of great animal magnetism (by his own account, at any rate) and there was always the feint hope that one or more new sources would be found that might reveal his to have been a different Fate from that of destruction at the hands of his enemies.

Could it be due to him that the world has not yet succumbed to an Alien Invasion? For in his last seconds, he (or another) may have done something that put them off the whole idea for now. Certainly, the Aliens for a time disappeared, as did PWN. If he defeated them, or caused them to be defeated, that's pretty good going in anyone's book and it may give us pause for thought; perhaps the old reprobate was, after all, 'A hero not a zero'?

And this is where the new source of material (the fourteenth source) has something fascinating to say on the matter. In a further note on the recently discovered hard drive is typed the following, which I have termed:

THE EPILOGUE.

'But–wait –what is this? Suddenly the Lissom Black Lovely winks at me, blows me a kiss, and turns against the mob, still brandishing her dagger. As the mob takes a few steps back, the Beautiful Blonde Bombshell and the Bountiful Brunette burst into action, throwing me a long, straight fallen branch they have together carried to the scene. (I had hitherto thought they carried it in order to knock my block off...)

I at once understand— it is the work of a moment for me to clutch the Lissom Black Lovely to my manly chest and middle-aged tummy and–with her arms around my neck– and, by plunging one end of the branch onto the bed of Lake Tina Superior, I pole-vault us onto the top of the spacecraft. (Gad—she is a bit more substantial than she at first appears!) We run over the wide top of that evil craft and then leap to the further bank of the Lake.

"You can't do that!" shouts the Chainosaur Carver King, "You are contravening the Social-Distancing Rules of Solemn Land!"

"Sod the Social-Distancing Rules!" shouts my Lissom Lovely. (To my surprise and gratification, she speaks English well —almost like a Native. Not only that but she swears like a Trooper.)

Then, the Lissom Black Lovely tugs the branch from my hands and with all her strength hurls the branch like a spear, end-on, through what the clever young woman has accurately judged to be the weak spot of a lower observation portal of the Alien spacecraft, and–gurgling–it begins to sink into the unfathomable watery depths of Lake Tina Superior.

Our enemies stand frustrated with no way of reaching us.

Then it is a long, joyful sprint (with just a little happy dalliance) back to Base Camp to freshen up and pick up some necessities, before setting out to cross the vast area of the Pestilential Provinces toward my Homeland and PWN Towers.

I told you I had been in worse scrapes, but I must say that rescue has come from an unexpected quarter and in the most romantic and unlikely way possible, I must admit. Why, it is almost unbelievable...

The Lissom Black Lovely will be a wonderful addition to PWN Towers! For such loyalty and devotion, she can be Number One Wife. She is a determined, resourceful, and beautiful creature and I may even make it her permanent post. I make a mental note to keep her well away from the Weaponry Room. She handles a dagger a little too professionally for comfort.

Oh–and I had better find out if she has a name; it is only polite and is quite the modern thing.

As for the rediscovery of King Solemn's Vines— alas, Reader, that must wait for another Expedition and another year. I must return — after all, I still have a Bountiful Brunette and a Beautiful Blonde Bombshell to add to the Collection at PWN Towers.'

—

Editor: Whether or not to give credence to this addition to that which was previously known, is perhaps a matter of personal choice, for it does not have the provenance of the other material. It has been investigated scientifically, however, and it does not appear to be a fraud.

AFTERWORD

Finally—on the same hard drive upon that which I have termed
'The Epilogue' was found, I have just come across the following (in the
virtual trashcan):

'On arrival back at Base Camp I have had faithful young feline
Meli draw the Lissom Black Lovely and myself a bath, so as to ease our
aching limbs and to (cough) get to know each other better. I reject her
initial pen-and-ink offering and explain my request in terms not even a
cat could misunderstand.

Eager with anticipation, we await the announcement that the
bath is ready, only to hear the most enormous splash! Together we run
into the compartment for bathing, only to find that my other devoted
servant Loopy has somehow contrived to fall into the water. The Lissom
Black Lovely stands there giggling and jiggling, wrapped only in a thin
silk robe I had brought across the Pestilential Provinces against such an
eventuality as my winning the heart of a Beautiful Lady. I–for my part–
assist my saturated old servant firstly out of the bath, and then the cat
flap, by the kindly employment of the steel-reinforced toecap on my
jungle slipper.

At that very moment there is a loud knock on the door which
the cat flap perforates. I open it to discover a liveried messenger, come
from my Queen. He retreats to a lawful and respectful distance of six
feet and kicks towards me a scroll decorated with the Great Seal of the
Kings and Queens of The United Kingdom. I immediately pick it up
with a pair of tongs and slip on a pair of handy latex gloves (latex gloves
are always handy if you think about it…). I break the seal and then
unravel it. It bears a short message, and it is as follows:

'Greetings to Our Appointed Explorer in the Guard-Lands and
Solemn Land! Henceforth let it be known that PWN is instructed, on
pain of death, to forward all Fauna and Flora–and not excluding human
specimens such as Lissom Black Lovelies and the like–to Her Majesty's
safekeeping, unharmed and untouched, not having debauched them, or

else face hanging, drawing, and quartering, plus anything even more unpleasant We may think of. '

Miserably, I go to pull the plug out of the jungle bath and urge a surprised and disappointed Lissom Black Lovely back into her clothes—*Curses!* I have been Subdued by a Sovereign and Restrained by my Regina.'

THE END

Although, at this time, there is no more known text by 'PWN', I am always searching. Should you come across anything which you suspect to be by him, please contact me at the following address:

Pavel Wanya Nevulski,
'Gallstones Magna',
Upper Mincingly,
Kent,
United Kingdom.

Pavel Nevulski is a published and broadcast writer of both humorous and serious poetry and short stories in the UK. He has contributed to many programmes on BBC Radio 4. He has also had a career as a musical instrument for The National Trust, English Heritage and many museums and private collections. He is now semi-retired from this work for medical reasons.

He lives in Norwich in the UK and had six daughters and two cats at the last count, but it may be time for a new census.

Lightning Source UK Ltd.
Milton Keynes UK
UKHW020007250921
391135UK00006B/355